Contents

DISCORDIA UNIVERSITY
COGERE EVOLUTIONE PER MUTATIONUM

DISCORDIA

UNIVERSITY

Zero SPARK

INTERNATIONAL BESTSELLING AUTHOR
CASSANDRA FEATHERSTONE

CONTENT INFORMATION

This is a *paranormal whychoose romance with poly elements*—our FMC, Kat, will not have to choose between love interests.

I *purposefully* include **all** pertinent information in this section from tropes to triggers to included content to silly things. It's an attempt to cover my bases which is probably futile since some will be upset with *and* without it.

However, it's my book, and I'll do what I want, so here we go.

There are many situations included that are intended for <u>mature audiences (18+).</u>

In this book/series, there may be instances/references (be they small or lengthy) that could trigger some individuals such as:

- a *lot* of discussion of mental illness
- demons
- attacks on the FMC (physical)
- crossover with *Faetal Attraction* and *Secrets of State U*
- discussion about past non-consensual sexual event in FMC's past (description not on page, not MMC)
- sexy shifting
- within series: MM, MF, MMMMMMFM, and more
- bullying (light from MMC)
- foster kid
- consistent discussions of consent

- non-binary MC
- alphahole/possessive MCs
- cinnamon roll MC
- girl disguised as a boy
- slightly unhinged chaotic MC
- big tough guy MC
- unhealthy coping mechanisms
- spoiled, rich MCs
- extremely aggressive boundaries
- age gap (unknown)
- cute familiar
- pre-existing pairings
- BDSM discussed (D/s relationship)
- horns, tails, and forked tongues
- traumatic childhood
- alcohol use and abuse
- threats of bodily harm
- death
- body modifications
- physical assault by non-MCs
- treacherous authority figures
- bullying (in person)
- PTSD
- blood
- emotional abuse
- body dysmorphia
- adult language
- pop culture references
- literary references
- emotional manipulation
- power play
- adorable nicknames
- physical intimidation
- emotionally abusive/manipulative parents (MCs)
- markings/tattoos
- Easter egg character cameos from other series in the universe
- family dysfunction
- shifting surprises
- absolute disrespect for shitty parents
- brief mentions of non-body positive dieting culture
- very liberal re-imagining of history
- ancient secret society who only cares about bigger picture

- official corruption
- discussion of arranged marriages
- rituals
- inappropriate professors
- name calling
- occasional misogyny
- shitty mothers and fathers
- discussion of parental physical abuse
- elitism
- bribery
- corpses
- drama
- physical threats to FMC and others
- species-ism

No practices in this book should be taken as safe or appropriate for real life application.

Content information is important to me and I do my best to include things people might enjoy and not enjoy.

READER'S NOTE
A FEW THINGS YOU SHOULD KNOW...

Zero Spark is book **three** of the *Discordia University* series. There are five books planned and they will start on Ream, then come to print/KU after they are re-edited and formatted. The books don't *change* from one medium to the other so much as get refined, etc.

This is a multi-book series, so *everything will not be revealed at once.* Some plot lines will continue through series in a larger arc and not get resolved in the first or even the third book.

I write lengthy books with intricate world building, strong character development, and *lots* of tiny threads that stretch throughout a series that may not always seem important at first glance. However, I promise nothing I put to paper and leave in the book is unimportant; it may simply become *more* important later on. There is no 'throwaway' detail in my worlds, so every scene will mean something eventually.

For information on the larger universe reading order, go to https://cassan drafeatherstone.com/pages/legends-of-the-ouroboros

I promise it will all get tied up and have a HEA; don't worry!

Zero Spark is a why choose/poly romance, which means our FMC will not have to choose.

I would consider it a **SLOW** burn—the slowest I've ever written. It will get spicier—slowly—in the following books as Kat's situation changes. If you're looking for porn with little to no plot, no judgment, but this isn't the series for you. It won't be closed door or FTB, so I believe the spice will be worth the wait. I realize spice scales are subjective and everyone has different opinions on it, so forgive me if mine and yours aren't totally aligned.

Note: In the South (where I'm from), it is fairly common to call people by their full names when you're being condescending to dressing someone down. It's not just family, and if they don't know your middle name, sometimes they even make one up! It's an authority flex to do so. This happens in my books a lot—even if they are not set in the South—so I'm just giving you a heads up that it's stylistic and purposeful.

There are some characters and creatures that speak in other languages. I made the *translations clickable end of chapter notes* to help.

There are some words that are slang, jargon, or foreign that may seem to be spelled wrong—*please email the author or find her on social media rather than report to Amazon* if you find a typo. This has been proofed and edited *several* times, so the error could be a stylistic or dialect choice. Every effort is made to find these pre-publication and since the publishing industry standard is below two percent of word count (and my books are almost always over 100K), I promise what you find is not out of the accepted range for the editors and teams who have reviewed it.

Please do not email critical feedback that is not a simple typo or formatting issue—this book is written and released. It will not be changed after publication to suit personal requests.

Note: If any artist/creator/real life individual/place/creative work/ thing becomes problematic after the publication of this book, please note that I will likely not remove them in the future. This does not mean I support whatever shitty thing they have said/done, etc, but reflects several realities about being an author.

First, I may have a subrights contract with a third-party (ie, audio, translations, etc) that keeps me from amending the text without their approval. Typically, that involves cost and agreement from them, which is difficult to come by. Second, my writing schedule is often extremely tight, and I am not able to comb through every book in my catalog to amend small details like references, playlists, chapter titles, or other minutiae that might be affected by such a thing. Not removing it does not equate to support/agreement with whatever awful thing was revealed, nor does it mean that I am problematic as well. Third, since I am not aware of everything that happens in the world every day, I may not even know about this atrocity yet. Please be understanding.

If you see this book *anywhere besides Kindle Unlimited or a library in ebook format,* please reach out to me via social media or email. Pirating kills my ability to write full time and I am so grateful for your help.

Contact my team for typos or to report piracy: teamcassandrafeatherstone@ cassandrafeatherstone.com

Author Ramblings

Readers,

I am so excited for the next installment of KK and her demons to hit your eyeballs!

This book *definitely* starts after the bonuses and books of *Faetal Attraction* and *Secrets of State U.* You **can** read this without them, *but* you may be confused about what happened between the *Quiet Burn* bonus and now. The early readers on my serial platform have *adored* the new book and the bonus. They are so very ready for the holiday crossover coming next and I hope you are as well.

Kit has more demons to show her true self to, powers to find, and healing to do as she makes her way towards the ominous, looming Games and the big scares that affect the whole LOTO universe. But you'll see her make friends and find support in this book, and that, too, will warm your hearts.

I got a **lot** of 'oh, my heart' comments if that tells you anything.

If you have issues with discussion of consent, her mental health, and the way that shapes her entire world, this may not be the series for you. I'm absolutely not willing to cheapen Kat's tale for anyone, especially when it comes to the way she behaves as a result of her trauma.

As usual, I've done a lot of research and added quite bit of mythology, depth, and information to my rich world. But if I get something wrong, know I did the best I could to make certain I had the right information.

*Plus, you know… magic. Magic explains everything. *wink**

While I definitely cannot ever make every reader happy—and that's *okay*—I'm so grateful for all of the people who enjoy my books in my group, REAM, and other venues. You guys are the sunshine in my day when I happen upon less than kind opinions on the internet by mistake.

For that, I can never repay you.

However, I never give up, so I'm going to be here with silly puns and smart FMCs who aren't afraid to show how big their hearts, libidos, *and* brains are.

Enjoy the next installment in this series in the *Legends of the Ouroboros* universe, and fall for the bad boy demons one by one.

Blood and guts,

Cassandra Featherstone

QUEEN OF SMART, SASSY SPICE

A Note To My Loving Family Members and Their Friends...

THANK YOU FOR SUPPORTING ME BY BUYING THIS BOOK!

THIS BOOK GOES A LITTLE FURTHER, BUT SINCE IT'S TIED TO ONES YOU CANNOT READ?

JUST PUT IT ON YOUR SHELF AND SMILE WITH PRIDE.

TRUST ME, IT'S BETTER FOR ALL OF US.

CAVEAT: IF YOU CHOOSE TO KEEP READING, KNOW THAT AT NO TIME WILL I EXPLAIN TERMS, POSITIONS, THEMES, TROPES, OR ANY OTHER PART OF THIS NOVEL AT FAMILY EVENTS, IN GROUP CHATS, OR ON SOCIAL MEDIA.

DON'T ASK.

ZERO SPARK PLAYLIST

CHAPTER TITLE SONGS

Zero Spark Chapter Playlist

To all of the readers loving and accepting Kat for who she is...
To the fans who are patiently waiting for her to be ready...

You are the truly amazing folks who get how hard mental illness is, and why people struggle so much with it.

Kat is brave, strong, and bold—not because of her struggles, but despite them.

Thank you for understanding her, and me.

Our girl is gonna make them all regret calling her whiny and weak.

*Sometimes, closure arrives two years later, on
an ordinary Friday afternoon, in a way you
never expected or could have predicted.*

*And you cry a little, and you laugh a little,
and for the first time in a long time...
You exhale.*

Because you are FREE.

~Mandy Hale

Start with:
Read this next!
BONUS SCENE #1
This timeline intersects with Veiled Flame
Bonus Scene
BONUS SCENE #1
Bonus Scene
Crossover Reading Order

Zero Spark
Starts Here

Intersects at
Chapter "Devil"
Bonus may
include things

Intersects at
Chapter
"Battle"
+ bonus

This timeline
intersects with
Suspicions at
the end.

Bonus Scene

Discordia University
Student Dormitories
Library of the Ancients
The Wastelands
Staff Housing

Canto V
Region: Hell
Arena of Lost Souls
agic Enclave
Knowledge Enclave
Administration
& Health Annex

CLASS SCHEDULE

All class schedules subject to administrative and professorial approval.

time	monday	tuesday	wednesday	thursday	friday
8:00 AM	Intro to Demons & Supes	Curses & Hexes 101	Intro to Demons & Supes	Curses & Hexes 101	Arms & Battle 101
9:00 AM	Lillibet	Wormwood	Lillibet	Wormwood	Eversore
10:00 AM	Deconstructing Human History	Mythology 101	Deconstructing Human History	Mythology 101	Free Period
11:00 AM	Alabaster		Alabaster		
12:00 PM	Free Period	Lunch	Free Period	Lunch	Dueling
1:00 PM	Lunch		Lunch		Lunch
2:00 PM	Ancient Demon Lineage	Free Period	Ancient Demon Lineage	Free Period	Dark Magic
3:00 PM	Kindervelt		Kindervelt		Salazar
4:00 PM	Literature of Dark Ages	Weapons & Tactics	Literature of Dark Ages	Weapons & Tactics	Intro to Fae
5:00 PM	Romero	Eversore	Romero	Eversore	Cedar
6:00 PM	Drama	Supe Law	Drama	Supe Law	Hackers Guild
7:00 PM	Dinner	Dinner	Dinner	Dinner	
8:00 PM	Thieves' Guild	Caliphate Mtg	Government	Caliphate Mtg	Dinner

COGERE EVOLUTIONE PER MUTATIONEM

WAIT!

A FINAL REMINDER BEFORE YOU READ...

My series typically have prequels, gap novellas/novels, and bonus material that are integral to your having a satisfying reading experience.

If you have not read the other pieces in this series, you may feel as though you have missed critical details, developments, plot points, and other information. This will cause the book to appear to have continuity gaps that it does not have.

If you have not read the bonus material for this series, it is available online here, in audio versions (if applicable), and in print special editions (if applicable).

I highly recommend consulting the bonus page prior to reading this new title so you're up to speed on all the things going on in this world.

Happy reading!

Previously On Quiet Burn...

We pick up right after the bonus from *Veiled Flame* (Kat's still hiding who she is from most of the guys), where everything detonated and then had the audacity to keep smoldering. Kat wakes to a relentlessly cheerful Salem, which would be adorable if she weren't trembling from exhaustion and pain.

She staggers into a shower with him and Dottie on hand, and of course half-dressed demon boyfriends under one roof means the bathroom is equal parts necessary hygiene and exquisite torture. She's weak, wired, and absolutely noticing abs. Her coping strategy is the only one that's ever worked—push forward and keep the snark razor-sharp so nobody notices the shaking.

Because the Games are looming and Discordia never met a power move it didn't want to choreograph, the guys formalize a campus-wide performance. Kat and the caliphate will 'fake date.' If predators think she's claimed, fewer idiots will try something. The snag is scheduling—Kat's got classes without them, and Lucian's not letting anyone rearrange a thing. She insists she can handle a few hours solo. The compromise lands with Salem and Dottie flanking her out the door.

Breakfast in the *Triclinium* becomes an intentional spectacle. Jasper directs the show so competitors read confidence instead of stress. Eyes track them like they're a live broadcast. The fake-dating narrative amplifies the attention until Kat is clinging to her center by fingernails. When they split for class, Slash walks her. He keeps conversation to a minimum and makes one point crystal clear. He'll protect her, and he's not pretending it won't involve violence if that's what it takes.

Oriel snares pickup duty after class. The vibe is good until an urgent summons hijacks the morning—Games announcement, *Triclinium*, now. The entire room hums with rumor and rubbernecking when they arrive, Jasper strung tight enough to snap. They brace for impact, gather food like it's armor, and wait. And then… nothing, because the rumor's a feint. Everyone stands down with frayed nerves and no answers.

Zavida walks Kat next and tries to pitch the 'Jasper's prickly, but he cares' defense. She's not in the market for excuses. They discuss what counts as 'boyfriend behavior,' reach class anyway, and Oriel is back on pickup to usher her through an elevator full of idiots who decide to perform homophobia within arm's reach of a crow demon. He nudges a little power and by the time the doors open the bigots are in the lobby clawing at each other over stolen trinkets. Kat tells him it wasn't necessary; Oriel tells her lessons matter when people choose cruelty. On that point, they align.

Elsewhere, Xerxes grumbles through a Kat-less day until the loudspeaker blares about a caliphates-only Games meeting in five minutes in the *Triclinium*. When the group converges, some brothers are there and others are sprinting. Slash needles Kat about eating; she snipes back. Jasper finally admits what's on his mind— Lucian is stacking the deck—gathering the biggest monsters early and coaxing them to clash before the Games even start.

Lucian staggers in like a cartoon villain and dials every sneer to max. Halfway through his oily speech, time misbehaves. The room freezes, and everyone halts, except Kat. She can move *and* talk. She uses the pause—cataloging faces, stances, tells, threats—then reality resumes. When she tests the guys, none of them noticed anything odd. Salem looks more tired than he should, which sets off internal alarms. Jasper moves straight into triage mode and starts assigning tutors and guards. Kat answers his orders with equal parts compliance and fire.

The next day in class, Slash whispers suspicions that something is off with Kat. Anton deflects, Kat arrives, and Salem nearly nods off. Professor Wormwood—wielding petty authority like it's a scepter—uses magic to jerk him awake. Kat defends Salem, and the professor retaliates by assigning Salem's punishment to her. The creep factor spikes, and a fast decision is made. They need Jasper to step in so Kat doesn't end up alone with a creeptastic teacher in a dungeon.

On the path to another class, Kat vents to Anton. It's too much, too fast. She's carrying a private wreck, and this performance—this pressure—rubs that old injury raw. Anton sounds, for one terrifying heartbeat, like he's decoded her entire secret. He hasn't. He's deduced a bad dating history, not the truth.

Zavida, waiting for class, tries to square two truths: loyalty to Jasper, and Jasper being a jerk. When the group finally lands in their seats, Kat calls all of them pretentious rich assholes because sometimes love is telling the truth. Class passes without incident. The next one, Jasper's, is another story. He's furious when they reach the arena. He barks at his own caliphate for speaking. Nobody knows what set the dragon off, but the through line is clear. Lucian is meddling with Jasper's curriculum and the prince is bleeding rage down the chain. They survive the gauntlet, but Kat promptly falls asleep in her next class from pure exhaustion, and Slash shakes her awake at the end.

Slash escorts her to the dorm for a dinner-slash-meeting. The walk is calm enough that Kat lets herself enjoy it. Inside, Oriel and Salem test-drive dating banter—awkward and ridiculous, but effective. Meanwhile, in Jasper's room, the dragon demands Zavida's rundown from the day and works out his frustration through consensual, scalding BDSM play.

Salem and Kat finish dinner prep. He praises her quick study in the kitchen, which flusters her hard enough to send her running to change and whisper frantically with Dottie about the boys, the day, and how to be a functioning human around praise. When she emerges, the entire caliphate has sprawled across the room. She gives Jasper wide berth and takes the seat that lets her breathe. There's sparring, there's needling, and then Salem hands out 'happy drinks' to grease the discussion.

It doesn't help when the prince announces that Lucian has scheduled a Samhain ball with all the demon universities—including the female ones. It reads like a powder keg with a dress code—even the idea of an open bar can't soften the dread.

A few days later, Anton narrates the emergency fashion scramble. They're in Jasper's class when he stalks in angrier than ever and escalates training to real-weapon sparring in pairs—an obvious step up from the week's plan. Anton kisses Kat lightly to ground her in the moment and reinforce the dating narrative, and Jasper seethes. He splits the caliphate across opponents, and they clock his absence by the end, can't find him, but settle for relief that Kat escaped with minimal damage. Slash retrieves her. She refuses a visit to Dank for surface-level injuries because she can't sidestep predator optics by broadcasting fragility. Slash ignores that and has Dank meet them in the dorm anyway.

On the way, Slash admits Oriel's built an informant network watching Kat's routes. Layered protection. Inside, Slash feeds her per Salem's instructions, which sparks a gentle fight about her appetite. Dank arrives, fixes what he can, and prescribes more food. The next class, Salem notices Kat's lingering soreness. She bites her lip, a dot of blood appears, and his demon rises on instinct. That forces a conversation about what she faced in Arms. They settle, they study, and then Oriel proposes something strategic: test Kat against Fae flora to predict what the ball and the Games might do to her.

They work through a list—some foods are fine, some plants prickly. A thorny one clears canines and Cubi from suspicion. Then they bring out the Bone Tree, the kind of specimen that reads bloodlines like a nosy aunt. Kat balks; they coax. She touches it and the room detonates in light. For her, it's like being electrocuted. When she wakes, she's spiraling into a panic attack until they pull her out with care. No one knows what the reaction means; it's unheard of. Kat agrees the caliphate can know, but no one else.

Slash carries her home again. The others return. X is worried; Jasper pivots to ball attire like he's trying to outrun what happened. They lay down the law: she can't wear a uniform to Samhain. Kat panics at the thought of Xerxes measuring her, then concedes—no scandalous cuts, nothing that screams for attention. Magical measuring gets done, and then the boys holler them into the common area for a special delivery. Everyone learns crowns are mandatory. Kat swears, then grumbles her way into wearing one Oriel had tucked in a stash—of course he did.

The next day, she opts for tactical silence. She and Dottie dissect bullying while she studies. Slash knocks with a tray and is too stubborn to go away. She waits him out, then caves, eats the meal, and finds little trinkets tucked on the plate from most of the guys. She smiles in spite of herself, deciding that she'll stop hiding, apologize for overreacting, and show up. When she steps into the common room, they're already there, studying. She tosses her trash, walks to her usual seat, thanks the ones who helped yesterday, and apologizes to the group. Even Jasper accepts, and they settle—the unit reknits.

Slash disobeys schedules to shadow Kat through a class where he isn't even enrolled. They're not letting Lillabet—or any other opportunist—corner her. With him there, nothing happens. They move to the next class. He drops her with a reminder that Oriel will collect her after.

Days tick by without incident. Xerxes sews in the dorm—ball outfit on a deadline and custom to Kat down to the last glitter. They talk through the realities of a mixed-gender event. X is optimistic; Kat is not. Girls from rival schools will read her as someone hogging the most eligible bachelors on the dance card, and she knows exactly how that looks to jealous monsters. They catalog the guys' proclivities while X pins. By the time Oriel arrives, Kat is wiggling out of the half-finished look. No one sees it but X.

Ball day lands. Jasper glowers about how fast the whole thing came together and how suspicious the scheduling is. He paces the lobby like a general waiting on troops. One by one the caliphate arrives half-shifted and lethal— except Xerxes and Kat. They descend together in complementary skirts that turn the lobby into a collective gulp. The boys don't fully understand why Kat looks that good; they understand it's exactly what X engineered for her.

At the ball they avoid drinks and food that aren't vetted. Mean girls snipe. Demon parents prowl. Lucian preens through an ass-kissing speech. Then Kat meets a constellation of parents, including the King. He's intolerable. Jasper retaliates by kissing Kat in front of everyone, the kind of deliberate provocation that radiates up the social ladder. They whisk Kat to a private room to breathe through the panic, then retreat to the dorm after she's steady enough to move.

Back in her space, Kat realizes she might be in over her head anatomically and makes a mental note to consult Dank. They tease Jasper about the kiss; the teasing makes Kat mortified and Jasper insufferably smug. Monday arrives with bad social media takes about the ball swirling in Kat's head like gnats. The guys find her at lunch, prod gently, and she admits she hates feeling like a burden. They shut that down. Jasper reminds her he's the heir to Hell and only does what he chooses.

Oriel walks her to class; she quietly slots a visit to Dank on the schedule. Salem tags along. She boots them both from the exam room so she can ask Dank questions she doesn't want echoed in the hall. He gives her a potion to keep her secret protected and a pamphlet that—later—will have her mind spinning.

Back in the dorm, Oriel and Salem ask to show her their animals—low-stakes exposure therapy. She agrees. The crow and the panda appear, and both love her. The rest of the caliphate comes home mid-cuddle and bristles because they wanted to go first. She promises they'll all get a turn. Jasper orders the shifts undone, which leaves two naked demons standing in front of Kat while she tries not to choke on air.

She's rattled enough to obsess over whether Salem deciphered the potion's purpose and to spiral about Dank's very educational pamphlet. A professor tries to embarrass her by asking about human-world sex education. She survives that too. After lunch she circles back to Oriel and Salem, ready to see their demons.

It's hard for them—they know their demons are attracted to her and that they're walking a thin line. The scene thrums with tension right up until someone pounds on the door. Slash and Anton stand there, insistent escorts to class.

Days later at *Triclinium*, the conversation swerves to uniforms. Xerxes shares the fight they had to wage for their own presentation. Kat is furious on their behalf, which turns into a wider compare-and-contrast about human school clothes. Slash shadows Oriel and Kat after lunch, suspicious they're avoiding the group. He tracks them to a quiet library floor where they sprawl and talk. He figures out Kat isn't moping over rejection—she's unnerved by hot-and-cold distance while the guys try to keep their animals and demons from stampeding.

Jasper's next class delivers Games uniforms and cruel conditioning. He runs everyone ragged. Zavida clocks how on-edge Jasper is and wonders if a geas is throttling his ability to warn them. That possibility chills the room. Most head to Kat's dorm, but Zavida hunts down Jasper to bleed off the fury.

Xerxes detours Kat to their room. They've put the pieces together and state it plain: they think the secret is real, not misdirection. Kat makes them promise silence. She'll tell the others when trust catches up to love. X promises stealth support—clothes, binders, whatever's needed—since destruction and accidents keep shredding her stash. They seal it with a blood pact. For now, that has to be enough.

Next day, Anton is prickly with suspicion and a little shut-out, but it's their usual game with X, so he lets it go. When Kat and Salem emerge, they pile into the elevator with Anton and head to class. Jasper lectures them on unity in public. In Wormwood's class, the professor hands out a list of spells including ones that shouldn't be in circulation. Everyone goes tight with alarm.

Lucian smirks through the next period. At lunch nothing explodes. In Weapons, Kat has to enchant a weapon like everyone else except she has no magic. Anton and X promise to help. The matchups are rigged to push Kat into danger and scatter the caliphate so they can't cover her.

An opponent threatens the exact wrong thing. It triggers the exact wrong memory. Kat's powers surge, wild and unchecked. The arena descends into chaos. Caliphate members rage out or fall. Jasper shifts full dragon and takes the sky. It takes dragging brothers from their classes to crush the riot, get Jasper back to human, and get Kat under control. They ignore other demons' injuries and deaths to haul their own to Dank's private office.

Dank treats X and Zavida first—they're worst off. Then he brings Kat in. She begs him to keep the others out of her bay. He sedates her to heal. While she's under, a Lady visits in a vivid dream—advice, destiny, warnings that won't hold still when Kat wakes. When she opens her eyes, everyone is hovering. They bring Dottie.

Dank portals her to bed once she's stable enough to move. The group agrees Kat and X will rest in the main room so people can rotate watch between classes. Neither patient loves it; both accept a compromise. Slash carries Kat to her room when it's time to change. Oriel appears to help with toiletries and admits how scared he was. Kat doesn't have a file for that emotion yet.

Morning brings X's private calculus about Kat's power—what it looked like in the arena, what it might mean about lineage. The boys compare notes. When they realize what kind of threat triggered her, even Jasper is incandescent. They plan to train smarter. Another day, a follow-up trip to Dank. On the way, Slash mutters that he would solve the people who hurt her in his favorite way if she'd let him. Kat is understandably startled by the blunt promise.

Meanwhile, Oriel turns thief for the greater good—breaking into Wormwood's office to learn why a professor is pushing forbidden spells. He snatches intel about snitches and compromising hookups, photographs a hidden compartment full of special items, and eyes a black book that might be spelled. Curiosity wins. He opens it, but he doesn't get caught.

At Dank's office, Kat confesses to Slash and X that she thinks she stopped time during Lucian's speech. They tell her never to say that out loud again because chronomancy paints a target on her back. X helps Kat through a small breakdown fueled by too many secrets pressing at once.

Back in Arms, Jasper's irritation turns volcanic. He's done being the administrator's marionette. He storms into the admin office to confront Darkstar and gets a front-row seat to Lucian and Lillabet having sex. Lucian taunts him mid-thrust because of course he does. Jasper delivers a warning, gets a counterfeit promise, and leaves more furious than he came.

He returns to the dorm to find Oriel and Slash painting Kat's and X's toes on the couch—symbolically sitting below them, which flips a demon power dynamic on its head. Jasper snaps, and when Kat asks why, he forbids the entire caliphate from explaining. Petty? Yes. On brand? Also yes.

After they clear out, X convinces Kat to see their animal. She watches them shift into a cobra, wraps around them, and is still petting scales when Anton arrives. His bird gets jealous. She lets him reveal it too. Oriel and Salem get home and shift. The pile grows—four demons in animal form curled against Kat. Jasper walks in and erupts. Slash and Zavida are jealous in quieter shades. Kat covers her eyes so brothers can shift back into clothes. Jasper furies that class was skipped for cuddles.

They table the fight and plan a surface trip. Jasper believes Lucian has backing from outside Discordia. They need to snoop, but Jasper's father must approve the pass. Before they go, Kat and Salem have a close moment in the kitchen that tips toward a kiss before footsteps cut it off. Xerxes appears with replacement school gear since disaster keeps eating hers. Oriel presents surface clothes from his hoard—unprecedented generosity. Everyone stares. Kat tries them on and they fit, because O hoards for a reason.

They portal to Bay City, where the streets are weirdly empty. Jasper orders a supe-rideshare, and the car drops them near a shuttered block where only Rigoletto's tailor shop glows. Inside, the tailor is a half-shifted brown recluse spider and Kat nearly passes out at the reveal.

He offers to outfit them for an Apalachin, and if Jasper didn't know whether they were walking into a trap, he knows they're walking into a world that watches. Laurel the raccoon shifter assists, and thankfully, Kat's secret stays safe. The outfits are tailored from available garments and they leave looking like the kind of people who belong anywhere they decide is theirs.

They find the keyed portal, step through, and land in an event with sections mapped to supe species. First stop is Fae-land, and the redcap gatekeeper demands a secret from each of them as toll. They pay. A market sprawls ahead, and everyone splits to investigate. Oriel leads Kat past a jewelry stall that hums against her skin. After hard bargaining, he buys a collar that sings to her—and to the place. When it clicks around her throat, something changes. As they move, the collar and Kat's magic pulse near specific tents. The caliphate shifts into ready stances as they investigate.

A group approaches that Jasper recognizes—including another dragon. It's Morgana and her men from State University. Kaspar and Jasper exchange taunts and recognize each other underneath their disguises. Prince Liam compliments Jasper for seeing through glamour. Cards swap hands, and future cooperation becomes possible.

The collar prickles again, and Kat warns them a beat before the world breaks. Crashes, cracks, the tearing of tents. Salem scoops Kat over his shoulder and runs for cover, following standing orders: get her safe first. She fights to be put down, but he doesn't stop until they're tucked into a hide.

Outside, chaos howls, but inside, Kat's panic spikes. Salem moves deeper and distracts her with touch that somehow calms instead of harming. It tilts toward heavy and real, and Kat realizes he's about to find out her truth by accident. She stops him, looks him in the eye, and says it herself.

That's the cliff we left dangling from before the bonus—her secret spoken aloud to Salem while the rest of their caliphate fights an unknown enemy.

Love In An Elevator

Kit/Kat

My lips twist as I look at the guys standing uncomfortably in the elevator. It's moving crazily, zipping around horizontally and vertically, which I've never seen outside of the movies. They don't seem perturbed by the odd motion though, only the destination we're headed for. Salem has his hand at the small of my back, his fingertips resting there lightly where the others can't see, but I can definitely feel.

It's both comforting and exciting, which is balancing out my anxiety spikes.

"I liked them," I blurt out. The silence was driving me crazy, and I don't know why I said that specifically, but someone had to say something.

Jasper grunts, eyeing me suspiciously. "That's twice today you've been nice to new people. It's probably a fucking record."

I open my mouth to retort, but I suddenly realize that he might be right. Ducking my head for a moment as I get myself together, I curl and uncurl my toes in my shoes. Once I've evened out, I meet his gaze, shrugging. "They weren't assholes to me from the second we met. It goes a long way, especially for someone like me."

Slash flashes my favorite grin at me. "Friends are good for you, little demon. But I will make them suffer if they do not behave."

Oriel chuckles, his eyes dancing with merriment. "I think that's fair, don't you, KK?"

"Probably," I admit as I think about it. "But I'm not sure your idea of behaving and mine are copacetic. I'd prefer he not eat anyone unless I give the go-ahead. Friends bicker sometimes, and make mistakes that hurt each other as far as I know. Morgana and Rogue seem pretty cool, so I doubt they'd do anything bad on purpose, but I'd like to make sure they aren't consumed for specious reasons."

"Check with Kit Kat first before taking vengeance—got it," X says cheerily as they wink at me. "Now that we've weighed in on the social register, can we talk about what the fuck we're going to find on the seventh level of this stupid labyrinth?"

My brow furrows as I notice the change in their stances. "Okay, I read the Inferno a long time ago. Refresh my memory, please."

"The seventh circle of Hell is supposed to be violence," Zavida says as he pushes his glasses up. "Obviously, the structure of our world down there isn't exactly described correctly in that work, but it seems like Gemini has this set up that way."

"Most of our atrocities get sent to either survive or perish in the Wastelands," Anton adds. "You don't know the geography yet, but there are other sections of the realm besides Canto IV, obviously. They aren't circles or levels—more like humans would define as small countries. It's a lot like… Europe, I think?"

I think about that for a moment, digesting his description and assimilating the information into my new reality. "Okay. So they aren't defined by the different sins or whatever? Keep in mind, I've never lived with a religious family, so I'm fuzzy on some details of that mythos."

"Ah, but they are." X grins broadly, their face lighting up. "Because we are, too. Each of us is the heir to a family line that sits on the royal court of Hell, right?"

I nod, tilting my head at them. "That's what people keep pointing out."

"Our families are the heads of each line—with our parents being the rulers currently. As you might imagine, the Strykers are the heads of the Sloth line," Salem says as he looks down at me. "And me turning out to have a panda side has always been something I get to live with other demons knocking on. It's stupidly appropriate, and I was lucky to be born an heir so I could bond with these guys. It keeps most of the bullshit from touching me."

"People are assholes," I say, my face pinching in anger at the thought of other demons giving the gentle guy shit. "I think your bear is cool as fuck."

Salem beams at me and Oriel elbows him in the side with a smirk. "Stop hogging the attention, bro." The dark-haired demon turns his intense gaze on me, looking amused. "I'm the heir to the Greed line. As he said, the crow portion of my blood is spot on, but no one dares give me crap about it. I'm far too good at stealing anything that isn't nailed down. They don't want me to find the things they desperately want to hide."

"That explains that stupid guild and that jackass who was being rude. You're both naturally and genetically inclined to be better than all of them. That was the first time you ever demanded the lead, though, right?" I squint at him curiously and he nods. "Man, did I step in it without knowing."

"I'm sure you did, KK," Xerxes cuts in. "Oriel's never wanted the spotlight, so they weren't used to him claiming the crown—regardless of how accurate it is for him to wear it."

"What are you, then?" I pause, licking my lips as I consider the possibilities for a moment. "Wait, you're a snake, and you're very alluring. Are you Lust?"

"Ding-ding." Anton winks at me, his rainbow hair falling over his eyes. "And of course, I'm the heir to Pride. It becomes more obvious as you go along, I fear."

My gaze roves over Zavida, Slash, and Jasper. "That makes him Envy, you Gluttony, and Prince Prickface is Wrath. All of which fit you so perfectly, that it makes me feel dumb not to have put it together by now."

Jasper opens his mouth to comment, but Slash stops him. "Do not, Prince. He was not familiar with the supernatural, nor the human writings about our realm. It is in poor taste to mock him."

"Fine," the dickwad grumbles as he sighs. "Since I can't tease you for missing what was right in front of your nose, I'll simply say that many centuries of intermingling and staying away from the surface have spread all the types of demons to the various lines. That's how you get an incubus like Anton in the Pride line, and hybrids across the board."

This is the most information they've ever given me and it's going to end soon when the damn elevator to Hades stops—I'm so pissed right now.

"The weather dragon and Morgana's people seemed confused about what kind of dragon you are. Is it some big secret?"

Jasper's eyes darken and he gives me a slow, sexy smirk that I want to bask in. "Sort of. I don't give weapons to those who might use them against me, so that is a well-guarded secret. Perhaps some day, you'll be worthy of it, but that is not today, shrimp."

Annnnd now I fucking hate him again.

"Whatever. Keep your scaly secret, then." I fold my arms over my chest and Salem's palm presses against my lower back lightly. That he's helping me stay level is kind of amazing, and I'm not sure how to respond to it… but I like it. "If you won't tell me that, then let's get back to what's going to be happening when this stupid door opens."

Zavida scratches his chin, his tails puffed around him, but not blocking my view. "As far as the text goes, it's about violence. Dante said it had three circles inside of it for criminals who hurt others, then those who harmed themselves, and finally, those who did their crimes to God and nature. I doubt the Geminis are worried about being that accurate, so my guess is that this floor will have the hunts, a fighting ring, probably some sado-masochistic set-ups, and stuff like that. But it will be pretty gory and hard to watch, no question about that."

Putting my hands on my face, I suck in a slow breath. Gore isn't really my issue; I've watched horror movies that were gross. There's really only one violent thing that will definitely cause a problem, and if I'm lucky, that isn't what this stupid bacchanalian event will be focused on. I look up at the demons carefully, licking my lips before I say, "I think I'll be okay for most of it. I'm not triggered by violence on TV or gory stuff in movies. I'm sure there will be things I don't expect and I might be grossed out by stuff. The only thing I really need you to watch for is… well, you all sort of know. If we happen on that, I won't fight anyone who whisks me away, so I don't draw too much attention. Okay?"

Slash's eyes meet mine as he growls, "We will make sure you are not harmed, little demon. Just like in the battle, someone will make certain you are safe."

I let out a relieved sigh, dipping my chin as I look at my shoes. I'm a pain in the ass to have along because of my bullshit, and I hate to think that they'll eventually grow tired of it like everyone else has. The amount of times foster parents or siblings accused me of being a 'woe is me' whiner or called my panic attacks tantrums or drama is significantly more than zero. It's a common insult to throw at people with mental health issues because the generations before mine weren't taught to treat them the same way they would diabetes or a heart condition. I can't stop my anxiety, my intrusive thoughts, or my panic attacks anymore than those people can stop their insulin from spiking or their arteries from clogging.

I've learned to ignore the shitty comments because I know they just don't understand because it's not happening to them.

But these guys have become important to me and I think having them turn on me that way would break me. So I force a small smile, nodding at the shark shifter as I push away my innermost fears. "Thanks, big guy. I don't enjoy thinking about being weak, but I'm not dumb enough to believe that demons acting out their darkest fantasies and violent behaviors might not cause a problem with my stupid brain."

"KK, stop beating yourself up," Xerxes chides. "No one is mad that you have issues. We put up with Jasper's rage and Slash wanting to eat everyone when they look at him funny. Anton and I sometimes lose control of our tempers and it makes people do… fascinating things you haven't seen yet. Oriel even steals from us, and we know it was him. And Salem falls asleep in the middle of important shit. Everyone has baggage, and if people don't get that, they can fuck right off."

Their words hit me in the chest and I feel heat spread all over me as the others nod in agreement. I wasn't prepared for this much acceptance in such a small space, and it feels like they're all so close that I'm drowning in their giant dude-ness. My fists clench at my sides as I figure out how to respond without crying like a dumbass, and I take a few long, heavily silent moments before I work out what I'm going to say.

"Since my… thing… I haven't really let anyone get to know me because I'm never sure that I can trust them. You guys are the first ones I've wanted to do the work to be able to connect with. So… thank you for saying that, even though I didn't admit out loud that I worry you'll tire of having to deal with my bullshit."

Salem snorts, his hand moving to grasp my waist lightly. "Oh, Kit Kat. As if you could get rid of a bunch of spoiled assholes who always get what they want, like us. Perish the thought."

His saucy retort makes the others laugh, even Jasper, and I lean into the panda demon slightly.

If I was gonna choose anyone to let in first, Salem Stryker might have been the best choice I could have possibly made.

CHANGES

JASPER

I won't admit it out loud, but I'm very conflicted about this plan. It's the most logical course of action, which is why I agreed with both the Geminis and my general when it was suggested. However, I have a leaden sensation in my gut that is making my dragon *and* my demon restless despite their satisfaction at getting to decimate that orc earlier. The feeling of dread sitting deep inside of me makes me look over at the shrimp when the doors to the dungeon open.

His lack of control over his developing powers and small stature worry me like Zavida's did many years ago.

The comparison makes me uneasy, so I cut my gaze to the darkness outside of the open doors. "Slash leads. Keep the shrimp in the middle, surrounded. Zav, be ready to illuminate if needed."

Anticipation ripples through my caliphate; except for Kit, we've trained together for many years, so they know what their roles are if we're attacked. That helps the gnawing concern a little, but not entirely. I won't be able to call on one of them to hide the kid like we did on Faerie lands—this place might not even *have* a safe place to conceal him. More than likely, safety is the only thing not available in Gemini's recreation of the seventh ring.

"You know, since you all revealed your demons and spoiled the whole 'slowly get acclimated' thing, I'm kind of hoping to yank the band-aid off the rest of the animals, too. Well, except Prince Prickface, because I saw his dragon, too." Kit pauses for a moment as we exit the elevator and start moving through the inky atmosphere in formation. "There's only Zav and the big guy's left."

Slash chuckles softly, and I marvel at how emotive he's become since this kid arrived. Prior to Kit's arrival, my second-in-command rivaled the Easter Island statues for silence most of the time. Now he's not only talking more, but laughing and smiling when he's not about to destroy someone. It's bizarre, and I have no idea how to handle it, either. His voice is low as he replies, "Sharks require liquid, little demon, not land. I could not fully shift here."

Not to be outdone, I interject, "And Zav frequently has his tails out, so you've seen plenty of him."

I sense the eyes on me as we stride forward, and I'm sure they're all judging me. It takes a moment before Xerxes speaks up, their voice full of amusement. "Are you concerned with how much KK sees of us in our natural forms, Prince? It's not as if we're posing for nudie mags."

The shrimp coughs and I swear, I feel the heat of his embarrassment radiating from him. My eyes narrow and for a moment, my focus wavers from our surroundings to wondering why he and several of my brothers seem to be suspiciously quiet after Xerxes' declaration. It's as if there's something that happened that none of them have shared and that makes me simmer with anger. Our caliphate cannot be united if we are all hiding things from one another.

I knew this little shit would be bad for unity—and here's my proof.

"Someone tell me what the unholy fuck is making you all—"

Slash stops short and I almost run into the back of my huge friend because I'm distracted. He turns, and my demonic eyes flash as our gazes clash. "Do not be foolish, Jasper. Can you not sense the waves of envy flowing through this chamber?"

"That's not it," Zavida mutters, and if we were alone, I'd paddle his delectable ass as red as his hair for the sass.

Anton clears his throat, his voice calm as he adds, "While I would never argue with our Envy brother about the effects of the line, I believe Slash is correct in his statement about the energy in this antechamber. My bird is ruffled inside, and he's unusually communicative with the incubus. That is causing it to be difficult to focus on the task at hand rather than what they are whispering in my mind."

The peacock hybrid is correct, I realize. My mind has been running over things I already know and honing in on things that soothe my dragon—hoarding what's mine to myself. Drawing in a slow breath through my nose, I close my eyes for a second while I speak to the inner monsters. Once I've commanded their submission, I can open my eyes and see much more clearly in the dimly lit room. Someone quite powerful embedded that little booby trap just outside of the doorway, and I bet it was to amp the newcomers up so they are simmering with emotion by the time they get to the main area.

"Fucking Gemini assholes," I mutter as I shake my head. "Guaranteed, there are cameras hidden here so they can watch the carnage while they wank off later on."

"Ew," Kit says and I spin on my heel to look at the kid who fueled my earlier turmoil. "What? I don't need to picture some random demon peeling his banana to a snuff film. It's gross, especially because I got the heebie jeebies about these dickwhistles from the way Rogue and the twins talked about them. I'm pretty prepared for these people to act like 'To Catch A Predator' featured targets."

Honestly, he's not wrong—the elder Geminis are well known for depravity.

"Fair enough," I sigh. The others look at me in surprise, and I shrug. "Slash is correct; if we cannot manage our emotions effectively, we will run into more surprises like this. The further in and down we go, the stronger they will be. Watching out for one another is paramount."

Zavida peeks out from behind the tails he escaped in when I snarked at him. "Code word, Jas?"

That's a good idea. I give him a pleased nod, and he emerges a bit more from the safety of his appendages. "Yes, Zav, I think we should have a word any of us can say to alert the others that they are being magically manipulated."

"Like a safe word for fuckery!"

Every one of us turns to look at the shrimp and he crosses his arms over his chest as he scowls. "Stop doing that. I used the term correctly, jackasses."

He did, and that's the entire issue. But instead of letting this get us off-track again, I clear my throat and reply, "So you did. Suggestions?"

"Inconceivable!" Oriel says, his face lighting up as he grins at the shrimp. I arch a brow, not getting it, but the way Kit and Salem look excited tells me this must be something they learned from him.

Slash tilts his head, then nods. "That is acceptable."

I wait until the others give their agreement, noting that whatever inside joke this phrase comes from is shared only between Kit, the crow, and the panda. Those three are getting awfully cozy, and—

Damn this fucking envy magic; it's not greater than my own, but it's pervasive if I don't keep my focus sharp.

"Fine. That word will be the signal that one or more of us are being affected by something and we need to wrestle free of it." That settled, I look at my general, gesturing to the darkness ahead. "Let's keep going or we'll never get home."

THE PATHWAY INTO THE MAIN AREA OF LEVEL SEVEN WAS LONG, AND WE HAD to pause several times to quell various inclinations of our animals or demons. It was obviously designed to ramp up emotions and supernatural sides as much as possible before guests arrived in the vast chamber we're standing at the edge of now.

My nostrils flare as they fill with the scent of blood, sweat, cum, and tears so strongly that I have to fight off an immediate shift. Sneering at the sheer amount of screams that echo off the walls, I grit my teeth and face my caliphate. Except for the kid, they're wearing similar grimaces. As demons, we're not turned off by the prospect of sex and violence—especially combined—but there's a current of evil running through the activities going on in this big ass underground coliseum of filth. All my instincts are rebelling against it in a way I've never felt before.

"I hate to be a Judgy Judy," Kit says as he looks at the group of demons and shifters experimenting with violently sadistic bondage toys in a nearby corner. "But that looks painful *and* like the people being whipped didn't agree to be there. We need to move somewhere else before I think about it too hard, please."

His voice trembles a little, but instead of commenting on it, I nod sharply. "Slash, lead us away from the posts. Whichever direction you feel is best, old friend, but make this view go away."

A feral grin takes over his face and I'm not sure if it's because he's enjoying the feel of unchecked rage like me, or because I didn't give his favorite trainee shit about his shakiness. I'd prefer it to be the former, but somehow, I doubt I'd get my wish if I asked. So I follow him, our pace casual as Slash diverts our path toward what smells like it's going to be a centurion pit. They're common in the Wastelands, and it's not a shock that they'd have one here. I didn't expect it to be as big as the one we're now facing, nor packed to the gills with half-naked, beaten supes of various species attacking one another as if their lives depend on it.

Which I'm certain they do because the wrath emanating from that pit is strong enough to make my dragon take notice.

"This is…" Zavida trails off as he scoots up next to me, the soft brush of his tails letting me know he's struggling. "… barbaric."

I nod, taking his hand behind the furry appendages and squeezing it. "This is how my line meted out justice in the darkest ages. Prisoners sentenced to death were sent to the Wastelands to be shoved into a pit with nothing but each other and the guards watched as they slowly killed one another, wasted away, became cannibals, etc. Now they use those pits for fights to the death, but not this."

"KK, don't. You don't want—"

Salem's voice is filled with worry as the kid elbows his way out of the middle to step up, even with Zav, Slash, and me. His eyes narrow on the screaming, fighting mass of supernaturals tearing one another apart and his lips press into a grim line. "Humans think demons are harbingers of evil. They blame their bad actions on possession or influence from them. But this looks as disturbing as things I've seen in history books, and I'll be damned if we didn't do this shit ourselves."

I expected him to lose it—to have one of his panic attacks and retreat into his mind until someone brought him back like usual. But I was incorrect; the demon inside of him is seeping into him more quickly than he's letting on. Kit prepped us to save him from the ugliness he won't be able to avoid in this compound, but he's doing much better than he thought he would.

"Evil is evil, no matter what species it is," Zav says as he looks at the kid. Shrugging, he jerks his chin at the pit. "There's always shades darker than what you have seen before. It's a bottomless well, Kit Kat."

The shrimp nods, letting out a slow breath as he continues to watch the mayhem as if he's trying to condition himself not to be revolted. A tremor runs over him, and my lips quirk when I see my Kitsuné reach his other hand out to lace his fingers with Kit's. I'm certain he'll pull away and Zav will be hurt, but miraculously, that doesn't happen.

Things are changing swiftly indeed, and I've been too damned full of my own shit to notice.

Start A War
Kit/Kat

The warm hand in mine comforts me and I squeeze Zavida's palm gratefully. I'm getting used to this gesture, especially since it's the preferred method of all the guys now. Well, except for Prince Asswad, but I think I'd be so shocked if he did that I'd forget my 'disguise' and make weird noises. It's probably for the best that he doesn't; I'm definitely not ready to accept anything resembling kindness in physical form from him.

But everyone else is okay, and that helps me ignore the bloody bodies more easily.

"You're right, Zav," I say absently. "And it doesn't have to take this form for it to be just as terrible. This is just less subtle and more aligned with what people think is 'acceptable' evil."

Jasper arches a brow at me, his expression curious. "Acceptable evil?"

I snort, shaking my head. "If you think people on the surface aren't paying to watch desperate beings kill one another for sport, you're seriously deluded. The rich fucks in the one percent up there have been slowly revealed as rotten to the core in ways the populace didn't expect in the past few years. I don't know if it started with realizing half our country wasn't worried if millions died with the virus or what, but it's pretty gross up there, too."

"Denizens of our realm have been working overtime, my father says." Slash nods, tilting his head at the writhing mass of new contestants in the ring. "The little demon is correct."

"On that note…" X winks at me, their eyes full of understanding about how much control it's taking me to keep myself level right now. "We should keep moving. I'm afraid if we don't, someone will notice that the big guy—"

He's cut off by a high-pitched yelp as the wolf shifter in the ring falls to the Minotaur. The crowd around us roars in approval, making the area echo with various sounds I can't assign to specific supernaturals. It's like I'm stuck by the fucking pit on Tattooine and instead of aliens, I've got all these demons and beasts surrounding me. The absolutely useless demon who is pretending to referee the match yells something I don't quite catch, but a wave of on-lookers part for him.

At least, I think it's a 'him'; I'm not sure in this demon form.

"Demons and guests, *look* at the size of this demon! You know he's a contender; make some noise to encourage an actual player into the ring!"

My eyes bug out when the guy points at Slash—of course—and the shark demon grunts in irritation. We were hoping to lie low on this disgusting level, but there's little hope of that if we refuse to play along. The crowd is cheering now, screaming their support for the enormous shifter who treats me like china to jump in that death circle. My anxiety skyrockets within seconds, and the Kitsuné grips my hand tightly.

"Kit, if he has to do this, Slash will be fine. You haven't seen—or don't remember from the class—but he is the fiercest warrior, even in half-shifted form." Zavida gives me a serious look as I force myself to nod. His expression softens as he leans in to whisper in my ear, "It's okay to care about him; we all do. But I promise, out of anyone besides the prince, he's the best choice."

When I turn to look at my 'trainer', he's muttering with Jasper low enough that I can't quite catch it over the din. Jasper looks pissed, and I don't blame him this time. We don't need Slash getting injured and we don't need the attention if he refuses. It's a Catch-22, and the prince is left weighing two shitty options. The other guys stay quiet, which I assume must be their default when command decisions are required.

I think I'm witnessing how the caliphate operates when they are in 'battle mode'.

They finally break their little tête-à-tête and Slash turns to the much smaller demon ref. "I will win one round, then cede my spot to the demon of your choosing."

The ref looks at the shark shifter as if he's insane. "Moab the Great is the undefeated champion. You won't last long enough to consider a replacement. But if you found the grace of victory, I cannot amend the rules of the ring to allow you to leave before defeat."

Suddenly, Oriel is standing next to the big guy, his dark eyes glittering with intelligence. He looks the lower demon up and down, then scoffs. "There is no visible contract stating that and my friend will not shake on that bargain. You're not a high enough rank to compel him to do so, either. Your options are to shake on his deal—since fighting until defeat in this game equals death, and he is not agreeing to that—or we walk. Your sponsors running the line in the crowds will be displeased, I think."

I follow the crow's gaze to several demons running around talking to people in the audience, obviously taking bets. The thief clocked every single one in our immediate area, and the ref's expression turns nervous as fuck. Jasper smirks at the guy, his arms crossed over his chest as he waits for the response to O's offer. This is clearly my emo friend's area of expertise because the prince didn't bat a lash when he took over.

My guys are working together like perfectly designed cogs in a machine, and it's fascinating.

"Are you afraid your fighter will lose?" Anton asks casually. There's a soft golden glow around him and I feel the magic brush against my skin as he sends it toward the ref dude. "It will damage your reputation equally if you chicken out now."

Remembering what they said in the elevator, I realize that he must be using powers from his Pride lineage to push the guy. It's working, I think, because now the asshole is rubbing the back of his neck as his gaze darts to some of the bet takers. I feel a tickle on the nape of my neck and turn slightly to figure out where it's coming from. My eyes finally land on a big, ugly demon that I can't categorize standing against a rocky column. I think this guy's the boss, so I carefully shift just enough that I can tug Jasper's jacket hem.

His eyes flash with his dragon as he looks at me and I cut my gaze to the Hulk-like demon watching the whole pit. The corner of his mouth quirks a tiny bit, and he nods ever-so-slightly before turning back to Oriel. I have to hide my grin when the look passes from one of my guys to another and I have to suppress the urge to fist pump. I think I just accomplished my first 'eyebrow conversation'.

Fuck, yeah, Kat—you're a rockstar.

I'm seldom that complimentary of myself, but having them all next to me is having a weird effect on that. Salem's praise, Zav's warm palm, and the reassurance all the guys have been giving me are definitely helping me find myself. That, too, interrupts the flow of my anxiety and fear about Slash competing, and I take a deep breath. If anyone can do this, it's the big guy who battles for sport, right?

"Fine," the grumpy ref says after a few moments. "I agree. You may leave the ring once you defeat my champion. You are not bound to the usual rules of play in our game."

Something about the way he says that pricks my brain, and I look at Slash as he nods. He's already locking himself down, getting ready to fight as he waits for the demon to lead him to the front. Jasper's jaw is set as well, and he follows his general as we all move. Biting my lip, I let go of Zav's hand, moving over to Oriel so I can speak to him quietly.

"I don't like that bargain." The crow grimaces, looking at me as he tilts his head. "I know I'm not… you know… versed in this stuff yet, but it's *bothering* me. Why say 'not bound by the rules of our game' specifically, rather than not 'bound to fight to the death' or whatever? It feels wrong, O."

Oriel looks thoughtful, his eyes landing on the boss demon, then coming back to me. "You might be right, KK. Your demon side is flaring because it senses a bad bargain—that's a good thing, but also a bad thing for our friend."

"I know," I whisper. "That's why *you* need to tell Jasper to yank him before this goes sideways."

An alarm sounds, and I whirl around to look at the ring. The muscled Minotaur is huffing through its bovine nose, his expression vicious as he gets into his stance. Slash ignores the dude, unbuttoning the rest of his dress shirt, then grinning at me with his sharp teeth. He tosses the jacket and shirt at me, which I scramble to catch, then winks. I swallow hard when I realize we aren't going to stop this now, and I have to watch him get hurt.

I want to kill the fucking demons hosting this damn party myself, but I feel Rogue's twins want that honor.

Gritting my teeth as I clutch the big guy's clothes, I try to slow my panicked breathing so I don't overload. Luckily, the scent of Salem and Oriel surrounds me as they position themselves close enough to touch me. That helps ground my anxiety and I lick my lips. I can do this; I can watch this violent bullshit and cheer for Slash because he's going to win. There's no other option—if he doesn't, I don't know which one of my caliphate is going to decimate this entire damn space first.

"Slash does not lose, shrimp," Jasper mutters to my left. "He was born for battle."

The Prince's comment is oddly comforting, and I nod, looking at him with fearful eyes. I don't enjoy sharing that emotion with him because he's likely to tease me. However, this time, he simply reaches down and ruffles my hair. My eyes widen at the touch, distracted enough that I miss the *ding* that signals the start of the fight. Once I'm settled again, I watch Slash dance around the circle with surprising speed as he assesses the Minotaur's style.

"He's figuring out how the guy fights," Salem murmurs. "We weren't paying close attention before and if Slash is gonna kick this cow's ass, he has to anticipate its moves."

I wrinkle my nose up at him with a tremulous smile. "I've seen Rocky, too, chef."

This time it's the panda's turn to gape, and he narrows his gaze on me for a brief second. "You, KK, might be a brat. I'm not sure how well that will go for you later on."

Crossing my arms over my chest, I spin back to the grunting fighters, my attention on the quiet guy who talks to me when we're alone. His blunt observations are always helpful to me, and I didn't even mind him carrying me those times—much. Being around the shark is easy and relaxing, unless he's smothering me with nutrition demands.

A loud sound comes from the bovine when Slash's enormous fist finds its target somewhere around kidney-level—though I have no idea if that fucker's kidneys are there or somewhere else. I'm having enough trouble learning the animalian and demon anatomy of my guys, much less other supe species. Slash snarls when the guy reels back, pressing forward in a flurry of punches that are definitely hurting the former champion. Since his hands are like a pair of damned cement blocks, I don't know how the Minotaur is still standing. He must have, like, armor or something.

Cheers and shouts echo off the high ceiling of the pit area as Slash continues to pummel the asshole, but it gets even louder when there's a flash of light in the ring. Squinting as it fades, I try to work out what the fuck is going on and once I do; I gasp. He's fully shifted into a fire-breathing bull, his eyes filled with rage. Panic races through me because I know Slash can't fully shift on land, but it stops short when our guy goes with a better option.

Holy Mother of Medusa, Slash in full demon form is easily four times bigger and a lot scarier.

Holy Mother of Medusa, Slash in full demon form is easily four times bigger and a lot scarier.

BATTLE ROYALE
SLASH

It is good that this chamber is large enough to allow my full demon visage. The others cannot hear the trash talk of this side of beef from their spot in the raucous crowd, but I can. His vile statements regarding my brothers—without even being intelligent enough to realize who we are—activated my darkest parts more quickly than normal. That is impressive, given my typical participation in competitive demon events, but it is not as if I do not know why.

This walking filet threatened the little demon and Zavida.

Roaring with the fury of a vengeance demon unleashed, I tower over the Minotaur with my razor-sharp teeth. In full transformation, my skin is a dark charcoal gray and my eyes flash with the red fire of justice. My caliphate brothers have very different horns and tails because of our animals, and I am not an exception to this rule. Twin horns shaped like white fins adorn my head and the long tail has both dorsal and caudal fins, just like my shark. I swish the sharply bladed tail around, clearing the space around me as they avoid the fins that, in this form, could cut off their limbs.

The giant bull bellows, and huffs steam, letting me know it is going to charge. Digging my feet in, I ready myself for the attack. This ridiculous fool believes he will toss me like a matador in Pamplona, but that will not be the case. Once I am set in my position, the difference in our strength and power will become evident. But I must be patient and keep my counsel rather than allowing him to continue to get under my skin.

"Here it comes, demons and guests…. Moab is preparing for the final blow!"

I snort, the corner of my mouth lifting at the announcer's claim. He has no idea who he made a bargain with and somehow, that's the least of his worries. I am going to destroy his best fighter so thoroughly that it will break up this entire fight ring. His benefactor in the back is going to be furious and it will not be at me. Or… if he wants to live, it won't.

"Take him out, big guy!"

Fire licks across the ring, and the Minotaur rears back before shooting forward at a gallop. The sound of the little demon yelling from the sidelines, so careful not to say my name lest someone identify us, makes my shark *and* my demon determined to defeat my foe. I would have shredded this bovine before, but now my supernatural influences want to show Kit that we can be trusted to protect him. That alone is making the magic burn under my skin and my magic swell into a dark ball between my palms.

My kind are not to be trifled with, particularly those of my line, and when the angry cow is within range, I unleash a torrent of magical fury at it. It makes a squealing grunt of pain as the force of my power smacks into it and sends it sailing through the air to slam into the barrier around the ring. Fire shoots in every direction as the beast slides down the magical wall like water, and I duck the flames as I stalk across the space.

Like my animal, my focus is singular and my drive is focused on one outcome—annihilation.

The crowd goes wild and I ignore the noise of the on-lookers. I'm certain the line has shifted and bets are being placed, but I cannot worry about the fools who came here to waste their time and money for demons like the Gemini. My brothers and I would not even be here if not for the impending coup—nor would any demon who wanted to maintain a reputation in Hell.

"A lucky shot from the contender, but Moab is most powerful on the ropes!"

Scoffing under my breath, I stop just short of the injured bull. He is struggling to stand, obviously feeling the effects of his head being slammed into the barrier by my magic. I do not enjoy seeing this supposed 'mighty warrior' so crippled with one blow, but the demon running this fight club oversold his champion. The Minotaur might have been able to defeat the dregs he's been battling, but he is no match for demons or shifters of my level—even without my training.

I stomp forward, grabbing the bull by its horns and swing it into the air above my head. Slowly, I turn around and give the audience a dark, sharky smirk of satisfaction. I want them to be watching what happens if they try to attack me or my caliphate, so I pause for effect as the idiot above me struggles futilely. The Prince catches my eye, nodding slightly in approval, and with a roar of triumph, I slam the mythical onto the ground. It's hard enough to shake the entire room, and the crowd gets quiet for a split second.

That doesn't last for long, because Moab does not even attempt to crawl out of the bull-shaped hole in the floor. I sniff in derision, looking down to make certain the asshole is dead. He stays still for another minute, and the bell sounds a victory klaxon. The announcer rushes in as the barrier falls, ignoring me to find his fallen comrade.

Smirking, I shrink down to normal size, letting the demon fade as I head for my brothers. I push my way through the cheering demons and their guests until I reach them, anxious to ensure that they are secure. When I get to them, Salem rushes over with a jacket that I recognize as Jasper's, holding it in front of me. I frown, not sure what he's doing, batting his hands away in annoyance.

"Dude," he says as he grabs my arm. "You didn't strip before the demon. All we have left of your *clothes* is your freaking shirt."

I blink as understanding smacks into me. The little demon is hiding behind Oriel, who is desperately trying not to fall apart in laughter. My jaw grits as I curse my temper, and I sigh in irritation. "Jasper's coat will not fix my problem entirely, Salem."

Xerxes and Anton are huddled together, the two of them looking like they're going to explode if they don't laugh soon. Zavida is much the same, but he's hiding behind his tails to stay out of my eyesight. The Prince finally rolls his eyes—despite amusement dancing in them—and growls, "Use the coat to tie around the front for now, Slash. We'll find something to cover you better somewhere in this fucking cesspit, so the kid can come out of the crow's tail feathers."

"He doesn't have feathers right now!"

The indignant retort, muffled by Oriel's back, hits me just right and before I can stop it, I burst into laughter. My brothers look at me wide-eyed, unused to hearing me express my humor quite so publicly, but I cannot help it. Kit often does things that make me respond in unusual ways, and this is no exception. His inability to see people naked without turning into a tomato, and the crow demon helping him hide from my dick are hilarious, especially in our current situation.

"What the fuck is with you, Scrum?" Jasper mutters as he shakes his head. "This is hardly the time to be jolly."

I can't stop guffawing, so I ignore my old friend as I take the jacket from Salem. He helps me secure it as best we can by knotting it on my lower back, then he calls to the little demon.

"You can come out now, Kit Kat. The one-eyed whale is out of view."

"I am a great white, Salem, not a whale."

He rolls his eyes and snickers as Kit comes out from behind Oriel. "Well, I *could* have said Coke can clasper, but I think *that* is a conversation for *later*."

Kit turns a color that seems to almost be purple as he makes a shocked face and I groan inwardly. The sleepy bear has gotten quite mouthy on this trip, and I don't know why, but I will figure it out. His raunchy description is making the little demon look like one of the funny stooge men we watched, and if we don't shut it down, it will become obvious to those around us.

"Anatomical discussions need to be saved for a less public venue." Clearing my throat, I arch a brow at Kit, holding my hand out to him. "Come, little demon. Walk with me until I can locate appropriate attire."

He gives me an unsure expression. "I don't know Slash…"

My lips curl up as I shrug and turn on my heel to walk away. "As you wish, Kit."

A strangled sound makes me grin to myself as he realizes what walking *behind* me in this ridiculous get-up means. Within a few moments, Kit is at my side, grabbing my hand and squeezing it hard. I look down, my expression full of mirth as he glares.

"That was mean, big guy. I mean, I even *cheered* for you and I'm the least cheerful guy you know."

The red tint to his face pleases me, but not as much as the fact that he's not breaking down. In fact, despite watching me kill the bull and seeing my ass a moment ago… Kit is more calm than when we were in the elevator. So I smile down at him fondly as I reply, "Not mean, and I heard you yelling. You were much more enthusiastic than I would have expected. Normally, you save that kind of glee for poking at the prince."

"It's weird, I know. But I sort of wanted to make sure you knew we believed in you." The little demon ducks his head and shrugs. "I know you battle and stuff all the time—or did before Dickhead Lucian cancelled the extracurriculars. But this is more serious, you know?"

"Indeed." I flash him a supremely pleased grin as we continue walking through the den of debauchery. "I am proud that you are handling this so well."

The heat coming off of him assaults my still raw senses from the adrenaline of the fight and my supernatural side having control. He is definitely going to turn into a crimson fruit if he keeps doing that; my crow brother is correct in his past declarations. I hear a distinct cough and turn my head to find Jasper giving me his usual irritated scowl. I'm not worried that he seems so pissy; it's becoming more and more obvious that he is struggling hard to reconcile his desire to get closer to the little demon and his ingrained distrust of everyone who are not our long time brothers.

"You performed as expected, General," he says in a very low tone. "However, I expected a debrief afterward. Learning who the money demon was would have been beneficial, and now we're leaving the area without doing so."

I'm about to respond when Kit snickers. The sound increases slowly as we both look down at him, and before long, the small pet has scampered out of his bag to chitter along with his good humor. That makes him laugh harder, and he claps his free hand over his mouth to stem the sound as best he can.

"What is so fucking funny, shrimp?" Jasper growls in annoyance. He puffs up, holding his wrath at being laughed at, as he demands an answer.

"It's... it's..." Kit continues laughing, trying to get the words out as he shakes a bit in my grasp. "It's just that... you wanted... a debrief... and you sure as fuck got one."

Jasper's eyes widen as the innuendo strikes him and I burst out laughing as well. My humor rings out loud and clear as I get it, the delight in his bawdy little joke apparent. He definitely has been spending too much time alone with Oriel and Salem, but I find myself even more pleased and proud of him as he continues to snigger like a normal teenage male between us.

This is what I call progress, even if the Prince is scowling harder than ever before.

Deal
Kit/Kat

I'm pretty proud of my little joke, and it seems like the big guy is too—which makes me inordinately happy. Dottie is perched on my shoulder as I let Slash and the begrudgingly quiet prince lead me through another section of shudder-worthy demon gangs doing violent things in front of cheering audiences. I'm not sure if it's all kink or if it's something else entirely, but I'm sure as fuck not going to ask. All I want to do right now is find some damn pants for the shark shifter and get whatever intel the guys think is enough, so we can get out of here.

I thought Discordia was nerve-wracking, but this is on an entirely different planet.

"Are you okay, little demon?" Slash says as he continues to watch everything he can as we move.

The tension in his form isn't from the fight, nor his nudity. I'm quickly figuring out how little supernaturals care about public sexual encounters or being bare assed where others can see. Historically speaking, that's the icky Puritan stuff ingrained in Americans rather than solely because of my trauma. But knowing something logically and reconciling years of conditioning are two completely opposite things. I'm getting better at avoiding a trigger moment when it happens, but I'm still not quite at the point where I'm totally comfortable with it.

I did well with Slash's ass, though, and I'd challenge anyone to see that rock hard muscled giant flash you without having palpitations. Salem's butt is fantastic, but holy fuck, the big guy is practically a mountain of marble. Not losing my grip is an achievement, and being able to walk with his hand in mine afterward should earn me a medal.

"You're thinking awfully hard down there, shrimp." Jasper eyes me, his gaze intense as he waits for me to respond. "Is that a sign I should be concerned with?"

He actually noticed something past the point of his perfect nose? I'll be damned.

I should definitely encourage that, but it's hard for me *not* to give the prince hell now. It's become part of our routine and it's almost as comfortable as having my kinkajou here to calm me. "Those of us who use our brain before our dicks often have reflective expressions, Jasper."

Slash snorts, not looking at his boss as he says, "You are doing well if your tongue is so sharp. That is good."

Jasper glares at him, then turns it on me as he veers to the right. I don't know what he senses, but his pace quickens as he guides the group off the main path. I can tell he wanted to shoot back a scathing response to my snark, but now he's laser focused on whatever he's hunting down. I can't decide if I should root for him to find his prey or if I should hope he doesn't. The Prince isn't sharing what we're doing as usual, and unlike the others, I don't have blind trust in his intentions.

We finally stop in front of a group of tents made of bones and some kind of animal skins. They look similar to nomadic structures on the surface, but their design is absolutely *not* human in style. The skulls and sharpened bones are arranged to both construct a temporary dwelling *and* to intimidate anyone who approaches. Dangerous vibes emanate from the biggest one, and I shrink back somewhat as the other guys gather behind us.

"Seriously, Jas?" Oriel groans as his eyes flitter from the smallest tent to the large one we're standing closest to. "This is such a bad fucking plan."

X frowns, giving me an uncertain expression before they nod. "I second that, man. Too much risk of being identified."

Slash grunts, his eyes flashing with the demon I saw in the ring, as he studies the small encampment carefully. "Nothing out of the ordinary for what it is."

My temper flares and I stomp my foot on Jasper's toe. "Hey! Someone tell me what in the fresh hell this is and why we're split on… whatever it is."

"Aw, shit, KK," Salem says as he rubs the back of his neck. "Our bad, dude."

"Still not telling me what's going on." I pull my hand out of the shark's grasp and cross my arms over my chest. Dottie moves closer, pressing her fur against my skin to help me stay in balance. "I want to be part of the decision, too."

Anton bites his lip and I know that means he's formulating his answer. The peacock shifter is very precise with explanations, and I sense he wants to be clear about this shanty town. "The Acolytes of Barbatos are a rare but powerful group of demons from every line who have sought various supernaturals who have the sight to breed with. Some are full-blooded and some are hybrids, but they are always present at large gatherings of our kind to visit—if you are."

Blinking rapidly, I swallow as I process his words. I don't fully understand the lore—how could I—but I know Barbatos was once a duke of Hell. He solved disagreements, but he also revealed hidden things and was said to have knowledge of the future and past. Demons in his legion breeding with… seers… would explain that mythos, I guess. But no matter how much sense that makes, this group of demons could be very dangerous for me.

If they find out my big secret and feel betrayed enough, they might leave me here and I wouldn't survive on my own.

Salem's eyes find mine as my pulse quickens, and the bear shakes his head slightly. I think that's his way of telling me I don't need to worry, but he's not the new guy hiding a very important piece of information from a paranoid prince. I look at Xerxes next and they don't seem as certain, but I could be misreading it. I'm not as good at eyebrow discussion as them, and this really isn't the place to test that skill.

"Why—why would we visit those demons?" I ask, hoping to distract the others from my escalating pulse. "Wouldn't asking them stuff reveal things we don't want known?"

Jasper grimaces, then sighs. "Perhaps. We will be required to provide payment for their services, but I know several things about these nomads from my father's incessant ramblings."

I wait, arching a brow as the Prince attempts to formulate his response. There can't be a benefit to seeking their knowledge greater than the risk of being exposed here or to the court. And for me personally, it would definitely need to be extremely beneficial to take the chance with them.

"The Acolytes ask for high prices because they are unerringly accurate—though their words must be untangled and analyzed to understand. They will insist that we don the robes of truth as we seek their guidance, which will cover Slash's ass until we get home. If we can bargain for each one of us to sit with one of their elder diviners, the amount of knowledge we'll eventually decipher will be enough to leave this mess afterward."

Okay, that's pretty fucking tempting.

"Damn, J," Oriel breathes as he looks around, then glances at me worriedly. "Talk about the pits or the Wastelands… We're smack dab in the middle of shitty choices all day today, man."

Zavida frowns and I know he's running variables in his head. His mind is calmed by logical processes and considering probabilities is likely a way he self-soothes. Unfortunately, I have zero clue how the fuck he's going to quantify this shit for his actuarial analysis. "The longer we stay, the bigger chance we have of being identified and thus forced to face the idiot running this. We don't know how emboldened he will be by this fiefdom and all the energy he's feeding off of everyone within."

"Gross," I grumble. I don't like the idea of anyone 'feeding' off my shit, much less the cartoon villain I've built up in my head to represent Luca Gemini.

"However, striking a bargain with the Acolytes has lasting consequences and could also reveal us if we do not craft the words carefully," Anton says thoughtfully. "They do not align with any side or species because of their powers; they're just crystal balls for hire. It's not likely they will share our details unless it comes up in one of their prophecies, and even then, the receiver will need a skilled interpreter to help understand their ramblings."

"You're saying they won't snitch, right?" Salem says as rakes his hand through his hair. "They're like… uh, what do humans say, KK?"

"Switzerland," I reply with a frown. "But, um, that's not actually a good thing historically. I mean, they didn't take a side, but they hid and profited off of Nazi stuff, which really isn't neutral. They were profiteers more than anything—is that what these guys are?"

"Yes." The big guy is eying the scary tents with a dark frown. "They are often descended from the Greed and Sloth lines because they place personal gain and power over action and loyalty. It seems Salem's comparison was apt, and it is why the royal forces, including my father, are averse to their use. The General has had many deeply fracturing disagreements with the King about them over the long duration of his rule."

"That's one vote 'no', then, I guess?" I ask as I look at the protective dude curiously.

He crosses his enormous arms over his chest, shaking his head. "I don't know, little demon. Zavida is also correct about the statistics of being in this place for too long, and Anton has made a salient point about their ambiguity. This is a tough decision."

For once, Jasper and Slash aren't the confident, blunt guys I've gotten used to seeing. It might only be this moment, but they're clearly caught up in both what they've been taught and a desire to achieve our caliphate goals. The other guys are being cautious about their advice—maybe because they, too, have concerns—and the longer we wait, the more eyes I feel on us from the Acolytes' camp.

These demons are watching us, waiting to see if we'll give in to the temptation of finding out things the universe doesn't intend for us to know yet.—for their price, of course.

"Fuck it," I mutter as I scrounge up every bit of courage I have in my body. Moving away from my caliphate, I approach the tent in the center. It's neither the biggest or smallest, but the energy seeping from it has been tickling my skin for the past few moments. I don't know if that means I should or shouldn't be using this one, but at this point? The choice has been made. "Yo, scary fortune tellers. Let's parlay."

"Mammon's never-ending buffet… Does he *ever* think before he does shit?" Jasper groans.

Ignoring him, I wait until an oddly pleasant looking robed demon exits the skull encrusted dwelling. He's short, rotund, and has a piggish nose with small, pointed horns. I assume his non-threatening nature is a guise—living at Discordia has taught me that even the least intimidating demons can reveal scary as fuck transformations. "Are you the acolyte I should speak to?"

The friar-like demon smiles, his mouth full of teeth as terrifying as Slash's, and then nods. "I am, young one. Come with me to my perch so I might read you. Then the bargaining shall begin."

"I'm coming with him—"

Salem's words are cut off by the sharp rebuke. "No. You will each walk your own paths, shining warriors. This one will negotiate with me and you will do the same with your prophet. Our order may only deal with individual demons and their desires—not entire groups. That is our way and has been since long before the Deceiver fell."

My caliphate is looking at me in consternation and fear as the weird guy leads me into his tent, but I can't worry about them right now. I got myself into this mess and now I have to be strong, so it's not in vain. If I can't handle a simple deal involving a Tarot reading—or whatever—I have much bigger problems on the horizon.

Which might actually be what Evil Friar Tuck is getting ready to tell me.

Get Out of Here

Oriel

"I don't like this," I grumble as we watch KK follow the odd little twerp into his tent.

Jasper gives me a knowing look, but replies, "O, you never like seers or soothsayers or prophets or—"

"Because they're either fake, which means their goal is to *steal* from us, or they're real, which means they are messing with the future," I shoot back as I cross my arms over my chest. "My line is greedy, but there's a limit to what acquisitions are not worth the risk."

Zav coughs, "Not for some of them."

Well, isn't he feeling his tails today.

"I know that many well-known cautionary tales used by humans and supes alike were actually demons from Greed, Zav. However, as time has passed, *all* of our family heritage has gotten smarter about limitations. Or, at least since our folks grabbed the throne."

Slash arches a brow at me. "You're saying *our* parents have tempered the extreme ends of their family lineage? I doubt that."

A small, thin acolyte in a billowy robe of red stops the conversation. I can't see his face, only a hooked nose, so I assume he must be a hybrid Fae—they have a lot of gnarly little idgits in their less conventionally attractive species. The being interrupts with a scoff before I can reply and that alone makes me want to throttle him. "The soldier is right—naught has changed but the setting, young Duke. However, Rakshasa will take him to read, then construct our bargain."

Jasper opens his mouth to protest, but like our favorite unemerged demon, Slash shakes his head. He looks down at the smaller acolyte with a toothy smirk. "I will join you, seer, but know that any shenanigans will lead to consumption."

"Y-yes," the now shaky hybrid says as his hood trembles. "Join me in the larger tent."

I watch them walk away, the growing sense of distrust in my gut making me huff. My crow is not fond of things I cannot swipe and no one can actually steal knowledge from a species with crystal ball powers. It's probably why I dislike them, but I'm sure there's some natural distrust of those I deem as fellow thieves who are too crooked to admit their gambits. It's complicated, but I don't have to explain it to anyone.

"Oriel, you're fluffing up," Salem says as he grins at me. "You've got feathers flying from your hair, man."

Shit, my bird is really pissed at this.

"Sorry," I mumble as I pat down my head. "I'll get it under control."

Xerxes looks at me pointedly as they click their tongue. "Everyone has buttons, Oriel. Obviously, this is one of yours, and well… no one is excited about KK being in that tent with the bald guy."

That makes Jasper growl with a hint of his dragon and we all turn to look at the Prince. His face is like a storm cloud, and I decide *not* to poke that beast as originally planned. He huffs a few smoke rings as he looks between the two tents our friends are in, then goes back to gnashing his teeth.

"Danger zone," Anton whispers as he moves closer to me. "Jas is *not* happy about those two being ensconced with acolytes outside of his control."

"Hello, young demons," a voice interrupts. "Batar is here to read the fiery fox. Please follow her to her abode."

Zavida looks worried until he sees the very short, rotund demon in a pink robe with fuzzy looking gray hair. This acolyte seems like an imp's grandma, and though I'm sure she's powerful, her visage doesn't make our Kitsuné lose his shit. "Um, okay. Where is it?"

My inclination to snort is tempered by the puff of pink smoke that reveals a flowered tent next to the one Kit Kat went into. It wasn't there before…

unless she was cloaking it. I could see that, especially because this Batar chick seems like she'd be a Hello Kitty fan with what we can see of her tastes. That's not very intimidating for the entire group, so it fits that her 'abode' would be cloaked.

"Come with me, gentle one."

Now our prince looks like he's going to go flying off the ledge, and I walk over to him. "Jasper, you gotta get a grip, man. This is probably on purpose. If they're the real deal—which is doubtful—then they know enough to pick and choose how they run this little con game. Your hot buttons are a good place to start."

"The shrimp stepped forward on his own."

"Uh, of course he did. Do you think grifters can't read body language and vibes and shit?" I sigh, shaking my head. "I know you and Slash deal with more… outwardly aggressive bad guys, but *my* duties often require finesse and subterfuge. I *know* those kinds of demons, man."

Xerxes gives me a weird look, and I frown. Why does he look like he wants to snicker? I'm not lying to Jasper; I really have to read people a lot. Turning to Anton, I notice he seems perfectly normal—albeit worried—but not smug like his lover. The dichotomy irritates me, so I turn to Salem and note that he, too, looks a bit amused by my declarations.

What the fuck is with my brothers today?

"Regardless of your experience, Oriel, I dislike putting our brothers *or* our futures in the hands of unknowns. But I did not see another solution to wandering this wanna-be hellhole for longer than I prefer." The Prince growls softly and crosses his arms over his chest as he struggles to push back his animal. "And the reward may well outweigh the risks, but…"

His words trail off when Slash stomps out of the large tent with an annoyed look on his face. The hooked nosed Rakshasa is following the enforcer as he approaches us. "Jas, it is your turn to bear the burden of this turd's company."

I blink, biting my lip to keep from bursting into laughter. Slash's description makes the hybrid tremble again, but I assume this time it's from anger, not fear. "I guess it didn't go so well, huh?"

"Come, leader of demons."

Jasper looks furious as his eyes cut from me to Slash, then back to the hooded seer. "Fine. Then Slash is in charge while I'm inside. Do *not* take your eyes off the tents."

Slash gives him a sharp nod, but he immediately focuses on the small tent where our newest member is still consulting with the chubby demon. "Understood."

Hopefully, Jasper's session doesn't go worse than the big guy's.

JASPER, LIKE KIT, STAYS IN HIS TENT FOR WHAT FEELS LIKE FOREVER. BY THE time he comes out, the rest of us have followed the small female acolyte into her abode and come back out. His jaw is tight as fuck as he stomps over to us, and I know he's been holding himself back so he didn't piss off Rakshasa. The first thing he does is walk over to Zav and check in, then he turns to the rest of us with an assessing look.

"Have you gone? Where is the shrimp?"

I sigh, knowing this will not help. "Still with the bald dude."

"Zaesil," the female says with a decisive nod. "He is the elder of our group. His readings last much longer and he chooses those who have much to discuss. It is not surprising that we have finished with the rest of your group before he is done."

That's just fucking fabulous—the kid has enough shit to agonize over.

"When will they be done?" Salem asks as he paces behind me. "It's been a very long time."

Slash frowns as he eyes the tent. "I do not like this."

Jasper comes over to glare down at Batar menacingly. "If any of you break the pacts that comprise our bargains, I will—"

"Now, now, young royal. We are not aligned with any players in schemes that can affect the cosmos." Batar shakes her fluffy head as she chides him. "We know far too much about too many things to tempt the wrath of those who are more powerful. The weavers would not allow us to remain if we did not comply with the ethos of their children."

Anton's head whips around when he hears her statement. He steps closer, studying the round demoness carefully. "I should hope not. There's not a demon in Hell who would chance the three who hold the threads of reality for all the realms."

"Indeed." Rakshasa bobs his head, the hood moving with him. "Not a crown, nor a pauper, a human, nor a god, not even a magical ancestor, may cross their boundaries without fear. The songs and poems stretch across the divides between to warn those who might try to defy the core of the universe."

Bullshit like this is why I despise all the oracle types; everything they say is so vague that no one can accurately understand what they mean—and it's by design.

"Demons can always find a way around things," I mutter as I run my hand through my hair.

My 'prophecy' wasn't very impressive, but it wasn't surprising, either. For all of this fanfare, Batar decreed I have secret feelings for someone in the group, my line will have a major disruption that will force me to take action, and that I am headed for tough decisions in the coming competition. All of those things were cloaked in a bunch of fancy fuckery and mystical mojo, but it's the gist of her reading. I offered nothing I couldn't handle—I will receive a message to retrieve an object stolen from the acolytes a century ago.

It could be something ridiculous or something that I'll have to bust my tail feathers to get my hands on, but once I realized she absolutely knows who the caliphate is, I couldn't say no. If the heir to Greed cannot find and return their object, it will reflect badly on the entire court. She's a crafty little shit, and I'm sure she used that with the others as well. It makes me wonder what Rakshasa and the friar demon got out of the others. I sense Batar is the least powerful of the three, despite looking the oldest in her humanoid form.

"They can if they are not practitioners of the divinatory arts," Rakshasa says sternly. "We must adhere to the rules or we will lose our ability to access our gifts. You may verify that however you choose when you leave this place, but you will find we are being truthful."

"Fine," Jasper growls as he looks at the two demons. "I accept your words for now. When will your leader be finished with our brother?"

Now all of us are looking at the breakable acolytes with determined gazes. They don't shrink back—I have to give them credit for bravery. The silence hangs for a few moments until, finally, Batar clears her throat nervously.

"Zaesil cannot be rushed. Your friend will be out when he is—"

The sound of footsteps pries our attention away from her and as Kit walks out of the tent, the tension among us lessens slightly. He doesn't appear to be harmed, nor having a complete freak out, but his shoulders are slumped as he moves toward us. The demon he met steps out, his hand folded at his waist as he stands quietly.

"KK, are you okay?"

Salem and I move at the same time, ignoring Xerxes's question as we rush over to our newest member to look him over. The panda reaches down, tipping the kid's chin up so he looks at him, then sighs in relief. I circle him as Salem rubs the back of his neck, my eyes checking every inch I can see carefully.

"I'm okay, guys."

Jasper's eyes narrow, and I wonder if he's finally going to admit he's been worried. Instead, he points at the leader of the acolytes, his voice dark as he says, "If there's one mark on my brothers, one scar in their psyche… you will regret the day you were summoned, seer. Know that."

Kit looks surprised, but he murmurs softly to us. "Can we go back to Hell now? I've definitely had enough of this fucking place for a lifetime."

"Little demon, it would be our pleasure to take you home."

That's when Dottie scrambles out of the bag again, perching on Kit's shoulder as she pumps a tiny fist in victory.

I guess that's her way of saying 'there's no place like home'.

HOME
Kit/Kat

We were extremely careful as we made our way to a bank of elevators opposite of the original set, and the guys got us in without fanfare. I wish we could have gone further so I could see Rogue again, but I wasn't kidding when I said I wanted to go home. My social battery is on its last legs and the stress of worrying about someone outing me, someone attacking us, or any number of other terrible things happening is exhausting. I've done exceptionally well for me, even when I had to tell Salem the truth in the middle of a battle, so I think I've earned some mental rest time. Dottie hugs me as that thought runs through my head and I wonder again exactly how much my companion knows.

I'll have to make them take me to that bestiary place this week to find out more, I guess.

"You called Hell your home, KK."

I look at Zavida, smiling as he hugs his tails while we wait for the stupid Suber driver to arrive. He's been as naked as me without his coping mechanism, and since we're in this damn serial killer spot again, I suppose it's okay that he's showing his demonic parts. Obviously, the driver won't give a shit, and I definitely don't. As long as Jasper doesn't scold him, I think it's fine for the nervous Kitsuné to comfort himself after all we've been through.

"None of the foster places were actually my home, so I've never had a real one. Discordia is close enough, right? I've got a family, sort of, and a room… That's what defines it, right? A space where you can feel safe and people who mostly support you?" I frown, not sure if I've understood the concept correctly now that he asked.

Oriel arches a brow at me, his brows furrowed. "Mostly?"

Jasper snorts, knowing what I mean by that, and I grin a little. "It's a lot like 'mostly dead'. Know what I mean?"

"You're right about it being your home now," Salem interjects, his eyes dancing with merriment. "Even if you've got a reluctant housemate giving you shit all the time, we're your family, Kit Kat."

The kisses from earlier make that description iffy, but I'll let it go.

"Thanks," I murmur as the car pulls up. "I'm still getting used to it, and to figuring out myself as I heal, but you guys help a lot. Truly."

That makes almost all the demons in my caliphate smile wide, and the prince rolls his eyes with a huff. I don't care if he likes it or not; it's true. These guys have done more for me in the short time I've been in Hell than most people have done in my whole life, and I want them to know how much I appreciate it.

"Stop blubbering and get in the car, shrimp," Jasper grumbles, and for once, I just follow his instructions. Surprisingly, he ruffles my hair as I do, and I have to swallow my shock as I find my place in the seats.

Miracles happen, and I think I just experienced one.

IT TAKES ANOTHER HOUR TO GET BACK TO THE PORTAL AND WHEN WE WALK into the weird room from earlier in the day; I breathe an enormous sigh of relief. The demons look at me with knowing looks and I flip them off, no longer able to keep the veneer of 'good behavior' up. That doesn't get me much more than chuckles, so I ignore them as we head back to the room. I just need all the damn stress of being in my old world around dangerous people to fade, so the knots in my back will release.

I definitely could eat, too.

"Feeling hungry yet, KK?"

My head swivels slowly to look at Salem, my eyes wide as his question comes out at a very coincidental moment. "What?"

He grins, nodding at the ding of the elevator doors. "We'll all change and get comfy, then I'll whip up some stuff. It's really tiring to be up there and I can only imagine how much you've burned yourself up having to juggle all the worries and anxiety. Not that you'd *tell* us that, of course."

"Right," I reply carefully. I don't want Jasper to mock me, but the panda demon is definitely on the money with his assumptions. I'm tired, sore, confused, anxious, and really eager to get out of these 'beautiful but way too fancy for me' clothes. "What do we do with the... outfits?"

Xerxes gives me a stern look. "Put them in your laundry bag and bring it to the living room when you come out. I'm taking *all* the stuff to the laundry myself so I can instruct them on how to deal with the fancy shit. I'll be damned if those dingbats are going to ruin *Rigoletto* originals."

Thank fuck they knows what to do because I am fucking clueless about couture.

"Excellent plan, X," Jasper says as he waits for Slash to hold the doors open. Once he does, we exit the carriage and I groan happily when we reach my door. "You really *are* happy to be back, hmm?"

I give him an incredulous look. "Of fucking course I am. This day was stuffed to the gills with crap I despise: danger, bad guys, fancy clothes, behaving, starving, and listening to you. If you added in much else, you'd have to dip into trauma to make it worse. I just want to get into my jammies and curl up in my chair, while I wolf down everything not nailed down."

The prince nods, tilting his head. "Your appetite is getting stronger. I suspect that is because more of your powers are developing, which is good. If we can encourage that, it will help immensely."

My lips curve up as Zavida takes his hand, looking pleased as he tugs the bigger demon away from my dorm. He winks at me before he murmurs, "Let's go, Jas. We should get cleaned up so we can eat. Even you have to be hungry after such a long time on the surface."

That gets the asshole's attention, and he smirks wickedly as he follows the Kitsuné's lead. "Yes, I believe I am... hungry."

For the love of frilly bathrobes, now I'm going to be imagining that...

"Aw, KK, your face is getting red again," Salem chuckles as he opens our door. "Don't worry, if they run over a bit, we won't wait for them. Jasper can get lost in his... devouring sometimes."

"Shut. Up." I put my hands on my face and scurry into our room as the others laugh and head for their own rooms. The teasing is even weirder now that two people know my secret; they know that I'm feeling girly about the two of them getting naked in there. "You're going to give me away if you're not careful, you know."

Salem rolls his eyes at me as we drop our bags at the entrance, shaking his head. "Firecracker, I can guarantee a few things for you. One, I won't be the one to give you away before you're ready. Two, until he's looking for it, Jasper will *never* see the truth because he's too busy worrying about you having other secrets. And three, the one you should worry about is Slash. That dude sees *way* more than anyone realizes."

I blink at the panda, dumbfounded by his very astute summation. "You're probably right. X won't give me away because he was worried from the beginning that I was trans and he'd be outing me. The others may notice weird things, but right now, they're chalking it up to being human raised."

"Bingo," he says as shoots a finger-gun at me. "So we'll carefully navigate how to keep you under wraps until you're ready to give up the goods—or you don't have a choice, whichever comes first."

That makes my teeth grind, but he's right.

"Yeah," I breathe as I walk towards the door to my bedroom. "I'm gonna change and put things away like X requested, then I'll come out here so we can chat until everyone else gets here. Is that okay?"

"Aces, dude…ette." Salem laughs and I roll my eyes at him as he opens his door. "Don't get all worked up about it, okay? I really meant it when I said I'm not upset, and I definitely meant it when I said I'm all in. So… take it easy on yourself in there."

Damn him for knowing me that well.

"Okay," I murmur as I slip into my room. "Thanks, Salem."

When I shut the door, I trudge over to my dresser and look in the mirror. I look like I've been *through it*, and I guess that's because I need to fuel up or whatever. Dottie makes a beeline for her perch, stuffing some of her feed in her mouth as she watches me peel my clothes off. I groan when I peel the binding off, so happy to have it loose despite the waffling on my skin from keeping it so tight for so long. One thing I have to do now that we're back is get Xerxes to hop on the replacements for the real binders. I'm not gonna last with this damn gauze shit.

"Put it on the list, Kat," I mutter as I dig out a sweatshirt and pants from the bags X brought this morning. At the very least, these have boxer briefs and regular lounge stuff, plus my uniforms. I'll need that for Monday, and they got enough that if I'm fucked up again, I should be good for seven days. "Smart, smart cobra. They don't give them or Salem enough credit."

Dottie pumps her fist, chittering her agreement, and I smile. She really loves most of the guys and the others, she's just getting to know slowly. I like that; it makes me feel good that my emotional support kinkajou has bonded with the demons who are becoming my found family.

"Salem will have fresh snacks for you, girl. Don't fill up on the seeds and stuff. You'll want the fruit." My warning makes her pause with puffed-out cheeks full of food and I laugh softly. "Or eat whatever, just don't vomit anywhere."

That seems to work for Dottie, so I turn back to my dirty pile and stuff it in the laundry bag from the closet. It has other shit in it, too, but if X will send it all to the cleaners, I won't complain. I have no idea how that system works and they all keep telling me to let them handle things.

Does it matter if it's my stinky socks? I think not.

"KK, I'm out here working in the kitchen. Ollie, Ollie, oxen-free." Salem's cheery voice makes my heart thump, and I have to blow out a slow breath to calm it.

"Be cool, Kat. He's super hot. He knows you're a girl, he likes you anyway, *and* he cooks for you. Most people would die on the spot to have that, and you cannot let the past fuck this up. Breathe, take it slow, and let him lead. You can trust Salem."

My pulse doesn't agree, but luckily, my kinkajou does. Dottie scampers off her perch and up my leg to sit on my shoulder. She looks at me seriously—as much as a small bear-rat can—and I know she wants me to understand that she thinks Salem is okay, too. Her soft chittering seals the deal, and I scritch her head gently. "I know, girl. It's just hard, but I want to try. That's new— I've never wanted to heal as much as I do now. I think it means I'm ready, right?"

I chuckle as she responds in her typical fashion, then look at the door to my room. When I go out there, we're going to talk and that's when everything will become 'real'. But I'm pretty sure I'm ready for it, and if I'm not? I'm also certain that Salem and X will help me. Not that Xerxes has really… Well, whatever. It's all jumbled up, but I know the cobra will help me figure things out.

All I have to do now is just open that door and leave this room—which is harder than expected.

WHISTLE

XERXES

"How do you think it went?"

I look at my love as he meticulously sheds his clothes and places them in our shared laundry, as I asked everyone to. "I think we met some good people—at least, it seemed like it. We'll see how Jasper handles the Fae prince and what happens from there. I liked that KK seemed to connect with those very confident chicks from each group. It's good for him to find friends outside of our nonsense."

Anton snorts, shaking his head. "I'm not sure everyone will be so excited about him consorting with outsiders, even if they're obviously taken by their own families. You know how some of our brothers are."

"I do, but Kit's going to do whatever he wants regardless, Annie. That's not something he'll make concessions about," I reply as I peel my shirt off. "If Jasper—or anyone else—gets weird about it, the kid's gonna lose his marbles."

My lover makes a face, but shrugs. "Possibly. He did a pretty good job of being good on the surface. Not nearly as many problems as I expected and by the end, Jasper was acting strangely proud of him. Zav was practically wagging his tails in happiness."

The Kitsuné was giddy as fuck when they headed to the prince's dorm; Annie's got that one nailed.

"Did you notice Salem stayed awake with almost no trouble at all?"

Blinking, I think about the panda for a few moments, scanning my memory of the trip carefully. "You know, I didn't notice, but now that you mention it… That dude was on it without a second's hesitation and I didn't see him chug any extra energy potions. What's with that?"

"I don't know, but it was fucking odd." Anton finishes stripping and I watch, my eyes coasting over his muscles as he walks to the dresser to grab boxers. "He was so awake that I hardly recognized him half the time. And KK *let* him guide him with little complaint. Those two are thick as thieves, you know."

I got that impression, and I know our newest initiate is close to the crow as well. They got to show him their other sides before anyone else, and though I'm not jealous, my cobra was until Kit let Annie and I do the same. We haven't revealed the full demon form, but his lack of fear when he had to witness the partial forms in the Gemini compound was encouraging. "Well, they live in the same room, Annie. And to be fair, Salem accepted him from the second Jasper shoved him into the second bedroom without a protest. That kind of shit forms a bond, you know?"

It's definitely how our attraction went from physical to actual relationship as we got older.

The peacock demon grins at me as he tugs on his sweats, and I remember why I fell for him. Walking over, I toss my clothes haphazardly as I approach, not paying a bit of attention to the couture I was worried about earlier. He arches his brow, his expression playful as he tracks my movements. "Aren't you feeling saucy? I love the look in your eye, especially since we're alone and Jasper's going to be late to the party."

"Anton, making others wait because you look especially delectable standing in nothing but those boxer briefs is rude."

Laughing softly, he turns, the shimmer of his bird surrounding him as he preens. "I love compliments; it's in my nature, love."

I roll my eyes at his blunt statement of the obvious. "Of course you do, baby. Your bird *and* your demon eat that shit up. However, *my* inner beings are more interested in the scent of arousal you're giving off like perfume. It's delightful."

Tilting his head, he waits until I'm pressed against his body before he says, "Speaking of which…"

"What?" I ask as I run my palms over his back. Neither of us looks as strong as we are clothed, but that's Slash's training regimen. The shark has been keeping us all in fighting trim since we were kids. "What about the scent?"

"Do you think KK is going to smell it soon? I mean, he's figuring out species better now. I assume he'll get the body chemistry changes soon."

Ah, he's worried our little newbie will figure out he's attracted to him before he's ready to admit it.

"I don't know, love. Kit's emergence is a mystery to everyone, even Dr. D. We don't have a frame of reference for an unemerged, over-age possible *tripleska* [1] who has unknown powers, lineage, and heritage." Reaching up, I smooth his rainbow hair away from his eyes, smiling softly. "But whatever happens, we'll work it out together. I mean, the poor guy doesn't even know what humans smell like when they're excited, I don't think. He's probably repressed it because of the trauma."

Anton nods, his face full of an unusual emotion for my mate: vulnerable. His family line being pride and his confident bird makes it incredibly uncommon for him to feel this way, much less say it out loud. "If you think so, it must be true. You're the expert on lust and shit."

I put my hands on his cheeks, looking into his eyes with a firm gaze. "I know it, and I *am* an expert on that subject. But truthfully, I'm fumbling around a little with this, too. Hell, I think we all are. No one expected some random kid to stomp out of the elevator with Jas and flip our entire world upside down within weeks. Give yourself a little credit, babe."

He darts in and kisses me hungrily, making everything in my body uncoil and stretch. The snake loves when he does that and I love him; it's a perfect answer to my statement. When our lips part, I suck his lower lip between my teeth, nibbling lightly before I let go. Anton hisses, his hands winding around my neck as our bodies heat. "Am I being graded or something? Because if so, I could definitely use extra credit. I've been slacking, it seems."

"Indeed, you have, darling." Grinning, I slide my hands down his back to the hem of the sexy briefs, toying with it as I nibble along the line of his jaw. "To get those points, you're going to have to earn them. Give me the demon, and we'll see how much you've studied."

Within seconds, Anton's frame is shimmering with rainbow colors, horns, and the feathered tail that whips back and forth eagerly. "How's that for skill? Seamless *and* quick."

"Only one of which is important to what we're doing now," I rumble teasingly, and he gives me a smirk. I allow my demon to rise, the long golden tail of my cobra trailing up his leg slowly. "You know I enjoy you demonstrating your knowledge of demon anatomy more than anything else."

Anton drops to his knees, taking the hint without even batting a lash. I look down at his rainbow locks, my eyelids fluttering as his palms settle on my hips. "Tsk, tsk, my love. I can smell how eager you are, yet I don't see the twins. Whatever shall I do to correct this situation?"

My hands settle on his shoulders, squeezing lightly. "I suppose you should show me how they're coaxed out if you're so knowledgeable. You may have to give lessons eventually, you know."

His eyes widen as he looks up at me, clearly shocked. "Holy fuck, that's hot."

"Is it? Then I suppose we'll just have to imagine how that would work." Anton groans darkly and I know I've hit the jackpot. "What would you do first?"

"I…" He pauses for a moment, then his sparkling eyes meet mine. "I'd show him that when we play, we enjoy switching roles depending on our moods. Right now, he'd need to be kneeling with me in front of you, waiting for instruction. That might be hard for him, but I think he enjoyed seeing you in cobra form and the twins interested him."

"Excellent," I coo softly. "What would you show him besides the correct position, my darling?"

My mate's thumbs brush over my hip bones as he slips my boxers down my thicker demon form carefully. The hemi-penes haven't made themselves known yet, but they will if he keeps doing this slow dance of role play. I'm enjoying the imagery as much as him, and the addition of KK makes it even hotter. "Once we get these off, we have access to all of your body. The piercings, the cloaca, the nipples… and all of it is important to arousing you."

His hands move up to tug on my single nipple bar, then he twists it until I snarl in pleasure. "Yes, that's definitely the spot to start my engines, baby. What would you tell our little inexperienced third?"

"That you enjoy a little more pain than I do, except for the fangs, and he can be rougher with his touch than he thinks is okay." To punctuate his statement, he pulls harder this time and my head tips back at the burn. "See? You look stunning when you're in that place, X."

I feel fucking amazing when I get the slightest flicker of pain, and I love that Annie doesn't mind.

"I do, and you're very good to mention it," I murmur when I look down at him again. "What next?"

Anton leans in, pressing his lips to my abs and starts a warm, wet trail over my lower torso. He licks, bites, nibbles, and raises marks as he tortures me deliciously. Burying my fingers in his hair, I let the sensations draw out the magic of my line. It flows out of me like liquid fire, filling our room with an aching atmosphere that I know has him hard as rock now. I can't help it; once I truly get aroused, the power inside of me spills out and claims everyone in the vicinity.

"There we go, my love," Annie murmurs as his lips drift down to the now prominent cocks standing at attention. He kisses the tips, making me shudder, and says, "I'd tell him we can work together until he's used to this. There's enough for us both to make you feel good."

Holy. Fuck. That. Image.

As my mind conjures a tasty picture of both Anton and Kit sucking my dual dicks eagerly, I tighten my grip on his head. Anton takes all of me into his mouth, and I moan his name as the sensation rockets over me. He's been doing this long enough that he knows every bump, every ridge, every vein, and how to flick two piercings just so. It makes me hiss loudly, and I open my eyes to watch him deep-throating my dicks with dark eyes. Humming and scraping over the soft skin with teeth, Annie works me so expertly that I can't keep up the premise of teaching, nor can I hold back the last thrum of my lust magic that crashes into him as I get closer to the peak.

"You… did… a good… oh, fuucccck, baby. That's it; right there… yeah…"

His hands squeeze my thighs, massaging as he wriggles and continues to give me a blow job that would impress a porn star. I'm edging closer to orgasm even more quickly than normal when he lifts his head, looking up at me with a smug grin that's full of wickedness. "Can I come when you do, baby? If so, I'll assign you an accessory to wear during the meeting that will make later a *lot* of fun."

I blink, thinking of the *many, many* things we have in our toy box and how much I'll enjoy prolonging the wait for fucking until after the group meeting. "Fuck, yeah, you can. Do it now, then we clean up, and you choose."

He swallows my dicks eagerly, and I let go of conscious thought to swim in the mist of lust magic that surrounds us. Within moments, I'm back on the edge of the cliff, hanging onto my lover with both hands. His distended claws scrape over my thighs, scratching enough to draw blood, and that's when my hips buck faster until I scream his name and tumble over. The blood makes my cobra even more eager and I continue humping his face until everything is drained out of me, making my posture limp and my breath ragged.

Looking down, I see the stain seeping through the brand new boxers and chuckle as best I can. "Oopsie."

"The only good way to ruin my shorts," he mumbles as my cocks soften and he lets them fall from his mouth to pull inward.

I will not argue with that; I'm too busy trying to breathe.

---

1. Triple-sided supe

FLIRT

KIT/KAT

"There you are!"

Salem's face lights up like a holiday tree, and it makes my stomach do flips like I'm on a trampoline. I smile back at him as Dottie and I come over to join him in the kitchen. "Sorry, I took a long time. I was—"

"Wigging out?" He smirks as he moves to the fridge, pulling out a wrapped slab and putting it on the cutting board. "No surprise there, Firecracker. Lots of stuff to make you get lost in your head today."

I step up on the stool he keeps in here, waiting to see what I can help with. Dottie scampers off of my shoulder, then jumps to the island where Salem has left some fruit for her in a small bowl. "Yeah. I didn't think I was going to see an orc, everyone's demons, and a giant fucking spider-dude within a few hours."

He arches a brow as he comes closer so he can loom over me. "That's all, huh?"

My face gets hot as I squint at him stubbornly. "No, it's not *all* that happened, but it's the weirdest shit for sure. "

His chuckle is low as he tugs my face up, so I'm looking into his eyes. I wrinkle my nose, having trouble pretending to be irritated when he looks so damn cute. "Now, KK. Don't be bratty. I'm only teasing you. Obviously smooching wasn't weird nor terrifying like a giant spider."

Speak for yourself, fur boy.

I'm surprised by the pouty sound of my own inner voice and look at Salem through my lashes. He's right, of course, and I don't know if I'm actually achieving my goal of being flirty or not. Maybe I'm being annoying? Fuck if I know. So I lick my lips and gather my nervousness until I say, "You're not scary, and it was nice, not weird. I liked how you helped me when we went to the stupid Gemini circus."

That makes him smile wider, and he winks at me, then tweaks my nose. "Get used to it. Now, hup to, woman. We have food to make and the other miscreants will be here soon enough."

I'm about to answer him when he swats me playfully, and I let out a squeal of surprise. "Don't *do* that! I'll give myself away."

My roomie does a wiggle dance as he walks away, and I can't help but laugh. Dottie chitters from the counter where she's stuffing her face again and I breathe a sigh of relief. I was worried this was going to be really fucking awkward, or I'd screw everything up completely, but so far? Salem's made me feel almost… safe. That's not normal for me—not at all.

"Stay cool. I won't mess up. If X can keep their big yap closed, I can, too." The panda demon comes back to me with a big bowl. "Now get stuff out of the fridge and throw together a salad while I season the meat. There's plenty of stuff in the fridge, but you might need to cut some of it up."

I can definitely make a salad unsupervised. Over the past few weeks, I've gotten much more familiar with the common foods, especially the ones Salem likes to stock in our fridge. I'm not saying I could identify everything on a buffet like at the Ball, but I'm getting better. Humming under my breath as I pull out ingredients, I realize I'm calmer than normal. Working on stuff with my new… kissing buddy… makes me less edgy. I'm not even worried about Jasper stomping in here to be a dick—for the moment.

"Salem?"

"Yeeeees, Firecracker?"

Ducking my head as pleasure fills me at the nickname, I have to cough to clear my throat before I answer. "I really enjoy cooking with you. It's relaxing and seems to always lead to good things."

"I would agree. Plus, having someone eager to hang out with me in the kitchen rather than bitching about it is pretty cool, too." I look over right as Salem does a hefty chop on the meat slab, and the sound makes me jump slightly. "Don't worry, I only use giant knives for food, not attacking people in the shower."

Oh, hilarious, dude.

"For fuck's sake, the damn bathroom makes me jittery enough without you putting *that* image in my head," I mutter as I finish tearing whatever the leafy stuff is and tossing it in the big bowl. "I don't think you understand how unnerving that is for me."

"Because you could get discovered if Prince Prickface yanks your door off? I wouldn't worry about that. He's only done it to Oriel once, and he was— oh." The panda demon coughs and looks away, making my eyes widen.

"He was *what*, Salem?!"

"Pissing him off?" he offers sheepishly. The expression is adorable and I want to comment on it, but he's inadvertently set off my panic alarms inside. He must realize it because he stops chopping and comes over, putting his big hands over mine, so I stop violently slicing my own Hell veggies. "Hey, hey. You'll be fine, Firecracker. Do you think X and I would let that happen? Absolutely not."

Sighing, I put the smaller knife down and turn to face him. "Probably not, but anxiety doesn't just *poof* because someone throws logic at it. It's like having a bagful of drugged up bees in your head, and they buzz around until they run out of steam. And trust me, that bathroom was already on my list of pulse pounding problems."

Salem's eyes crinkle as he smirks. "Because you're scared of being discovered or because everyone's mostly naked?"

"Pick. A. Card. Any. Card," I grind out as I frown up at him. "I mean, *yes*, I worry about the secret. Then I was worried I was, like, unintentionally assaulting you guys somehow because of it. Then, that stopped because X said no one would care, but also, I still have to see you all naked. That's an old fear, but it's paired with… new stuff now."

"Mmm. New stuff, huh?" His hand reaches up to brush a hair off my forehead and I bite my lip to keep from making a silly noise. "Like what new stuff?"

"Oh, no, Salem Stryker. You're not getting me to fall for that." I point at him, wagging my finger accusingly. "We have to finish this food, and we have no *idea* when any of them are going to barge in here. That… *stuff*… is not for public knowledge right now."

"Aw, KK, but we could hear them coming…"

My eyes narrow. "As if I'm naïve enough to fall for that. I know little about our… new thing… but I know guys are about as observant as Mr. Magoo when they're focused on sexy things. That much I've seen in horror movies and the like, so it has to be true."

"That's just not fair, Firecracker." His face pulls into an honest-to-Satan pout and my eyes widen as I feel my resolve crumble like a damn cookie.

I'm going to have to learn how to deal with that—fast.

"You promised to call me chef if I let you finish your salad, yet I haven't heard it once since," Salem grouses as he stands at the stove cooking something that might be his version of mashed potatoes. "I've been hood-winked… bamboozled, even."

Rolling my eyes as I put away the last of the salad stuff, I pick up my bowl and step down to carry it over to the island. "You have not. I wanted you to finish the starches before you got distracted."

He turns on his heels, grinning broadly. "Roast in the oven, potatoes staying warm, and the bread is rising. I'm owed my dues or you'll be in violation of that deal."

Dipping my chin, I ignore the heat crawling up my chest and shoulders at the slight rumble to his tone. I'm aware of how much he likes that, and though I didn't originally mean to arouse that part of him by saying it, I'm feeling oddly giddy knowing that it does. I hop up on the stool, putting my elbows on the counter, and look over the large expanse at him shyly. "I'd never do that to you… chef."

His eyes flutter closed, and he tips his head back as he looks up at the ceiling. His hands grip the edge as he groans softly. "You're trouble, KK. You know that?"

The pleased sensation his words stir in me vibrates through my frame, and I have no idea how to handle it. I place my face in my hand, using the casual position to keep myself upright, as he finally opens his beautiful eyes again to pin me heatedly. "I don't know how to be anything but me, so if that's who I am…"

His smirk makes my thighs tremble a bit, and I press them together. "Oh, I'd never want you to be something you're not. Hell, Firecracker, I didn't even care if you were a girl or a guy—just that you're cute, awkward, funny, and the first person I've paid attention to in that way."

This dude is killing me; I'm actually considering blowing my cover because I want to kiss him again.

"Stop that," I say as I sit up and wave my hands at him as if brushing away all the emotions and butterflies making my common sense pack up and head for the hills. "Don't... be mushy. I don't know what to do with mushy."

Salem chuckles, rounding the end of the island to stand next to me again. "I can't figure out if you're more worried about sexy stuff or mushy stuff now. But it seems like the latter tames that bratty attitude fairly well."

My nose wrinkles and I cross my arms over my chest as I glare up at him. "Well, now I'm not going to tell you a damn thing, jackass. You're not supposed to do a Jasper impression; you're the nice one!"

"Oh-ho, my little sous chef... You are so very misguided." His eyes twinkle and he leans down, whispering in my ear, "Before you arrived, I was *not* the nice one. Jasper tossed you in here because I scared the piss out of prospective roommates all throughout my lower school years. That's why he chose this room."

What?!

Pulling back, I squint at him as I process that tidbit. "He thought you'd be mean and make me run away? *That's* why everyone kept looking at us weirdly when I showed up at the meeting with you?"

Giving me a toothy, demonic smile, Salem shrugs guilelessly. "I don't like people in my space and they don't like my cooking and hyperactivity paired with a narcolepsy act. What can I say?"

My lips curve up, once again feeling victorious. "So I did good, then? I made you enjoy having me around and you didn't send me packing?"

Something changes when I say that, and my adorable roomie's expression turns downright wicked. "Oh, yes, Firecracker. You were so *very, very* good—in fact, good enough that I started trying to figure out how to get you to notice me within days. And by that, I don't mean just see me, but... see me like you did in the tent."

I swallow hard, gathering my thoughts before I reply, "I do... I mean, I did. Well, both. I see you like that, I mean. And I like... that you want me to.

And when you get all squirrelly because I say the 'c-word'. That's… it makes me feel things."

"That's absolutely perfect, KK, because I definitely see you that way. And I want to explore those things more when we don't have impending visitors."

"Me, too," I whisper as I reach over to put my hand on his lightly. He leans down a little, and I know I'm going to give in when a loud pounding on the door makes me jump away.

Salem looks like he's going to murder someone as he pulls back and I sigh softly.

I knew it would be just my luck for one of the others to arrive just in time—I just knew it.

Hey, Good Lookin'

Salem

My brothers have annoyingly terrible timing.

Kit gives me a shy, but mildly frustrated smile when I pull away. Despite wanting to throttle Oriel for interrupting, I'm still happy to see her look eager to kiss me again, so I decide to spare the crow—this time. I wink to let KK know it's okay, then stroll over to the door to disengage the system so we don't have to stop fixing the food for each arrival. I only had it on so we'd have privacy to talk—and maybe smooch a bit—and that's not an option now. No use making everything more difficult and the rest of them cranky.

"Food smells tasty," O says as he pads in. He's wearing casual clothes, too, and his feet are bare.

KK waves at him from her perch on the stool as she keeps an eye on the pots and timers. I didn't have to ask her to do so , and that pleases the shit out of me. Dottie chitters, and my roomie grins. "I think she's happy to see you, Oriel. You're probably not on the 'grape up the nose' list."

The crow shifter smirks as he drops his stuff next to his chair, then heads over to grab a drink. "I'm honored and grateful. As funny as that was, I don't want to be on the receiving end of the little gal's vengeance. She's fierce for such a small animal."

"A bit like me, hmm?" Kit grins broadly as she crosses her arms over her chest.

That makes me marvel again at how dumb I was not to figure her secret out without that moment in the tent, and I chuckle under my breath when I think about how annoyed O will be with himself. He notices so much because of his line and his role, but this seems to have coasted right over his punky head. "Definitely like you. Hey, we should do that bestiary thing tomorrow. I almost forgot about it."

"Can we?" KK pops out of her chair, obviously excited as fuck. She rubs her hands together as she waits for us to respond, clearly plotting something —though I'm not sure I want to know what.

"Tomorrow's pretty packed," I say as I grab the trays out of the oven. Kit blinks at me, her eyes on my hands, and I shrug. "I thought you realized I don't require mitts and stuff, dude. Demon, you know?"

Oriel elbows her as he passes by with his drink. "You're more observant than that, KK. Come on now."

I blink, my eyes cutting to my new kissing partner as I try not to snort. The annoyed face she's making is adorable, so I have to look away before I fuck this up. I swore I wouldn't, but *damn*, I didn't think O would give me an opening like that right off the bat. Coughing as I pull the bread out, I shut the oven so the roast can continue cooking and put the hot tray on the stove-top. "*You*, however, Kit… You need to use the mitts to get the bread sliced, so it cools flat. It'll be easier to put the spread on."

She gives me a salute, her eyes twinkling, and I growl softly as I stalk over to where Oriel is now stretched out in his seat. The little brat is taunting me, and I can't do a damn thing about it. However, I can definitely needle my brother a bit to take the edge off. "When do you think the others are gonna show? Slash should be soon, I'd think, but the couples are probably still fucking like rabbits after all that nakedness and danger on the surface."

Kit chokes on the soda she's drinking, and I grin as she wipes her mouth on her hand. "Salem!"

"Yeeees?" I ask, batting my lashes playfully. "I mean, ask Oriel. He'll tell you I'm right. That kind of violence and arousal combined with risk and magic, makes our demons super horny."

"*Salem.*" This time it's O and I raise my hand to rub my hand over my mouth so he doesn't know how amused I am. "Be nice to Kit. He's not quite ready for such blatant guy talk yet. He's getting there, but…"

Wrinkling her nose, Kit sniffs her agreement. "That's right, buddy. I'm still figuring this stuff out and you're being a Pushy Panda. Today was a lot for me; be nice."

Oh, for fuck's sake—now she's purposely pouting.

Oriel's eyes widen as he tilts his head. "KK, are you… pouting? I don't know if I've seen you do that quite so… appropriately timed before. You *are* getting more comfy with us!"

I let out a sigh of relief when he jumps to a conclusion that doesn't raise suspicion on his own. "You don't live with him, man. This dude knows how to get what he wants when he feels like it."

"Who doesn't?" Kit shoots back as she gets up again, rounding the island to finally start slicing the bread like I asked. "Besides, you guys always say you *want* me to communicate better and I'm trying to do that. Am I doing it wrong somehow?"

"Not at all," I reply with a smirk. "You're just a wee bit sassy, given the lack of Jasper in the room."

This time, Oriel arches a brow, his expression thoughtful. "You know, he might be right, KK. Though, to be fair, I enjoy the smart mouth. It's fun, and it tells me you're feeling confident in what you're saying. That might not be true with Prince Pissypants, but I can tell the difference between the fake confidence and when you're really comfortable. You have tells."

She does? Now I feel dumb because I don't know those. Damn him and those sharp fucking bird eyes.

"Well, keep that to yourself, bird boy. I don't want everyone knowing all the shortcuts yet." Kit hops down from the step stool, wiping her brow from the steam. "The veggies are almost done, Salem, and the bread is sliced. What's next?"

Frowning, I wag a finger at her. "Now you come sit down and relax. I let you help because we both enjoy it, but you're exhausted from the shit on the surface. You need to let your body and your brain calm down some more. No more chores for the night."

She rolls her eyes and sticks her tongue out at me, making both O and I blink in surprise. He's definitely right about her comfort level with us, and I can't wait to explore that at some point. But first, I want her to myself, so I'm keeping my damn mouth shut.

It won't always be just me, but I'm going to fucking soak up the time that it is.

"YOU LOOK MUCH BETTER, LITTLE DEMON." THE SECOND SLASH IS IN THE door he's headed for Kit, his eyes narrowed on her like he's a guided missile. He's laser-focused on my roomie, and I'm pretty sure it's only *partly* because Jas assigned him to see to her welfare.

I have zero clue what Slash does or doesn't like in that arena because he is the most myste-rious of us all about sex; I've tried a million times, but no one ever talks.

Oriel looks up from his book, squinting for a second as he grins a little. "Calm down, big guy. Salem and I didn't make him run circuits or anything. We're not stupid."

"Sometimes, I question the limits of your intelligence in matters such as this. You are both fond of risks." Slash drops down to his knees, getting even with KK's face as he examines her. "But you seem truthful at the moment."

"Slash, I'm fine. See?" KK holds up the arm that was injured prior to our trip, moving it to show him the wound has healed well and didn't get fucked up on the surface. "Whatever Dr. D gave me and the rest took care of most of the problem, and since I did nothing strenuous today, it got better. Cross my heart."

The huge shifter grunts, watching her movements, then nods. "Okay. But I want to make certain you remain cautious for the first couple of days this week. We will start working on endurance again after Wednesday. Does that sound like it will work?"

"Yep." Kit smiles at him, then jerks her head at the kitchen. "The food smells fucking awesome, right? I helped Salem cook and now we're finishing up some work while we wait for it to finish."

"It does, little demon. You did very well." His hand reaches out to ruffle her hair, and I hide my grin when she flushes the pretty pink that is one tell I'm aware of.

That means she's having less than pure thoughts, and when I inhale slowly, I can almost smell a change in her scent. It's weird that I can't grasp it fully, but I bet there's a reason. I'll have to ask her about it later. For now, I'm kind of enjoying being in on her big ass secret, and I refuse to spoil it. "Kit Kat, you are *so* much easier with him than Jasper. If you were this calm with him, the two of you would stop butting heads."

"Truth," Oriel adds as he looks up from his book. "However, taunting him is amusing as fuck, too. I can't decide which one to root for."

Slash shrugs, moving from kneeling to sitting at Kit's feet. He picks one up and starts rubbing it absently. "I think he can do whatever makes him feel comfortable. It would be less trouble if they got along, butI know that my old friend and leader can be abrasive. He's often that way when he loses control of things around him, and it is the only thing he can do to get it back."

What the hell?

"Slash, you're almost waxing poetic, dude. What gives?" I look at O, who nods in agreement, and then back at our brother. "And you're not kissing Jasper's ass, which is unheard of."

Kit chuckles, his eyes sparkling with mischief. "The big guy talks more around me than normal. I guess it manifested even with you jokers here this time. That's why I don't look shocked."

Our general grunts in irritation—likely with himself for forgetting his audience—and goes back to working on the foot in his palm. "You listen, and it doesn't feel excessive when we are alone. Get back to work, all of you."

I shake my head, knowing that he's embarrassed about the slip, so I let it go. I'd love for him to interact more in the group, and I definitely wish he'd break from our cranky dragon leader more often. If he feels like we're poking at him, he might not show that side again. "Fine. The roast only has a little longer, anyway."

"Plus, the mattress bouncing quad will get here soon. We won't be able to focus once X gets here. They'll want to talk about *everything* that happened in great detail." Oriel's jab is friendly, but he's right about the cobra shifter. Xerxes will want to chat, and Anton will insist on analyzing every detail as they do so.

That's why they work so well together, in my opinion.

"Jasper will also be eager to discuss the events and the possible allies we met. The Fae and the Gemini twins could be strategic."

Kit puts his book down again, leaning forward in his chair. "And I want to get contact info for Morgana and Rogue. They seemed cool as fuck, and I'd like to at least be able to text them sometimes."

My grin is huge; Kit trusting *anyone* is a big deal. I don't know if we helped her do that or if we just supported her well enough for her to get there on her own, but I love that she's actually interested in making friends.

I'm going to do everything in my power to make sure she gets to do that—and if they hurt her, they'll have to deal with me.

One of Us

Kit/Kat

The rest of the guys slink in eventually, and I can tell they've all… calmed themselves. Jasper looks much less on edge than he did on the surface, and Zav isn't even clutching his tails. Whatever they do in private is clearly beneficial to both, and that thought comforts me a bit. I'm not one to judge their dynamic if they're happy and healthy; it seems silly. I wouldn't want people commenting on whatever the fuck I figure out I like just because it doesn't fit in their neat little boxes.

I'm kind of amazed that I could think about having preferences related to that without a single shudder—that's some serious fucking progress.

As Slash and Oriel help my roomie get the plates and stuff set up, Dottie and I curl up in my big chair. They all *insisted* I'd done enough repeatedly, so I quit fighting the overbearing dudes because I honestly am very exhausted. Not having to mask that is helping my energy store immensely—or I think it is. My brain is definitely less fuzzy, and my limbs feel less heavy than when I first emerged from my room. Slash's preaching about eating and keeping my reserves up is also smacking me in the face pretty hard right now; he wasn't joking about how different it is when you have this thing inside of you trying to wiggle its way free twenty-four-seven.

"Little demon, I'm bringing your plate first. You are looking better, but still pale." He turns to Salem, his gaze narrowed as he grunts. "Watch more closely, panda. You are here with him most often and need to help him learn to manage his energy levels."

Salem smirks, then winks at me. "I promise I will *absolutely* keep very close track of KK's energy and exhaustion from now on, big guy. In fact, I'll monitor so closely, he'll think I'm breathing down his neck."

Ooh, that sneaky son of a bitch.

I snort, tilting my chin up as I mutter, "So you think, sleepy boy. You're not my keeper anymore than the others are."

"Ah, but I *am* the chef," he snarks back and I feel my eyes widen as color floods my cheeks. "And what I say goes in this kitchen."

Emotions flood my veins as I fight off a multitude of sensations and feelings coursing through me as the clever panda strikes a very surreptitious blow. He wasn't lying about keeping my secret, but he definitely left out how much he's going to tease and taunt me. I swallow hard as I sink into my chair lower, ignoring the suspicious laughter-like chitters from my kinkajou. They can both suck it—I'm fighting for my life here.

"That's correct," Slash says as he pours another glass of my juice. "Assert your control, and remain vigilant, my brother. I am pleased with your dedication."

Oh, come on! The big guy is supposed to be on my side.

Xerxes looks at me, biting their lower lip as they dart between looking at me, then Salem, and suddenly, they press their fist against their mouth. I'm not great at reading people, but I'm pretty sure they just realized Salem is 'in the know'. Shaking my head a tiny bit, I hope they get that this isn't a topic we can discuss now. In fact, we need to wait until absolutely no one else is nearby. The cobra finally lifts their hand, a knowing smirk forming almost immediately.

"Shit," I mutter to myself as I tear my eyes away so I don't fuck up this very delicate balance of 'I know he knows you know he knows' game. "Slash, are you done piling my plate full enough to feed all of Hell's armies or what?"

That distracts everyone long enough for Oriel to add, "Don't forget the crunkleberries."

"A point to the crow. KK loves those and he'll be much less cranky once he has eaten a few," Salem says as he finishes loading the dishwasher. "They make him giddy."

Anton looks up from his book for a second. "They make everyone giddy, Salem. However, I do believe they affect KK a bit more than us. Probably because his demon isn't quite done baking, so to speak."

"And no one checked me to see how I'd react to the food down here before feeding me; don't think I forgot that tidbit from our visit with the fortune teller tree." I glare at the guys, and Jasper finally stops grading papers to give me a shrug.

"Because at first we didn't give a shit what happened, shrimp. Perhaps not the answer you'd *like*, but it's the truth. Those aren't always pretty in Hell, as you know."

I can't decide if he's a bigger dick when he's just being honest or when he's aiming for my kidneys, but the Prince is a pain in my ass either way.

"I'm aware my safety was of little concern until some of your better demons decided not to be huge asshats, Jasper. You don't have to rub it in every time I say something that highlights your poor choices."

Zavida gives a reproachful look as he pushes his glasses up. "He wasn't really being mean, Kit."

"Oh, how the spines soften when they've gotten some," Oriel snarks as he and Slash walk into the living room with what I assume is my food and drink. The crow follows the big guy over to me, handing me the glass and silverware first, then Slash waits until I'm situated to give me the full plate. "Jumping back to Prince Pricklypants' defense, mmm?"

"No," Zav says firmly. "At least, not like that, Oriel. I'm simply being fair. He was being blunt and truthful, but not mean this time. It's a step, right?"

Fuck. The bushy-tailed gamer is right.

"Okay, fine. Sorry that I snapped a little when you were making a minor effort."

Slash gives me a toothy grin of approval. "Excellent, little demon. Now eat while we get our dinner, so we can finally discuss the trip and the fruits of our labor."

I should tell him to fuck right off, but strangely? I don't want to. The more I get to know my caliphate and understand why they behave as they do, the less I want to defy every single command simply to be ornery. Sometimes, it's because they are used to speaking a certain way and it isn't about controlling me. Other times, it's about gentle reminders that are firm, but also not trying to force me. And I don't mind that as much as I did when I first arrived. The care they show me is like a warm blanket wrapped tightly to help me feel safe and supported—something I haven't ever had in the past. So I let things go and the reactions I get from them make me feel ridiculously happy.

There has to be a name for that and the only person I can ask without feeling stupid is X.

Making a mental note to talk to them about my newfound emotion later, I nod at Slash so he'll go get his own food. After he goes, the others rise from their chairs and I dig into my plate hungrily. The food Salem and I made is delicious, and I marvel again at the fact that he never uses a recipe or looks a damn thing up. Salem's style is all vibes and on-the-spot decisions that never seem to have negative consequences. It's not to do with his demon magic—his stuff is all dreams—nor his lazy panda. I don't know where the cooking instincts come from in his line, but damn, the dude should have his own fucking restaurant.

"Taste good, KK?"

My head lifts as Oriel chuckles, then Anton and X follow suit. "Um, yeah? Why?"

"Because you're making *insane* noises and obviously don't even realize it," X says smugly. They pile roast on their plate as their eyes sparkle merrily at me. "They're porn noises again, if you're wondering."

Damn it, how do I stop that?!

"Doesn't bother me in the slightest," Salem announces as he pulls a bottle of the Fae wine from the cabinet for the others. "I think it's almost musical."

"You would," X shoots back as they take the bottle, pop a fang, and uncork it. My eyes widen because I haven't seen them do shit like that yet, and their tone is much less laid back than it was before.

Wondering what happened to the laid back cobra from a moment ago, I pause eating so I can study their face. The fang has receded as they pour, but there's a dark flashing in their eyes that I recognize from the snake form. For some reason, X's cobra is an unhappy nope rope and I have no idea what changed so abruptly. I lick my lips as I fret internally, hoping I haven't messed something up big time without realizing it.

"Everything okay, Xerxes?" I murmur softly.

Salem snickers, shaking his head as he ignores the dig. "They're just fine, KK. Don't worry your little mop-head. Sometimes, our animals get temperamental and it's hard to explain why."

"No, it's not," Jasper says as he grabs the wine to pour his glasses. "Don't be dense, Salem. The animals are motivated by the four 'F' words, mostly. Other emotions they feel all boil down to the basics in the end. They're animals, after all."

Gee, thanks, Prince Fuckface—there's two 'fs' for you.

This time, I keep my sarcasm inside, though, because the prince is trying to be helpful, I think. Zav turns and gives me a thumbs up, which tells me that my assessment was correct. "Fear, flight, feeding, and um…"

"Fucking." Salem grins wickedly as he says it.

Xerxes hisses under their breath, taking their plate and glass to the living area without comment. Scales shimmer in a few places on them, and I fret again as they drop into their chair. Anton ambles over not long after, joining them in the same chair and arranging their bodies so they can share the space. The bird demon is also frowning as he looks at his mate, so I'm not sure that he knows why X is being weird, either.

"Don't be crass, Salem," Slash says as he bumps the panda. "You'll make the little demon uncomfortable while he eats. That will not help our objective."

"It's okay," I say with a small smile. "I'm getting used to it. I promise I'll say something if it's really bothering me, but… I have to get used to some of this stuff so the other competitors can't use it against me. And um… I think I'm doing well."

"Yes, yes, you're amazing. For fuck's sake," Jasper grumbles as he joins us in the living room with Zav on his tail. "Will you all get your shit together so we can debrief?"

Slash heads for his chair, settling in, and waits until O and Salem bring up the rear. "Now we can begin, Prince. Where would you like to start?"

"Telling me orcs exist would have been helpful," I mutter before I take another bite of my potatoes.

That makes the shark grin, and he shrugs. "There is no possible way for us to communicate how many supernaturals, hybrids, and other variations *could* exist, especially given that ones in the realms other than the surface are very tight-lipped about numbers and species proliferation. It's a hold-out from before the Society banded everyone together; no one wants to share their true kingdom statistics in case there's war."

"Great." I take a drink, then frown. "I'll never know what the hell I might run into anywhere, then?"

"No different from the rest of us, shrimp," Jasper shoots back. "I was surprised by the fucking thing, too. I didn't think Faerie had a lot of giant-sized shit like that hidden, but now I'm reconsidering that assumption."

"Think the Prince will share with us?" Oriel asks suddenly. "He and his little family seem fairly decent. Not trustworthy yet, obviously, but I got a good vibe from them."

"Slash and I will continue working with that new channel to see what it brings," Jasper replies as he scratches his chin. "And perhaps the shrimp will make friends with the gargoyle hybrid."

"I get an actual assignment?" I blink as I look at the demon royal in shock. "Seriously?"

He shrugs. "Don't act as if you didn't intend to contact her or the Geminis' mate, anyway. This is simply a task to go along with your own desires."

I don't care what the fuck he calls it—Jasper Eversore just included me in the caliphate business and I'm not letting that go for a fucking second.

What's Up?

Anton

The way everyone behaved last night made me feel as though perhaps our caliphate is coming together as it needs to. Adding Kit into the group was supposed to help protect him, but afterward, Jasper fought his inclusion even harder. It didn't matter that he was on board with the induction; he simply seemed determined to trample all over our new member in a way he never did with the rest of us. Of course, shared history and family ties probably play into that dynamic, but no one other than the prince got the vibe that Kit was a plant—at least, not after the first few days.

Jasper's trauma is so deeply buried under his guise of leadership and control that it manifested as semi-abusive behavior when his world view was questioned.

Shaking my head, I decide the books I've been reading to understand KK's needs may be infiltrating my brain. I'm analyzing everything like a human, and that's not normal for our kind. To be honest, though, much of it makes sense when you relate behavior to the concepts the books present. None of my brothers would enjoy those observations, though, so I keep them to myself. It won't help to get anyone else's back up by dredging up their past. Right now, our focus has to be on the Games and figuring out the bigger picture with Lucian and whoever else is pulling his strings.

"Annie, are you heading to the bathroom or what?"

X is holding their bucket of products, tapping their foot impatiently as I stand in front of my dresser spacing out. I grab my clothes and shit, giving them an apologetic look. "Sorry, love. I don't know where my head is this morning."

"Where it always is," my mate says as they head for the door and open it. "Going over everything relentlessly until you plan the right courses of action. We just have a *lot* more bullshit on the tray than normal."

They're on the nose with that for certain.

"Did you get the order placed with the pass-through app last night? You were dead set on getting the Hellscape thing to work when we got back to the room." It's not unusual for them to be focused on some random thing they absolutely have to have *now*, but Xerxes was damn insistent on making the demon link to the human online marketplace work for some reason. I've learned not to question their whims with that over the years. It's never anything worrisome, but it definitely gets them hyper as fuck when it won't work right.

"I did. Zavida had to help me get around the stupid blocks on the service at this Satan-forsaken school, but I was eventually successful. My package should arrive before we get back from classes today." X grins broadly, their world right again now that their hyper-fixation has been appeased. "I'm all taken care of."

We walk into the hallway, meeting Oriel as he carries his stuff toward the large shared bathroom as well. The crow demon looks tired, and I wonder if he went off on one of his thieving jaunts after we all split from Salem's dorm last night. The desire to pilfer and acquire shit forces him to do so fairly often, and his favorite time to wander around swiping things is night time. Not surprising, but it can make for a grumpy asshole if he's out late enough.

"Anyone else feel the odd weight to the air this morning?" he asks as we tug open the door and head into the large room. "It's like… anticipation or something."

Jasper's eyes cut from the mirror where he's standing in his towel as he messes with his hair. "You're all *late*. Even Salem and the shrimp are in the showers before you. Get a move on."

I roll my eyes. Of course, he's going to tighten up again the minute we're back to the normal routine. Hopefully, he doesn't slide back into kicking Kit while he's down, too. "We're five minutes off the normal schedule, Jas. It will be fine."

"Maybe for O and you, but we know Xerxes needs their time." The prince arches a brow at my mate, who waves their hand dismissively. "Don't forget we're still eating breakfast in the *Triclinium*. I want to observe the other teams as much as possible, especially since we believe some of them have ties to the fuckwaffle in charge of this place."

"Hey, guys." The voice of our newest member gets my attention as he emerges from his stall fully dressed with wet hair. I feel bad for him—not because there's something wrong with the guy, but because he's so traumatized by his past that he's rarely comfortable in his own skin. "Don't let him get to you; he's back to Pissypants mode."

Jasper opens his mouth to retort, but before he can, Zavida walks up to him and hands him a bottle of cologne. He pauses, rolling his eyes to the ceiling before muttering, "I want to be on time, for fuck's sake. The shrimp has a class on his own first and it's the fucking predator. Do we really want to give her a reason?"

"I will be there. No bullshit will happen when I'm present, Prince." Slash comes out of the actual toilet looking imposing and full of lethal power in his small towel. Kit makes an odd sound as he scurries away from the showers to the very last sink. The shark demon grins hungrily as he faces us. "She risks her life if she displeases me and I will take my punishment happily, if that's necessary."

"Slash," KK says from his spot. He doesn't look our way; instead, he's rubbing lotion on his face and pretending to look at his reflection. "There's no need for anyone to get in trouble. Having you there will be enough, I think."

Slash huffs, stomping over to his sink to brush his sharp ass teeth. "It had better be. I am in no mood for foolishness after what the prince witnessed with her and Darkstar. She's an enemy on all fronts and as my father says, 'if you don't put down the stray that bites, it will do it again and again until you do'. I think it is one of the few things he believes that is ultimately true."

"What in the hell..." Jasper looks at his general, his expression puzzled. "Are you getting paid by the fucking word this morning?"

Kit grins, finally turning for a moment to look smug. "I like it when he's talkative. Fuck off, Jasper."

And now it's time to head for the showers before they all start bickering again.

ONCE WE'RE ALL DRESSED AND READY, WE STOP FOR OUR BAGS, THEN TAKE the elevator to the main floor of Canto IV. It's full of students this morning, which is odd at this time of day. We're usually not surrounded by random fuckers from the other floors when we leave because Jasper makes us leave so early. However, today, a throng of demons are milling about.

Maybe Oriel was right about the weird vibe in the air?

"I knew it," Oriel mumbles as the crowd parts for us to walk through it to the front entrance. "Something is fucking weird, guys, and it's been bothering me since my flight last night."

Jasper eyes him carefully, tilting his head. "What did you sense during your gathering?"

"Like I said before, when we came into the bathroom. The vibe is off. As I flew around campus, I felt it. It didn't emanate from a specific location or I would have investigated. It's just something I feel, and I'm surprised the rest of you don't, too."

Kit frowns, putting his hand on Salem's arm to make sure he doesn't trip over something, then closes his eyes. "I'm trying, O, but I don't feel it." His eyes pop open as we head into the main quad and he makes a soft sound. "Um, I smell something, though? Do you guys smell that? It's... new. Like, I have no idea how to describe it even because this is completely new."

That makes Slash growl low and the shark demon sniffs the air a couple of times. "I do not smell it, little demon. It is not normal for a scent to be one I cannot find. I have the best receptors in the caliphate."

I'm about to question that when Zavida's tails pop out, swishing in irritation back and forth. The Kitsuné nudges the prince, pushing his glasses up as his expression turns to one of confusion. "And I hear something... something far away, but very intense."

What the actual fuck is going on?

"Fuck," Jasper snarls as he puts an arm around Zav to keep him close. His tail drops, letting us all know the dragon is on watch now. "Oriel is right; something is going on at Discordia this morning. Keep your heads on swivels; it seems to lurk, but it's not here—whatever it is."

"You know, we just came back from a risky, life-threatening weekend of bull-shit. Couldn't whatever this is wait a couple of days? I'd like to have a fucking break," Kit says as he kicks a rock across the ground. "It's like we've got a magnet drawing bullshit to us."

"Perhaps a magnet named Kit Kat who has unknown powers and hasn't emerged yet?" Salem grins as he pats the kid's hand. "That's not to blame you, KK, but it's possible."

"It's probable," I agree as I sigh. "The university picked you on its own, after the invitations went out last spring, and your murky provenance has pointed to that from the beginning and we all know it."

"Great. Now I feel guilty for putting everyone in danger."

"Stop that," X says as they lean around me. "If this was some weird ass prophecy shit, it would have come no matter who the chosen one was. And if the people involved are the ones we suspect, it was inevitable—those people have been furious with their lots in Hell for a very long time. You're not really the lynchpin, especially if our new friends are right about the bigger picture."

"This is so damn annoying," Oriel mutters. "There are so many layers and whatever the fuck this thing happening this morning is, it's something we couldn't possibly have planned for. That we're all having different reactions based on our senses means it's triggering the animals, not the demonic bits. Given that the King and the courts don't allow a lot of visitors here from other realms, that means we're going to have a problem like we did up on the surface. Something is *not* where it belongs."

"Please don't let it be another smelly ass orc," X groans. "We're all clean, and I thought that stench was going to hang about forever."

I chuckle, shaking my head at my mate. "You really focus on the important things, huh?"

"I mean, they're not wrong. How many fucking uniforms have I had to replace already? I'm not eager to do it again," Kit says with a shrug. "I didn't get to see much last time because *someone* rushed me away like a fucking cave demon, but..."

Salem smirks, looking so pleased with himself that it trips my wires. Why is he so damn happy about Kit complaining about being spirited away? The panda just keeps smiling as he says, "And you were much better off for it, now weren't you? I know it's hard to admit when you're wrong, KK, but sometimes you have to."

"Shut. Up. Salem," Kit growls as he wrinkles his nose and yanks his arm away. "Don't make me remember how mad I was at you for treating me like the weakest link."

"I did no such thing and you know it, KK. In fact, I treated you incredibly well during our little camp out. Not a single complaint was uttered about how good I was to you."

That just makes our newest member make a frustrated sound as he stomps toward the *Triclinium* without waiting for the rest of us. Salem laughs, his eyes dancing as Slash speeds up to catch KK, so he's not on his own. I tilt my head, curious why he's being so outwardly aggressive; it's unusual for him. Before I can ask, Xerxes tugs on my sleeve, nodding at the huge shark and the small, unemerged demon.

"They're kind of adorable next to each other, right?"

What does that have to do with anything? Why is this morning so fucking weird?

Dumb Dumb

Kit/Kat

Breakfast was both annoying *and* anxiety inducing—which isn't far off from normal—but the unidentified thing we can't find, made it ten times worse. By the time we finished and split up for class, I think Jasper was ready to call it a day and force us to hide in our dorms until the weirdness passed.

Unfortunately, there's only so much of that we can get away with, and even he knows we can't waste that leeway on bad vibes.

"You are thinking hard again."

I look up at Slash, grinning a bit as he bumps me, and I stumble slightly. His eyes widen comically and I laugh, waving his concern off. "It's okay, big guy. You were just being playful, which is kind of a step for you. I'm just less solid —obviously—and we have to adjust your physics next time."

"I didn't hurt you, right?"

Man, he looks worried, so I won't drag this out. I don't want him punishing himself for something that didn't happen.

"Slash, I'm fine. I know, I know. I'm breakable where the others aren't. It makes me irritable, but I know it's true. Your big nudge just threw me off balance; I didn't even fall. I'm all good, buddy." I give him a bright smile, one bigger than my norm, to make sure he knows I'm not hiding anything.

When he finally stops scrutinizing me as we walk to the building my Intro to Supes class is in, I breathe a sigh of relief. Scratching his chin, the shark demon repeats, "But you were thinking too hard."

"Well, yeah. It's all I do because my brain is… wired that way." He nods, and I wrinkle my nose. "It concerns me that some invisible whatever the fuck is running around campus and no one but us seems to even notice. That's weird, right? This isn't like a royal thing that I've somehow been 'gifted' because of the caliphate shit? Like you guys can sense danger like some demonic form of Lassie?"

He blinks at me for a second, then holds the door open to the building. "I don't get that reference, but I think the correct answer is no. I have no idea why we are sensing something that the other students and staff do not appear to be sensing. I think that worries Jasper as well; he didn't say it, but I can read his brooding."

Walking inside, I look around the main entryway, hoping to see other students looking disturbed, but no. There's just nothing going on but normal buzz to class shit, so I head for the elevator with Slash on my heels. He scares people away from joining us and when the doors close, I look up at him. "I thought he was going to say we couldn't go to class, honestly. And I know that's, like, not good to keep missing. It'll get someone—probably me—pulled into Darkstar's office. I *really* don't want that to happen after Jasper's gross story."

Slash grimaces and nods. "I would not want that either—not for you or me. However, should someone try to fetch you, I assure you, little demon… None of us will allow you to be taken to his lair alone. They will have to take great pains to separate us, and that would draw attention I believe Lucian does not wish to have on him."

"I hope so," I murmur as the bell dings and we exit. "Because I don't want to see his bare ass *or* whatever magic he'd use on me if he thought it would get info about you guys. I have a feeling it wouldn't be pretty."

The shark demon frowns, his eyes narrowing and his jaw gritting in determination. "I will make it my goal to ensure that never happens. When I promise things, it is not a casual statement, so I will ask Zavida to help me with some sort of alarm on your phone that will summon me."

Ducking my chin, I do my best to hide the flush on my face as I mutter, "You don't have to be at my beck and call, Slash."

Snorting, he pulls the classroom door open. "Again, I remind you I do not agree to things I do not wish to, little demon. I should have insisted after the prince saved you earlier in the year. I am the one in charge of our safety, after all."

And he takes it very seriously—which I kind of like... a lot.

"The most common type of supernaturals are shifters, of course. They are plentiful in many variations on the surface, and governed by individual groups that have leaders in local, regional, and on the national level. Since they are part of the larger treaty between supernatural realms, they also fall under the governance of the Society, which their leaders have representatives on at various levels."

I sit up straighter as Lillibet continues her lecture, very interested in this topic. My trip back to the human world revealed a lot of this, but I'm hungry for more information. I can't keep running into shit like a fool because I don't know the same stuff as the other demons surrounding me, including my caliphate. My stylus flies over the screen as I take notes carefully, despite knowing that Discordia's professors will have their own slant on this.

"Shifters are also the most common hybrids amongst *all* the realms because they often have a drive to find what they call a 'fated mate'. It's a magical and biological imperative that drives them to seek a perfect match that will help complete them. It may be one being or several, but the likelihood of their finding that match is widely varied. Since shifters are composed of both very common types like wolves and much more rare types like mythicals, it is claimed that the Fates stopped pairing them *only* with their own kind and expanded the possibilities to include all other species and hybrids."

Leaning in, I look at Slash with wide eyes. "They can find their soulmate... anywhere? In anyone?"

"Fated mates is a much more complex situation than she is describing." He glances down to the front to make sure Lillabet isn't watching us. "Many species have their own version of it, and yes, most can find them amongst their own kind and many others."

"So it's destiny, not biology at all, right?" I whisper.

Slash gives me a crooked grin. "While demons rarely interact with those deity loving crones, they are tied inextricably to the timeline of *all* supernaturals since time immemorial. They are only called by the most recent names because the Greeks somehow got the world to acknowledge their convention most eagerly."

Fucking wow.

"You mean they're older than the deities? Like how old?"

"Primordial old, little demon. The descendants of the original creators who were escalated to a higher status to ensure they could continue to be fair and even-handed throughout the entire span of the universe—or so we were taught as children." He holds up a finger, pointing to my notes, and I realize he's signaling that we have to be quiet before the bitch notices.

Lillabet pauses, turning to look at the room haughtily. "Shifters are not amongst the strongest supernaturals, and therefore considered one of the lower levels of hybrids. Most of them are abandoned and left to the Society to be raised in enclaves at a *much* higher rate than any other hybrid."

I wrinkle my nose at her obvious species-ism. That's definitely no different from the ugly ass racists at home, and I highly doubt the fucking royal court of Hell would have kept their hybrid children as heirs if they weren't extremely powerful. Out of the seven demons set to inherit the thrones here, all seven are shifter mixes. This petty woman knows that and she definitely knows one of them is sitting next to me, fuming at her audacity.

"She's doing it on purpose," I say in a low tone. "Don't let her get to you, big guy."

He grins toothily, his light eyes sparkling with malice. "I'm not, Kit Kat. Better demons than her have tried to force a confrontation when it would not be advantageous and they were also not successful. Jasper will have a field day with this, though."

I have to cover my mouth so the snort isn't audible. "Jasper has a field day with *anything* that allows him to strike out at people who piss him off. He needs anger management, man."

Slash doesn't reply, but I can tell by his smirk that he agrees. Turning back to my notes, I highlight things I have questions about so far and underline what I think will be important. This is the most useful class Lillabet has given so far, and I'm *very* anxious to expand on it.

"Mr. Queznar," the Cubi says as she struts across the front row. "Please list at least five species of common shifters and five species of mythical shifters. If you did the reading from last week, you should be able to do this with ease."

I squint at the dude who stands, then roll my eyes when I realize it's that fuckwit species-ist from the Thieves Guild. This should be good; he's going to say something awful and I'm going to have to let it go.

"Common types include big cats like lions or tigers, canines like wolves or coyotes, birds such as eagles or hawks, large reptiles like crocodiles or constrictor snakes, and aquatic animals like sharks or whales." The dude turns slightly, shooting a smug look towards us, then he goes back to simpering at the succubus. "Mythicals are rare, but the species who are found most often are dragons, phoenixes, mer-folk, griffins, and centaurs."

Lillabet leans in, giving the odious little shit a long peek down her blouse as she feeds off his lust. "Very good, Mr. Queznar. Now, can someone else tell me five uncommon shifters and mythicals? I want to see how many of you skimmed versus actually read."

I want to raise my hand, but I *definitely* do not want her to come up here. In fact, I don't want that predator within twenty feet of me if possible. So even though I did the reading, and absolutely know this answer, I'm not trying to get noticed.

"Yes! Mr. Aloysius, please show us how closely you read," the blond Cubi says as she wiggles her way up the stairs. I shudder involuntarily, knowing she's going to fill up on him next and he's probably looking forward to it.

But I guess ugly ass pit demons can't really be choosers, right?

"Uh, so uncommon regular shifters would be, um…"

"For fuck's sake, he doesn't know," Slash mutters. "He just wants a hit of her horny juice."

"Go ahead; dazzle me and you'll be rewarded." Lillabet's purr is loud enough for everyone to hear, and it makes my skin crawl.

Before I know it, I've turned and buried my face in Slash's shoulder, not wanting to witness this spectacle. It's just too gross, and it's too damn early in the morning.

"Don't worry, little demon. She'll spoon feed it to him soon enough." Slash pats my head lightly. "She wants the energy, too."

"Uh, maybe leopards?"

Lillabet sighs happily. "That's one. What other ones can you name? Think hard about the answer Mr. Queznar gave."

"Yeah, like… dogs. Um, hyenas?"

"Very good!"

I groan into the hard muscles I'm pressed against. This dude has the IQ of a donut and there's no way this is going to go any more quickly unless someone helps him. Unfortunately, all these idiots want their turn on horny-go-round, so they will not help him out. "Slash," I mumble into his arm. "Just kill me now. I can't take this. It's actually worse than Jasper running his mouth, I think."

The shark shifter chuckles, patting me again and allowing me to continue to cower in his strength. "It won't last forever, no matter how much it seems like it. Just stay calm and quiet so I can keep you safe from her wrath. I'll protect you while you bemoan how mono-syllabic my fellow demons can be."

I think he just made a joke at his own expense… Slash is definitely my favorite today.

Safe

Zavida

"This is interminable," I whisper to Oriel as he stirs the potion in front of our group. Xerxes gives me a knowing look, but I don't let it stop me. "I really hate that Kit has classes we're not in. Every time we discover something new about this conspiracy or his powers, I feel like it gets more dangerous for him to even sit in classes without someone beside him."

X tuts quietly, putting their hand on my arm. "Zav, you know we can't get KK moved into our classes; that douche in the admin office won't approve it. Plus, he doesn't want us to smother him all the time; it will reinforce the belief that he's too weak to make it on his own."

"Ugh, I knowwww." We both look at the crow shifter as he groans his agreement. "What? I don't like him being on his own, and though Slash is in this period with him, the next one is uncovered. Alabaster is a dick, but he will not assault the kid—that's what helps me not molt over it."

I chuckle, smiling a bit as our brother expresses more concern than normal. Neither X nor I have seen him molt over stress in a long time, so he's definitely the next in line to fall for the newbie who's thrown our group into chaos. "Oriel, don't pick at your feathers; it won't help. I get it because I struggle to keep my tails from popping out constantly, but at least they don't hurt me."

Xerxes sighs, leaning their hip against the counter as they watch the hex potion out of the corner of their eye. "Guys, KK is improving a *lot*, even if it doesn't seem like it. The magic is coming slowly, but he's asking for help, trusting people to protect him, and even trying to snark less with Jas. I see his issues fading bit by bit as he gets more comfortable with us. Just keep showing him we're safe; isn't that what we all had to do for each other?"

Thinking about that for a moment, I nod. "You're right, X. None of us were predisposed to trust one another because of all the court intrigue—other than Slash and Jasper. One by one, those two brought us into the caliphate fold by sharing our struggles and trauma. They didn't *call* it that; they simply said we were bonding by fire or some shit."

"Maybe we need to work on that with KK, so he gets even *more* comfortable," Oriel replies, tapping his lips with his painted fingernails. "Carefully, of course, because he's still trying to heal properly, and not without asking if he's cool with it. We don't want to take away from his ability to cope by dumping on the poor dude."

Such emotional intelligence today—I'd say I'm shocked, but I actually believe my brothers have more than they show on the daily.

"You want to get Kit on his own and have a guy bonding over the bad stuff?" X says as they wrinkle their nose. "I don't know about that. Feels like it might go super sideways if he feels pressured to reciprocate. I'm pretty sure he hasn't repeated his story to anyone outside of his shrink or whoever his fosters were. At least, not in full, you know? That might fuck up his progress."

"Or help it," I murmur. "Maybe only talking to adults who likely blamed him and then discarded him is why he can't heal. He's been made to feel like he should have known, should have done something different, and that he's a burden. You can tell by the way he's constantly explaining his issue and defining his boundaries; he's had to re-iterate them so many times that it's a reflex to do it now."

"Well, fuck," Oriel says. "I sort of figured that he was just doing that because he's mouthy. Fuck knows, our prince thinks that, Zav."

Ducking my head, I whisper, "When Jas and I first… you know… he had to devise ways to get me to actually give him boundaries. My trauma worked the *opposite* direction as KK's, and he was always on me to stop apologizing for having them. I noticed Kit was over explaining and being *not* apologetic about it in the same way I was holding back. It felt familiar, and I'm pretty sure it's because he *has* to in his mind or someone will violate him again."

"I agree." Xerxes reaches over, stirring the concoction for a moment before they look at us. "When I measured him, I was very cautious, but besides the new tattoos he's hiding and the small scaly patches… he has scars. Not a crazy amount, but enough to concern me, so I didn't ask. I don't know if they're related to the incident or some other heinous BS, but he definitely has seen some shit."

Oriel nods, digesting that information as he adds a few ingredients to the bubbling liquid in the cauldron. He's quiet for a moment, then he sighs. "That's not unexpected, I suppose, but it doesn't mean I like it. In fact, I really fucking hate it and some of the others will, too."

"I don't feel upset he hasn't pried into our shit, though." They both look at me and I shrug. "The guy is keeping his pain to himself, and his obsessive need for boundaries means he wouldn't ask if we didn't offer it up. I think he's trying to be respectful, in his own way, and that's unusual for the demon world."

"So many things here differ from how KK was raised—both in the 'normal' human world and the bullshit he grew up with. It's honestly surprising that he is adjusting without a lot of craziness. I don't think I'd do nearly as well were it me." Xerxes grabs a handful of herbs, tossing them into the simmering pot with a satisfied expression. "Which is why I'm also not worried about that situation. His hands are full and he's doing the best he can with the tools he has, hmm?"

Our glitzy brother is right—Kit is definitely trying, and even his quirks have become endearing—so we can be patient, even my irascible lover.

By the time we finish Curses & Hexes, the three of us have talked shit out like a coffee klatch, and I think it helped *a lot*. I wish some of the others had been there, but given that we don't share every class, it's just not possible. None of us share the next session—it's specific to our learning paths, so we part ways knowing that the guy we're worried about is being escorted by Slash. I agree that the demi who runs the Human History class is more of a smug tool than a threat, so while I have a tiny bit of concern, it's manageable.

My phone buzzes as I head for Complex Algorithms in the computer lab, and I pull it out to check the screen. The OG caliphate chat—without Kit—comes up immediately and I arch a brow. We don't use this one as much as before, but I assume someone is doing so now to report to our prince.

Prince: How was Intro, Slash?

Enforcer: Fine. Headed to his HH class now. Who will be there at the end?

Thief: Me. I'm taking KK somewhere for lunch. We won't be at the table.

Prince: When did this get decided and why?

Thief: Calm down, man. I want to show him something to cheer him up. It's no big deal, and it's perfectly safe.

Enforcer: I should be the one who decides that.

Chef: No, Kit Kat should be the one who decides that.

Spy: Agreed. *high five Salem*

Prince: You two… shut up. I don't want to manage a disaster today, O.

Thief: Cross my heart, Prince Pricklypants. No disasters. We'll hang out, then I'll drop him off at Demonic Languages afterwards.

Hacker: That's another one on his own. Who's got that?

I asked because Mondays and Wednesdays are nightmare fuel with Kit's schedule. He's in a ton of shit we're not, and we don't have free blocks to deal with it. Knowing what we do about the breadth of the conspiracy—or what we think it is—makes that even worse than before. We have no idea who Lucian has *here* that is gunning for Kit without making it known. The bullies all make their idiocy known, and we can monitor them with my trackers. Unknowns are *my* biggest fear; they could be anywhere, hiding behind a disinterested look or pretend smile.

Prince: I'm waiting…

Enforcer: I have Cardio after my quick lunch at that time. I will go.

Chef: Then he has Lit with O and me, so we've got him from there.

Thief: Where's dinner tonight?

Prince: Dorm unless there's an unscheduled change of plans.

Thief: Aye, aye, Captain Crankypants!

Prince: ...

With that decided, I move swiftly to the class I need to get to. It's way below my skill set, but jumping one course was the most the comp sci professors would allow when I registered. I won't have to focus for long on whatever we're assigned, which means I can use the time to work on things that will actually benefit my caliphate.

Plus, it'll please Jasper, and I like when he's pleased—it's good for both of us.

Once I get up the stairs to the tech floor, I head for the lab with renewed purpose. I need to program web crawlers for accounts of the rest of the 'Apalachin' thing the supes on the surface called that weird meeting. I want to know if the general public has gotten wind of the orc attack, if any gossip is floating around about the rest of the event, or even if people know my caliphate was there. That will be the first thing I tackle after I zip through whatever Turing has us doing.

"This is odd," I mutter as I open the door to the lab to find a *very* sparsely attended class. "Where the hell is everyone?"

The spectral form of the professor raises his hand to shush me, and I roll my eyes once he's turned back to his own computer. Professor T isn't really a ghost, but he's been co-opted by Discordia from his proper home in the Legendary realm to teach. I assume he's being paid a fortune because storybooks and legendary types aren't fond of coming to Hell versus the deity's place. He's fucking amazing, though, and when I'm really allowed to learn from him, I know it will be amazing.

Since I will not get an answer to my question, I plop down at the computer I favor in the corner and log in. Once I'm into the system, I look up at the whiteboard to get the assignment and fly through it as fast as my fingers can type. It only takes a few minutes to complete and email, at which point I look at my screen with a hidden smirk. One flick of the app on my phone shrouds the lab computer in my own security, and I get to work.

The web spiders for the surface don't take me long—I've been doing that shit since I was a wee demon. After I have those set up to notify me of any findings, I code a series of malware that I'm going to *try* to infect the intranet at Discordia with. I want to use it to trigger alerts for specific words and phrases that might help us identify who the fuck is helping Darkstar, and who might be after KK. There are more basic ones that monitor social media in Hell for our names and families, but those are mostly to keep track of what's being said. We've never needed them to keep someone from doing terrible things to us because we're so damn strong together. Kit doesn't have that and I want to do my part—as small as it may be—to help him stay safe.

After all, I promised to make it up to him and I'll be damned if I'm going to fail.

Magic
Kit/Kat

I'm a bit surprised when Oriel shows up by himself at the end of Human History. My free period/ lunch time coincides with a couple of the guys' over the two-hour stretch and I expected to see at least Zavida with him. Instead, I see a sharp-eyed crow demon leaning against the wall opposite the doorway with a nervous expression that is *not* the norm. At least, it's not in my experience so far, and I'm very curious why he looks like he's ready to bolt.

"How was class?"

I shrug, stepping out of the room and closer to him before I reply. "Same old. The shit I knew isn't remotely correct, and we're only in ancient times. My solo reading is further along—I'm in the Middle Ages—so it's not surprising, just really hard to reframe with the new lens. It all makes more *sense* with the supernatural context, but relearning things you've been taught since you were little is *hard*. You know?"

"Freaked out by the fall of Rome, aren't you?" he smirks and I'm glad to see the worried look leave his handsome features.

Making a face, I snark, "Uh, *yeah*. Romulus and Remus were wolf shifters, Nero was a fucking demon, the deities were real, mythos fell along with empires because of other deities meddling, and Pompeii being less of a volcano and more a dragon? Little weird for me."

The crow demon nods and offers his arm. "Well, I can't say whether it will get weirder for you or not, KK. I'm also biased, but from the other end. Every time I have to hear the stuff they told the humans about history in that class, I marvel at how damn gullible they are. It's just as worthy of head shakes to supes as it is from your side."

I take the arm, twining mine through his as he leads me down the hall. "So what's up with you being here all by your lonesome? I figured Zavida would have raced his tails to join you. Is he with Jasper or something?"

The smirk fades and Oriel scratches his jaw, his eyes going back to the nervous look from before. "Well, he might have if I hadn't declared this lunchtime mine."

What?

"Why… why would you do that?" I ask carefully. I'm not sure if the nervousness makes sense now or not. Salem was a bit like this until we… found a rhythm, and now he's smugly confident. But Oriel will not do what Salem did during lunch, right? I swallow around a dry throat, feeling my stomach drop as I consider all the possibilities that it could be as my mind flies off the handle.

Turning to look at me, the dark-haired demon gives me a crooked smile. "I have something to show you, and those assholes aren't invited."

I blink, not sure what to say to that.

Does he mean what I think he means? If so, what the hell am I going to do?

As we head deeper into the building, I realize I haven't been to this part before. That's not remarkable by itself, if I'm honest—outside of the doc's office, my classes, the dorms, and the *Triclinium*, I don't wander around the campus. The one time I did resulted in Prince Pissypants rescuing me from a fire that we still don't discuss. No reason for me to repeat the scariest night I've had at Discordia so far.

But I am curious where the fuck O is taking me.

When we hit the ground floor from the twisty back staircase, I tap the arm I'm holding. "Are you ever going to tell me where we're headed? I mean, I don't know Discordia very well, but it seems like we're taking a really round-about route."

"That's because it is." His eyes dance with mischief, and I huff softly. "Don't get all puffed up, KK. I don't want anyone following us here; in fact, turn your watch thingy off."

Oh, damn, I forgot about this thing.

"It's kinda funny that I disabled the tracking on your phone and laptop after Jas had Zav do his thing when you first got here, but now you wear that shiny trinket without pause." His grin is knowing and I roll my eyes as I hit the button to turn it off with my free hand.

"Shut up," I grumble. "You know that was to keep him from controlling me, and this thing is actually about safety. Though it wasn't an *easy* transition to accept, I'll grant you. I have trouble accepting help, especially when it makes me feel caged, but um… I also don't want you guys to worry and something to happen to you because you're distracted. It's a *Catch-22*, I guess."

"We appreciate your sacrifice, KK. However, I'm glad you turned it off. I don't think you'll remember the route since you don't roam the campus, but I don't want them to know where we're going. I even considered a blindfold, but I didn't know if that would activate a trauma, so I discarded that plan."

My face heats and I have to clear my throat before I answer. His care in making sure he doesn't accidentally trigger me is sweet, and it reminds me of how carefully Salem is treating me. Once I'm good, I murmur huskily, "I appreciate that. Though, um, for future reference, I wouldn't… I mean, blindfolds aren't an issue. Just… so you know."

Oriel stops, giving me an absolutely sinful grin. "They aren't, huh? Good thing you told me; I'll tuck that away for later. I'm sure I'll want to remember it.."

Oh, my. Now what do I say?!!

Choking back a squeaky sound, I squeeze his arm, so he leads the way again. "Get a move on, birdman. I'm hungry as fuck. The big guy's regimen has my body trained to know when I'm s'posed to have food. That might have been his plan, come to think of it."

"Slash would be *extremely* happy to hear that, you know." He opens the door to another staircase, this one darker and more foreboding. "In fact, I think he'd be tickled pink to know you insisted I feed you. You had to be dragged to food when you arrived, KK."

I dip my chin so I don't have to look at him as the blush gets hotter, mumbling, "Whatever. Did you bring food or what? 'Cause if not, we won't be able to stay long. I definitely can't make it through the rest of the day without eating a good meal. I snacked on my morning snacks already."

"Damn… Slash is going to be super fucking happy to hear that." Oriel pauses, then adds, "But yes, I have food here and once we're here, you're gonna be so entranced that it won't matter what anyone else thinks, anyway."

Was that him convincing me or himself? Either way, it's pretty cute.

"You're setting yourself up for some pretty big expectations." I pat his arm, my lips curling up a bit. "Are you sure whatever you're taking me to see is spectacular enough to withstand the build up?"

"I'm fairly certain I more than meet expectations."

Blinking owlishly, I stumble over words again because, given how my roomie is acting now, I think Oriel just flirted with me. The tinge in his voice was definitely suggestive—at least, I think it was. I could have been mistaken, though the words he chose were hard to misinterpret. "I… well, I uh… I…"

His laugh is dark and husky, which makes me tingle from head to toe. "KK, I think you're going to pass out if you don't breathe. Relax… I promise you're going to enjoy my surprise."

"Oh? And how would you know? Is it a *highly rated* surprise?" I shoot back. My eyes widen when I hear myself; I didn't *mean* to take that petulant tone. Oriel has done nothing wrong and I don't have a right to even insinuate that he can't enjoy… whatever… with whoever he wants.

These demons are rotting my brain and making everything confusing—more so than usual since we came back from the surface.

We reach the bottom of the stairs and Oriel winks at me, completely ignoring my little snit. He opens an enormous door with a key he produces from his pocket, then holds it for me. "Watch your step now, KK. We're in the older part of the university now. There's a system of tunnels that goes underneath everything, but you have to know someone to get access. Lucky for us, I do."

"Lucky for us?" I echo, hoping to move on from my oddly possessive episode.

"Yep. It'll be hotter than you expect because of the underground lava deposits, but it's Hell, you know?"

I nod, thinking about that. Since I haven't explored the campus, much less the realm, I'm pretty ignorant about the geography, much less the geology of my new home. "Good thing Dottie is hanging in my bag, taking a nap. I wouldn't want her to jump down and burn her little paws."

Oriel snorts. "No, you would not. But where we're going, there will be places for her to explore."

"Are we going to a secret jungle gym? A hidden amusement park? Maybe an underground bowling alley like the White House had?" My curiosity is killing me, but it's been taking a back seat to the uncertainty about flirting and double entendres.

"Well, we're using the underground to get where we're going, and it will have things for you to play with," he says with a bob of his eyebrows.

Damnit, what is with *these guys now? Am I putting out a vibe or something?*

I say that like I'm mad, but surprisingly, I'm not. Anger and fear aren't part of the equation, strangely enough, but anxiety and nervousness are. My lack of experience doesn't seem to matter to Salem, but I don't know what to expect from Oriel—or any of the rest, if that becomes a thing. Wait, do I want it to be a thing? Am I actually entertaining a seven guy dating situation for real? With *these* ridiculously hot, patient, and mostly kind *demons?*

My heart thumps in my chest as I swallow to get the dryness in my mouth to fade. I sort of ignored that idea because it was so incredibly silly to me previously. How can I avoid thinking about it now when a second dude is maybe probably sort of flirting with me as we walk down a dimly lit secret passage to his secret surprise?

"KK, you're white as a ghostie, man. What is going on in your head? Is it too… tight down here? Do you have claustrophobia and I didn't know? Or maybe you didn't know until now?"

Oh, for fuck's sake. He's such a decent guy under the dark makeup and cutting sarcasm.

"No, no… Oriel, I'm fine. I'm *not* claustrophobic." I think for a second, then add, "At least, not if I'm not already in an episode? I get panicky when closed in if I'm mid-attack. I think that's because of the incident. But it's okay now. You don't make me panic."

His brow arches. "Your pulse says differently, Kit Kat. I can feel it racing against my arm, you know."

"Well, fuck," I mutter. "Okay, I'm a *little* nervous, but that's not the hallway, it's just surprises. I trust it won't be bad in my head, but I'm working on knee-jerk reactions, as you know."

A huge set of doors appear in front of us and he stops just before we get to them. His smile is gentle as he looks down at me. "I'm thrilled to hear that you're just working through an involuntary reaction, not worried about me. And the trust thing is… uh, really cool."

I watch him rub the back of his neck, waiting for him to address the ornate purple doors. When he doesn't, I wrinkle my nose as I squint at the intricate designs on them, then turn back to ask, "Are you going to tell me what the hell these open up to? I'm dying here."

His eyes widen, and the look on his face is priceless as he gapes at me. "You…. You can… *see* them?"

Uh-oh. I get the feeling I'm not supposed to—and it's a huge deal.

Secrets
Oriel

I'm more than stunned as I stare at the guy in front of me. He's giving me a look like I'm crazy, but he has *no idea* what this means. If I was looking for a sign about whether I should shoot my shot with him… *this* is the big flashing one I can't ignore. No one… and I mean *no one*… can see the entrances to my hoards because they're created from my shadows and sealed with Greed line magic. The only person who could subvert that kind of power is a fated mate, and I think I'm going to lose feathers in a few seconds.

Shit, shit, shit. Is it really possible that he's fated to all of us?

Some supes, especially shifters, have a handful of mates, but it's not normal for demons to have them at all, much less seven. But KK is *definitely* part demon, but his origin is nebulous enough that none of us has truly landed on what we think he's going to be. The powers he's shown so far—chronomancy, that weird darkness thing, and a few other quirks—don't match up with most of the options. The scales would lean toward a dragon, obviously, and the tattoos are… unusual and not easily attributed to anything as far as I know. He's just a huge fucking question mark all around, but… *he can see the goddamn doors.*

"O, you're freaking me out now," Kit whispers. "Mostly because you're gaping at me and not speaking, which makes me worry I've done something wrong. That's probably just me, but honestly, I can't help thinking—"

I grab his face and grin crazily at the babbling dummy I'm growing entirely too fond of. "KK, you gotta breathe. I swear, I'm going to make you put a nickel in a jar every time I have to say that, you know? It'd make for a nice little savings account for you."

He blinks, giving me an owlish look. "Oriel, I don't have nickels to use and um, it's hard to breathe when you're squishing my cheeks like that."

Oh, fuck. That's true.

Letting go, I suck my lower lip through my teeth, chewing on my lip ring for a second while I think. "Okay. So I'm gonna say something that will sound really weird, but.. those doors are invisible."

"Uh, no, they're not. Why are you yanking my chain? I can see them plain as day—all purple and spiky and sparkly like you. What the hell are you talking about?" Kit frowns, crossing his arms over his chest as his brows drop. "That's not funny, Oriel."

"I'm *not* lying, KK. But I might have been unclear, so here it goes…" I suck in a sharp breath and then blow it out. "That door is invisible to everyone but me… normally. See, it's made from my shadows and sealed with my family magic to keep people from finding my… um, well, *one* of my hoards."

His eyes widen as I feel my face get red, and I rake my hand through my hair, tugging on it a little. Kit reaches out, pulling my hand away from the anxiety coping mechanism, then gives me a lop-sided smile. "Well, why the hell can I see it, then? Because it's very clear and I didn't even know it wasn't an actual door in the middle of this damn hallway."

Okay, I'm not having this discussion out in the open—not a single fucking chance of that.

"Come with me, then, and we'll chat," I say as I wave my free hand, making the immense door open enough for us to get inside. "I don't want to talk about it out here."

KK grins a bit, nodding at me as he accepts my proposal. "Alright. But I have to admit that everyone talking about these famous hoards and how you don't share them has made me really curious about this topic. Am I sworn to secrecy?"

"Uh, *yeah*," I reply quickly. "None of those dickheads are *ever* coming in one of my doors, thank you very much."

"Then why me?"

I'd love to tell him, but he's not ready for that much honesty yet—but someday, I hope.

"Don't you want to see what's *inside* the special room?" I tease gently. "We don't have all day, you know."

Nodding, Kit shakes his head and straightens his posture up like he's preparing himself. "Okay, lay it on me. Open the doors, Oriel."

I press my lips together in an amused grin, then reach out to grab the ornate handles of the doors, throwing them open as I walk in. Sensing that he's following, I stride deeper into the outer chamber of the Gothic-style space that fits in between the light and the dark. It's all shadow magic, of course, and it's how demons like me can slip from place to place without being seen if we choose. Some of my kind prefer to always travel this way, but I use it when it's necessary and avoid being here when it's not. I've always felt like too much time in a liminal space like this drains the 'humanity' out of my fellow demons, and we have less than other supes to start with.

"I see nothing but a fancy entryway, O. So far, mildly impressive, but not a five-star experience worth hiding."

Turning to face him, I sigh. "You know, I miss when the magic stuff filled you with wonder, KK. You're getting jaded."

He chuckles and shrugs. "Bound to happen, I suppose. I mean, if I'm always gaping, I'm not ready to fight, and that's no good, right?"

Fair point.

"Come on, then. This is the more exciting part," I say as I offer my hand. Kit takes it, and my bird caws with happiness inside as his warm palm meets mine.

Leading him to the smaller set of doors ahead, I press my free hand to the surface and they open, revealing a room filled to the brim with pilfered treasures of every conceivable kind. Crows aren't picky, truthfully, so this room is not only stuffed with *actual* gems and artifacts, but also treasured items from random demons I've encountered throughout my life. The Greed part of me is why I have several hoards—I can't stop myself from stealing things everywhere I land to hide away—but the animal portion of me enjoys loot that fits a myriad of definitions. It doesn't have to be monetarily valuable for the crow to see value in it, which is why I had the tee-shirt I gave KK when we went to the surface.

"Holy fuck, O. This is... enormous." Kit looks up at me with wide eyes. "You have *more* of these?"

"Quite a few," I admit with a sheepish expression. "Between the heritage and the bird, this is probably my biggest fixation. The others have their own foibles like this, you know. It's not just me—though, I'm definitely better at hiding mine than the rest. It's part of our blood, you know?"

"Mmm. Yours is greed, they've said, so this makes sense." Kit lets go of my hand to walk over to a section that is a giant pile of precious stones and metals of every type imaginable. "I am impressed that you seem to have organized your sinful desires."

If only he knew…

"Makes it easier to find shit when I want it," I mumble. "Sometimes, I give things up to get things I want more, like at the Fae booth."

His hands fly to the collar he hasn't removed since we were caught in the Orc-fest. "I remember. You gave up something for me, and it looked stupid valuable. Why?"

I can't very well say because I've just been proven right about you being my damn mate, so I chew on my lip ring for a moment to buy time. His eyes track it, which makes me want to preen, and I have to smack my brain back into focus to find words. "Because our little family is that important, Kit Kat. *You're* important, and that was a trinket in comparison. Don't fret about it."

His brows furrow as he turns away from the glittering pile to face me, then steps closer so we're inches apart. "I am? I mean, yes, I get that most of you guys have accepted me, especially since that stupid ceremony, but… I guess it's the BS from my past that keeps me questioning why I'm even a blip on your radar. That's not fishing, so don't feel you have to compliment me so I don't shatter or anything. I'm just musing out loud, really, and—"

Before he can finish, I reach out and grab his arms gently, pulling him against me. I don't even have a second to process the move before my animal brain takes over and I dip my head to kiss the babbling guy I've been dancing around for weeks. Our lips meet, and I wait just a second until he goes pliant, then slip my tongue into his mouth to explore. Even the impatient bird inside of me knew Kit had to give his permission to make this okay, and now that he has, it's open season.

I feel his hands move to my shirt, grabbing it to hold on, and every part of me practically sings in happiness. This is what my demon *and* my animal have wanted, which means they're in an unusual harmony. Taking advantage of the calm within, I let go of Kit's arms to wrap mine around him as our kiss deepens. He's hesitant, but I sense the spark of brattiness when he suckles my tongue for just a brief second before letting go. When we break for air, his face is adorably flushed, and he bites his swollen lower lip shyly.

"Oriel, that—"

"Was perfect, KK." I squeeze him in my embrace, hoping to let him know that he's safe and I will not push him somewhere he isn't ready for. It's going to fucking *kill* me if I have to let go, and I'm going to need to find something to shield the raging hard-on I'm sporting, but I'll do it so I don't fuck up this chance. "I've kinda been waiting to do that for a while."

"Really?" His eyes widen and he blinks. "That's what Salem said, too."

Oh, that bi-colored son of a bitch—I'm going to thrash him for hiding that he got to our KK first.

"Did he now?" I smile gently, making sure the kid knows we will not fight over him or make him choose. That's important, especially because humans, unlike demons, are *not* prone to poly family units. Kit has to feel secure in exploring his feelings for all of us or he'll run for the hills, so he doesn't get hurt. It helps that it's true that we'll accept his decisions about who he wants, but it doesn't mean I'm not kicking that furry ass for hiding shit. "Well, I'm not surprised. While some of our bros are outspoken, others are more… introspective about their emotions."

"That's me, too," he whispers. "Not because it's a normal state—though I'm not sure about that because I just don't know what I *could* have been, you know? But because of the other stuff."

My hand raises to cup his face, and I look down at him with a soft expression. "Yeah, I know. And I know why you always have to bring it up—you've been made to excuse your behavior for so long that you don't even think about it, right?"

He nods and I sigh. This damn guy may not have been totally physically abused—I don't know what the scars X mentioned are, so I'm not ruling it out—but he's definitely been emotionally abused so badly that he doesn't know what end is up. What he doesn't know is how fucked up *our* backgrounds are because demons are taught to channel it into our demonic nature and keep our mouths shut, especially those in the royal court.

I'm going to do something perilous, but since he's definitely my mate, it doesn't technically break any laws.

"So I'm going to tell you something about my shit, and um… you can't repeat *anything* about it if we're not in one of these hoard rooms. Got it?" I look at him seriously and he swallows hard, but nods. "The Greed line, like all the others, has existed since Hell was created. My father is a direct descendant of the line, and my mother is a hybrid—though she will deny it with her dying breath. Greed *needs* hybrids, of course, because breeding with animals and supes who are prone to that kind of proclivity strengthens the demonic inclination of our line. However, they hate it with a passion because hybrids are considered 'lower'."

Kit frowns. "How come all the heirs are hybrids, then?"

"Because we're all the strongest progeny, including bastards, that our respective families have produced. We were all powerful individually, but once we bonded as a caliphate, no siblings could touch the raw power we have. It's a bone of contention, and it lead to a lot of bad shit in our pasts." I pause for a moment, then murmur, "Some of us had it worse than others, of course, and my parents' mildly abusive shit isn't really as bad compared to theirs. But those are *their* stories to tell, so don't ask me."

"I wouldn't!" The kid in my grasp looks horrified at the thought, and I have to suppress a smile. He really is a good fucking person, and I hate that all this shit is falling on his head like a piano in a cartoon.

"Okay, well… I spent most of my childhood proving myself—my thieving mettle, I guess—in very dangerous situations, trying to earn my parents' respect. Failure wasn't an option, but if it was a reality… the reactions weren't good." I cough, looking away as I shrug. "The tats cover a lot, especially because they're old. But my old man is not someone you want to disappoint, and I paid for it until Jasper brought me into the fold when I was eight."

"I'm sorry, Oriel," Kit whispers. "But, um, I promise—just like you did— that you're safe with me. And your secrets, of course. That, too." He blushes, and I smile softly at the adorableness of his shy behavior. "But I… I *like* this. Seeing the hoard and um… the kiss… and um…"

Damn it, if he doesn't stop that, we're going to be in real trouble because I will not be responsible for how I react.

SHADOWS
KIT/KAT

The look on his face is familiar—Salem had a similar one in the tent, and it makes my stomach flutter with excitement. I know the chances of finding *two* gentle, understanding guys amongst the demons I'm surrounded by weren't great. However, in contrast to my usual bad luck, I've somehow attracted both beautiful guys and they're not put off by my inexperience *or* my issues.

Maybe I've been saving the good luck my whole life until now? That would make this easier to believe.

As our soft breaths fill the silent room, I try to stay calm when he doesn't respond right away. Admitting I like what we're doing is tantamount to admitting I like *him* out loud, and my anxiety is sparkling in my veins like electric glitter. It should get easier after you've done it once, right? Once you've had the courage to tell someone you like them, even if it's not direct, doing so isn't as hard each time afterward. Right?

"KK, you look worried. Don't be," Oriel says in a raspy voice. "I'm quiet because… knowing you're enjoying this and that you want to share secrets with me…"

I blink up at him, my eyes confused. "That's bad?"

"*No.*" The dark-haired demon chuckles huskily, and I watch his pupils dilate. "No, it's not bad. But it is… hard to control the parts of me who enjoy that very much—who enjoy *you* very much. And I don't want to scare you or push you too far. You're doing so well; it would be a crime to set that back."

Biting my lower lip, I smile a little, then murmur, "You do crimes all the time, though."

That makes his grin widen, and he looks even more handsome when it reaches his eyes. "Good point. But that one? I *never* want to do that, Kit. I promise I will *never* intentionally hurt you."

I frown for a moment, then look at him seriously. "You're very smart to realize that you can't really promise never to hurt me…you could accidentally and that would make what you said a lie. That would hurt even more, I believe."

"Plus, I'm a guy," Oriel chuckles. "We're wired to fuck up, especially demon males. So yeah, I qualified my promise, but it's because I want you to trust me. I want to be close with you like this and more, eventually? So we have to start with honesty, and I get—"

My eyes widen and before he can finish, I push up on my tiptoes to kiss him one more time. I know what he was going to say, and that means my charade has to end. He was going to say that he's baring himself to mind my boundaries—or something like it—and much like Salem, I've run out of road with my disguise. If I don't come clean now, everything will be tainted, and that's not who I am. So I enjoy the gentle, yet hungry kiss until it breaks, and pull back so I can gather myself.

"Oriel, I have to… There's something you need to know."

His eyes are a little glassy, making my chest puff with pride, though I'm not sure why. "I can't imagine what would be important enough to stop *that*."

Famous last words if I've ever heard them.

Making sure that I'm not touching him, I rake my lip with my teeth one more time, then meet his gaze. "Oriel, I'm not a guy."

He blinks for a moment, then bursts out laughing. My eyes dart back and forth as he snorts and doubles over, clutching his stomach as his hilarity continues. I don't know if this is a good or bad thing; he's just about crying in laughter in front of me. Or is he losing his shit? Fuck, I don't know. I mean, Salem was so relieved that no one emasculated me that I suppose it took the edge off of the reveal. But Oriel and I are just here, alone, and he shared something deeply personal with me.

"Um…"

Oriel finally takes a huge breath, then blows it out as he stands straight again. I think he's trying to calm his amusement so he can talk, but it's making me itch all over. Wiping tears from his eyes, the crow demon blows a loud raspberry, then his shoulders slump as his body relaxes. "Okay, okay. I'm fine. I'm fine."

Good for him, but I am not, and he'd better say something before I puke.

"I'm not laughing at you, by the way." The way his eyes sparkle is encouraging, but I'm loath to believe body language versus words. "I mean that."

"Okay…"

He shakes his head, then says, "I'm laughing at *us*—every damn one of my brothers and I for being so fucking blind. Like… when you said that… everything came together. All the little things I wrote off or ignored because you're human and you have so much trauma. I discarded the weird shit without a second thought because fuck if I know how humans behave in close quarters, right? But I *did* notice shit; I wasn't crazy."

I shrug a little, still unsure where he's going with this. "No, you're not crazy for that reason, at least."

"But you know what, you devious little shadow?"

Shaking my head, I wait for him to go on because I don't have a damn clue where he's going with this diatribe.

"I'm proud of you," he says as he moves within centimeters of me again. "It had to be scary, coming here with all that on your back and such a big secret, too. But you stood up to the Prince of Hell and his friends without batting a lash, and even took not being human in stride."

I swallow hard as I look up at him. "People are capable of wonderful and horrible things when they feel like they don't have a choice."

His grin is boyish, almost delighted as he nods. "That, my little shadow, is spot on. You're definitely as wise as Zav, and certainly as sneaky as me. I think you might have all the good stuff my brothers and I embody wrapped up in… what I assume is some sort of restrictive under things?"

My face turns bright red, and I look away. I don't have those back in my grasp just yet—X is working on it. But I am bound up mummy-style under my clothes and it's very *not* sexy unless your name is Amun-Ra or something. "Sort of."

Oriel blinks, then snaps his fingers. "They keep destroying your fit! You've run out of boobie slings, haven't you?"

No, no… never that phrase, I'm going to die on the spot..

"I… uh…" All I can do is sputter. Oriel is very into *how* I pulled off hiding, but he hasn't said a word about whether that changes anything. Since we just had a *moment*, his acceptance or denial is more important than my lack of binders right now. But I can't go farther out on that limb until he gives me a clue what he's thinking.

His brows furrow, and he holds up a finger. "Just a minute. I think…"

The crow demon takes off into his lair, muttering to himself as I stand, rooted in place by my fear that this is all for show. Maybe he's using the puzzle master persona and compliments on my ingenious plan to cover the rejection I'm going to get. All this praise for being strong might be to soften the blow when he tells me I've crossed a line I can't come back from.

Fidgeting with my ring, I stare at the floor and spin it, willing my brain not to follow that thread to its inevitable conclusion. Unfortunately, my luck has run out for the day, because pictures of his kind but firm face flash through my mind. I see Oriel apologizing and putting me back in my place as a friend, while being distant until…

I have to stop. I have to stop now. If I don't stop, I'm going to—

My breath hitches as the constriction in my chest spreads, making it hard to fill my lungs. Fingers sparkle with numbness and the sensation crawls up my arms as I dig my nails into my palm to break the flow. It doesn't work, and I wrap my arms around my torso as I beg the universe to let me just get through this so I can nurse my wounds in private. I won't survive being rejected *and* having to be carried back to my room because of an attack. The humiliation would be more than I can handle when I've been this vulnerable.

"Hey! Hey!" Prying my lids open, I see O standing in front of me again, dangling what looks like a sports bra about my size from his fingers. "What the hell happened? I just wanted to help you and I knew I had one of these —or maybe a few. Don't ask, because I *hate* when the jobs send me to Brimstone, but I always find a way to amuse…"

A long shuddering breath escapes my lips, and he blinks, the babble paused as he peers down at my face. I swallow again, trying to get my dry throat to allow me to respond to the unusually talkative demon. "Um… I'm… sorry. You… I…"

This time, his eyes widen as it hits him. "Shit! *Shit.* See? I told you! Guys are dumb, KK, and I just did *exactly* what we talked about. I hurt you because I said nothing before I took off! *Motherfucker, I'm so stupid!*"

His monologue is somehow completely external right now, and that's not normal for Oriel. So I risk myself one more time to reach out with a shaky hand and place it on his mouth. He blinks as I cover the words spewing from his mouth like a fire hydrant unleashed, but there's finally quiet again. I take another moment to find my voice and when I do, I whisper, "You're not stupid. But I did lie, so you have every right to be angry with me. I will accept whatever consequences come with that."

A dark brow arches at me, and I remove my hand, dipping my chin as he stares. After a second, another warm chuckle slides over me as he grabs the hand I pulled away. "Don't you dare pull away from me, shadow. I want you to focus on breathing, then look me in the eye so I can tell you the truth."

The truth? That sounds ominous.

But I look up at him as instructed, my eyes fearful as he holds my hand between us. "I'm ready."

"KK, you look like you're waiting for a firing squad," Oriel says softly. "Don't be afraid."

"Easy for you to say," I mumble. "You're not the one who did something shitty and had to admit it."

"Ah, ah. What did I say?" The demon winks at me as he places his other hand on the one between us, holding on tightly. "Now that you're able to focus, I need you to understand that I didn't walk away because I'm angry with you. I walked away because I wanted to find that damn bra for you. I wanted to help you… because what I don't want is for you to be discovered."

I don't react; I can't until he's done.

"If you were discovered, they might send you back, and honestly? I don't want to spend four years or even four more days in this damn place if they do that. I *like* you, Kit, or whatever your name is… Is it Kit? That's not the point. The point is… I didn't care if you were a guy before and I don't care if you're a girl now. You know?"

"Um…"

Oriel leans in, putting his nose against mine as he says, "I don't even care if you turn into a smelly orc, little shadow, because you aren't getting rid of me unless someone fucking kills me, okay? *That* I'm gonna promise without a clause because I'd stake one of my hoards on it."

Holy shit. I don't even know what the fuck to say to that, much less what it should make me feel.

Talk

Jasper

Slash and Xerxes purposefully stayed quiet most of lunch. My mood was volatile, and though the silence helped me simmer internally rather than externally, the tension was almost corporeal. When his lunch period ended, Xerxes took off like a shot, leaving my general to handle my ire. Unfortunately for me, he's staring at me like he's considering consuming me like one of his enemies, and that's not a normal thing for Slash.

"Out with it. I grow tired of your silent disapproval," I say before I take another drink of my fizzy soda. I'm typically more fond of coffee, but I don't need the extra energy Hell's finest beans would give when I'm agitated. My tail is already twitching like mad, as I struggle to process my perplexing fury.

The shark demon arches a brow, looking at me with such condescension that I nearly lose my temper on the spot. His smirk is sharp, like his teeth, when he finally deigns to speak. "You are being immature again, Prince. While it is common to the throne at present, I do not believe it's how *you* wish to rule when it is time."

Damn. Right to the jugular with a dig about my fuckhead father.

"I don't want to be him. But I don't see how that applies right now." I lean back in my chair, crossing my arms over my chest as I stare back at my closest friend. "I'm hardly ruling from above at school."

His grunt is irritated, but he simply stares. "Debatable, but not what I meant."

"Fuck, you're a pain in my spiky tail, Scrum. You realize you don't get charged per word to fucking speak, yeah?" My sneer is meant to provoke him, especially since he's being frustratingly vague about his criticism.

"I don't feel the need to say my every thought out loud, Jasper. That's not a crime, nor is it your *real* problem. Throwing shade at me will do nothing to quench the fire within you." Slash turns away from me, picking up a napkin to put items into it from a small plate he hasn't touched.

His casual rebuke rankles me more than someone yelling would. This is my oldest and most loyal brother, yet he's not being remotely helpful when I need it. It's not normal—except since the damn shrimp moved into Salem's room. I growl softly as I consider how differently my brothers are acting since his arrival, including my general-to-be when I'm the king. That damn unemerged demon is fucking everything up, even my ability to keep my caliphate in line.

Slamming my fist on the table, I ignore the clatter of the dishes as I rumble louder this time. "Don't make me command you, Slash."

A flash of silver and icy blue in his gaze, followed by a few sharper teeth showing in his grin, let me know I've gotten back at him. "You won't do it. That is not how our relationship works and never has been. Perhaps with others, but not me."

"Does that matter when things have so clearly changed?"

Slash chuckles and shakes his head as he finishes gathering the food, then carefully ties the napkin closed. "Ah, here we are. I wondered when you might get to the root of this tantrum."

Tantrum? What the fuck is he talking about?

"Watch how you speak to me, Scrum. I'm still—"

"Yes, yes. You're the prince—which is a shield you throw up when you do not wish to be honest with us or yourself. I have heard that before, Jas." My friend shrugs, placing the napkin into his bag, then looks at me with an unsympathetic expression. "It is long past time for you to stop being your own worst enemy."

My jaw drops and I sputter for a moment before I finally come up with a response. "What the fuck does *that* mean?!"

Not the most original thing I could have said, but the shock of Slash judging me *and* saying that sort of shit is making it hard for me to think straight. I would expect this sort of behavior from Oriel, or maybe Salem, but not the stalwart shark who has stood by me since we were toddlers. Like his father does with mine, Slash has always had my back, even if he disagreed, without complaint for our entire lives. I don't know how to handle the emotions I was feeling *before* he did this, but now I'm inches from blowing my top in the middle of the goddamn *Triclinium*. We don't need this many demons to witness a battle—which is the only reason I'm holding back.

"Jasper, I have been quiet every time you were heading in the wrong direction for two simple reasons. You are my prince, and we all need to learn hard lessons. Those ideals were enough for me to follow you anywhere most of our lives." He shakes his head, his expression hard as he meets my gaze. "But you are struggling right now when you do not need to. You could be happier—we could *all* be happier—if you would get to the finish line sooner. Your permanent shitty mood is making everything much harder than it needs to be."

I suck in a breath, ready to blast him when he holds up a large hand, shaking his head. "No, we will not have this out here. We both know that would be a terrible strategy. Now, I must go to Octavian's class before I am late. The ex-Caesar does not enjoy tardiness, so I will leave you with a suggestion: go see the Doc. I believe it will be helpful."

Gaping at my best friend as he rises, I watch as he nods at me once, then heads down the dais to cross the cafeteria on his own. He's never left me anywhere before unless instructed to do so, and I can't fucking believe it's over that damn *kid*. My fury lights a fire in my veins even more now, forcing me to grit my teeth before my scales break loose. I'd prefer to burn this away with a long, fire-filled flight, but I cannot do that here.

In fact, I have Sovereign Law next and I should head there, so I also don't get my ass kicked, but I can't. I won't be able to function later in the day if I don't get rid of the feelings plaguing me, so I don't think I have any other options.

I guess the apples today will not keep the doctor away.

BY THE TIME I REACH DR. DANCKWARDT'S OFFICE, I'M NOT SURE ABOUT this solution anymore. He's technically loyal to the crown, not me, and I don't know if my questions will get back to my father. That would be incredibly dangerous for me, my brothers, and that infuriating shrimp. I don't want the King to send the Daggers after us. It would be insanely easy to blame our deaths on the upcoming games, and he'd be free to rule for as long as he can remain physically and magically viable without an heir.

Honestly, I'm surprised he hasn't done it yet, rather than the pitiful attempts from amateurs Slash has foiled over the years.

I look at the door, still indecisive, then raise my hand to knock on it. Before I can, it creaks open, and I see the familiar plague mask peeking out of the crack. The vibe in the air changes to something far less adversarial when the old demon realizes who it is, and I let that calm me.

"Prince Jasper," he rasps as he steps aside so I can come in. "While I am always honored to see you, I hope you are not injured or ill. That may be the main reason to grace me with your presence, but my wish is for you to be secure."

"Thanks, doc," I reply as I wait for him to direct me to the spot he prefers. The gloved hand points at the first table and even though I'm *not* hurt or sick, I hop onto it. I'm not sure what I'm doing here, honestly, but Slash doesn't say things that he doesn't mean. If he believes this is the answer to my problems, there must be something to it.

"May I inquire what I can assist you with, Your Highness?" The doc stands in front of me, still masked as he waits for me to give him orders. It's very different from how the physician behaves when we bring the shrimp here, and it didn't bother me until now.

Why is he so stiff and formal when he's been our doctor since I was summoned?

"You don't have to be so…" I gesture at his attentive posture and the mask, hoping to convey what I mean. "I don't need that… ever, really."

The surprise wafting through the air is palpable, but the ancient demon nods. He removes the mask, walking over to his apothecary area to place it on the counter. He then removes the gloves to reveal the bony, feathered hands that patched everyone up last time, and suddenly, I feel lighter myself. I don't know why, but when he returns to face me, the sight of his fiery bird skull is actually comforting.

"I…"

Dr. Dankwardt lets out one of those crusty laughs he rewards the shrimp with and I bristle for a second before my shoulders untense. His glowy orbs seem to know what I'm feeling, and that's strange because I don't have a goddamn clue what the hell is going on with me. I'm more mercurial than ever before these past months, and while there's a lot of fucking bullshit going on, I know how to handle that. I've been dealing with that kind of pressure my entire life.

"Prince Jasper, may I be so bold?"

Someone has to because I'm so fucking lost, and I can't admit that out loud. I've *never* been able to admit that kind of weakness aloud, not even to my brothers. The future ruler of Hell does not have the luxury of showing vulnerability in the same way others can. To be honest, fury and fire are the only things I can comfortably express without giving people an edge that could lead to bad shit. So I nod at the doc, my gaze sharp as I wait for his assessment.

"There are very rigid roles demons must play in this world, particularly if they have burdens such as yours. You and your bonded have risen to levels many did not want or expect you to achieve. However, *all* beings—even demons—are susceptible to the common occurrences in this world. Our destinies bring us closer to those events in different ways, but it is no less confusing for those who are born with royal blood than those who are not."

What the fuck does that mean?

When I don't respond, another rusty chuckle and a horrifyingly grim smile takes over his face. "Ah, so you are still in the dark about the situation. That is probably because you have suppressed so much in your life, young dragon. You need to allow yourself to feel as strongly about the rest of your life as you do with Master Zavida. Do not fight the emotions, my prince; instead, embrace them as they are without tainting them with the weakness of spite."

"I have no idea what you're talking about, Doc," I sigh as I let myself fall back on the table to stare up at the ceiling. "But I can't let everything out—because of my position, my future… all the things you said. I got that part, I think."

The demon floats over to me, standing at my side as he looks down. With a snap of his fingers, a tall chair appears, and he makes himself comfortable, then gives me the scary smile again. "We can discuss that, Prince Jasper. Let us try to unravel this together. I believe it will be very beneficial."

I hope to fuck so because my brothers are revolting one by one; I have to get this under control.

Love To Hate Me

Kit/Kat

Oriel's declaration made me feel like crumbling *and* a bit like I could fly, which totally fucked with my ability to process. He didn't seem surprised, though, and we spent the rest of our free periods snacking on the food he'd squirreled away for me while I sat in the circle of his arms. I worried he would be upset that we weren't… exploring… but he seemed content to talk about his hoard, pointing to various sections with glee.

It helped me center myself—both the food and the gentle support.

By the time we finished and O led me out of the weird magical pocket, I was settled and able to grab his hand to lace our fingers together. That made him light up with happiness, his dark features full of a joy that was in direct contrast with his goth-y appearance.

"KK, this was the best lunch I've had in a long ass time," he says as we make our way out of the maze that he took me down to get to his secret spot. "I'm glad I demanded to whisk you away, even if it pissed His Royal Pissypants off."

I frown, tilting my head to look at him in confusion. "Why the *fuck* would Jasper give a shit if you wanted to hang at lunch? I'm his least favorite student in the entire place most days. I'd think he would be happy to see the back of me."

The crow demon tsks, shaking his head as we leave the building, heading into the main quad on our way to the arena. "Little shadow, I don't think I can answer that question any better than he could. Jasper has deep-rooted issues around expressing anything outside of anger. That was the only thing rewarded positively in his house, and he learned to embrace it as self-defense."

Jasper's shitty home life was evident when I met his father, but I can't ask Oriel to betray his trust by explaining further—it's not fair.

"I don't think anyone with an ounce of awareness could miss that," I reply with a sigh. "But the dude *hates* me, despite knowing I'm not a spy or a plant. Honestly, other than my dickhead foster brothers, I've never met anyone who pushes my buttons this hard."

"Hmmm," O replies as we cross the last part of the main area and head to what will surely be the scene of a disaster or my humiliation as always. "I don't think those two reactions are the same."

Snorting, I pull Dottie out of my bag, letting her climb to my shoulder and get some fresh air. She napped most of our sojourn to his hoard, and I'll want her alert while I'm on the field for Weapons & Tactics. I trust my demons not to accidentally harm her, but the other idiots? Not a chance. I realize I called them *my demons* and my face heats, so I focus my eyes on the ground as O guides me to our destination.

"Well, Blake and Bryce scared me and Jasper doesn't, so that's sort of true."

Oriel laughs and squeezes my hand gently. "While that's hysterical and I wish everyone else had heard it, I don't believe that's why it's not the same."

I wrinkle my nose, sneaking a look up at the amused demon. "Jasper obviously has issues, you know? But… I think somehow I know that while he's mean as a defense mechanism, it's because he doesn't know how else to react to shit. It's been drilled into him, and I get that sort of trauma response."

"You fight him at every turn, little shadow." His fingers flex around mine and I duck my head again, smiling at the ground. "You're not exactly oozing empathy, mm?"

"It's one thing to have baggage and learn how to either stow it or drop it at the door," I finally say after a brief pause. "It's another to pick it up and throw it at other people to protect yourself."

"I'll give you that. Jas has never tried to sort his shit, except for when he finally admitted his feelings for Zav. He had to do that, or we were all going to kick his ass." I look up, surprised as fuck, and Oriel shrugs. "I can't get into their shit, but Zav was conditioned—like all of us—by his idiot parents and there was only so much unintentional trauma we could allow Jasper to recreate."

"Someone stopped him? I find that hard to believe. He doesn't listen to any —ohhhh." My eyes widen and I look at him as realization dawns.

Oriel nods, his eyes dancing. "Yep. Slash told him to get his shit together in a way that conveyed what would happen if he didn't. No one else has that kind of sway over him... well, except the Z-man now because... dick."

My snort is so loud it almost hurts and my crow demon beams. When I recover, I purse my lips at him. "That was not appropriate, Oriel Blood-stone. I don't need to know about their... crotch Olympics."

"Oh, but I think you do, KK." My flush deepens, and he laughs darkly. "It may be extremely relevant information someday—you never know."

Fat fucking chance of that, buddy.

IT WAS HARD TO FOCUS FOR THE REST OF THAT DAY AFTER THAT LITTLE TRIP, but I managed to successfully do it without revealing what went on.

Unfortunately, today has been less easy because inquiring minds definitely wanted to know, and I'm not ready to share.

The second gift Oriel gave me from his hoard—the sports bra—is probably one of the most helpful things I've been handed since I arrived here. He assured me it's clean, and a sniff of the material confirmed that it's not teeming with someone's fluids, so I took it into the bathroom to change. Unwinding the damn bindings makes me sigh in relief; they're not the best method and it's hot as fuck being mummy-wrapped with this stuff. I look down at myself, noting that the potion Dank gave me is working.

The kindly demon's 'girly bits' potion has kept me from being scented—at least, by the demons here—and hiding the sparkling kawaii tattoos that popped up after the damn initiation. I didn't realize it would serve double duty, but the fiery headed doctor refused to tell me *why* the damn things disappeared after a week of taking his meds. He simply said that the potion was crafted to conceal all traits that would identify me as a demon capable of reproduction.

Whatever the fuck that meant, I can't tell you.

I can, however, state that having what feels like the best engineered sports bra in existence holding me in place under my gym shit is light years better than the gauze. I could kiss Oriel—you know, again—for thinking of it, despite the bump his squirrel moment caused. Dottie chitters on my shoulder as we walk out of the locked room to face the dudes, and I almost laugh at her agreement. That is, until I come face-to-face with half-naked caliphate members and I have to scramble away before I embarrass the shit out of myself.

"Okay, Kit, you're gonna have to rein it in," I mutter to myself as I make a beeline for the field without them. "Especially because of the… stuff… with two of them."

Ignoring everyone else as usual, I take a seat on the farthest bench with my kinkajou. Dottie perches on my knee, giving me a knowing look that I can't decide if I'm misinterpreting. My voice is too low for most to hear as I say, "Don't judge me, Dottie. You've seen it. I mean, even the tiny Kitsuné is muscled, and it's ridiculous how fit X is when they're not clothed. You'd never know. And yes, I feel like a creeper, so shut up."

She just looks at me with wide eyes, and I press my palms into my eyes to rub them in frustration. If only that could remove the image of my guys topless, that would be amazing. But alas, it doesn't, and when Salem, Oriel, X, Annie, and Zav emerge from the locker room, I want to sink into the earth like a worm. Every cell in my body sings and sparkles, distracting me enough that I miss the looming shadow standing over me until he growls.

"Why are you sitting by yourself? Didn't we discuss the rules?"

I am not in the mood for Jasper's bullshit at the moment; I am having a crisis of hormones.

"Fuck off, Jasper." That's all I got right now. My brain is way off the track, whizzing around in a combo of panic, desire, confusion, and embarrassment that trumps the prince's pissiness.

The frown he gives me is so severe that I *feel* it despite not looking at him. "That's it?"

My head whips up and I glare at him murderously. "Yes."

"What the hell did Bloodstone *do* to you? I'm going to beat the absolute—"

Huh?

Before I can stop myself, my hand shoots out, grabbing the prince's wrist before he stalks over to Oriel to do whatever he's threatening. "Stop."

The heat coming off of him in waves surprises me, but I guess it shouldn't. He is a dragon, after all, and though I don't remember a lot of what happened when he intervened in the study room, I have touched him before. In fact, that's when I—

Oh, no.

Jasper looks at me in terror as the heat intensifies where my hand is clutching his arm, and I blink rapidly. A low snarl echoes out of his chest, then he wrenches himself away, his eyes full of flames. I realize that's his dragon, but I don't know why his dragon would be angry at me. I just wanted to explain, so he didn't lose his shit, and now it looks like I've made him even angrier. That's not good at all.

"Don't. Touch. Me."

Licking my lips, I nod mutely as the other guys arrive. Their faces fall as they catch the vibe between Jasper and me, especially Zavida. He immediately heads for the royal, cozying up to the furious dragon. That seems to help, but the looks on Annie, O, X, and Salem's faces aren't encouraging.

"Hey, guys. Um, sorry I came out without you. Jasper already scolded me, so uh… no need," I mutter as I look at the ground. I don't know why, but there's something deep inside of me squeezing my airways and even though it's *not* a panic attack, I feel like I can't breathe. I force the air out in a fake cough as Dottie scrambles up to my shoulder, putting her tiny arms around my neck.

"You okay, KK?" Salem asks carefully.

Nodding, I squash all the rioting emotions inside of me down, imagining they're at the soles of my feet so I can walk on them like I did back home. When it feels like I can speak, I lift my head to give the panda a smile that I hope doesn't look as fake as it is. "A-okay, man. We had a good lunch and now I'm ready to have something shitty happen that sends me to the infirmary. I mean… I'm ready for class."

That gets laughs from everyone but the Pissy Prince, who huffs loudly before extracting himself from Zav's grip. "If you can't handle classes, there's no way you'll be able to handle the Games, shrimp. Toughen up."

With that unhelpful advice, he stalks off to stand in front of the line-up space on the field and roars his instruction for the class to begin. All the demons line up, even me, and I look down the line nervously. Whether he's being a jackass or not, Jasper isn't wrong about the Games. I'm getting better at a lot of stuff, but every time we make progress, a big ass distraction knocks us off-kilter and we lose focus. So much so that I realize I don't even know anyone in this damn school other than my caliphate, some staff, the bullies in class, and Dank.

How would I even know who can do what and how to strategize about their teams if I don't know their names or species?

My revelation makes me groan internally. Between hiding my secret and my issues, I've been consumed by fitting in with the guys who semi-adopted me. That's good, but if I don't have a damn clue who is operating around us, then I won't have the same ability to use my brains as I did at Woodlawn. Until my demon shit is under control, *all I have* is my brains. I have to pay attention to the other people at Discordia, especially because I have an outsider's perspective.

Otherwise, it won't matter if Jasper crushes me under his boot… because we're going to get killed.

Get It Together

Zavida

When we got to class, Jas seemed quieter than he has been lately, but I thought it was a good thing. His energy was less spiky, and he didn't give the four of us who arrived early a ton of snarly shit. I thought it would make Weapons class better until Oriel and Kit showed up just in time to change before it was time to line up. They weren't late, but they definitely looked like O's 'lunch excursion' went well. I could sense the camaraderie in their behavior, which made KK less tense and worried. However, the second my brothers and I joined Kit in the arena, it was clear that the somewhat muted Jasper was gone.

He barked dismissive criticism at the kid, then sent the entire class on a grueling warm up of laps around the stadium with heavy weapons in tow. I know he's been concerned about endurance—especially with our new member—but this felt retaliatory. I can't imagine against what, though, as KK gave in to his snarky commentary without a fight before Jasper commanded this nightmare.

Well, it's a nightmare for the others—I tapped my Kitsuné and went speeding through my set of circles around the stadium quickly.

My lover is glowering at the recruits as they finish the assignment, while I sit on the bench and hydrate. I haven't asked why his mood flipped so dramatically, but following his narrowed gaze tells me it's about Kit and Oriel. The former is doing better than expected—some of his demon power must be developing because his endurance is increasing. He's not lagging so far behind the rest of the group that it's laughable, and he doesn't look like he's going to keel over mid-lap. That can't be what is pissing Jas off; he *needs* all of us at top form for these stupid games.

No, Jasper is angry about something other than Kit performing better than expected, and I'm not sure what it is. The prince loves to pretend he's unreadable, and he might be to people other than his caliphate. To us, especially me, his emotions are often as subtle as flashing billboards and this one is saying 'danger, danger, ready to explode' so clearly that it might as well be screaming it. I'm not sure anything I can do in public will bring him back from that edge, so letting him stew is for the best.

"I suppose Slash is doing *some* of his fucking job," Jasper mutters as he paces back and forth along the line we were all standing on before the laps. "At least that's not being thrown in my face."

That feels more like petulance than anger, and I will not engage.

Anton passes by us, his eyes meeting my lover's briefly before he's gone. Jasper snarls and rakes his fingers through his hair, muttering to himself as he continues his frenetic pacing. I shake my head when he's facing away, unsure what's crawled up his ass and died. Annie and X *absolutely* did nothing, not in the locker room or on the field. Xerxes kept the conversation away from our missing brothers at lunch, redirecting our focus to talking about when the admin might make another announcement about the Games.

Jasper is projecting his frustrations onto everyone, though I doubt it will stay equal when the running is complete. As if he heard my thoughts, the dragon demon stomps over to me, his eyes flashing with the beast. "Why are you so quiet? Usually, you have commentary."

I give him a noncommittal shrug. "First, that's not true, and you know it. I'm very internal, and it takes me time to process things. Second, I don't know what you want me to comment on. Obviously, you're having a hissy about something, but you don't feel open to discussing it. Since we're in public, alternative methods of soothing you aren't available."

That makes him smirk, a rough chuckle escaping his lips before he can stop it. "True."

"You were calmer when we first arrived. I'm not sure what made you flip the switch to asshole, but I figured if you wanted to talk about it, you would." The corner of my mouth quirks as I give him a pointed look. "And here you are, talking. I was right."

His features cloud with darkness for a second, then he shakes his head as if to push that emotion away. "Very intuitive, Zavvie. You're getting better at reading people, I believe."

"I'm *always* good at reading you, Jas. That's part of being yours." Pushing to my feet, I stretch my muscles, not wanting to tense up after the grueling warm-up. "But you are not as good at communicating, especially with feelings that conflict with how you were raised. Our caliphate has gotten used to the volatility and your outbursts, but Kit is still adjusting to us, this place, and his new reality."

"I said nothing about *him*," the prince shoots back and I have to look away to hide my grin.

He's so fucking clueless about expressing anything but the anger adjacent emotions his father rewarded throughout his life.

I'm about to reply when a loud chittering sound gets our attention. Dottie is perched on top of the water station, bringing her close to face height for me. That's still quite a bit lower than Jasper's face, but the small animal is shaking a fist at him. When he snorts and rolls his eyes, I watch as the kinkajou scampers down the dispenser to run across the sideline. I frown, surprised by her acquiescence, then look at my lover.

"She's not happy with you. Did you do something bad?"

"It's a rodent, Zavvie. I don't care if it's a familiar; I will not give it credence." Jasper crosses his muscled arms over his broad chest and I sigh. Stubborn as a fucking mule rather than a dragon, and powerful enough to demand that everyone give him his way. The Prince is often his own worst enemy, and nothing I've been able to do has changed that.

Suddenly, a much louder squeaky sound comes from behind us, and when I turn to look, I have to cover my mouth. Dottie is back on the water cooler, standing on her back legs as she lobs small pebbles she must have found on the sideline at my lover. He blinks in shock as they bounce off him, and I can barely keep the laughter from escaping. It's not even close to being harmful, obviously, but the tiny animal is so clearly unafraid of him. He has no idea how to handle something with so little power attacking, so he just stares in mute shock.

"What… What in the fresh fucking *Hell* is that thing doing?!"

Wrinkling my nose, I swallow the amusement, hoping it won't escape when I speak. "Uh… I think Dottie is mad at you. Why, I'm not sure, but she's definitely making her displeasure known."

Jasper scowls, stomping closer to where she's perched. "What's your problem, you little shit? I haven't been nasty. Sending the class on laps was completely legit and not remotely a punishment for anyone, especially your unemerged friend. I cannot *believe* I'm talking to this walking winter hat."

He makes a disgusted sound as he stomps away again, and I look at Dottie curiously. "What *are* you mad about? He's been a much bigger ass before and you didn't seek things to hurl at him."

The small creature settles back on her haunches, looking at me like I'm an idiot. Her tail wraps around the spot as we stare at one another, then it finally breaks when Jasper paces past. That's when her expression seems to change to one of derision, and I laugh softly.

"Okay, he's definitely gotten under your fur, and you aren't able or willing to make it clear why. Got it."

Now I'm stuck with *two* uncommunicative pissy beings, and I have no clue how to get either of them to give me a hint on how I can help. My eyes cut to the rest of my caliphate as they finish their assigned laps, while muddling through the best way to approach this so it doesn't drag on all night. Once Weapons is over, we only have an hour until dinner break, then a caliphate meeting slot after that. If I can convince everyone to meet outside of the main building after their six o'clock classes, we might take a detour to the one place that *might* hold answers for at least one of the furious creatures on the sideline with me.

I grin to myself, pulling my phone out of the special pocket in my gym clothes and send a private text to all my brothers *except* for Kit and Jasper. It will be difficult for either of them to protest my field trip if they aren't aware I'm orchestrating it. Slash can bring KK from their law class, and I'll scoot off to meet my love after his least favorite class—Human Diplomacy. Jasper will be grumpy after that, of course, but if I'm careful, I can soothe him before we meet the others.

This plan is perfect, and if I'm very lucky, it will accomplish more than just discovering what the damn kinkajou is trying to tell us.

THE REST OF WEAPONS WENT BETTER THAN I ASSUMED IT WOULD, GIVEN THE mood of our professor. Jasper backed off of Kit to focus on grinding the entire class into the ground. He made everyone use large broadswords and practice a variety of attacks and defenses with groups that mixed every twenty minutes. By the end, no one was spared the ache in their arms and legs, even Salem and Oriel. Being bigger and stronger than Annie, X, KK, and I, they're not as easily pushed to the brink of their endurance.

Today was an exception because the prince was grueling in his demands for perfection.

I damn near limped to Supernatural Law with Kit, and once Slash joined us, quiet fell over our small group. They both seemed really comfortable with no chattering, and I soaked in the feel of not having to keep track of conversation that zings back and forth. It was actually nice and I see why our newest member is so damn comfortable with the big guy. He doesn't demand attention, nor does he talk simply to fill the air. So our trip to Holmes' class and the subsequent calm during it were extremely soothing for me, especially with my nervousness about arranging the secret trip.

As soon as Holmes dismissed us, I gave Slash the nod, and took off, eager to find Jasper before he heads for our dorm. Using the extra burst of speed from my partially re-filled reserves, I zoom to the graduate level in the Knowledge Enclave. It's important to re-direct him before he's made a firm decision about the rest of the evening; Jasper Eversore is stubborn as fuck normally. When he's struggling with emotions, he digs in further until he's almost as immovable as a damn mountain.

I come to an abrupt stop when I see him, letting a bright smile come over my face. Tricking him is not my usual *modus operandi*, but I'm fairly certain I can do it long enough to get him where we need to be. "Jas! Hey, Jas…"

The dragon turns to look at me, his brows furrowing in confusion. I don't meet him after this session—at least, not in the classroom—so it's out of the ordinary for me to be here. "Zav? What's going on? I thought we were all meeting in the dorm for dinner. Salem is making some… hell, I don't know. It's hard to focus when he's talking about cooking."

Not for you—you can usually focus on every single one of us, taking in every detail like a savant.

But I don't say that because it would give away that I know he's having a problem with shit. Instead,. I nod, falling into step with him. "Change of plans. We need to make a detour to the main building first. I have to grab something for my class tomorrow, and since you said none of us should travel alone…"

His eyes narrow. "*You* came here alone."

"Only the last bit. I had company until I got to the building."

One more white lie won't hurt, right? Especially since I'm going to fix this so we can all deal with genuine issues rather than interpersonal shit.

Surprise!
Kit/Kat

"Where are we going? I thought we were heading to dinner," I say as my stomach growls.

Salem chuckles, bumping me with his big shoulder and knocking me off balance a little. Once I'm in control of myself, he pulls a granola bar with my ribbon on it out of his pocket. "Don't want you to be hangry, KK. You get hard to handle when you're all… riled up."

Heat floods my neck, spreading toward my face unbidden. This fucking guy… I clear my throat and mutter, "Thanks. Sorry, my stomach was rude. Slash has sort of trained me."

"Lucky him," Oriel says as he flanks me on the other side and I have to force my eyes to the ground to keep anyone else from seeing the mild panic in them.

Now there's two of them and I'm definitely going to die on the spot one of these times they're poking at me.

"I take my job as a trainer seriously, it's true."

My hands cover my cheeks as I let O and Salem lead me wherever the fuck they're all avoiding telling me about, hopelessly trying to get a grip on my reactions. Slash missing their innuendo is funny, but I can't even enjoy it because I'm so filled with that hot, itchy feeling. I'm not stupid; I know it has to do with my body having a physiological reaction to the gorgeous men taunting me. But it's new and different, so I just don't know how to deal with it. Hell, I don't even know if it's going to give off some.... signal that the others will pick up on. Dank's potion works on a lot of things as far as I know, but what about… arousal?

That makes my anxiety spike a bit, and my pulse jumps as I try to figure out what I'm going to do to get that answer. Obviously, I can't control how my body reacts; I'm not a Cubi. Although, I guess they can't really do that until —I shake my head, pushing out the intrusive ADHD thoughts so I can focus. *This* I can do; I learned coping skills. But my pussy isn't my brain; telling it to shut up won't work. It might make me feel better, but it won't fix a genuine issue that could give me away before I'm ready to admit stuff.

Gahhh. why the fuck is everything so damn hard to wrangle? I'm such a mess.

"KK? I can sense you spiraling from back here."

X's voice is soothing, likely on purpose, but it's not patronizing. They're just trying to help, especially because they *also* know the four-one-one. So I cough to make sure my voice isn't a dead giveaway, then respond. "Um, well, you guys know that being unaware of my surroundings is difficult for me because of the stuff, so…"

"Wait! I know what to do," Oriel says and my gut clenches. I have an idea what he's going to suggest and I don't know that I'm ready for that with a full damn audience. My pulse spikes again when I imagine all of them— except for our pissy prince—watching me while I can't see them.

Unfortunately, the reaction I get isn't the one I thought it'd be—no, it's more heat in my veins and a clench inside that is *not* fear. "I don't think—"

Before I can finish, O whips out a blindfold and is standing in front of me, lifting my chin to meet his eyes. "I promise it will be okay. Even though this is a lot of trust, you know that Salem and I won't let anything bad happen, right?"

I nod, swallowing hard as I look at him.

"Hey! I will not let bad shit go on, either," X growls indignantly. "Nor will Annie or Slash. Don't be an asshat, O."

The crow shifter rolls his eyes, then tears his gaze from mine to the offended cobra shifter. "X, that's not what I meant. He's already had one discussed and shit was fine. Salem is around him more than anyone. It's different in terms of familiarity, okay? I wasn't making a value judgment, you big diva."

"Well… I guess—"

"He had a blindfold on with you previously?"

Annie and X speak almost simultaneously and I have to tighten my fists at my side. I don't want the guys to fight, especially about me. Biting my lower lip, I cough again before they can devolve into bickering. "Hey. Hey. Shut up."

They all stop, looking at me as I turn to face the group. Slash is studying me carefully, as if he's trying to find out if I was harmed by what Oriel claimed. X and Annie both have odd expressions on their faces that I can't place. Salem is glaring at the crow demon with daggers in his normally sleepy eyes. This is so fucking weird that I can hardly stand it, so I hold a hand up.

"Sorry. I'm not being rude, but you're not giving me time to think. I need that in order to consent, and the potshots distract me." My smile is sheepish, but it makes their spiky emotions recede almost immediately. That lets me breathe more easily and I let out a sigh of relief. "Thanks. I needed that."

"Did us being calmer actually help you?" Salem asks curiously.

"Yep. My chest got looser and I can breathe better," I answer immediately. "I could sort of feel your emotions pressing in with my anxiety and it was… a lot."

Anton's gaze narrows on me. "Feel us, you say?"

"Mmm hmm." I breathe out again, shaking my limbs one by one to dispel the sparkling sensation in them that often precludes a panic episode. "Now I can do my things to help keep on an even keel. But thinking you were going to really fight over me was definitely not good."

Slash snorts, shaking his head at me. "Little demon, we will never truly fight over you. That would be ridiculous. You are one of us, and that means you belong to all of us."

"Even those who don't have a clue yet," Salem mutters to himself. Oriel's eyes sparkle and he raises a fist to bump it with my roommate's.

Surprisingly, I let out a hiss at them, and my hands fly to my mouth to cover it. I mumble behind them, "What the hell was that?"

Xerxes throws their head back and laughs, but the others just stare at them. Once they're done, they grin. "KK, you just hissed at those two goobers like a cat. I fucking *love* it. I don't know *why,* obviously, but damn, that was funny as fuck."

My face turns beet red, and I shrug. "I don't know why, either. But… take it as a warning, I guess."

"That would be in line with how it sounded." Anton smirks as he tilts his head. "We should get moving, so we're not late. Kit, if you're going to allow Oriel to provide his estimation of help, then say it now."

I look at all of them, biting my lip nervously for a moment. Finally, I nod. "Okay. Do it, O. But you and Salem better not fucking let me trip on something or I'll skin you alive."

"Now *that* is something I enjoy seeing," Slash says mildly. "And an excellent demonic threat, little demon. Very good."

His praise makes everything light up within me as the crow brings the blindfold to my eyes again.

I have got to find time to talk to Dank about this shit before I get into trouble with these guys.

WE WALKED FOR ABOUT TWENTY MINUTES, THOUGH I FELT THE ATMOSPHERE change at one point, and I don't know why. It was odd, and I felt like I was in the Arctic because of the chill in the air. When we actually stop, I wait for Oriel to remove the blindfold, but he doesn't.

"Hey, when do I get to see? And what was that weird… vibe… in the middle of the trip?" I frown, rubbing my hands on my biceps. "It was freezing for like three minutes."

"Don't freak out, okay?"

Oh, that helps a lot, thanks… said no one with anxiety disorders ever.

"Telling me not to panic is never *ever* going to keep me from freaking out, Salem." I aim a stern expression in the direction his voice came from, hoping it's effective. "That's like saying 'don't think about it' when you have to piss."

"Huh. I didn't think about it that way. Good metaphor, KK," X chirps as they come closer. "But to answer your question—since everyone else is too chickenshit to do it—Oriel shadow traveled us, so the trip was shorter. For those of us *without* those powers, it feels weird. Though, I can't say *cold* is what it felt like to me."

"It feels like that to me."

My entire body goes rigid as Jasper's amused tone comes from a few feet away. The cloth over my eyes now feels like a binding, and I make a soft sound of panic as I reach up to claw it off. I didn't know that he was coming, nor that I'd react quite so keenly to him if he showed up while I was that vulnerable. My eyes dart around the circle of demons, noting Zav has arrived as well, and when I get to the prince, he looks strangely upset.

Why the fuck is he upset? I'm the one who was shadow traveled, blindfolded, and snuck up on.

"Uh… yeah. So um…" I fumble my words as I mentally run through every mantra I know to get myself under control. "Not to be a pain in the ass or anything, but where is here? And why did we have to shadow travel? Oh, and why the fuck didn't anyone *tell* me?"

Anger floods me, and I know it's just trying to combat the panic about Jasper being here while I could not see him. Logically, I'm totally aware that the prince could have hurt me *many* times before now if he actually intended to. And I *don't* think he'd do something like my past trauma at all—I really don't. But I don't feel entirely safe around him yet because we can't seem to find stable ground, so my brain is running through emergency protocols.

"Don't be mad, KK," Oriel says as he steps closer to untie the blindfold with gentle hands. "I didn't want to scare you. But we needed to move more quickly once we covered your eyes. The terrain would have been dangerous in that state."

"Just… *tell me*," I grit out. "I know you probably had good intentions, and maybe didn't even think I'd notice." His sheepish expression tells me that's spot on. "But I did, so that should be a lesson about assuming things when we don't know what the fuck I am or what powers are still developing."

"He's right, actually," Jasper says and I whip around to gape at the typically dickish royal. "We shouldn't assume anything about his abilities until he's fully emerged. He could be any combination of things; we've all agreed on that. That means anything *we* do might not affect him like us, but like the others, or even things we have no experience with."

"I… I…" That very smart statement, said with zero snark, has me speechless.

Did Jasper get a personality transplant since Weapons class?

Zavida pats his hand, looking proud. "Good point, Jas. You're absolutely correct,"

"I concur," Anton adds. "I believe we should actually be *actively* looking for signs like Kit feeling the tension before… in the vein of X's lineage. But also, I do not believe any of us besides Jasper feel cold in the shadows, do we?"

They all shake their heads, and Jasper gives me a smug smile. "See? That's more of my lineage, as Anton is suggesting."

I wrinkle my nose. "So you believe I may come from Wrath or Lust? I can see the first one, but, uh, not the second."

Xerxes laughs, their eyes sparkling with mischief. "I think your past may have more to do with that than it being a sign that we're mistaken. Once you get healed enough to give that theory a test drive, you may find out otherwise."

"No shit," Oriel and Salem say at the same time. I gape at them, but they don't see it because now they're eyeing one another like they're getting ready to compare dick size.

Yes, even I know what that looks like on guys… I had two asshole brothers who did it all the time.

That *Poe-reading motherfucker* knows.

Realizing he's been let in on the secret changes the dynamic a little, but it doesn't make me mad. Obviously, I enjoyed that brief period where I was the only one being *aggressive* about my play for my Firecracker. But Oriel has been with us when demons and animals were revealed, and I think he'll be a fabulous partner in crime for romancing KK. I'll still want her to myself sometimes, but that's going to be true of anyone who gets into the inner circle of trust.

"If you two are done staring at one another, we should probably go *into* the Beastiary so the shrimp can talk to the Keeper," Jasper says drily. "I'd prefer not to be here all night, especially since I was hoodwinked into coming."

Zavida flushes at his comment, but he focuses on KK rather than seeking forgiveness from the Prince. "I knew you wanted to find out about Dottie, and we discussed coming here. Things just keep getting put off because of weird stuff, so… I sort of hijacked our schedule to make it happen. I hope that's okay."

I watch Kat's face light up with a smile that is genuine and my Kitsuné brother gets even redder. He's definitely crushing hard, and a quick glance at Jas verifies he will not make a big stink about it. That's a fucking miracle in itself, and before he changes his mind, I bump KK's shoulder. "Let Dottie out and we'll go see what this grumpy fuck has to say, hmm?"

Kat's smile flips into a frown as she looks up at me nervously. "The… Keeper… is mean?"

"Hornclaw is brusque," Jasper corrects him. "He is ancient, like Dank, and has little patience for most students because they do not respect his purpose or his animals. Demons generally interact poorly with non-familiar creatures unless they have been raised to be less…traditional."

"Okay, he *comes off* as mean," I say. Jasper nods curtly, and I take KK's arm, waiting for Dottie to perch on her spot. "But I think you'll be fine. You have a familiar already, and she's well-trained. You don't treat her like shit, either."

"Plus, KK has wrangled most of us, and we're not the most pleasant sort." Oriel grins and KK dips her chin shyly.

Oh, he's done some serious ass-kissing; I can tell.

"Come, everyone. We are wasting time."

I chuckle as Slash looks at us impatiently, walking past Kat and me to knock on the big wooden door sharply. The shark shifter is both patient and impatient with helping our newest member. I believe that's part of his indecision about her and it's caused because he doesn't *know* she's a 'her'. He's processing some interesting feelings and thoughts at the moment, which means unless he's interacting directly with Kat, he isn't in the mood to fuck about.

Though, I could be totally off-base on that and I'd never know because Slash will tell no one.

"Don't make this grumpy demon mad, big guy," Kat murmurs as we approach the bulky demon. "I want him to like me just in case this familiar thing is… you know. A thing."

"Very astute, shrimp."

"Jas, come on, man," Oriel says as he puts himself between the prince and Kat. He's on the other side of her, giving our leader an annoyed look. "I know you're hungry, but stop ping-ponging between halfway decent and cranky dick. Zav set this up to be nice; it would be shitty to ruin it for him, hmm?"

I whistle low as O calls Jasper out with just enough accuracy that it's a direct hit. Anton and X smirk at one another, joining the crow near KK. "Damn, dude."

"Fine," Jasper grumbles as he rolls his eyes. "Slash, what the fuck is taking so long?"

Right as he complains, the slot on the door opens to reveal one cloudy eye and one scarred one with a metal patch over it. "Who's that? No classes today!"

Kat shrinks back into my side, and I narrow my eyes at the crusty old fart who made her worry. Slash, however, just laughs as he looks at The Keeper. The shark demon isn't intimidated in the slightest, especially with Jasper approaching from behind him. "Slash Scrum and the Royal Caliphate seek entry to The Beastiary, Keeper. Your Prince wishes to visit."

The eyes dart around until they light on Jasper. Then the only one we can see rolls to the heavens. "Baphomet's balls, boy! Why didn't you say so? I thought you were the demons ditching. Fucking freshman are always out here screwing around with my door and the animals they can taunt from outside of my wards."

"Open the door, Arces. We have someone we want you to meet."

Before he's even finished speaking, the slot slams closed and I hear a series of locks disengaging. It feels like a *lot* of them, given how far out The Beastiary is. I'm not sure I believe many students are taking the time to come all the way out to the edge of campus near the Wastes to piss off this old fart. More likely, he's paranoid and set in his ways, so anyone who comes near is some kind of threat.

"Salem, is this guy crazy?"

"Point of fact, unemerged one… I am most certainly not." The large, imposing demon fills the doorway, and I blink in surprise. He's easily as large as Slash and Jasper, but Arces wears his millennia in a face full of scars that continue into the neck of his warrior-style clothing. He has a bright red beard like a Viking, and short fuzz on his head to match. "I am ridiculously old, and very short-tempered, but I am not mentally unwell."

Kat tilts her head, looking at the giant demon, then nods. "Okay. Well, I like honesty, and do really badly with so many things that it's laughable. I wouldn't *mind* if you were unwell, I just needed to get a baseline so I can interact with you and feel safe."

Damn, that was gutsy; I want to tell her how proud I am of her, but it would make her embarrassed.

Arces looks at Jasper, his imposing face splitting with a smile. "You don't bring me boring, do you?"

"Jasper has brought you demons before?" Slash says, his brow furrowed. "That seems… unusual for our Prince."

"Aye, it is," The Keeper says as he moves out of the way to allow us all to come into his home. "Your Prince may be unyielding and harsh, but he is not stupid. His assistant position allows him to be with his caliphate—he was given that position because he made the right moves when he was a student. Those included mentoring and discovering powerful students for the staff."

We all look at him this time, even Zavida. The Prince glares at us, snarling low as he pushes his way into the very open and airy living room of the ancient animal whispering demon. He drops into a big chair dramatically, crossing his arms over his chest. That just makes the weirdly jolly warrior dude laugh as he gestures at the other seats. I tug Kat along with me, settling her on the wide couch carefully. Oriel takes her other side, resting his hand on her knee lightly.

"Arces, this is our newest member, Kit. He was dropped into our lap unexpectedly by Darkstar, but that's why we're here." Jasper watches as the big man fusses around until we're all seated. "You don't have to play the host because I'm here."

I have to cover my mouth when the Keeper whirls around and gives our Prince a ball-shriveling look. He inhales deeply, then shakes his head at Jasper reprovingly. "You pups never want to do things the right way. It's fucking annoying, Eversore. When people you don't despise visit your home, you offer them a rest and a refreshment. How are you going to run a castle someday if you can't be trusted to know how to act in a humble hut like mine?"

Uh, this guy's house is anything but small, and it's definitely not a hut, but I will not correct him.

"Your home is very spacious," Kat says as she looks around. "Not a hut, by anyone's standards, Keeper. But it is very welcoming and I wouldn't have expected that from your original greeting at the door."

We all look at her in unison, eyes wide, as she takes Dottie off her shoulder and lets the kinkajou scamper onto the low table in front of us. I wouldn't have spoken to the legendary Arces Hornclaw like that, but then, I also wouldn't push Jasper the way KK does, either. She has an extreme disregard for her health and well-being that borders on daredevil levels sometimes.

But luckily for her, the ginger demon bursts out laughing again. "Oh, I love this new kid. Means what he says and says what he means, eh? Now, give me a moment to put the kettle on, and when I return, I'll take a look at that tiny little creature. Not from around here, so I'll need to be up close and personal."

Once he's gone, Jasper slouches in his chair, his expression relieved. "Zavvie, you were right about coming here tonight. This is important, and I'd let it slide."

The Kitsuné looks happy and his tails pop out, swishing back and forth as he looks at the prince. "I thought if we got Dottie confirmed as a familiar, we could use her to track what kind of hybrid Kit is. Not every species or line draws them, after all."

Oriel frowns, looking thoughtful. "I don't know, Zav. More than one thing means either or all of the pieces could attract a familiar. Might not be the key to everything that you're thinking."

"I think our theory…" Xerxes says as they look around, then turn back to us. "is the right one. If that holds, then this won't change our current path. However, everyone knows the Keeper can help demons learn to work with their familiars more smoothly. I think that would still be worth it, don't you, KK?"

She gives them a bright smile, nodding. "Dottie and I do really well now, but if the Keeper can help me work with her even better… it would be good. I'll take anything I can get until the powers I don't have control over… manifest or whatever… fully. Especially with the Games coming."

"Those bloody things!" Arces booms as he stomps in with a tray of very well-made tarts and a stack of tea cups. He sets it down on the sideboard, then grunts as he heads back to get the teapot. "Why in the Seven Realms the King let this go on, I can't fucking imagine. He will not stand for a coup like your families pulled, so there's no reason to kill off a bunch of service-able elite demons by the barrel-full."

Anton rises, walking over to quietly assist the Keeper in his tea time ritual without being asked. For a second, it looks like the big demon is going to shoo him away, but he hands him the cups to pass out begrudgingly.

Kat elbows me, leaning in to whisper, "Those tarts look great."

"They *are* good, new friend of the Prince." The Keeper strokes his beard, giving us all a pointed look. "I was summoned in a time where even the nobles were taught basic life skills. I had options for what I would dedicate my life to—until that bloody coup. When it finally ended, the King showed his gratitude by placing me here and allowing me to *choose* what I wanted to do for eternity."

I'm not sure if that's sarcasm or not.

"You chose to work with the animals?" Kat asks curiously as Anton hands her a cup. "That's kind of cool, especially when you're obviously a war hero. I would have expected someone like you to take over the classes Jasper does the assisting for."

Arces walks around behind Anton, pouring tea carefully as he responds to her. "I considered it… Kit, was it?" When she nods, he continues. "But I'd had enough of fighting and animals have always responded well to me. My familiar is doing his rounds over the fields, but he'll be along, eventually."

Kat scoots forward, her posture eager as she asks, "Oh, cool! What is he?"

The slow grin of the Keeper makes me almost shiver, and when he answers, I know why. "A Stymphalian bird."

KK doesn't know what that is, but I sure as hell do, and it's impressive as fuck—this guy might be more useful than I thought.

Mysteries and Mayhem

Kit/Kat

Everyone looks really impressed, but I haven't gotten to that species in Mythology yet. I have no idea what it is—beyond a bird—or why it's awe-inspiring. So I sit up straighter and ask a question guaranteed to make me look dumb. "What's a Stymphalian bird? Sorry… I'm still learning about Hell."

Arces blinks, then looks at Jasper with a dark frown. "Your new inductee is completely new to Hell? For fuck's sake, Eversore… Were you going to let me act like a fool forever? Beelzebub's hairy legs, boy, you know better than that!"

I shrink back a bit, waiting for Jasper to hurl snark at me, but the prince simply shrugs. "I thought you'd figured it out by the animal, Keeper. I wasn't hiding shit from you."

The big man sniffs in indignation, then looks back at me. "Well, Kit… I suppose I'm going to be the one to educate you even though they didn't place you in one of my classes. Seems like a shitty oversight if you arrived with this little gal because anyone who comes here with an animal obviously *has* a familiar. They're not all that common, and few demons have a true partnership with animals like us."

"My animal likes me just fine," Salem says with an annoyed look. "He just happens to be on the inside, not out."

The bearded demon gives my roomie a stern expression. "We're not talking shifter hybrids, Stryker. That's someone else's department, thank fuck. But before we end up on a long-winded rant about this school's idiotic schedulers or your bear, I want to answer Kit's question. Stymphalian birds are much like any mythical bird in that they are inexorably linked to an element of the universe."

I bite my lip to keep myself from making a Pokemon reference, and even though I don't look, I hear Zav's quiet chuckle. "So… um then… you mean phoenixes would have fire?"

"That's right!" Arces moves to pull his huge chair closer to the table so he can see Dottie while we talk. "Mind, there's a difference between a phoenix shifter and a phoenix familiar… and not every mythical has non-shifter cousins. As I said, the shifter/animal line of inquiry isn't my area of expertise—outside of being one. That doesn't mean I study theory and historical biology, though, so don't think I'll be able to go into detail about it. My affinity is with the companion animals that some of us can be gifted by Fate or simple happenstance, like your furry friend."

"Her name is Dottie," I say, as my brain tries to wrap around the existence of both normal animals and shifter variants. How would I ever fucking know if a wolf or some random cat is a *person*, not an animal? This is bullshit, and I'm frustrated to death with all the things I have to learn suddenly. "But I'm… mostly sure she's an animal?"

Arces laughs, smacking his palm on the table and Dottie jumps, then shakes her fist at him. Her chitters are angry, and the big man immediately coos an apology. I'm not even sure how he's making those sounds, but it definitely calms my kinkajou down. "Sorry about that, little one. I didn't mean to frighten you. I'm a lummox, you see, and sometimes we're not the most cautious of beings. We're heavy of hand and foot without thinking about those who are small."

Dottie stops, giving him her signature chastisement at his words, settling back on her haunches and holding her tail as she looks around carefully. The other guys stay still and I let out a sigh of relief that no one is making a stink about her panic. Being scared doesn't mean she's weak or useless anymore than it does in humans or demons. I don't want Jasper nitpicking my biggest comfort because she didn't want to be squashed.

If he does, I'll shove more than grapes up his fucking nose, that's for damn sure.

"So…what element does your bird have a connection to?" I ask as Arces holds his hand out to Dottie. I think he wants her to climb onto it so he can study her close-up, but I don't know if she's ready for that after his table pounding.

"Metal." The Keeper grins broadly as my girl moves closer, bit by bit. "She has metal feathers, a razor sharp hybrid beak, and her shit is actually poisonous. You wouldn't think that'd be an advantage, but it is. Saved my bacon plenty of times on the fields of war long ago."

"That's cool as fuck," I admit. My eyes stay on my kinkajou, anxiety flowing over me as Arces attempts to get her to warm up to him. "I don't think Dottie has any special powers… Well, maybe she seems to understand me when I talk, and she's quite good at telling Jasper off."

Xerxes holds up a finger. "She also shoved grapes up his nose, so her bravery is fairly off the charts."

Arces looks at me, then the others for confirmation. Finally, his eyes move to the prince, who rolls his in response. "I'll be tarred in wastes and covered in Black Cow dung. You *are* a brave little nibblet, aren't you? Most grown demons wouldn't risk attacking the Prince of Hell, and here you did it and lived."

Dottie chitters happily this time, then alights onto his palm. The Keeper brings her up closer, tilting his head as he looks her over. "I see nothing that marks her as dangerous, though we knew that because she protects and comforts you, Kit. I assume that's why she put fruit into Jasper, and I'd guess it's why she has such a fighting spirit."

"I didn't even consider that," Zavida says, his eyes wide. "Dottie defends Kit so much that none of us thought she could be a problem."

"See, that's where schools are failing you whelps." The Keeper looks up, pinning us with a one-eyed glare. "They don't teach you rich little bastards that bad things come from everywhere, not just shit you'd expect. Someone could have sent a handful of magical things to pretend to be a damn familiar."

Jasper growls softly, slapping his hand on his face. "Damn it. I should know better. We *all* should know better."

"It's my failure, not yours," Slash says with an angry frown. "I should be punished for my carelessness."

"I didn't think of it when I did the checks—" Zav shrinks into himself, clutching his tails.

Oh, we're so diving into deep, ugly waters here; I have to stop it.

Shooting to my feet, I clap my hands loudly. "Hey! Hey, shut up. All of you."

The big hybrid holding my familiar gives me a pleased look, but the others stop and gape at me. I suck in a big breath, then blow it out before I speak again. "Blame doesn't change what happened. No one needs to prostrate themselves or get upset. Dottie is *not* evil and we're all fine. Plus, now you're… I don't know, more aware for later."

"Right you are, unemerged." Arces turns to Jasper, his scarred face ruddy with excitement. "I take back my former fury, Eversore. Even though you withheld information because you're a sneaky shit, I very much approve of your new member. The kid has spunk."

"Oh, he's got more than spunk," Jasper drawls as he makes a face. "But I suppose your stamp makes me feel marginally better about it."

Zavida pokes his head out of his tails to shoot a dirty look at his lover. "You promised."

"Fine," the dragon grumbles as he sinks further into his chair like a sulking child. "What do you think he is, then? We don't know because his heritage up there has been muddled by the foster system and some ridiculous shit that's preventing Zav from finding anything online."

Leaning back in his chair, the Keeper strokes his beard with his other hand. "I'm not a seer, young royal, nor am I skilled in deceit, like your thief or your hacker. I don't have the answers you're seeking simply because I am good with animals. Though, I suspect you believe Kit is a hybrid shifter as well, which is why you asked."

"We believe he is a hybrid, yes," Oriel says. His fingers are steepled in front of him, and he's observing the big man. My darkly handsome crow isn't sure that he trusts Arces yet, even if Jasper does.

It's because of me, and I don't know how to react to that.

I just dip my chin and look at my hands, unsure of what I should say now. Fortunately for me, I don't have to wade into that discussion because Anton does it for me. "It follows that you might get a sense of it because of your affinity. I see where his train of thought was going."

"Yes, but I am of more use to you when I say that few surviving demon lines can bond with familiars." The red-headed man smirks when I whip my head up to look at him curiously.

"Surviving lines? I mean… I know there are a bunch of demon types, but… no one mentioned that there were some that no longer exist." I chew on my lip nervously as I wait for people to expound. Again with more info that everyone else knows and I'm woefully behind on. It's making me feel like I really am going to get people killed by accident.

"Aye, Kit. When we entered the last war after Jasper's father and his caliphate won the Games, there were some rare demonic lines that were hunted to extinction. People who are not me, mind you, said they were executed to prevent them from helping defeat the current leadership's run for the throne. But as I said, I would never say that because suggesting a minor genocide was perpetrated by the crown to win the war would be *treason*, you see."

Jasper groans as he looks up at the ceiling, and his tail twitches back and forth in agitation. "Arces, there's no possible way any of those species survived. You know, they scoured the entire landscape of Hell to make sure the 'traitors' were found and eliminated."

The Keeper shrugs, his expression full of mischief. "Ah, but that's the key, isn't it?"

"What's the key?" Slash asks with an annoyed grunt. "Don't be cagey. It's counterproductive."

Arces strokes a finger over Dottie's head gently as he sighs. "Scrum, I wasn't being cagey. This conversation is a minefield and I'll thank you to remember my words about being a big oaf earlier. Dancing around delicate situations isn't my forte."

"You don't need to worry that we're going to rat you out," Xerxes says firmly. "We're not fans of that style of management."

I nod, looking at the professor seriously. "And no information is bad information with this mystery. I mean… I can't talk about what things I think I can do, but… I would like to find out what else might be coming. *Please.*"

"Wait." Jasper holds his hand up, looking around for a moment, then back at Arces. "You have this place completely warded, yes? That's what you've always said in the past, but this… is edging toward extremely sensitive territory. I need to know if Annie and X should add another layer before you continue."

"Aye, but if you want to throw extra on before I speculate wildly about something that would paint an enormous target on your newest member's back, I won't be offended. It's probably not remotely true or possible, but we risk much to discuss it."

Jasper nods, then gestures for the two magical demons to do their thing. His expression is pensive as it darts between Arces and me, and I have to lean against Salem to help calm my thrumming pulse.

This man has a theory about me that's so dangerous, he's afraid they'll kill us for speaking it out loud—of fucking course he does.

Uh-oh!

Slash

The Keeper must be trustworthy if our prince has been slipping him promising demons throughout his tenure at Discordia. However, I am still unsure about sharing our theories and concerns with Kit outside of our circle. I have difficulty allowing *anyone* other than my brothers and the doc near him because of my animal's instinct to protect the small demon at all costs. It's a war within me, especially paired with my curiosity about *what* the Keeper is doing with the demons he mentored over the years.

I prefer not swimming in gray areas like this and it's making it hard for me to concentrate.

"While they create a field, I must ask why the prince was bringing you promising young demons. Jasper would not hand weapons to just anyone, in my experience."

"Very nice, Scrum. I see a glimmer of your father in you, but not enough to make me worry." The one-eyed demon gives me an assessing look, but I see the sparkle in the good eye. "Young Eversore caught my eye when you were all but pups. Through a lot of careful planning, we've been able to keep our association out of the public eye."

A bang at the door makes Kit jump and I snarl as demonic power rushes to my extremities in preparation to defend. "Stay down, little demon!"

Arces throws his head back and laughs heartily and Jasper waves his hand at Salem. "Go let Rook in before she destroys the door again."

"Again?" Kit says as he watches the panda move to comply. "Does… Rook… do that often?"

"Aye," the Keeper says as a flurry of what sounds like slicing knives and squawking streaks across the room towards the kitchen. "Rook is like most mythical birds in that his patience is very limited. They are given the powers of elemental magic and it makes them short-tempered like those elements. It's best to allow them to be what and who they are—something that is actually common in familiars."

Jasper huffs an irritated breath as his eyes cut to the kinkajou still sitting in Arces's hand. "I haven't forgotten, even if the little rat is asking for it."

"Hey! Dottie is *not* a rat. It's not her fault that you take such joy in berating me and she has to defend my honor."

The little demon glares at the prince and I have to stifle the snickers threatening to break free. He gives my best friend such impassioned sass that I can't help enjoying Jasper's discomfort. No one in our long lives has done such a good job of calling him on his shit, and I respect it immensely. Plus, the prince *needs* someone to force him to curb the learned behavior from his shitty parents. We all do in this caliphate and I have noticed that our newest member balances that perfectly.

I will let no one screw up that new equilibrium, for any reason, even someone as venerated as The Keeper.

"Let's not argue, children. I'd prefer to discuss dangerous and forbidden topics that apply to the situation you find yourselves in *right now*. Is the field complete? If not, your magicals need more training, Prince. They are too slow for the field of battle the new Games will be and you will die waiting for them to help you."

Xerxes looks ruffled as fuck, and Anton's eyes shine with pride of his lineage as he glows even more brightly. The peacock shifter's voice is dark as he shoots back, "We are not moving slowly, and this is not battle. This is a safe place that we are reinforcing, with no preparation or supplies. Our efforts are to ensure the privacy needed."

"Are you finally done, then?"

Kit reaches out, putting his hand on X's bouncing knees when the red-haired ancient questions them again. "I don't think he's being a jerk as much as he *really* wants to talk about this stuff. The face he's making appears to be eagerness, not condescension."

"I'm with KK," Oriel says and I snort.

"Shocker." The crow glares at me, but he and Salem are easily the closest to Kit. They often take his side in disagreements—none of us expect either of them to desert him.

"I'm not with KK just to be contrary, Slash. My agreement is because I am more gifted at reading other beings than anyone in this room, other than Xerxes. The two of us have roles that require us to observe others and act based on those thoughts. They do it in the light and I do it in the shadows, but notice that Anton is more irritable than his slithery companion."

The gloomy bird is right, but that doesn't mean their allegiance isn't obvious.

"I see your point." I nod, turning back to the Keeper. "Your bird is not the only one who has such spirit. Ours do as well."

"That they do, Scrum," the demon says as he grabs one of the cookies from the plate and shoves it in his mouth. Once he chews, he tilts his head. "Now, are we ready? Your young initiate was accurate about my excitement to finally discuss this with someone other than the grumpy royal."

"We're good," X confirms as they let go of Annie's hand. "Or as good as we can manage with the time and tools available. Go on, Keeper. Tell us what you and Jas have been hiding under a bushel for such a long time."

Jasper rolls his eyes. "We haven't been hiding everything he's spinning, X. Obviously, there are recent developments that have sent Arces into a tail-spin. I'm just as confused by this extinction talk as you are."

I arch a brow. The Prince rarely admits when he's mistaken, and even less often, that he's surprised. This theory and whatever they've been sitting on is significant. In fact, it must be vital for him to have kept this association a secret even from me. I'm the only person Jasper Eversore has confided in since childhood, and despite his love for Zavida, I'm still number one.

Or I thought so until he brought us out here to No-man's-land to meet this weird ass animal whisperer.

"As I was saying before, the current court staged their coup in the name of making Hell a better place. However, that noble vision disap-peared quickly once they were in charge and realized that it is more difficult to hold on to that level of power than they assumed." Arces leans back again, and his oddly dramatic bird flies in to perch behind him. "Their noble aims flew out the window and instead of replacing the exhausted indifference with enthusiastic change, they settled on an iron fisted dictatorship."

Kit frowns, looking at us, and I shrug. "Before we were a twinkle in their eyes, little demon. We have to take him at his word."

"Right you are. Now, let's see… oh, yes. They put harsh laws in place, and with a single edict, they sent their most loyal and elite assassins and mercenaries to hunt down the rarest demons. No one is certain what the reason was; that was never explained, only dodged by every single court leader when asked. In fact, it became illegal to ask or discuss those lines soon after they were declared extinct. Certain power sets became non-existent, and others were regulated to working solely for the crown."

Oriel tilts his head, looking thoughtful. "Which ones? That seems arbitrary given the amount of inter-mingling the demon types have done over the millennia. Both species and lineage have melded in ways that force us to define ourselves very young, so I don't understand how they could just… blink some skills out of existence in that fashion."

Arces grins, tapping his nose. "Exactly, thief! So what do you believe happened, then?"

"People stopped talking about the types the crown said were extinct because it was illegal. So anyone who might have shown traits or powers hid them. They didn't want to be executed," Anton says thoughtfully. "Which means those demon species probably weren't completely eradicated."

"Exactly." The Keeper looks smug as he lets Dottie scamper onto the table again, so she can snitch a treat. "This coincided with a *lot* of other things that, separately, did not seem important. However, I have a theory that they were."

"Like what?" Jasper asks.

"Hell pulled further away from the other realms, and became more isolated. The mishmash of reasons wasn't satisfactory to anyone with half a brain. Also, the rise in disgust for hybrids got its footing. If you all weren't heirs, you'd have far more trouble with your peers, you know."

Kit snorts. "I've been trying to tell them that. Everyone at that school hates me because they think I'm human or some weird combo, and it's worse since these guys jumped me into their boy band."

"Not surprising, Kit. Your admission was late and probably controversial, then the Royal Caliphate adopts you instead of destroying you. You have made more waves than Discordia has seen in a very long time," he muses as he strokes his beard.

"Awesome. That's just… awesome," the little demon grumbles as he leans into Oriel. "No wonder I have so many friends."

"You have us." My gaze is steady as I look at him, hoping that he knows I spoke because I felt it was important.

A shy smile comes over his face, and he looks at me through his floppy hair. "Thanks, big guy, but I think Arces is saying that's part of my problem."

"Aye, but it's not the biggest part. I'm not done with my theorizing yet. More tea?" I blink as the large man pours more tea into Kit's cup, then hands it to the kid. "Trust me, it will help."

The new guy's eyes narrow and he huffs. "Why do all the ancient demons insist on me drinking their tea to solve my problems?"

"Because tea is one of the greatest inventions the humans ever offered," the Keeper replies seriously. "Plus, it works very well for dispensing various medications and potions that can help patients."

"Get to the point, for fuck's sake," Jasper groans. "Tell us the rest."

I grin, enjoying his impatience. He forgets that my original question about why they've been partnering with talented demons has been thus ignored. "I would like to get home at some point tonight; I agree."

"So antsy," Arces says with a sigh. "My theory is that the court attempted to wipe them from Hell because they were a threat and many of them escaped the purge by hiding—either in other realms or in plain sight, by pretending. They've been dormant, and their purpose hasn't been discovered yet because the royals commandeered everyone with seer powers to their private use."

"You and Jasper have been what? Hunting for them? Since we were kids?" Salem frowns, scratching his head. "That doesn't seem likely."

"Ah, but it *is*, young bear. I met your prince as an incredibly smart, empathetic, newly summoned demon in his first two decades. He hinted even then that his father was… less than optimal, so I kept in touch when I was called to the palace occasionally. We had to keep that hidden, of course, as the king would have me beheaded in a second if he knew I'd breathed a word about the true slaughter that marked the beginning of his reign."

"Spells, right?" Xerxes chimes in. "You've used illusions and spells to keep your communication secret, even from us. Right?"

"Yes." Jasper looks at the whole caliphate seriously. "Even after we were bonded, I had to protect you. This is beyond *our* discussions of things that *might* be called treason. It is flat out defiance to locate and help hide demons who may be in violation of Hell's laws."

Kit is quiet for a moment, then he meets the prince's eyes steadily. "I want in."

To the complete surprise of no one, the little demon I yearn to keep safe just threw himself into the fucking fire again.

Truth Hurts
Kit/Kat

They all look at me like I've finally jumped off the cliff of sanity, but I'm serious. I want in because it's *right*, but also because whatever the hell I am is probably linked to this extermination. On Earth we'd call it a genocide, and people would pretend that it's bad unless it's people who don't look like them. But in Hell, it was part of their 'take over strategy' like some jackass CEOs gaining a competitor's companies and then dismantling them. I can't decide which is worse—killing entire swaths of people for hate or for business decisions.

Either way, I want to find out if Jasper and the Keeper have anyone hidden that knows what I am.

"I know it's dangerous and scary and blah blah blah, guys," I say as my eyes meet each of theirs. "But you know we're unsure about my heritage and Zav could not crack things in both realms that he should be able to access. Perhaps that's because those who have enormous amounts of power have made certain to obstruct those inquiries." I lean back against the couch, brow arched as I stare them down. "Possible, right?"

Zavida pipes up first, his eyes bright. "Yes! It is *possible*. It's actually possible in a *lot* of ways if we consider that the cover-up could have been instigated by the royals *or* the secret survivors. We know what the royals can do— mostly—but we do not have shit for records of the species who were eliminated."

"Son of a bitch," Jasper mutters as he rubs his hand over his face. "That makes finding your birth info out before the Games start very unlikely. I was hoping you were just like any other lost one, abandoned on the surface to the fuckers up there. But I was incorrect."

"Aye, Prince. You didn't consider that he wasn't raised in an enclave—so I assume because you didn't bring it up. That means the Society bastards weren't the ones who buried him." Arces taps his fingers on the arm of the chair as he thinks. "Someone buried him *away* from all of that with no records and no one to watch him; I say it was deliberate."

I frown, my body tensing as I mumble, "You think my parent or parents… left me there to protect me?"

"Perhaps," he replies easily. "It could have been your birth givers, or friends of theirs, or damn near anyone who didn't want you to be killed off for more reasons than I can list. The world is full of times when beings make the best decisions they can at the time, even if it doesn't feel like the right one. I don't want to get your hopes up that you're going to find a bunch of old rebels who escaped for this long, kiddo. That might be a pipe dream, but there are those the cranky royals and I suspect have blood outside of the laws."

Swiveling to look at Jasper, I make an annoyed face. "Is there some reason you didn't bring me here earlier? Or say anything useful rather than be shitty to me?"

His face gets red, and he looks at his hands, then coughs. "I didn't realize you were one of them. We had all the talks about you and powers and what's odd… but somehow, my brain never connected *this* to *you*. I don't know why—maybe because you hide shit and piss me off. Until we started chatting Arces up, it just… didn't even occur to me."

Oriel tilts his head, and so does Anton. I know what they're doing now— they're doing that bird sense thing where they try to figure out if he's lying. When O finally sighs and pats my knee, I know he's decided that Jasper is telling the truth. "Jas, you've been kicking KK's ass from the second he got here. You knew all the pieces, but you couldn't put them together because you were sure he was a spy."

Arces bursts out laughing, slapping his leg as the metal-winged bird makes a weird cawing, clinking sound. "Bloody here, boy! Neither your father nor that slimy Darkstar would send a demon as weak as this to watch you. No offense, Kit, but until you emerge, you're just not the threat those two would require."

I wave my hand. "None taken. I don't have the power those villains seek and may never come close. Plus, I have a slew of other issues that practically make living impossible."

"That is why you would make the best spy," Slash says with a shrug. "No one would fear you, and since we were forced to have you amongst us, we'd likely write you off as harmless. That would be a good gambit—if they'd never met you, little demon."

His smirk makes me blush this time, and I squirm in place. "Aw, Slash. You *do* love me."

"What does that mean, Scrum?" The Keeper looks at him in confusion and the shark demon laughs.

"Kit is not compliant, vocal as fuck, and has zero sense of self-preservation. The amount of times he's gone nose-to-nose with the Prince despite the enormous imbalance between them is impressive. He would not have faded into the shadows, as those like Oriel do to cover their tracks."

"Hey! I didn't shove the grape up his nose; Dottie did."

"You have told him to go fuck himself more than any other demon in Hell, though. And without a single mark to show for it," Salem interjects. "Plus, you've kicked him out of places, insulted him, and somehow threw food in his face."

I guess that's true; I have been pretty harsh to him in return.

"It's fine," Jasper says, shaking his head in irritation. "I saw no need for violence in response because he's so tiny. I'd feel like I was beating up the skinny nerd and that's beneath me."

"Uh-huh," Zavida mutters as he hides in his tails. "That's definitely why."

Slash snorts, his icy eyes glittering as they meet mine. "He be little but fierce. Do not count Kit out, Prince. The practice field would disagree with your biased assessment."

I groan, slapping my hand over my eyes. "I keep telling you guys I don't know what happened there."

The Keeper pours himself another cup of tea, then looks at us expectantly. "What, pray tell, happened on the field? Perhaps I can use that to reference my knowledge of those who fell after the coup."

Great, now they're going to spill my ridiculous, uncontrolled power spike. I'll never live this shit down.

"So you all shifted, and many of you lost your grip on your animals?" Arces muses as he strokes his rough hands over the bird now perched on the arm of the chair. I don't know how he's doing it without slicing his palm open, but I guess he's lived with the damn thing long enough to know how. "Very interesting indeed. Others felt the call?"

"We managed to get some texts out once Zav and X were secured. They were injured, and I think between that and Kit's injury, the animals had too much control of our brains." Salem looks chagrined and I know he hates that he was so violent. He prefers this calm, laid back guise to that, but as the guys have all explained, your animal knows what it needs to do. Sometimes, you have to let it go.

And sometimes, it tells you to fuck off, like that day.

"I was too deep in the shadows and the dragon to tell you anything." Jasper scowls, but I know that's only because he despises being sidelined. He wasn't the leader at that moment, only an infuriated dragon looking to take shit out.

Slash grins toothily. "I brought him back once I arrived. It was difficult, but with the help of Oriel and Anton, I got to the sky. However, when I came down, it was very messy. We had to help calm Kit and guard the injured until Jasper returned to himself. All the other demons were… bloodthirsty."

"An accidental death in combat class would pass muster," the Keeper mutters. "Yes, it could have been an attempt on someone's life. Which, I am unsure, but your theory holds."

I open my mouth, but I see Slash tapping his wrist pointedly out of the corner of his eye. That's a symbol for a watch or the time, but I don't—*Oh.* The corner of his mouth quirks when he knows what dawned on me, and he shakes his head slightly. He doesn't want me to mention the time bending thing to Arces. I don't know why, but I trust Slash a lot, so when I speak, I say, "They think I had some empathetic, emotion pushing powers or something. I can't really describe how it felt, except that I was definitely *not* at the wheel."

"Hmmm." Arces strokes his beard, then leans back in his chair with his hands clasped. "I believe you, Kit. But I will have to consult my journals to be certain of my theories. Will you allow me to request your Human

History class be swapped for Familiar Training 101 after the holiday? I don't know when they will start the first Games trials, of course, but in the meantime… I think you've seen enough of that history from their point of view—ours isn't necessary."

"Uh, yeah, I'd be fine with that. Guys?" I look at them, knowing that class is one that I don't have them with me. "Does that seem like a good plan?"

"Yes." Jasper steeples his fingers in front of him as he nods. "I think finding out what your rat can do besides assault me with fruit is helpful."

That makes Salem laugh, then Oriel, and before I know it, they're all snickering at the beleaguered grumpy dragon. "She was only trying to protect me, Jasper. You know that."

"I do, which is why I didn't skin her for a hat."

His threat makes Dottie get up from her comfortable position, stalking to the edge of the table and shaking her little fist again. The bird near the Keeper looks at her for a moment, then turns to send a blast of ice-dagger filled air at the prince. He yelps, leaping up as they embed in the chair where he was sitting a moment ago.

"Fucking hell, Arces!"

The Keeper throws back his head to howl, and I cover my mouth as a pissy prince plucks the icy projectiles out of the material. "Rook has been working on manipulating water through our bond. I have a wee bit of skill with it, and he obviously decided to practice on you. I suppose it was in camaraderie with your wee rodent, Kit."

I snicker again, then look at the odd metal bird. "Thanks, dude. I appreciate the support. I'm sure Dottie does, too."

My kinkajou moves away from the edge so she can wave at the bird. I think she's being friendly, so I don't worry about it. Jasper, however, finally finishes dusting his seat off and growls as he plops down. That makes Dottie turn and blow a raspberry at him—which is when I lose it.

"Oh, for fuck's sake. The damn animal is worse than you, and that's saying something."

Salem's arm wraps around my shoulder as I double over, enjoying that the prince has spent much of this night being poked and prodded without recourse. Oriel was *not* wrong about how much I'd enjoy this trip, and I'm grateful as hell that they made me come here. Not only did I get to see Jasper humiliated over and over, but we've gotten solid clues to follow up on.

A loud roar echoes through the house, shaking it as my eyes fly wide open. "What the actual *fuck* was that?"

Arces grins, his eyes full of anticipation. "That, new demon, is the Wastes telling me it's time to go find my dinner. Rook probably came home after seeing it and I was too busy gossiping with you to notice. You should all take leave—it's not good for demons of your age to be here after dark."

I look at Jasper, then Slash, and they both seem perturbed, so the Keeper is telling the truth. "Okay. We'll take off. I, um… I'll try to get back out here before Solstice or Yule, okay?"

Arces stands, towering over me as he grins. "You do that. Make them bring you to visit."

"I will!" The others stand, too, scooping up Dottie and ushering me to the door as the bird caws again.

I guarantee I'm not coming here alone just yet, buddy, so be ready for the crowd.

Secrets

Xerxes

K was quiet as we headed back, and I don't blame her. That was a *lot* of information, even for me, and I've been in this caliphate most of my life. I get why Jasper kept us in the dark—in his own mega controlling way, but he was trying to protect us. If Slash and Zav can understand that, I think the rest of us can let go of our frustrations as well. Those two are the closest to him and have been for a very long time, yet he still did what he deemed necessary to save their lives if he was found out.

Jasper Eversore has a beating heart deep inside of him, but he hides it under layers of trauma and snark that scares most demons away.

Of course, that doesn't excuse his shitastic behavior at times. He's been shoving Kat out the door from the second she walked through it and it wasn't because he was being noble. It was because of his father's absolute fucking inability to care about anyone but himself and his accumulated power. That attitude being mercilessly drilled into Jas through a mostly stick and occasional crumb of carrot reward system has him completely fucked in the head. He suspects everyone will hurt him and rarely changes his mind once it's made up. The six of us were lucky to fight through that barricade over the centuries, much less mere months.

As we approach *Canto IV*, I make a small noise to get everyone's attention. When things get *this* introspective, it's usually my job to bring them all out of their heads. "I suggest we change and gather in Salem's room as normal.

We can eat a decent meal, regroup, and discuss this mess without outside company so that tomorrow, we emerge united once more."

KK looks at me for a second, her expression unreadable, then nods. "Alright. Dottie, Salem, and I will host if everyone promises *not* to be jackasses."

That's meant for the prince, who only huffs in response.

I smile gently, appreciating what that concession had to have cost her. She's probably reeling from all the shit she learned and really needs safety and privacy. But as is her pattern since she arrived, Kat is adapting to the needs of the group as best she can while still honoring her own boundaries. Her flexibility alone should have proven to someone up there that she wasn't human, but perhaps the isolation she forced on herself kept anyone of consequence from noticing her. Either way, I'm grateful once more that she found her way to our group.

"I've got stuff that won't take long to heat, but it's not fancy. This will be self-serve, basic fare because we're all too tired to do more," Salem warns. "Don't bitch about it, or I'll toss you out on your asses."

Slash frowns as he holds the door open to the dorm, allowing Kat to enter. "Your efforts are always appreciated, Salem, especially now that the little demon is helping."

Kat snorts as she enters with the big shark shifter hot on her heels. Salem and Oriel follow closely, hovering behind them. I squint at the two typically quieter demons, realizing that they've been glued to her since our trip above. I wonder if they have been initiated into my small club; that would explain why they've been much racier and clingier than normal.

It could simply be that they admitted their attraction, but I don't believe KK would continue hiding her secret if that happened, so it's both or neither.

"You're thinking awfully hard," Annie whispers to me as we follow Jasper and Zav inside. "What's going on in that gorgeous head?"

I lean into him as he wraps an arm around me. "So many things, my love. It's hard to nail them all down, in fact."

Anton hums softly as the group files into the elevator. His solid presence at my side is comforting, and when I look around, I note Zav is doing similar to Jasper, while the other three are tightly ringed around Kat. I wonder if that will expand to include everyone else eventually, and what will happen when the prickly leader of our group is forced to admit his attraction to the small woman who is evolving our caliphate without trying.

"Food will be ready in about ten minutes," Salem announces. "Or the beginning of it will. I'll change quickly so KK can take his time, and once he's ready, he can help put the rest of the shit in to cook. Don't fucking dawdle about getting your knobs waxed."

His vulgarity makes Kat flush, but no one seems to notice it as she ducks her head. I bet her imagination is running wild, and she doesn't even know the right way to imagine such a thing. It's kind of adorable, and I look at my mate with a knowing grin. He arches a brow, following my gaze to the red-faced newbie, then chuckles softly.

"Salem, behave," Annie says firmly. "We get your drift. You're going to make KitKat turn into a fucking tomato, man."

The panda demon looks down, his expression devilish as he bumps her shoulder. "Don't worry, Annie. KK is used to my dirty mouth; he can take it."

That gets a snort from Oriel, and though it didn't seem possible, Kat turns even redder as the crow winks at her.

Oh, there's definitely something rotten in Denmark, and I'm going to find out what as soon as possible.

"Jasper has to learn to trust people," Anton says as he hands me a fresh set of lounging garb from the dresser. "His reticence will only make Kit pull further away because he continues to get only pieces of the picture."

I tug on the comfy skort I designed from the original athletic gear I was given, then I add the tee shirt. I usually cover a bit more, just in case the scales appear. However, since KK met my snake, he's been a lot less willing to stay under a basket. Annie is waiting for my response, so I turn away from the mirror to face him. "I agree, but we both know that getting Jasper Eversore to do *anything* he's not ready for is like pulling teeth from a fucking hellhound."

My mate chuckles as he finishes stripping, then bends to find his own sweats. I modified his as well, though not to be as frilly as my own. Anton likes things to fit to his form, falling in precise lines to show his body in detail. That's not about being vain as much as his need for definition and sharp lines in everything from his art to the way our bed is made. I've never minded his 'quirks', but in my research into what humans diagnose in one another, I've found a great deal of information about the way his mind works.

I'm far from qualified to be putting a label on him—and even if I were, I wouldn't—but I believe I've figured out new strategies for helping my love function optimally.

"Did you mess with my clothes?" he asks as he looks at his reflection thoughtfully.

I nod, padding closer to wrap my arms around his waist from behind. Setting my chin on his shoulder, I murmur, "Yes. Do you like my alterations?"

"Very much," he says as his eyes skate over the image in the glass. "This is… more satisfying than any casual wear I've owned thus far. I don't feel… like I'm wearing the wrong skin."

Beaming brightly, I kiss his cheek, then let go. "That's exactly what I was aiming at. I'm pleased that it worked."

Anton tilts his head as he turns away from the dresser. "What made you decide to do this? I didn't even mention that these things were bothering me, X."

Now it's my turn to flush that tantalizing crimson. "I was reading the books about human psychology that we got to try to understand Kit. There were things in them I was able to recognize in myself, then in all the members of our caliphate. Once I recognized certain traits and behaviors, I sort of just… extrapolated? If it didn't work, I would have had them replaced, obviously."

Annie licks his lips, his mouth quiet, but the expression on his face tells me that his mind is racing. He finally speaks, his eyes earnest. "Will you do the same to the rest of my uniform items? I believe it will increase my ability to focus in classes and effectively optimize my emotional state."

One thing I've learned over the centuries? When he talks like a robot, it's because he has too much emotion to process it quickly enough to respond to people.

"Absolutely." I tilt my head and hold my hand out. "Are we ready to face the circus?"

He nods, smoothing his hands over the tailored clothes, then takes my outstretched palm. "Yes, I believe I am."

I don't make a big deal of his obvious overwhelm; he will be okay in a bit when he's had time to let his brain run whatever mental hoops it needs to. With our hands linked, I pull him out the door and down the hall to Salem's room, knocking lightly. There's a muffled curse from behind the door, then I hear another door shut before heavy footsteps come to yank the impediment open.

"What?!"

Anton blinks at Salem as if he's lost his mind, and I don't blame him. Salem is rarely so brusque, and he's glaring at us like we weren't supposed to be here. I clear my throat, looking at the panda demon curiously as I say, "We're here for dinner, not late, and with unpolished knobs, man."

My joke hits as intended and the big chef is silent for a second before he bursts out laughing. The sudden flip in attitude is a bit jarring, but his eyes are dancing with amusement when he says, "Fuck, man. You hit the nail on the goddamn head. My bad.... come in and make yourselves at home."

I share a confused look with Annie, but we file in to find our usual seats. There are drinks placed beside them as if someone was already preparing for company, but KK is nowhere to be found. "Uh, where's Kit? Is he okay?"

Salem whips around from his position at the counter, his eyes narrowed. "What do you mean 'is he okay'? Of course he's okay. I'm not a jackass."

Huh?

"I mean, after the big reveals and theories and stuff? That had to be really hard to take in all at once," I reply carefully. The laid back demon is weirdly ping-ponging between various emotions, and I'm simply not sure what to do to prevent him from getting all pissy.

"Oh." The panda runs his hand through his messy, two-toned hair as his posture relaxes. "Well, he changed and came out for a few to help, then he went back in to, uh, get some shit for our discussion. You know how he likes to take notes and shit."

Anton nods. "He does. Kit is very much like Zavida and I with having his things organized in a specific fashion. I would venture that, also like me, it is a calming influence."

That's putting it mildly.

"I'm here; don't worry," Kat says as she comes out of the bedroom in her baggy sweats with Dottie and her tablet in tow. She looks a little rumpled and her eyes are a bit glassy… she might have been crying—which I can't blame her for if it's the case. This shit just keeps piling up on her and she's really doing the best she can not to break.

Frowning, I ask, "Are you okay, though? You look…. frazzled."

Her face heats again as her eyes dart to the kitchen. Salem is facing the oven as he fiddles with dials and I arch a brow. KK ignores my questioning look, walking over to place her tech in the chair before she gives me a crooked smile. "It was a difficult evening, but I think I'm doing better now. Salem and I have been getting things ready for you guys and that helped a lot."

The puffy-chested smirk our chef has on his face as he turns is a dead give-away. "I'm very soothing. Someone write that down for when Jas says shit about me."

Somehow, I don't think that's the important information here, bro.

Smooth Operator
Kit/Kat

Salem and Oriel will be the fucking death of me with this… flirting.

I know they promised to let me tell the others on my own time, but neither of them seems capable of being careful about their newfound closeness to me. Just before X and Anton were knocking at the door, the previously laid back panda had me backed against the counter kissing my breath away—*again*. When he finally let go to stomp away, I was rumpled and messy, but my entire body was on fire. Salem might act like he's got all the time in the world to do things, but he kisses as if that world is going to end any second now.

That's why I ran to my room like a scared rabbit; I had to calm my pulse and my heart so they wouldn't know.

X is looking at me suspiciously, though, which means I may not have hidden my riled-up state as well as I hoped. Of course, Salem is still teasing me gently, and that's making it difficult to maintain my cool. It's his favorite thing now, apparently, and I've got to figure out how to get used to it. I'd ask him to stop but… I love it and hate it at the same time, so my brain refuses to make that request. This shit is so damned confusing, and I *definitely* do not remember it being like this with… the guy from the past, even before the incident.

"I'm uncertain Jasper will give a shit if you've been helpful," Anton says before he finally gets comfortable in his chair.

He takes a moment to get settled when he comes into someone else's space, I've noticed, so he occasionally seems like he's behind in the conversation. I *think* it's because he's figuring out if things are clean enough and how to arrange himself in a way that doesn't irritate him somehow. I get having quirks that make it hard to adapt, so I usually ignore his fidgeting until he's ready. Which he apparently is now, and I should probably stop analyzing shit in my head to avoid my squirming embarrassment from before he and X came into the room.

Not about Salem, just… I need to wrap my head around this new stuff before I can have it be a group topic of conversation.

A loud thud at the door makes me jump and I have to re-settle before I can turn back to Annie. Once I'm good, I smile at him. "You're probably right about that."

His response is a shy smile that surprises me, but I don't have time to examine before Slash and Oriel come barreling into the room. Salem winks at me from the doorway and I extrapolate that he must have yanked the door open just as they were poised to bang on it again. The two demons trudge over to their seats, but not before each pass by my chair to ruffle my hair or pass me a…shiny rock?

"Oriel, what is this?" I ask as I hold the large, rough looking blue crystal up to look at it. "I mean, it's pretty, obviously, but does it do something? Why are you handing it to me?"

Salem takes one look and throws his hands up, stomping back to the kitchen as he grumbles, "Fucking. Cheater. Goddamn. Bird."

Now I'm even more confused than I was before—these dudes have more mood swings than people say women do.

"I believe," X says as they squint at the item. ".. that's an uncut sapphire the size of a racquetball." They whistle low as they tilt their head towards Anton, who nods in agreement. "Bitchin'."

Having never been given jewelry *period* prior to the collar still around my neck from our trip to the Fae realm, I would never have known if Xerxes didn't tell me. However, I also didn't live in a cave, so I realize this is really fucking big for a gemstone. I bite my lower lip, not wanting to make the crow upset, but 'what the fuck' is a fair question right now.

"Oriel, you have made Kit nervous by not responding." Slash glares at the darkly handsome demon accusingly. "Do not make me come over there."

I give the big guy a grateful look, but shake my head. "No one has to bully him because O will tell me what I want to know. Communication is important; we all agreed with that, right?" Using his words against him right now may not be quite as fair, but I do want to know why he handed me this damn thing.

"It's… er… it's for you. Nothing more, nothing less." Oriel sinks into his chair with a petulant pout and my eyes widen.

He just gave me a 'crow' gift; this is some weird bird-demon courting thing, isn't it? Shit!

I may have made a tactical error in drawing everyone's attention to the damn thing. Once I realize that, I stuff it in the pocket of my pants, hoping like hell I can keep the redness away from the exposed parts of my body. It now occurs to me that's why Salem stomped off yelling about birds; he thinks O is one-upping him or something. I mean, maybe. Damn, I don't know! I've never done this girly shit before and I don't have anyone to—

My gaze flicks to Xerxes, who looks as though they're the cobra that just swallowed a naughty mongoose whole. Sighing, I grumble, "Pop goes the weasel, I suppose."

That gets a snicker out of them, and I wag a finger at the smug snake demon. They shrug, leaning back in their chair as we all wait for things to cook. Dottie scrambles over, leaving Salem in the kitchen as he hums to himself. She perches on my chair above my head, chittering a bit at the newly arrived demons happily.

"They'll be along soon, girl. And Salem's food won't take too much longer." I turn to look at the others with a sheepish grin. "It's just a heat-up of something we made and froze just in case there was a need for a quick meal. Salem says I should have options all the time here since I didn't have them before."

Oriel arches a brow, his lips curved up. "He said that, did he?"

Before I can answer, the dual toned chef comes into the living room brandishing a wooden spoon. "People with smart mouths often get whacked in the back of the head, Bloodstone."

I frown as I consider that. My mouth is pretty damn snarky, and I've managed to avoid getting clocked with wooden serving equipment so far. Amazing given the fact that I was in the system my whole life, but it's actually true. "I don't think you need to whack him for being a jackass. Otherwise, I'd spend all day every day whacking—"

The door flies open without a single request for entry, and the very subject of my sarcastic sentences stalks in like he owns the place. He looks *extremely* amused as he heads for his throne-like chair with Zav trailing behind him, and once he flops down onto the cushions, he arches a brow at me. "What were you saying, shrimp? I'm *dying* to know what the end of that sentence is."

Uh, weird, because I was being snotty about him, but okay.

"I was instructing Salem *not* to clonk Oriel for being a smartass. I said if everyone with a smart mouth got whacked for it, I'd spend all day every day whacking… you…" My entire body freezes when I hear my words out loud. I certainly did *not* intend to convey the meaning that has him smirking so hard that he might injure himself. "Oh, fuck off, Jasper! That's not what I meant at all."

The other guys look back and forth between us as if they are terrified to respond, but it's X who breaks the quiet with their giggles. Anton snorts, followed by Slash laughing, and then everyone joins as the hilarity of my mistake fills the dorm with humor. I turn to Dottie, pleading with her for relief, but she titters as she, too, understands my gaffe and finds it funny.

"Traitors everywhere," I mutter as I hunker down in my chair to hide my flaming face. "I hate everyone."

"Apparently, not Jasper," the voice says wryly, and when I catch him, I give the sly Kitsuné a double dose of my middle finger for his trouble.

Jasper just stacks his stupidly muscled arms behind his head, looking so impressed with himself that it's stifling. That asshole is going to lord this over me for at least a week, and I won't be able to do a damn thing about it. I might as well prepare myself for the fury now.

"Ha ha, Kit said something silly," I mimic as I roll my eyes at them. "We should definitely make him feel as self-conscious as possible so his anxiety doesn't kick up. Oh, wait…"

Salem points his spoon at me with a stern expression. "Bad, KK! You're just embarrassed, *not* anxious. I can tell the difference and you're getting way better at dealing with entendres. Don't be a faker."

"I'm not…" I say weakly, and even Dottie looks at me sideways. "Okay, okay! You win. I'm fine, just dreading that royal asshat making fun of me for saying that for weeks on end."

The prince in question arches his brow, looking at me suspiciously for a moment. "Now, why would you think I'd do something mean like that?"

"Because I've *met* you?"

Jasper's smile broadens as he dips his chin. "Nicely done, but it won't win you enough points to prevent your eventual torture, little demon. What else do you have to offer?"

"He's got a honking great sapphire," Anton says wryly. "Though I realize now that might not have been what you meant."

"Does he now?" The prince looks intrigued, but I don't answer. "What if I said you could trade it for my good will? No teasing about your desire to… whack me all day, every day… ever."

Man, that's tempting, because he's definitely going to make me suffer for tripping over that phrase.

"Nope," I say regardless. "Not for sale, Eversore. Do your worst—I've seen better, I'm sure."

The twins were ruthlessly devoted to making me look stupid, pathetic, and useless whenever they could back home, so I'm not pulling his leg. Bryce and Blake weren't ever satisfied with overshadowing my accomplishments with their sport glory—no, those budding psychopaths preferred to make sure everyone knew I was a loser. So yeah, I have some experience with this shit that will help me get over whatever he plans to do.

Xerxes looks at Oriel, then at me before they say, "But that's worth quite a bit, KitKat. Maybe you can barter for more from the prince if you'd be willing to part with it."

I snort, giving them a dirty look I reserve for snitches and meddlers. "Probably could, but he has nothing to offer that would be equivalent to its value to me."

That makes the stormy-eyed crow demon perk up, and he looks up from where he was playing with his rings while the rest of us chatted. "He doesn't?"

Pretending to think about it for a moment, I sigh audibly, then shake my head. "Nope. Not a damn thing. It's just too important to waste."

The declaration sounds pretty firm, and I pulled off some pretty good acting, but inside? I'm full of jelly and shivers because I admitted that I treasure something he gave me. I don't like letting people see possible weaknesses, and I didn't *just* flip Jasper off by saying that. It also gave the rest of them a weak spot, should they choose to aim for it, and the crow a vulnerability he desperately wants.

These fucking demons do weird shit to my 'smart' brain and send all my decisions south of my fucking neck—it's a real issue.

PROTECTOR
ANTON

The crow looks like he's about to burst with giddiness, and my love is holding onto the edge of their chair cushion like they're physically stopping themself from clapping. I recognize that Kit often struggles with expressing vulnerable emotions and that statement was unusual for him. It must be why X is happy and Oriel is practically vibrating, but I'm uncertain I grasp the significance completely.

Jasper, however, seems nearly as clueless as me. He frowns at the smallest member of our caliphate, tilting his head. "I didn't expect you to say that. I find myself a tad bit flabbergasted."

Oriel smirks at the prince and I wonder if he's going to get up and do a victory dance. "See, Jas? Some people can't be bought or bribed; Kit's one of them."

Kit shrinks in his seat a bit, his confidence deflating as he mutters, "I mean, I probably could be if the right circumstances are in place. I'm not perfect, O, and there are things I'd compromise my ethics for—I think."

Interesting, because that is not how it seemed when he first arrived.

"That's not unusual," X says as they sit back again, their eyes flashing with what definitely appears to be pride. "Lots of people have shit they'd sacrifice themselves for, KK. You probably haven't felt that before because you've been so isolated. It's not a bad thing, just something you have to be careful about revealing to potential baddies."

Salem walks over, wiping his hands on a towel. "Exactly. I'd do some less than savory shit for the people in this room, and lofty ideals wouldn't stop me for a second. That's what being in the caliphate means, right?"

"Right," Zav says firmly. Jasper's head turns to look at the Kitsune, but his chin is set stubbornly. "You don't have to feel bad that you'd protect anyone you care about, and definitely not that you'd risk everything for them. That's a human savior complex; demons aren't burdened by such mores."

"Really?" Kit says as he sits up a little straighter. "You guys don't think it's bad that I don't give a shit about anyone else in the Games as long as we're all okay?"

Is that what was bothering him? Fuck, even I could have told him that we'd like to save Hell, but it will take a back seat to our brothers every time.

"No," Slash says, his icy eyes meeting the kid's intensely. "We do not."

Jasper sighs heavily, making a face as he grumbles, "Slash is right. That's what the damn ceremony does—binds us to one another above everything else. Hell can fall, the surface can be ravaged, and whatever the fuck else happens can be dealt with later. We protect each other, even if it means burning the entire planet down to do it."

Kit's eyes widen and I can tell he's running frantic mental calculations in his head, trying to re-arrange everything he's been taught is right to compensate for that statement. I smile a little, then murmur, "That's hard to reconcile for someone raised where you were; I'm sure. But it's true, and it's part of who you are now and who you will become when all your power is free."

He makes a face, then throws up his hands, upsetting the kinkajou at his shoulder. Dottie scrambles down the chair, racing over to climb up Oriel's leg to perch on his knee. Kit winces, his voice full of regret. "Sorry, girl. I didn't mean to almost smack you. But man, this whole 'powers are free' thing is bullshit. I keep displaying hints of things without trying, but nothing that breaks me out of the cage. Is it always like this? Because if so, it sucks ass."

Slash gives him a toothy grin before shaking his head. "No, little demon. Usually there are a few signs it is coming and it just… happens. But that is not the experience of someone like you who has fully grown without manifestation."

"That's true. He functions as a 'lost one' like those surface Society jerks call them. I can do research on how their powers typically come about. Maybe we're missing steps or something, especially if he's got more than one thing floating around inside of him."

Jasper's phone buzzes, distracting us all despite Salem bringing in plates of hot food. The prince looks at the screen, frowning for a second, then turning back to us. "Oddly enough, this is one of our new acquaintances. They've run afoul of a demon hybrid broker up there who gave them some information."

"It's Morgana?" Kit says excitedly. "I liked her; her men seemed great, too. Well, except for the dragon, but I guess that's just a species trait. Being a dickhead, I mean."

Oriel snorts as he takes his plate from Salem, winking at KK. "It absolutely is. They're *all* insufferable."

"Says you, thief," Jasper grumbles as he goes back to his phone. "Ah, I see why they're having trouble. Celestara works for some of the oldest demons in Hell, though her real master is—"

"The original occupant of your father's seat," Zavida finishes for him. "But... he's with the deities or the primordials now—at least, that's what the stories say. No one really knows since the rest of his court was killed in the war."

"She is not a demon to take lightly," Slash says, nodding a 'thank you' at the panda when he receives his fully stacked platter.

"What do they want to know?" Kit asks curiously. Salem brings his plate, giving him a firm look as he hands the new kid the utensils. "Yes, I know. I have to eat. Don't worry, Salem."

X chuckles, their grin fond as they look at KK. "You really don't have a chance, do you, man?"

"Nope," Kit replies before he scoops up a bite, then wipes his mouth. "Some of you guys are like old nanny goats."

Salem distributes the other plates one by one as Jasper stares at the phone and Kit continues eating. I set mine aside, thinking about the woman who helped us fight the orc requesting help. She and her wealthy surface dwellers would be very good allies, especially since we know that some of this is coming from Faerie. One of her mates is a prince of Daybreak, though he and his guard seem to be in the dark as much as everyone else. But their reach is undeniable, and put together, that family will be a great resource.

"I think you should respond with information, Jas."

The prince arches a brow at me curiously. "Why?"

"Because we said we would!" Kit proclaims with a frown.

I nod. "That, and because the Games are likely a symptom of the bigger plot in Hell, as we've discussed. The possible coup here is a symptom of the bigger picture up there and across the realms. Having our own powerful contacts from multiple realms who have resources to help is invaluable. That is why we made inroads with the Gemini twins as well, right?"

"Anton has a point," Slash says as he looks at Jasper. "Strategically, forming alliances such as that could only aid us in fixing our immediate problem—surviving the Games—to the larger ones looming."

"Plus, I had a very good feeling about them," X adds lazily. "They're good people."

Kit gives them a grateful look as he sips his drink. When he's done, he pulls his legs up, sitting crossed-legged in the big chair. "I did, too, Xerxes. You have like… powers like that, but I've spent a lot of time in places with people I don't know if I can trust. My radar is pretty good, too."

Jasper gives him an amused look. "Is it now?"

"Stop that; it's shitty," Salem says as he finally passes Jasper with his own plate. "No one expects to be harmed by people they trust, and having that happen to him a few years ago doesn't make his instincts bad. Don't be a dick."

The growly snark surprises all of us, most of all Jasper. The Prince sniffs, eyeing the normally docile bear suspiciously. "Okay, fine. That's a low blow, and it's not true."

Again, almost an apology from the never regretful Prince of Hell; will miracles abound?

Kit bites his lower lip as he murmurs, "He was very convincing, and they said I was drugged."

The atmosphere in the room changes almost immediately, and I watch as both O and Salem move to the new kid's chair. Their food is abandoned as they shift into a fat, happy bear and a large sharp-eyed bird who sit in front of his chair and on the cushion behind him protectively. X definitely claps this time, and I turn my gaze away from the fur and feathers to arch a brow. They just grin, reaching over to place their hand on mine and squeeze.

"Oh, shit! I'm sorry!" Kit says as he looks at the two shifted demons in a panic. "I didn't mean for that to happen."

Slash leans forward, his hands clasped and elbows on his knees as he eyes the three of them. "You were in distress."

"*Are* in distress," Zav mutters as his tails swish around him. "You *are* in distress. The animals feel it."

Clenching and unclenching his fists, Kit looks at Jasper pleadingly. "I swear I wasn't trying to make anyone upset. I just… it's important that people understand that situation accurately, even when I don't *want* to discuss it."

"That's a trauma response; I read about it," Zavida says as he lets go of his tails to push his glasses up. "People must have tried to blame you for the situation and now you *have* to ensure they know what really happened. Otherwise, you spiral, right?"

Xerxes clucks their tongue. "Oh, KK. That's just awful."

My love is spot-on, as always, though they know a lot about being blamed for shit that is out of their control. "It's very damaging to have those who are supposed to protect you accuse you of being responsible for your trauma. I assume it's no different if it's birth parents, foster parents, or even medical personnel."

Kit nods, biting on his lower lip for a moment before he speaks. "At first, the nurses were the only ones who believed me. Well, one nurse they brought in from a bigger hospital who had training, I guess. The others, including the police and social workers and stuff… they didn't."

"Was the guy rich? Popular? Royal? What?" Jasper demands and I squint to see threads of his dragon emerging.

"I…" Kit swallows, digging his fingers into Salem's furry ruff before he responds. "Middle class, but you know. Popular. Good family. Basketball. Smart. Funny. It was one of those 'I should have known better' moments every… one… goes through when bad things like that happen."

That was an interesting pause—I wonder what he was going to say originally?

"They believed him and not you," Slash says with a low snarl. "With no evidence to support his side?"

Shrugging, KK says softly, "Evidence doesn't matter when *you* don't matter in comparison up there. Hell's not perfect, I'm sure, but neither is up there. It's just as much about power and money and all that shit. Anyway… we should… I mean, should I do something so they go back to normal?"

Panda Salem tosses his enormous head, making an annoyed sound, then he turns and puts his chin on the kid's knee.

"I think that's a 'no'," X says with a smirk. They look at Crow Oriel, who hops closer to Kit's head, his eyes glittering with malice. "And so is that look the bird just gave me. Get used to them being all Animal Planet until your aura calms down, KK."

"How are we supposed to discuss this shit if they're like that?" Jasper groans and Zav moves quickly, dropping to the floor next to him to press against his leg comfortingly. That gets his attention, and he sighs as the tails brush his hand. "For fuck's sake… okay. We'll do it with those two being clocked out, and the rest of you can explain it to them later."

"Thank you," Kit says to the dragon in a soft voice. "For, um… not being you for a little bit."

Jasper blinks, his eyes flashing with the shadows of his animal for a moment, then nods. "You're welcome, shrimp."

I honestly don't even know who the fuck that is sitting there, but the contrast is making my head spin.

Bad News
Kit/Kat

It took a bit to get Salem and Oriel calmed down, but once we did, the rest of the dinner/meeting went remarkably well. I wish I could figure out what made Jasper act so uncharacteristically decent so I can replicate it today—however, I fear it will remain a mystery. He was subdued in the bathroom when we got up, and behaved at breakfast, though the occasional snarky retort reared its head. I suppose I can't complain, though if I could, I'm not sure my current companion is the one to do it to.

"I hope they get back to us soon," I murmur to the hulking shark shifter as we take seats at the back of the Intro to Demons class. "I'd like to know what Morgana and her guys think about everything we laid out."

He nods brusquely, watching as I unload my stuff onto the desk so I can take notes. Slash has been quiet since the whole 'animals popping out' deal last night, and I'm not sure why. I guess it would be frustrating to have a shifter animal that can't really emerge unless there are specific conditions—which might explain his withdrawn behavior. Dottie chitters as she gets comfortable, and he finally says, "Yes, I am also eager to get their take on the provided intel."

Damn, dude. Way to make me feel like I'm bothering you.

I wrinkle my nose at my tablet screen, not wanting to seem like a whiny brat by commenting on his reticence. If he wants to be a super-stern guy again, it's not my job to police his behavior. Plus, it's possible I'm just being overly sensitive, and given my issues, that option is more likely than Slash actually deciding to be mute today. At least, I think it is, and I don't have the spoons to fight with my brain on it in *this* class.

"Good morning, my gorgeous students!" Lillabet calls as she wiggles her way to the front of the lecture hall in her skin-tight pencil skirt and tank top. She's gotten less and less dressed as the semester has ticked by, and I worry that by the time we hit the break for Yule, she'll be fucking naked.

Slash grunts as he shifts in his chair, his lip curling up in disgust. He doesn't give a fuck that she's a professor, and I kind of love him for it.

"This morning, we will have a surprise visitor from the Games committee! Isn't that *exciting?*" she coos as she walks around the lectern to turn on the projector. "Now, I know you aren't in your teams, but the administration is eager to get the ball rolling, so to speak. Your teammates or future teammates will see and hear the same information in the other classrooms during this period as well."

Somehow, I doubt that highly, but I will not say it out loud.

The enforcer next to me has his phone out immediately, his large fingers flying over the screen as he texts the group to notify them of what we're hearing. I ignore the buzzing in my pocket as he does so, knowing that whatever they're saying will have to wait. I'm actually *in* this class, unlike him, so I can't look distracted. Lillabet hates me as it is, and I wouldn't put it past her for a second to report that I wasn't paying attention to important Games-related bullshit.

A hum starts as soon as the very tall, very broad man walks onto the dais to meet the Cubi. He's clearly been around a damn long time because the ambiance of power radiating from him stretches back far enough to brush against me. It's ice cold and threatening, making me shrink back in my chair. Dottie climbs up to wrap herself around my neck, tucking her head behind my ear to comfort me as I shiver. My eyes dart over to Slash, whose jaw is gritted tightly enough to bite through steel if he chose.

"This is Major Diabolus of House Scrum. He is the right hand of the King's general, and a war hero in his own right. His heritage springs from the line of Gluttony paired with Wrath many eons ago, and today, he is here to discuss the structure of the Games." Lillabet practically swoons as she leans over the furniture, obviously trying to show off her assets to the enormous demon glaring at the classroom intently.

Slash seems to get angrier as she drones on, and I realize he must have some very bad history with this dude. The demon is his father's second, like he is to Jasper, and as his father is to the king. That means whatever nastiness the general does flows out to the public via this fucker. I don't know if that applies to his heir or other children, but since the shark shifter is rigid enough to become stone, I'll bet it does.

"Listen up, cretins," the huge demon booms in an impossibly low bass tone. I shiver again at the onslaught of power, and before he continues, I feel my caliphate brother slip his hand over mine. "You are *all* spoiled, selfish, poorly trained little shits who think *far* too much of your power and ability because of your names. Names that you were *born* with rather than earned as the old ways dictated. Therefore, I will treat you with the disrespect that you deserve until you prove otherwise. Is that clear?"

No one responds—they're probably just as worried as I am that his question is rhetorical. When the room stays silent for a few more moments, the soldier pounds his fist on the lectern, shaking the ground beneath him with the force. "Is that clear?!"

"Yes, sir!" is the loud, echoing reply as everyone catches on that he wants the class to vocalize.

I don't join in; I only mouth it because, fuck if I'm letting some rando I've never met say he doesn't have to respect me. There was enough disrespect on the surface to last me a lifetime, so I'm not giving up my power simply because he yelled like a tyrant. Slash's fingers lace with mine, keeping me balanced as I look the Major over carefully. Lillabet didn't tell us what he is —only who he belongs to and what his history is. I have a feeling that it's important, especially since my sulky shark friend is staying silent.

"Excellent. During the next few weeks, the official Games committee will visit your classes to apprise the royals of your progress towards readiness. The King wishes the start date to be set, and until we are certain that no one will embarrass His Majesty by flailing around like a commoner, that cannot happen. We were leaving it to the staff at Discordia, but they obviously cannot be trusted."

I feel Slash suck in a sharp breath and I wonder who the hell is on this damn committee that is making the least fearful demon I know worry. Leaning in, I whisper in a very low tone, "You're scaring me a little bit."

He doesn't respond. Instead; he lets go of my hand to trace letters in my palm very slowly. It takes a moment, but I get the gist. "T-H-E-R-E A-R-E B-A-D T-H-I-N-G-S A-F-O-O-T."

Awfully poetic for him, but I guess he's having a hard time.

"Now," the big soldier at the front continues as he moves to the left side of the platform. "I realize that you all have not been prepared as well as others in this school. Some families have grown complacent since Hell has not had a war in millennia. That will change, and quickly. Those who have bonded caliphates will be pulled into separate training programs from those whom we need to pair up to form the appropriate-sized team. We do not care if you have already chosen teammates; our vizier is far more skilled at matching demons by their strengths and weaknesses than you could ever be."

I blink, looking at Slash again. They let people pick groups and start training only to rip them apart now? What the fuck changed since last week? Dottie rubs her cheek against my skin, and I close my eyes for just a moment so I can absorb the calm she's attempting to provide me. When I feel less edgy, I let out a breath slowly as I chant my mantras in my head. I hate to say it, but Jasper's insistence on inducting me is paying off right now for certain.

Damn that asshole for being right.

The finger on my hand starts again, and I focus on it as Slash spells for me. "T-H-A-T I-S V-E-R-Y D-A-N-G-E-R-O-U-S."

"No shit, Sharklock," I mutter, and he gives me the first grin I've seen on his face all day. "Why?"

Slash frowns, clearly wanting to respond but having trouble with our archaic form of communication. I assume he's not speaking because it will bring the Major's attention to us, and he wants to keep that from happening. But I'm not sure why I can get away with it while he can't. The finger moves again, and I wait. "V-I-Z-I-R O-W-N-E-D B-Y C-R-O-W-N."

Now I get it. The royal family patronizing this douchebag means he or she can say anything they want, and based on reputation, it will be followed. But that gives them the power to set up political or business rivals for their own benefit—allowing them to kill major wealthy heirs before they can take their spots in the world. It's dangerous because they will wield it like a weapon, and very few people will be safe.

"Does this hurt us?"

My question is interrupted by the Major stalking to the right side of the stage and looking around the room with sharp eyes. They land on me, then Slash, and I get the worst chill yet. I don't think it matters if Slash is spelling or not now; it's obvious this guy has some idea of who I am. "Those of you in caliphates, no matter how foolishly chosen, will be tested and assessed by the committee's preferred adjudicators. The most elite members of the royal guard and guilds will check your abilities to measure you for the Games. My proctors will arrive by the weekend, and within the week, we will know if you are worthy."

Fuck, fuck, fuck! Is he kidding me?

That makes Slash's finger on my palm shake a little, and I don't have to ask why. While the others are well-trained and ready to fight long-time caliphates of lower levels, I'm nowhere near the point of vying with that kind of group. I have no idea what my magic is entirely, nor how to reliably use it. This motherfucker just announced my goddamn death sentence, and we can't do a fucking thing about it.

"Can't help feeling like this bullshit is on purpose," I mumble.

Slash nods, his finger moving to spell, "S-M-E-L-L-S L-I-K-E K-I-N-G."

Of course it does. Jasper gave his father the bird at the Halloween party, and now we're going to be caught up in his vengeance plot. I blow out a long breath quietly, trying to keep my body and mind from locking up completely. I definitely *cannot* let this fucker see me have issues; that will make it to the wrong people within nano-seconds, and it will hurt the guys. I have to keep my shit together long enough to get out of this damn classroom on my own two feet, and once I do, I can head straight for Dank's office.

The kindly old demon will write me a note, and he might have more information to help me navigate…. everything that seems to happen to me at once. He gave me the pamphlet on scary demon penises, so I assume he has more shit stored in there about animals, and mates and… magic?

Fucking hell, I hope so or I'm really screwed.

You're My Best Friend

Slash

The little demon was adamant that I take him to the Doc's office when the class let out. Since I could sense his fear and tension throughout Major Diabolus's ego-driven lecture, I agreed. Kit has a free period and lunch back-to-back today, so I will arrange for someone to pick him up when he's ready for food. I have been consistently surprised by his relationship with the previously cranky old demon physician, but the prince trusts him. Now that he's taking such conscientious care of our new member, I am also solidly behind the plague-masked doctor.

Much like the Keeper, I will accept allies who are fond of the little demon and seek to help him adjust.

"I really appreciate you escorting me to see Dank," Kit says as he looks up at me.

I know he's worried about my reticence, but I am struggling with my inner animal *and* my demon. When Oriel and Salem could shift to comfort him last night, my own beasts were furious. The shark because I could not physically do the same, and the demon because we have not been given permission to do so in private. Yes, Kit saw us all in various forms out of necessity at that ridiculous party, but the only people who he has specifically consented to meeting their other sides are Salem, Oriel, Anton, and Xerxes. I will not disrespect his decision to meet our alternate selves when he feels ready; he's been violated enough in his life.

So, I consider my words before I respond. "The doctor is trust-worthy, according to you and our prince. And I would never refuse to keep you safe from harm on your travels between locations."

He looks slightly vexed at my answer, and I'm not sure why. "Yeah, I know, big guy. You're a big supporter of 'Kit goes nowhere alone'. I'm just sorry you're stuck with it this time."

That seems very self-deprecating, and he's been so much better about confidence in us lately.

We cross the lobby of the admin building without being accosted as I mull over what I can say. "Little demon, no one is 'stuck' with you. We all agree that you are a target, and we wish to keep you unharmed. You know that because we have discussed it. No one is being forced."

"I know, except…" he trails off as we get in the elevator and I flash teeth at anyone who tries to join us until the doors close. "…I feel you are really distant today. I guess that is triggering that foster kid thing of being a burden. It's not your fault, though; you aren't doing anything bad. That's my shit to deal with."

His admission is insightful, yet shows how vulnerable he is when his past comes into the present.

"Kit," I say as my mind races with possible responses. I don't know how to deal with my emotions without putting pressure on him when I tell him the issue. "I have been quiet because… because…"

The elevator dings, and we exit it, walking down the hallway to the door of the doctor's office. He gives me a sad smile as I struggle. "Because I'm a pain in the ass and now your father's henchman is here to make us even more miserable?"

"Well… Yes. The Major's presence is not a good indicator of how this is going to play out." I frown, shake my head, and then lean down to look him in the eye. "But you are correct in assuming that something else is bothering me. I simply do not know how to express it."

His soft laugh should make me angry, but it's not mocking. His expression tells me it's in surprise, and the hand that shyly reaches for mine confirms that. "Slash, I know you're not… effusive. I don't expect that, but you can tell me things like I do with you guys. If it upsets me accidentally, I'll tell you and we can work it out. The only person who doesn't seem to get adult communication is Jasper, so don't take a page out of his book, okay?"

My eyes narrow, and I squeeze his small hand before I say, "You must promise that if I do, you will not internalize this as something that it is not."

"I mean, I'll try?"

I suppose that's as much as anyone can promise truthfully.

"The other night, Salem and Oriel could shift and comfort you when you were upset. I cannot do so for obvious reasons; that makes my shark angry. But my demon was frustrated as well because I could have partially allowed them to emerge, but… You have not given us permission, and even if you had to see things at the demon house, that does not change your wish to be prepared for our other sides revealing themselves here."

The little demon blinks for a second, looking surprised, then he beams. "Slash, you are a very good man underneath that vicious shark demon facade. Do you know that?"

I scoff. "That is highly questionable."

"Not even a little bit," Kit insists as he continues smiling in a way that makes me very confused. "But whether you agree with me or not, I am sorry that honoring my request was giving you discomfort. I'm not sorry for setting a boundary; don't get me wrong. However, I get that you guys have beings inside you that have desires and needs that ignoring makes you fairly unhappy."

"Unhappy isn't quite the word, but yes."

He chuckles again, shrugging. "I don't know the right words for it yet, but I do get the general concept of feeling like something is trying to crawl out of your skin. So, before I go in and visit Dank, I want to make something clear, okay?"

I nod, waiting quietly for whatever it is he needs to get off his chest, even if it will frustrate me.

"You have been endlessly kind to me, and you work hard to show what a good person hides behind the demon mask. I would like to meet both of your shifts—or whatever—in a more official way." Kit licks his lips, pushing up on his toes to say the last part right in my face. "You don't scare me, Slash. That isn't something I say often, but it's true. I like you for who you are, and whatever those revelations show me won't make me fear you."

Blinking, I gape at him as he lowers to flat feet, squeezes my hand, and winks.

"Now I have a doc to chat up, and you have class. We can talk more later after you've… digested this." That said, he lets go of me and opens the door to go into the office.

I'll be damned—it was like an entirely different person came out once I admitted feelings. Is that what our brothers are doing to curry such favor?

I've been sleeping on watching the bird and the bear, but I won't from now on.

THE BRUTALITY OF THE ARMS CLASS INCREASED TENFOLD TODAY AS THE Major watched from the sidelines with a grimace. Jasper obviously received the message about the speech early enough to adjust his curriculum, something I'm grateful for. If he hadn't upped his game past the point of some of the weaker students, the Major would have reported his 'largesse' to my father, who would have run straight to the king.

Jasper doesn't need his father meddling anymore than he already is by sending that asshole.

By the end, I've broken a slight sheen of sweat—unusual for this class because of the lackluster competition—and Jasper is practically grinding his teeth to dust as he waits for me to get cleaned up. He has a TA-free period and lunch, but I have Human History, so we won't have a lot of time to strategize as I head to my session. However, I will not go there smelling like a fucking barnyard animal, and he has to wait until I'm ready whether he likes it or not.

"Since when are you this prissy, Scrum?" he growls impatiently as he stands in the doorway of the locker room.

My eyes narrow, and I arch a brow at his perfectly coiffed and outfitted form. "Pot. Kettle."

Jasper laughs and shakes his head. "I'm *always* nitpicky about my appearance; it's part of being the prince. You, however, have become much more interested in staying well-groomed. I'm curious why."

He's exaggerating—I was neither smelly nor dirty before, nor am I X-level fussy now.

"I think you're worried about our fathers and their pets invading Discordia. That's why you're picking at me like a scab." I frown and then point a finger at him. *"Don't* go back to transferring that negativity to the little demon. It's counterproductive and will only hurt the caliphate's unity."

His lips curve up, and he tilts his head. "Interesting that *you're* now standing in front of the shrimp, too. Who will be next, I wonder?"

Sighing, I roll my eyes to the ceiling and pull the clean shirt on. Once it's buttoned, I turn back to the idiot I call a friend. "You're woefully behind with emotional intelligence, Jasper. It's your biggest weakness, and there's a good reason for it. But continuing to drown yourself when people throw you a life raft is stupid and unhealthy. Ask Zav to tutor you or something, but stop making everything harder than it needs to be."

"Says the man who barely looked up from inhaling his food at breakfast." The dragon blows a shadow ring of smoke at me with a smirk. "Pot and kettle, yes, old friend?"

He's got me, but I doubt he knows why *he has me on the ropes.*

"I was hungry and focused on day one of the days I hate the most—ones with Jasper classes." Sniffing as I finish tying my shoes, I grab my bag and slam my locker shut. "My job is to keep track of the little demon on those days when he has too many unobserved classes. Focusing is how I get into the mindset that allows me to succeed."

"Oh?" Jasper pushes off the doorframe as I approach, his expression amused. "Is that why you wouldn't look at the kid? Methinks you are lying or fooling yourself, Slash."

I suck in a breath, then blow out quickly. Of course, the only thing he'd notice is when I'm not following my own advice. He definitely missed how close Oriel and Salem seemed to Kit last night, and he's not noticing the soft looks coming from the pride and lust heirs. "Jas, I don't need to have this conversation with you, either. Fuck off."

His eyes flash with his demon, and I realize my mistake almost immediately as we walk through the arena hall to the exit. "You've already had this talk, hmm? With who?"

"Don't be dense, asshole." I stride ahead of him, determined to ignore this line of inquiry unless he forces me. Jasper is my prince, but he does not need details of my personal conversations or experiences with others. He especially doesn't need to know about them with the little demon. It would be ungallant and a betrayal of Kit's very clear boundaries.

"Slash, I could *order* you to tell me, you know," he says as he catches up. The

Prince looks smug, and I glare at him hard enough to wither his balls. "Okay, okay, fine. I won't."

"I would make you regret it."

Jasper snorts, shaking his head. "We haven't scrapped for a long time, friend. I'd probably enjoy the challenge, but I don't think I'd enjoy the mutiny that would follow. Even if you didn't lead it, I feel certain that the others would be angry with me. I don't quite get why, but perhaps that's something else Zavvie will need to explain while he's calming my ire later today."

The heir to Envy is going to have a big knot to untangle—literally—when Jasper gets home this evening.

Battlefield
Kit/Kat

Slash was not kidding about his dad's lackey causing problems. Human history is typically an enlightening class for me because I hear what *really* went on, versus what I was taught for the first half of my life. Alabaster isn't great, but I usually make notes about things I need to research to be caught up to everyone else's level. He's a jerk when I don't know shit; that won't ever change. However, that's where this class helps me pinpoint the most important gaps in my knowledge. The demi-hybrid is often most snide about things, places, and people that every demon should know by now, and he clarifies that I'm deficient for not knowing.

He's a dickwad, but his dickishness helps me focus on the right shit, at least.

Today wasn't like that at all. The Major wasn't in our class, but one of *his* minions was. A tall, broad demon of indeterminate gender who never spoke —other than grunts and scoffs—but watched everyone in the room like they wanted to stab them. Alabaster was rightly nervous in their presence, and it made everything I use this class to accomplish go out the window. The lecture rambled, our professor was too shaken to snipe, and he ended up letting us read ahead for a nebulous 'project' that I'm certain doesn't exist. I think he couldn't stand the mercenary-looking observer glaring at him any longer.

Of course, this atmosphere not only fucked up my actual learning but made me sit there on the edge of panic for the remaining hour after Dank dropped me off. Poor Dottie did her best, but I had to stay laser-focused on the front of the room. Our watcher was threatening enough without pissing them off by texting or indulging in self-care methods. My notes are fractured—disorganized and messy—because of the pressure and my racing mind. All I want to do now is…

Oh, thank fucking Mammon.

Oriel is here to pick me up, and I feel the tension leave my body as he approaches. His brows are furrowed as he studies me with the avian head tilt, and when he's close enough, he mutters, "Rough class, little shadow?"

A shiver runs through me at the new moniker, but I ignore it to nod. My eyes plead with him not to ask here, and he smiles before offering his arm. Once I take it, we turn, heading down the hall to the elevator so we can go to the *Triclinium.* "Thank you for being… you, I suppose."

He arches a brow, smirking through his shiny piercings. "You thought I'd show up in costume, pretending to be someone else? Amusing, I'm sure, but definitely not the day for expressing our 'furry' sides, KK."

The humor is to get me to relax, I know; he's not making light of my obvious stress to be a jerk.

"Well… I think it would be fun to see you dressed as Big Bird, but it's not really my *thing.* Don't get any ideas, okay?" I grin a little, letting him lead the slow unraveling of my knots of panic and fear.

"Hmph. I'm a *much* bigger bird than that yellow motherfucker. Just you wait." Oriel puffs up, giving the impression that if he were shifted, his feathers might *actually* be ruffled at the idea.

It's adorable, and if I say so, he'll get even more affronted.

"I'm sure you are. The few of you I've seen in the private shift sessions have been holding back, I'd wager. None of you wants to scare me accidentally, which is very considerate." I frown as I think about this morning, then look up at O with a curious expression. "Slash asked me if he could go next."

That gets a snort, then a full-on laugh from my companion as we enter the elevator and head to the bottom floor. Once it opens, Oriel guides me out into the lobby of the building with his hand on my elbow. When we're clear of the front doors, he looks at me with sparkling mischief in his eyes.

"Did you acquiesce?"

"Should I not have?" His response is another rumbling laugh, and I yank my elbow free to dig into his side as we walk across the quad. "Tell me."

"Slash is an odd duck, little shadow. He doesn't mince words and looks at things differently than anyone else I know, even Jasper. I think it's because of how the General raised him to look at the entire world like a giant chessboard, but I could be mistaken."

I give him a wry look. "I'm very aware of that. I *have* met the guy."

"Yes, but you have *not* met his animal, nor his demon. Not really." Oriel grins crookedly. "It's an experience you won't forget, so make sure you find some sort of swimwear. Also, remember that he doesn't hide who he is in humanoid form and won't in those forms, either."

Squinting at him, I ask, "Are you trying to tell me you guys are all being… gentle with your reveals and Slash will go balls out without a thought?"

"I don't know about *balls out…*" The crow snickers and I whack him in the arm indignantly. Once he's done laughing at his own dick joke, he sobers up. "Look, I know I'm being silly, KK, but I'm not lying. Slash wouldn't ever hurt you because you're one of us, but he is always exactly who and what he is. So, you know… be prepared that he won't cushion the blow."

Huffing, I try to think about what that will mean for a shark and a vengeance demon, but the latter has so many different visages. I've seen a few around since I arrived, and I don't know what his is going to look like since they can occur in several of the royal lines. As for the shark? I mean, I've seen *Jaws*, so it can't be too much worse, right? If no one starts the French horns and the strings playing the theme song, I should be fine.

Of course, those are famous last words, especially when I say them.

Lunch went surprisingly well, but that was because the group chat got a message that Jasper and Zavida were 'tied up' with work—something that made Oriel act like a very typical guy as he re-directed our path to *Canto IV* to have lunch in our dorm. I'm not naïve; I know he believes they're fucking and doesn't want to say it. But honestly? I'm not really as touchy about that stuff now—plus, I have to admit I'm curious, if only to myself.

Jasper and Zav's dynamic is a mystery to me in practice, and I know the media doesn't portray it correctly.

Not that I'm going to *tell* anyone that because I'm definitely ready for the explanation. For the moment, I'm okay with my less-than-knowledgeable imagination and the bite of mystery. I have enough 'new things' to deal with now that I've kissed both Oriel and Salem—two dudes who know my secret and seem completely fine with playing tag team. They like jabbing at one another playfully, but I believe them when they say they'd have no problem working together.

"Yet another thing I'm not ready for," I mutter as we climb the stairs to our dorm. Oriel opens the door, letting me pass as he tilts his head.

"What was that, little shadow?"

My eyes widen. "*Nothing.*"

"That was a very strenuous protest. Doesn't seem like nothing," he replies as we wade through the other demons filling the entryway and common space. "I told you that you can—"

"Suck his dick, right?"

We both whirl around to see our old friend Bastion standing there with a group of similarly beefy-looking fuckers as they smirk at us. Dottie scrambles out of my bag, perching on my shoulder immediately like she's ready to throw down with the asshole. It makes Oriel chuckle, but the dumbass from the *Thieves Guild* just glares.

"As if some stupid rat could help you thwart me."

Dottie chitters loudly, her small fist shaking as she gives Bastion a piece of her mind. I reach up and pat her head lightly in thanks, then shrug as I look at the homophobic shitstain with a bored expression. "Bastion, if the Games hadn't been announced, O would be running your shit. You lost; get over it. This little scene is so... 90s high school movie, man. Homophobic slurs? Demons don't even give a fuck about that shit."

"Alas, he's right, Queznar." Oriel angles himself so his bulk is between me and the furious bigot just slightly—a move not missed by the troupe of *Beavis and Butthead*-esque demons standing next to Bastion. "You tools are just *dying* to use cockwaffle to get ahead in the ranks, but you don't realize that you are cannon fodder."

Bastion sneers. "What the fuck are you talking about, Bloodstone?"

I'd like to know as well, but fuck if I'm going to say it.

"While Queznar is high enough that there are limits to the damage I can do outside of class without declaring an official beef... you are not." Horns sprout from his head, and his wings and tail appear as he stares down the group of hecklers with an eager grin. "I can wipe the seven of you off the face of Hell without breaking a sweat, and no one will give a single fuck because you're from the bottom of the barrel, boys. Do you think Queznar missed that fact when he formed his little boy band?"

I blink, watching the crow demon, who's been kind to me from the beginning, morph into the dangerous royal heir to the Greed Line as he confronts the bullies. "Oriel…"

"Don't worry, Kit. They know I'm right. Look at their faces—full of realization that they're disposable pawns too late."

"You can't kill all of us," Bastion huffs as horns sprout from his head as well. The others shift, and I suck in a breath at the various forms before me. "You're one demon, Bloodstone, and not even the most powerful one from your stupid group."

"You're a drude, and most of your powers require us to be asleep, asshole," I retort then clap my hand over my mouth.

I did not mean to say that out loud.

"Oh, the little human wants to play, too? That's perfect because when you're out cold, I can break your mind just as easily as if you're asleep. Comas work for me, too." He licks his lips, and the ice cold hand of past trauma wraps its fingers around my gut.

Oriel flaps his wings, and his size, even in the humanoid form, grows with the fury radiating off of him. "Consent is sexy, fuckwad, and unconscious people can't give it. If that's how you get your kicks, no wonder there are rumors about your… lack of staying power."

I want to laugh, but the hungry gaze of Bastion and his minions is triggering something inside of me. It's not just the fear again, though, and as the black and red energy moves through my veins, I whisper to Dottie, "Get out of range, girl. Now."

"What are you yammering about over there?" one meathead growls. "I don't like mouthy food. Let's get this over with."

That comment is the last thing I register before the power inside of me takes hold and my body aches from head to toe. I let out a loud sound that reminds me of being at the zoo, then I see Oriel's jaw drop as he spins to check on me. Head heavy and bones aching, I throw my head back and let the sound escape again to echo off of the walls. Screams and yelling follow, but I pay it no mind as I stalk towards the group of guys foolish enough to threaten me and the shifted demon next to me.

I want to say something snappy, but I can't seem to make my mouth work except for the continued bursts of sound I'm emitting as the inches between me and the bullies close.

Whatever the result is, I'm not in control again, and the energy inside of me will not be sated until they have been taught a lesson in respect.

FIRE
ORIEL

I couldn't have predicted this even if I tried.

Fuck, I don't think a damn seer could have foretold this damn mess.

Looking at KK, I'm stunned as my gaze roams over the preternaturally large, gorgeous, and furry *lioness* that's getting ready to pounce on that idiot Bastion. She's eyeing him like a nice demon flank steak as a golden aura of power shimmers around her leonine body. No one has said a word about her lack of mane yet, and my brain finally clicks on the fact that I absolutely *have* to distract them before one of these goobers notices. They're not the brightest bulbs in the box, but this scene is way too public for someone else not to open their big, fat mouth.

"*Kit*," I say in an urgent growl. I let the demon help me push against her; he's the more dominant half of my supe sides, and I need her to respond to that. "You need to calm down. Focus on me and ignore them. Think about yourself, what you look like normally, and push all that energy into that picture. Do it now before this gets so much worse."

The lioness looks at me curiously, then goes back to glaring at Bastion and licks her chops.

Damnit. I need someone with a dominant shifter *side to pull this shit off.*

Before panic sets in, a loud roar—louder than the one Kat let out by far— echoes through the entire common room, shaking the fixtures with its strength. I look up quickly and blow out a thankful breath because I know exactly who that belongs to. He's probably going to make the aftermath a *lot* worse, but Jasper Eversore is definitely one of the most dominant shifters I've ever met. Kat won't have a choice but to obey a command from him— even if it's going to send her over the edge later on.

"Shift…. now!"

I swallow hard as the Prince's command reverberates through my bones, forcing even *my* animals to fade without complaint. Kat's body shimmers again, immediately shrinking, and I strip my coat off, rushing over to get her covered before anyone can see what's coming. Her clothes are in shreds on the ground, so I shuck my pants, too, as she lies prone on the stone floor. I feel Jasper's frown from the top of the stairs, but I don't give a shit what he thinks. Someday, he'll get it, and for now, he can assume I'm coddling the traumatized kid.

She's out cold; no surprise for a first-time shift and forced return by an alpha. So I gently work her legs into my baggy-ass uniform pants, getting them on her while I crouch close in my boxers and button down. Once I get them buttoned, I slide her arms into the coat sleeves and wrap it tightly around her so not a peep of skin shows.

"What the *fuck* happened in here? Someone tell me *now!*" Jasper is definitely channeling his dragon because he sounds like a goddamn fantasy villain. His voice is so loud, deep, and resonant that it makes my skin tingle with the power.

"That little shit insulted me, and I was teaching him a lesson when he turned into a fucking lion. Are you daft, Eversore? Your pet has less control than the other weakling you're fucking." Bastion wants to die, apparently, because he's poking the least amiable staff member on campus when he's already infuriated.

As I lift KK off the ground, cradling her in my arms, I see Zav speed out from behind Jas in a red and white streak of motion. He picks up both of our things, his expression angry and his tails twitching with the intensity of his emotion. I didn't know he was this attached to our newbie yet, but it explains why he's been so eager to defy Jasper without backing down. "Thanks, man."

"You did well, O. He would have been stricken if everyone saw him naked."

You have no fucking idea, *Zavida.*

"I know. This is going to fuck with him enough as it is. He doesn't need to slide into an episode about that, too." I give the Kitsune a nod as we move aside as Jasper leaps over the railing and lands on the floor with a thud. "Plus, this is going to get ugly. Let's get out of his way."

"Should we stop him?" Zav whispers as he pushes his glasses up. "He could start something very bad if we let the dragon lead."

My lips curve into an evil smirk. "Honestly? I gave that motherfucker and his little minions a chance several times before KK lost his shit. Jasper can do whatever the hell he wants. That kind of disrespect can't be tolerated; his father will agree."

Zavida nods and we move in unison, climbing a set of stairs to be out of the blast radius enough that I feel comfortable. Jasper is stalking over to Bastion with murderous intent now, and the hangers-on look as though they might run. I could tell them that's a bad idea because Jasper's dragon *loves* to chase, and there's nowhere they can hide that he won't find them. His hunting skills are goddamn top-tier.

"I believe I've made it clear that the 'shit' in question is under the protection of the Royal Caliphate." His head turns as he looks around the room, probably memorizing the faces of the demons present. "Was I unclear about that declaration? Did it not reach every corner of this fucking place within hours?"

The crowd murmurs, and people avert their eyes. We all know that it did because people started whispering about Kit fucking us. Rumors and gossip move as quickly here as anywhere else in hell or the other realms. His question isn't meant to be answered, especially because not a single one of these cowards stepped forward to correct Bastion and his off-brand boy band.

"*Was I unclear?!*"

Shock runs through the room and suddenly, a lot of murmured 'no, Prince Jasper' responses create a fearful chorus. I chuckle, keeping Kit close as I watch the chaos descend into Jasper's favorite emotion. He's likely gorging himself on the terror, so he'll be charged up demon-wise for days. Zav should get himself hyped up before tonight and keep it going or he's going to limp for the rest of the week. The Prince's appetites will be multiplied by a bazillion after this shit.

Jasper's wings flare out around him menacingly as he growls, "Then why did I find a crowd of you scumbags watching a mid-tier demon threaten two of my brothers? Did you mistake Bastion Queznar for a royal? Were you more concerned about his approval than my *wrath*?!"

Clutching Kit tighter, I brace myself as the prince lets out a wave of wrath strong enough to bring every demon in the room other than Zav and me to their knees. He didn't even need to *touch* them—only send the power of his birth line into the universe—and they're all howling in pain as they tear into themselves. I hear his breath heave as he stalks up to Bastion himself, and I know he's grinning through his fangs as he watches the dumbass scratching through his uniform to get to his skin.

"And you…" Jasper pauses as he spits on the ground and a fire starts at his feet. The effect is terrifying to people who don't know him because it will crawl over his entire body, yet not harm him a bit. Fire scares everyone in Hell, because its power is linked most deeply to our realm and our creators. "You *dare* to ignore my commands, and flaunt it in the face of a royal? Where did you gather up the audacity to believe you'd survive hurting anyone that belongs to me? Hmm?"

Bastion is trying vainly to think of an answer, but Jasper blows a stream of fire at him that sets his hair on fire. Once it's flaming, his screams take the place of any response, and not a single being in the room can fight the control Jasper's wrath has over them. I feel the prince's glee at the scene, his glee at their suffering, and I know this is going to get much worse before it gets better. We might lose him to his dragon and his demon if we don't intervene.

"Jas, I think you've made your point," I say as I turn KK away from him just in case.

Our leader spins around, looking at me through his slitted eyes and half-transformed features. "They deserve worse."

"Agreed, Sir," Zavida replies as he peeks around me. "But this will only bring trouble when there's trouble enough visiting right now."

The mention of the Major makes Jasper sneer in derision, and I realize that Slash's dad *definitely* did some shitty stuff to our friend when he was a kid. I'm guessing he helped beat the shit out of the mouthy royal and that hatred has festered all these years. Zav was doing the right thing by bringing it up, but Jasper's fucking tight-lipped behavior about his past has led us to step in an even bigger pile of shit. The dragon-demon whirls back around, his size growing as scales crop up on his bare chest.

Big mistake. Huge.

"How are we going to keep him from going whole lizard and destroying the dorm?" Zavida asks worriedly.

"I think we need to wake KK up," I whisper back to him. "If the dragon was worried Bastion would hurt him, maybe seeing him conscious will help back the cranky fucker down."

It would probably work for me—I think—so I'm willing to try it. We have to be very careful about it, but I don't have any other ideas. Unless Zav has a stroke of brilliance, she's the best we've got.

"Maybe? I can't confirm that his dragon is fond of Kit, but… Jasper doesn't talk about emotions very much other than anger. It took forever to get him to discuss our relationship outside of sex. He's so terrified of being hurt by people he cares about that it bottles everything good inside of him up."

Grimacing, I shake my head. "I'm going to move closer, but I need you to be ready to zip off to find more of the guys if this doesn't work. Slash would be best, but fucking anyone would help. Got it, Zav?"

He nods, and I hold on to Kat tight enough to bruise as I make my way down the stairs slowly. Jasper is playing with his food, so to speak, making Bastion and his friends harm themselves badly enough that they will definitely need the infirmary. His power hits me by the time I get to the bottom, and I grit my teeth against it. The Prince could control any of us if he chose, but his intent when he did this was only towards the people who took part in the bullying.

When I get close enough that I think he'll pay attention, I look down at Kat and turn away from the crowd. Leaning in, I tap her cheek with my palm lightly, hoping it would work. "KK. Little shadow. Wake up. We need you. If you don't wake up, Jasper might burn the damn dorm down. Show us who's really in charge."

Her lashes flutter, but she doesn't wake up, and I groan as I rack my brain for another way to get her to come out of the 'post-first-shift' coma early. I know from experience that it doesn't happen this quickly, but there has to be *something* that will get her conscious. An idea hits me, and I snort at my own corny bullshit as it runs through my brain. It's stupid and definitely risky, but what the hell? It can't make anything worse, right?

My head drops, and I press my lips against hers lightly, giving her the less creepy *Sleeping Beauty* treatment. Suddenly her eyes pop open, and I feel her entire body tense like a goddamn statue. Before she launches into a panic, I pull back and look down at Kat seriously, murmuring low. "This is probably confusing, and you're going to feel you should have an attack. I can't tell you everything right now because we *need* you to do your 'ass-kicking' thing to Jasper. Something happened after Bastion taunted us. He showed up, and we're getting ready to lose him to his demon and dragon. He might take everyone here but us down, and the building, too."

Kat looks at me wide-eyed and trembling, then nods without speaking.

"I'm going to carry you over because you're weak and dressed only in my damn uniform. That's not for a nefarious reason, but again, the explanation has to come later. You *have* to convince Jas that you are okay and he's done enough to punish these fuckers. Got it?" I blurt.

Licking her lips, Kat nods, then whispers, "Did anyone… do they know?"

"No, I covered you in time. That's why I'm walking around in boxers and a fucking uniform shirt and tie. You're welcome." I grin a little, my eyes dancing as she lets out a long sigh of relief. "Now, let's get him back so we don't draw anymore negative attention to ourselves before we get you out of here. Okay?"

"Okay. I trust you, Oriel," she says softly. "Take me to the lion and we'll see if I can tame him."

Oh, if only she knew how ironic that statement is.

Born Under A
Bad Sign

Kit/Kat

My body is aching and my brain is muzzy, but Oriel said I have to help calm Jasper or everything is going to explode. I'm not sure why that's happening or how I'm going to do this, but I can't refuse to try. Blinking as my vision comes into better focus, I see the chaos around us as he moves closer to the Prince's back, and shock floods my veins.

What in the fuck happened between now and the last moment I remember looking at those nasty assholes?

Oriel's lips press to my ear. "Don't worry about the rest of this shit; it will be fine. Just keep your energy focused on Jas."

I lick my dry lips, pushing away the feeling of dread lodged in my gut as the screams of agony echo off the high ceilings. Blowing out a slow breath, I close my eyes for a moment to compartmentalize, but they pop open immediately when a thought occurs to me. "Where is Dottie?" I croak in panic. "You don't have her!"

The crow demon stops and looks down at me again. "You're right, little shadow, I don't. There was a lot going on when this all went sideways, but the last time I saw her, you'd told her to scram and get out of the line of fire. She's a smart girl; I'm sure she did exactly what you told her. Familiars are good like that—at least, that's what I've been told."

Trembling a little as my concern battles with my brain, I nod. "I know I can't do anything right now, but once we get Jasper… whatever… we have to find her. *Promise me, O.*"

His expression is both gentle and sincere as he replies, "I promise. For now, though, we have to avert disaster, okay?"

I don't know why he's so damn certain I am the one who's going to save us, but I have to try—no one's ever had faith in me like this before.

Nodding, I wait for him to inch closer to the raging dragon and the bloody mess in front of him. Once we're within hearing range for my less-than-powerful voice, I say, "Jasper. Jasper, listen to me."

Nothing happens, and my hands shake as the fear that I'm going to fail everyone tries to wrestle me into an episode. Suddenly, the energy that was pushing at my skin earlier rears its head again, this time the red and black meet a deep purple that worms its way into the mix as if it's always been there. They all shove at one another, and I squeeze my eyes shut, internally yelling at whatever this is to fucking stop like the energy is a bunch of recalcitrant toddlers. To my surprise, they stop when pain slices through me, as if taking notice that something is wrong.

"You can do this, KK," I hear Oriel murmur from what sounds far away. "Take control and use that to get his attention."

Easier said than done, my guy. I don't even know what the hell is going on inside me, much less how to wrangle it.

I ignore the physical issues that precede an attack and the voices of doubt in my mind that normally help it manifest at his words. If this demon thinks I have the strength to figure this out, maybe I do. After all, I've survived a shit ton of nastiness before and I can do it again. This year has been hard, but it's shown me I *can* heal, and I owe it to the guys and myself to stay on that path. So, I suck in a shaky breath and yell at the battling prisms of energy again.

Only this time, they seem to really listen.

The pause gives me time to let in hope—something I rarely do—and I use it to push another command to the power. I ask it to help me convince the prince to shift back, to regain his control, and most of all, to *hear* me. Babbling for a few seconds, I finally trail off when the three opposing forces seem to stop fighting one another and pay attention to my words. Then, something crazy happens… they bundle together like a magical DNA strand.

By Lucifer's sweaty nutsack, I think I've got it.

Opening my eyes again, I look at the prince's back, then my voice comes out stronger than before. "Jasper Eversore, you self-centered fucknugget, *listen to me!*"

The room goes silent almost immediately, and I feel panic creep in. Before it can take hold, I speak again. "Turn around and look, you jackass."

Insulting the infuriated dragon demon isn't the *best* plan, I'll admit, but in times of uncertainty, you gotta go with what feels right. Telling Jasper he's a fucking douchebag has worked the entire time I've been in Hell, and I will not stop now just because he's gone loco. If I'm going to lasso all this shit, I have to be me, and Kat Camponella is the only person who gives the Prince of Hell as much shit as he throws out.

Hopefully, I don't die doing it...

Luckily for me, the dragon/demon/humanoid version of Jasper is angry or amused enough to turn around and rest his slitted eyes on me as I rest in O's arms. His lip hitches in a sneer, but I can see past that to what's really got him spinning out of control—fear. It's not the human part of him, I don't think, and maybe not even the demon. The *dragon* is upset, and lashing out as violently as it can to resolve the problem the way it knows best. That's why he's not listening to anyone, and it's why he isn't making the logical decisions he makes more often than not.

"Jasper, look at me. See me. I'm begging you to get control of it." The reptilian eyes study me closely, roaming over every inch of me as I hold on to his brother. "Out of anyone, I *understand* this reaction. The primal part of you is in protection mode—it has to make certain that you and everything you care about are safe. It hungers for vengeance against those who harmed or sought to harm those things. It wants to destroy everyone who allowed the bad things to happen."

Oriel's arms tighten on me, and I swallow hard as I draw on those damn colored strands for the strength to continue on this path in public. I don't even like admitting this shit to my fucking therapist, but the dragon isn't tearing everyone to pieces right now, so I have to continue.

"That part of you is right—it shouldn't let shit like that happen and it *should* be able to take the pound of flesh it desires. Because it *knows* in its gullet that no one will avenge this wrong with the ferocity and equivalence that it demands." I suck on my lower lip, biting it with my teeth to feel the sting for a second. The slight pain helps me focus again and push away my own fear before it gets a hold on me. "The truth is, *nothing* can actually make wrongs like that balance out. You can only take what petty revenge you can and the rest is about making sure it doesn't happen again. I *know* that and I think you do, too."

Tilting his head, Jasper moves close enough to lean in and sniff me curiously. I want to pull away because I'm not quite comfortable enough to be this damn intimate with the prince yet, but I can't. Something in my brain is shouting that I need to let him figure out that the immediate danger is over or he won't be able to wrest control from the animal inside. A skinny, long as hell, forked tongue flicks out as if tasting the air, and I'm reminded of X doing something similar in his cobra form.

The prince is verifying me for some reason, and I can't reject it—everything in me is screaming to let him.

"See?" I say shakily. "I'm here. Oriel's here. Everything is… well, it's not okay, per se, but you know. It's um… less dangerous except for… you?"

Jasper blinks, then looks around the room as if things have snapped into place. The oppressive feel to the air pauses, and I let out a breath of relief. I don't know what he was doing before, but I definitely felt like it was amping up the fight between my own internal bullshit. Now, they're not only intertwined, but feeling *much* less combative. His wings flex as he turns back to me, and I note his tail isn't whipping back and forth like a pissed-off feline anymore.

"That's good, KK. You're doing it. Keep it up."

O's whisper of encouragement has me swallowing around the dry ache in my throat as I look the dragon in the eyes again. "I wasn't lying, was I? Those slimy shitballs are cowering, right?" A slow nod is my answer, so I press on. "They've probably been punished pretty well for… whatever. I smell a lot of blood, so I guess you dealt with all the passive idiots, too. You can come back now. It's safe."

Scales shimmer on his chest, and I'm stuck for a moment staring at the intricate tattoos littered with dragon attributes, and piercings sprinkled over seriously muscular bulk.

Not now, stupid female brain! I don't have time to ogle him.

Of course, that part of my brain is as much lizard as he is at that moment and doesn't give a solitary *fuck* what I say. I shiver a bit in the crow demon's arms, and a low chuckle rumbles against my back. His lips brush my ear again as he says, "Don't worry, little shadow. I won't tell anyone your deep, dark secrets… including that one."

"Especially that," I mutter before I grit my teeth and look up at the fading dragon in Jasper's eyes. "You did your job and protected people. Let him have the reins again before we're all hauled in front of some really unpleasant committee or slammed in a jail cell."

That grabs its attention, and within seconds, the slitted eyes and wings are gone. It leaves an angry, shirtless royal looking at me in utter disbelief. He runs a hand over his hair, then looks around the room quickly before he growls, "Son of a *bitch*."

"Yeah," Oriel says. "You had a *moment* again, and Zav and I couldn't get the big guy to back off. This is a shitshow, man."

Before Jasper can answer, I feel a rush of air, and when I look down, Zavida is standing next to us with a worried look on his face. I would ask if he's okay, but my eyes catch the small bundle of fur in his arms and my heart seizes in my chest.

"Dottie!" My kinkajou uncurls, chittering loudly as she escapes Zav's clutches to run up Oriel's arm and look at me carefully like she's waiting to see if I'm hurt. "Zavida, you're a *hero*."

The Kitsune flushes bright red, and his tails swish up to engulf his frame. "Not really. She found me when O took you to Jas. I've just been keeping her from getting hit by debris or magic or whatever."

"Focus, people," Jasper snarls, and we all look at him to make sure he's not slipping back into crazy reptile mode. "We need to get the fuck out of here before Darkstar or any of our *guests* arrive. If we can get upstairs and appear to be doing normal things, we might be able to claim that—"

He's cut off by the dorm's heavy doors flying open like we're in Helm's Deep, revealing the conniving fuckwhistle himself, along with his demon flunkies, and the exact emissary from the Court we hoped to avoid in tow.

"What do we have here?" Darkstar says as he smirks gleefully. "Violations of the behavior code involving the royal caliphate—how shocking."

Born under a bad sign, indeed.

STAND UP

ZAVIDA

The first thing to run through my brain is that this fucking mess was a set-up. But as I study the Major, I realize he doesn't look bothered or even remotely smug. In fact, he seems… bored. The royal 'assessor' walks around the gleeful headmaster without a word, his eyes darting around the room as if he's grading the aftermath in his head. While Lucian is practically vibrating with dark joy, he is carefully stalking through the bloodied students as if they're not worth his time.

"It appears we have a cadre of your students learning what happens when you cross royalty," he finally says as his eyes zero in on our nemesis. "They failed miserably. This does not bode well for the enjoyment of the Games by the Court or even the writhing masses, Darkstar."

Lucian's face goes pale as the bulky demon gives him a toothy smile that says he's pleased with what he will report to his commander. "But… Major. This is not a battle scenario; this display speaks to a lack of discipline and control by—"

"I would consider your next words very carefully," the ancient demon says as he smirks. "The laws of Hell outline the responsibilities of bonded caliphates in responding to threats—and they apply to the Prince of Hell as easily as the poorest wretch in the streets. Though… I believe that someone who has never attracted one would not realize how it works."

Ouch. That was aimed right at his pride; the Major doesn't pull his punches in public.

"Outrageous!" Lucian hisses as he stomps over to the soldier with his stupid cape flapping. "I am in charge of this school; it was an honor bestowed upon me by the King himself. My judgment is supreme, and you cannot suggest that I do not understand the structure of caliphates in front of my students."

The Major snorts as he shakes his head in derision. "You'll find the emissaries of the Court and those in their command are not required to do anything, but follow their orders. Your indignance is registered and discarded as I see fit. This is a disgrace, Headmaster; there's no reason a crowd this large should capitulate so easily to being conquered, even if they are first-years. You and your staff have been slacking for centuries."

Beccarus hisses, then immediately hides behind his slimy boss when the Major's eyes light on him. Lucian ignores the little shit as he looks around the room to memorize who he's going to take his anger out on. He doesn't say it, but I know that expression. I've seen it on my parents and the others'. Life at court teaches you to read people quickly and to know when to stroke egos and when to retreat to avoid being made an example of.

"This sort of thing never happened until *your* caliphate arrived, especially that ridiculous human," Lucian says as he whirls on Jasper.

That was a mistake; the Prince is not *in a place to be diplomatic.*

My assessment is proven correct when our half-dressed leader gives him a feral grin. "You haven't had this kind of power within these walls in a long time. Dust-ups are bound to happen; there's no reason to pretend demons don't solve their problems with bloodletting."

"Good answer," I murmur to myself. "Keep him on the defensive, Jas."

My tails wrap more tightly around me as I look at Oriel and the bundle in his arms. He pulled Kit closer when the newcomers arrived, but the last thing we needed was for the Major to take notice of him. It's going to be hard enough to deal with this new side of him—especially since it appeared to be a very young shifter form that hadn't matured yet—without that fucker gunning for him.

I guess, given how much younger KK is than us, it's not surprising that he's manifesting that in his supernatural sides as well.

Making a note to do some research on late-emerging 'lost ones' and how their forms age compared to their previously humanoid bodies, I bite my lip. I hope that doesn't make it even harder to train him; the Games will wait for no one once the officials announce the date. We need to get him in basic fighting shape by then with every bit of power he can access. I make another mental note to check into the administrative files to ensure The Keeper requested that class change. Dottie is another source of strength Kit will need, and that guy is the only one who knows how to wrangle that.

When I come out of my jaunt in my mind, I notice Lucian is still fuming as he inspects the demons on the floor. I don't know if he berated Jasper more, but my prince looks as though he's handling the affront of such a weak demon dressing him down better than I expected. I don't know if that's the influence of Kit's request before or if it's the Major's presence, but I'm grateful, regardless. I can't exactly touch him in this situation or it will set off more sparks with his father when the asshole emissary puts it in his stupid reports.

The door opens again, flying wide hard enough that I expect the damn thing to come off of the hinges. The rest of my brothers enter with grim expressions except for Slash, who looks ready to eat the entire room even if he regurgitates it all in the end. Our general stomps so hard the fixtures rattle as he joins Jasper in facing Lucian and the visitor from court.

"What the fuck is going on in here?" he demands.

Shit. Slash is pissed—*like supercalifragilisticexpialidocious pissed. This is bad.*

"You don't have the right to speak to me in that tone, Scrum," Lucian growls. His ridiculous minions come out from behind him, fanning out a little as they present a threat to the enormous shark demon. "Know your place."

Oriel's voice is low, but I hear it. "Some people are so stupid that it's painful."

I chuckle, peeking out from my tails to get a good view of what comes next. X walks over, standing to my left, while Salem takes my right, and I sense Anton behind me. No one wants to miss this, especially because Darkstar has been a thorn in our sides since we arrived.

Slash's hand shoots out, grabbing our headmaster by the collar of his ridiculous ruffly shirt and lifts him into the air. The guy is huge, so when he extends his arm, Darkstar is easily ten feet off the ground with his legs scrambling as he makes noises of outrage. I watch as Slash allows just enough of his animal to bleed through that his teeth are sharper and more plentiful as he grins up at his prey. "My place in the food chain is well above yours. Do not test that fact."

The Major breaks the silence by clapping slowly, his face reflecting delight as he looks at our second-in-command. "*There's* the spirit of my leader and our King! Scrum, your father would be proud. *Never* let a weaker being control you, no matter why they believe they can."

Jasper snorts, and I feel the derision in him through our bond. He knows that both the King and the General happily smash anyone who questions them to bits. They don't admire displays like this; they make certain the person standing up is punished to within an inch of their life. That includes the prince and the general's son—and the Major knows it. He was part of the training those two endured for most of their lives to make them 'strong enough' to lead.

As if the King ever intends to allow that to happen.

"Put me down!" Darkstar yells, his voice changing from the faux haughty tone he usually affects to one that is panicked. "You will suffer the consequences of this insolence. I don't care what this demon says; you are in my school, not at Court. Your entire caliphate will learn to respect the authority of my office."

"Dude, no one has *less* power than someone backed into a corner that screams 'respect my authority' and threatens punishment like that."

"Lilith wept, Kit," I mutter as I slap my hand on my face in defeat. "Why?!"

Salem chuckles, putting a hand on my shoulder. "Because that dude is the biggest badass in this fucking *room*, Zav. Balls the size of boulders and not an ounce of self-preservation, but damn, he's brave."

"That will not help when—"

The Major stomps through the mess at his feet and around Slash. He gives the prince a dark look as he maneuvers past him to face Oriel and the bundle of uniform that just risked his hide to zing our asshat headmaster. "And who is this clever yet hidden demon?"

Jasper whirls around, looking at O and the rest of us in an infuriated panic. His dragon flashes in his eyes, then he grits his jaw, and it disappears. "That is our newest member, Major. He does not appear to be strong, but he is fiercely intelligent and clearly has the mettle you were describing earlier. Darkstar placed him on our floor despite his newness to the realm, and I could sense his potential immediately."

You could knock me on my ass with a feather right now, and I'm fairly certain that extends to my brothers as well.

"Interesting," the Major practically purrs. Slash's shoulders move at that sound, and I know it's a very bad sign. The shark is enjoying his taunting of Lucian far too much to be affected unless it's fucking terrible news. "I look forward to meeting this inductee, especially if he's the one your father spoke of at the Samhain."

"That's even worse," Anton says quietly. "You know what it means."

"However, if he's so brave and wise and has such *potential*... Tell me why he's balled up in a discarded uniform, hiding from the world during your victory, Prince Jasper? I find it so... *baffling*."

Lucian's body hits the ground with a bang that echoes through the common room as Slash turns to the emissary. His eyes are icy, and I see the struggle in them—it's akin to the one Jasper gets when he's fighting one or both of his supernatural sides for control. But Slash almost *never* has to fight for control, so this situation is going downhill fast.

"I do not believe my father or the King gave you orders to doubt the Prince of Hell's assessment."

"Slash..." That was Kit, and I curse under my breath as he draws attention to himself *again* instead of letting us handle this. The guy is determined to get himself killed, I fucking swear.

But The Major just stares creepily at the lump in Oriel's arms rather than doing anything.

"He'll never let someone threaten one of us without attempting to defend," Salem whispers. "It's not in his nature; he can't stop himself."

X sighs and tosses their hair over their shoulder. "It's true, Zav. KK pretends to be this prickly-ass fucker to protect himself, but that skin is something he developed. He wasn't born with it. Instinct always wins; you know that."

"Lions aren't particularly forgiving creatures," I reply in a low tone. "It's another part of him."

"Indeed," Anton agrees.

Finally, the demon's lips curve up in a dark smile, something that seems to make Slash even angrier. "Right you are, Prince Jasper. My job here is to qualify the competitors for the Games and report back to both of your fathers on the progress at Discordia. I feel I will have more information to relate as my stay continues—at least, if today's events are any indicator of the future."

Jasper snarls softly as The Major turns his gaze to Oriel. "You should get your brother to the doctor if he's injured, Bloodstone. Wouldn't want to give the impression that other than his mouth, he's weak."

That said, the Major looks over his shoulder at Lucian. The head is dusting himself off still, his pathetic minions helping to get the pieces of flesh and ick from the floor off his cape. "Take me to the arena, Darkstar. Of course, that's only if you're capable after the General's heir shook your brain out of your candyass."

Lucian gives my caliphate a sneer that promises retribution as the Major heads for the door. Great, now both of them are gunning for Kit, and we have no idea what they're going to do in retaliation.

Just what we needed.

Surprise, Surprise

Kit/Kat

All this drama is really fucking hard to follow when I feel like I've been hit by a damn building. I'm sleepy, achy, and my brain is so much slower than normal—even after I've had an episode. But I did the best I could to talk Jasper off the ledge when Oriel pleaded with me, and I stuck my nose in when Lucian was giving my guys shit. That definitely burned off what little energy I had to spare, but fortunately for me, O is now walking away from that scene with Dottie and me safely in his arms. I close my eyes as I feel him starting up the steps, and my body relaxes a bit when the sounds of the others following his lead hit my ears.

It might be okay to rest now—everyone is here and unharmed.

So I let myself drift, catching only the merest snatches of their conversation as the caliphate moves through our dorm to our floor.

At least, I think that's where we're going. I'll find out later.

⚜

My eyes flutter open, and I squint into the dark room as my vision slowly adjusts to the lack of light. I don't know if it's dark because the lights are off, the time of day, or both. To be honest, I don't actually care because as much as my head is throbbing, I think it's best that this is the atmosphere

I woke up in. I breathe in, then out, letting the calm vibe in the atmosphere settle into me as my mind comes into focus as well. I'm glad we're in what I'm pretty sure is the dorm room Salem and I share rather than a bay in the doc's office. I already saw him recently, and I haven't really had time to process the info he gave me about the guys' animals and demons regarding sex.

Dank wouldn't rat me out, but I feel ridiculous having to go in and out of there so often.

That's *my* hang-up, I know, but no matter how supportive and kind he is, it's hard to move past the judgment I felt at most medical offices after the incident. It's yet another layer of bullshit that came out of that damn night that pops up when I least need it to. People simply do *not* understand how many intricate, complex webs of trauma can result from a single event—medical, legal, parental, sexual, physical, emotional, therapeutic… The list goes on and on because up there, the system is set up to pretend to protect victims while it mostly re-abuses them.

I shift a bit, pushing the thoughts of the past away so I can focus on the here and now. The scent of incense or candles tickles my nose, and I inhale it, my lips curving up a little as it soothes me. Someone took great pains to make certain this space was set and maintained with care so that when I woke up, I'd feel safe and secure. My initial guess would be X, but after the recent behavior of O and Salem, it could have been them as well. Or maybe a combo…

"You're awake," a raspy voice under me murmurs, and my eyes widen.

How did I not realize I'm lying on someone? Who the fuck am I right now?

My frame tenses, and the arms around me tighten just a bit. "Careful. You've been in and out for a while, and you might not want to just jump up."

I move my head a bit, just a tiny shake, to clear the cobwebs and purposefully calm the atmosphere so I can identify who has me in their grasp. When I finally look up, I sigh with relief when I see Salem. Swallowing around my dry throat, I reply softly, "Two fucking days? Really?"

"Really," he says with a gentle smile. "We've taken turns being here to make sure you had what you needed, but no one missed too much class."

"The professors are going to give me such a hard time," I groan. "I keep missing classes for 'medical' shit."

The panda chuckles, his hand patting between my shoulder blades gently. "They won't. Not only do they know you're attending without powers—to their knowledge—but your bestie, Dr. D, personally visited them the morning after that damn fight."

"Dank went to my *teachers*?" I ask incredulously. "In person?"

Salem laughs again, his expression filled with mischief. "He did, and from what I understand from Zav, it was made crystal clear that any pressure placed on you for medical absences would be considered an affront to his position as royal physician. Zav said some of them looked like they were going to quit on the spot and hightail it the fuck off campus."

"I'll be damned."

"We all will, KK, but not because you somehow gained one of the scariest fuckers I know as your ally." I frown at him, not agreeing that Dank is scary in the slightest. "I know he's acting like a kindly old man with you, but trust me... that demon is *terrifying* to most people, even Jasper."

Jasper probably deserves it; I can see him giving Dank shit for no good reason.

"Now, now," Salem says as he shifts me a bit in his arms. "Don't get feisty. You're not ready for that yet. Two days is a good start to handling what happened, but it's not enough. It will take a couple more days for you to be at normal strength and to process this."

His words make my panic rise, and I lift my head this time, looking him directly in the eyes. "What do you mean, 'what happened'? What will I need to process, Salem? I know I sort of blacked out, but... what happened when I lost time?"

"Oh shit," he mutters as he takes in my rigid posture. "You don't... Fuck, man. I've never heard of anyone forgetting when—damn, damn, damn."

That doesn't help me at all, and my breaths come faster, signaling the need for me to get a grip on myself before this escalates. "Five fingers I see.. four windows covered..."

"KK..." the panda demon says as he takes my hands in his. "Look at me. You are safe, and nothing *bad* happened while you were out. At least, not to *you.*"

I pause in the slight rocking motion I was using to soothe as I listed things. "Then why... Why did you seem so freaked out?"

A dark, rumbling voice at my back answers for him. "Because you shifted for the first time in public and the lion inside of you was going to tear Queznar to pieces for his insolence."

Swallowing around the lump in my throat, I turn to see Jasper standing there, shirtless and barefoot as he stares at me. "L-lion? Shifted? Like… you guys? That's my…?"

The prince shrugs as he drops to the floor in front of our chair, sitting cross-legged so he's at the same level as my face. That alone is fucking weird, but I don't have the bandwidth to snark at him about that right now. "It's one of your abilities, yes. Is it the only one besides your demonic blood? I don't believe so, but we have no idea at this point. I do know that Zavida and I have discussed it at length, and we believe that your shift, though late in your life, has manifested in a juvenile form because your demonic lifespan will be long like ours."

My brows furrow as I ask, "You're saying I'm a baby demon and my lion is a baby, too?"

Jasper actually snorts, then shrugs at me. "Perhaps not a *baby*, shrimp. But younger than us by far, obviously." He arches a brow, his smirk deepening as he looks me in the eye. "You *do* understand that despite our appearance being that of college-aged humans, we're *much* older than that in human years, yes? Compared to ancient demons, we're at this stage of life, but to humans, we'd be dust by now."

Of course, I knew they were much older by the way they talked about things and the way human history is taught to the freshmen, but I didn't ask because… that makes all of this even more real?

Huffing, I look back at Salem. "Why does he seem so determined to think I'm stupid?"

"I don't know, KK. You've been obviously intelligent since I met you." The panda chuckles as he pats my back again. "Though, to be fair, Jasper treats *most* demons like they're beneath him in some way or another. It's how the asshole in the big chair raised him. He's better now than he was when we first met as kids, though."

"Oh fab," I retort wryly. "So in another… thousand or so years… he'll realize I'm no less capable than you guys?"

The prince's lips twitch, and I can tell he *wants* to laugh, but refuses to allow himself to. Instead, he coughs. "I don't believe you're intellectually inferior, shrimp. You're simply not educated about demons, Hell, and the world you now live in. I have to assume you don't know things, so you're not missing important context if that's the case."

"Awfully big words for 'I act like you're a rube on purpose', Prince."

He scowls at me, opening his mouth and then, like magic, he stops the insult I know was coming. Sucking an annoyed breath in through his nose, Jasper breathes out slowly and then turns back to me. "Zav set this room up for maximum comfort and the feeling of balance and safety. Arguing with you will defeat his intentions, and I don't want to do that to him. It was important to him that you awaken in a non-stressful environment, so you could process this without fear."

I arch a brow, surprised that it was the Kitsuné who did this and even *more* surprised that Jasper is honoring his wishes despite his absence. "Why?"

Rolling his eyes, Jasper shrugs, looking irritable. "I don't know; he's soft like that. Zav didn't have the best emergence with his animal, unlike most of us. While our parents were disappointed with the lack of full blood sometimes, none of them were as furious with the animal we gained other than his. He wanted to make sure you didn't have one of those panic things or whatever."

Jasper Eversore, Prince of Hell, and my eternal fucking critic… did all this to make someone else happy.

You could shoot me with a damn arrow and I wouldn't feel it through the shock running in my veins right now. Something ridiculously important happened down there besides my stupid animal coming out at the worst possible moment, and I really want to know what it was. However, I think this is probably stretching the limit of Jasper's ability to be nice as it is, and I will not risk fucking up Zav's kindness by pissing him off until he breaks. So I tuck that question away for later, knowing that Xerxes, Salem, or Oriel will answer for me in private—I hope.

"Why do I need a couple more days here out of the public eye?"

The Prince sighs with relief when I don't push him on the emotional stuff, his expression clearing up. "Because the first time you shift, your body has to get adjusted to it. You went in and out pretty quickly, which is harder on you; hence, the two-day coma. However, we *have* to work with you on how to do it on *purpose* now that people have seen it, and how to *prevent* it when you don't want to do it. Otherwise, you're going to be exposed to much more dangerous attacks by people who expect you to know what the fuck you're doing."

"Knowing how to talk your animal down in high emotional settings is something that will take time, though," Salem interjects. "It's difficult to gain their trust, and even harder when your animal is known for a volatile nature… like, say, a *dragon*."

Jasper glares at him murderously, and I feel the air shimmer. "Shut up, Salem. You know damn good and well I have to deprogram him from the way they raised me. I've spent decades unlearning the things I had to do to survive there and—" He stops, taking a deep breath and grits out, "But this is not the time for that. He is correct about needing to work with your animal versus against when possible. The latter is quite difficult and will drain you until you have more strength built up."

"What you're saying is that you guys arranged the rest of the week off via Dank so it would flow into the weekend to help learn this? Is that what I'm hearing?"

Jasper grins toothily for a second, then nods. "Yes, Kit. You're going to spend a *lot* of time with us in the gym, starting with the fucker with the absolute most control I know."

It doesn't take a genius to figure out who that is, and if Jasper thinks it's disappointing, he's a fool.

Bury Me Face Down

Jasper

This morning, I'm feeling *extremely* pleased despite the upset yesterday. When the rest of my caliphate trickled into Salem's dorm for dinner, the shrimp was doing better and his mood was stable. That alone meant my brothers were happy, and Zavvie was very grateful for my beneficence when we retired to my room for the night. All that good vibes shit allowed me to wake up with less weight on my shoulders, even though I realize this bubble won't last.

Between the crown, the games, and Darkstar, the world will go to shit again soon enough.

However, for the moment, I'm showered, sexed, and fed, which makes my entire cadre of beings inside calm. Our caliphate meeting after we ate last night went more smoothly than usual, and we could come up with an amenable schedule for us to keep tabs on the resting kid in his dorm. Zav is staying with him to eat and get dressed for the first two hours, but Kit will be alone with Dottie and his phone for the next class session. I didn't like that idea, but Oriel insisted he might need some time to himself, and when the others agreed, I was outvoted. Normally, that would piss me off, but the look on the shrimp's face made me back down and consent.

I look over at my brothers as they finish their meals, asking. "At lunch, Oriel will join him until the full block is over. Correct?"

The crow demon nods, wiping his mouth. "Yep. I'll bring him some snacks from the store as well, though I doubt Salem's cabinets and fridge are empty."

"As if, birdbrain," Salem retorts as he smirks. "KK has plenty of food and drink to make sure he's feeding that expanded hunger from shifting."

I nod, pleased with his efforts. "Good. Anton will take over for the next block since O has a free period, and that will give him time to snoop in his crow form. He can check out our recent visitor and our old enemy."

"I plan to dig until I find the dirt; trust me." Oriel grimaces as he pushes his tray back. "There are definitely things we need to know that we haven't located yet, and I intend to find them."

"The next slot is mine," Slash interjects firmly. "The little demon is recovering, but since many of the first-year students will be in your Weapons class, I will guide him to the gym to work on strength and shift. It will not be as fast as you wish, I believe, but I *will* get him trained, Prince."

The forceful way he says that makes me believe, but there's more to Slash's insistence; I just don't know what.

"Excellent," I murmur as I watch him closely. "Anton and Oriel will escort him back to the dorm for dinner since they are free in the next block of time. They will await our return there, and we will make sure the shrimpy has his make-up work for the study session. Anything he finishes, we will divvy up to turn in the next day. Got it?"

Salem frowns, grumbling into his coffee. "I hate that this is two of my packed days and I don't get a shift, but I know we have to maintain a presence here at lunch to make sure no one oversteps."

Chuckling, Slash claps him on the back. "You share a room with Kit, old friend. That gives you plenty of time to catch up if need be. Do not fret about being left out."

I give my second an odd look, then shake my head. He's so fucking weird about Kit. "Right. Plus, we'll all have dinner and study time before bed. We can break up Friday's shifts then as well."

"I don't get a shift, either," Xerxes says as they shrug. "Life is rarely fair, but we will survive."

He doesn't look *like he's fine with it, but his words say differently.*

"Everyone needs to switch off their 'worry for the injured' bullshit and switch *on* the suspicion of everything lever," I say firmly as I stare at them from the head of the table. "Without Kit in the mix, we will *all* be able to listen, watch, and learn as much as possible during the day. There's no limit to what we can glean when we are laser-focused on the task; I expect results when we reconvene at lunch and dinner. Got it?"

X sighs heavily, flicking their long hair over their shoulder in irritation. "Yes, Your Highness. We *live* to serve."

I frown, narrowing my eyes at the cobra demon. "Snark is unhelpful. If we want to survive the Games and keep the shrimp safe, this is not only important, but *necessary*. Use powers or strategies you would normally reserve for emergencies only if you must."

Anton arches a brow as he stands, picking up his tray as he looks at me seriously. "You'd like us to tap into the lineage abilities? For recon and surveillance? Is that not overkill?"

"The Major was chuffed yesterday because he humiliated Lucian. He will be less easy to control in other situations. It is warranted, especially if he fixates on the little demon." Slash's expression is full of suppressed anger, and expressing it here and now is not normal for him. He wants us all to know that we *must* do things that are not usually our modus operandi in day-to-day life.

"Kit will be unhappy with that," X says softly. Of all of us, their hidden gifts are the most intrusive and boundary-crossing. They will have to explain the use of those powers to our injured brother, and it will not be fun. "He might not mind Jasper, Slash, Oriel, or Salem's skills. However, Zav, Annie, and I have more… emotionally manipulative gifts that will leave marks on our prey."

I nod, understanding their concern, but before I can respond, Anton cuts me off. "Yes, love, that is true, but he will understand that we need to do it to protect him and each other. Our enemies are vaster than we assumed at the start of this year, and the schemes have crossed borders to other realms. It is simply foolish to waste our most coveted abilities when we are trying to ensure the safety of our caliphate, Hell, and the rest of the realms."

I couldn't have said it better myself—it's bigger than a handful of demons being coerced, especially if we want to stay ahead of the bad guys.

Once we parted ways outside the *Triclinium*, I headed straight for the arena. Tuesdays and Thursdays are a mix of various-level Weapons classes with a few graduate-level classes of my own. They're packed tightly, and like Xerxes, I have no room to go back to check on the shrimp either. I'm not sure why that bothers me, but I suppose it's because I prefer everything within my sphere of control. Kit in his room, injured and occasionally on his own, feels like a risk. I don't like it, but I also cannot skip anything with that motherfucker from the court on campus. Yesterday was bad enough, but at least he determined that we were victorious.

That report should keep my father from lashing out from his gilded throne room—I think.

The quad is busy despite the early hour, and I attribute it to the Major's presence. Every demon is rushing to their classes, not dawdling for fear of being late when the ancient soldier or his minions show up. There are always a few poor souls who end up being made an example of, and I'm sure there will be a bloody scene in that vein soon. The Major lives to strike fear in the hearts of his men, and he can't strut around campus if he doesn't put his money where his mouth is.

"Probably going to happen in one of my fucking classes," I mutter to myself as I speed up when I get close to my destination. "That would be a double lesson, meant to prove that my father has blessed whatever he's here to do. Fuck."

I don't give a shit about random demons at Discordia; the General's pet commander can do whatever he wants to them. However, after lunch I have the 101 block that Oriel, Xerxes, Anton, Zavida, and Salem are in. The shrimp should be there, too, but luckily, he's on granted leave because the royal physician favors the little shit. I've yet to be glad for that quirk of Fate so far, but now? I'm fucking *chuffed* that the old demon likes Kit so much. That will save him from seeing what I believe will be a seriously terrible display in that class this afternoon.

Of course, it might gain him a buddy in the dorm if people get hurt—which is almost guaranteed if the Major shows.

When I enter the tunnel, the noise coming from the field is noticeably absent, and I groan internally. My first session is a second-level training block, and the returning students are usually chatting as they change. I almost always have to shut them up to start, but the silence echoing in this hall is deafening. Even if I'm right about our guest later today, *someone* in authority is out there, and I will have to deal with them when I emerge. My tail swishes as I psych myself up, moving from concern about my caliphate to detached royal asshole in seconds.

"Ah, there you are, Prince Jasper! I wondered briefly if you might set a poor example by being late to your own class." Darkstar's voice is like claws on a chalkboard, but I don't let it show as I stride out onto the field.

Arching a brow, I check my phone to see that I'm five minutes early as planned. "Perhaps you need Beccarus to wind your watch, Lucian. The hour has not yet passed, and I am early—admittedly, less than is my normal routine, but not late in the slightest."

The icy blond is dressed all in black like a fucking pirate with that stupid cape swirling around his ankles in the morning wind. The scent in the air tells me there's a sandstorm in the Wastes sending the breeze this way, and our headmaster is heartily enjoying the theatrical effect it gives his ridiculous attire. No wonder my father and all the Court leaders scoff at this dumbass —he's more a cartoon villain than a serious threat.

Or he was until he found a bunch of other losers to latch onto; now he's dangerous by association, and I hate it.

"If I didn't know better, I'd say that was insolence." Lucian's eyes glitter as he shoots a knowing smirk at me. He knows the emissaries from Court could pop in, and I can't shoot back a retort as safely as I could before they arrived. "However, I choose to believe you did not consume enough coffee in that dreadful cafeteria instead."

"That cafeteria is run by you," a voice mutters in the crowd, and Darkstar whips around with murder in his eyes.

"*Who* said that?" No one responds, and he flicks the cape over his shoulders as he strides toward the gathering of second years menacingly. "Come now. If you had the rocks to say it, claim it, gentlemen. Don't be so weak and predictable."

A hand raises, and I groan, looking up at the sky. That demon is from one of my father's favored houses within our line, and though I agree it was brave, the kid doesn't have the power or skill to go up against the head like this. "I did, sir."

Before Lucian can open his mouth, I stomp over and roar, "Laps! *Now!* Being disrespectful to the headmaster of the college is not acceptable in this arena. You'll run until you cannot move or I will find a better punishment, Irascus!" The kid looks at me wide-eyed, but he takes off running toward the circle around the arena as instructed. "That goes double for the rest of you slugs. Now get moving on warm-ups!"

Once my students are occupied, I turn back to Lucian. He's observing me, like a spider with a fly. It would be funny under most circumstances; his power isn't remotely close to my own. He's not a threat—in that way. But he has power and sycophants in other places, and I don't need to piss him off enough to send one of those ridiculous office demons scuttling after my brothers in my absence.

"Excellent discipline, Eversore. You've quite a hold on your students."

I snort, rolling my eyes as I watch the class warming up. "Good order and respect often breed loyal soldiers—that's something the General and the Major taught when we grew up at the palace."

With sharp blades, powerful fists, hot pokers, darkness, captivity, and punishments that haunt me, but fuck if I'm going to tell him that.

Sharks

Kit/Kat

When Anton left me for Weapons class, I only had a few minutes to myself to get changed into something suitable for the gym. The plans made last night regarding who would stay with me had left me panicking, but luckily, X crept back to my dorm after the others left with a large bag full of uniforms and other clothing they'd ordered when we last spoke about my… predicament. It didn't have *everything* I needed, but I have five new binders and boxers to wear under the uniforms so I'm not wrapping myself in the gauze I got from Dank.

That shit is hot and painful after a while—I owe Xerxes big time.

However, a session with Slash in the training gym means I'll probably get near water—he was quite firm in his request to show me his animal, and I believe that his smirk when Jasper gave him the assignment conveyed that it's time. I'm nervous as fuck—for many reasons, including no experience with killer sea life and because if I get in the water, I may have to admit my secret. I chose dark shorts, boxers, and two tees with my sweatpants, but that may not be enough. Slash is no fool, and he's quite observant when he's paying attention; sometimes, he is even when he's *not* paying attention. I won't be able to keep this from him if I get in the pool.

Truthfully, I'm not sure I *want* to. The big guy had been a quiet supporter for a while and started treating me with respect pretty quickly once he was away from Jasper's influence. He's even spoken up in person a few times now, despite the prince's scowls of disapproval. I think he'll stay in my corner when I explain how I came here in disguise and why I kept it a secret once I was inducted. Jasper's insistence that I'm a spy is a big part of that, but the opportunity to get away from my old life being yanked away is the largest portion.

Slash knows my life up there was shit, and I think he'll get why I couldn't risk it.

Salem, X, and Oriel have understood; I'm pretty sure Annie will, too. Zav is a toss-up because of his co-dependence on Jasper, but I have faith that he's working to be stronger. I mean, mostly, and I can't very well criticize him for waffling when I'm hiding shit, right? I frown as that thought muddies my normal concrete boundaries and expectations. Since I began admitting the truth to the guys and getting to know other sides of them, my hard lines have softened slightly. I may have been *too* demanding of people because of my assault trauma and the behavior of everyone who didn't support me. Though, to be fair, I had to protect myself when no one else was willing to.

Now I'm here, with enemies abound, and seven guys who are equally damaged. Most of them are exceeding their own trauma-informed boundaries to be respectful, and I have to give them the same courtesy. There are requirements I won't bend on, of course, but that's normal. Healing together is what caliphates *should* do based on all that ritual and brotherhood shit, right?

"We're here."

I blink, looking around to find that Slash is entirely correct—we are at the double doors to the training gym. He had my arm and led me across campus, into a building, in an elevator, and to this very spot while I stayed lost in my goddamn thoughts. I can't remember the last time I was transported from one place to the next while *conscious* without being aware of my surroundings every step of the way. Yet I trusted this huge dude to do so, without my brain screaming in protest even once.

He has to be okay with this or I'm definitely going to freak out.

"I… Did you just walk me here without saying a word so I could just think?" I ask as I look up at the shark demon.

Slash tilts his head, then nods. "Yes. You were very focused, and I believed it to be a good thing that you were not worrying about the whispers and looks. Was I incorrect?"

"Fuck, no," I mutter as I flush bright red. "I didn't need to see all the people staring at me; I'm self-conscious enough as it is. And… because I hear more now…"

"That was my opinion as well, little demon." He grins briefly and lets go of my arm to push the doors open. "You did not require all that pressure their stupid gossip would have put on you. It is a sensitive time when you first shift; hearing people make stupid commentary on it is not useful to your progress."

I walk in behind him, looking around the room to make certain we're alone. "I'd argue that petty gossip is *never* useful and *always* something that should wave a red flag about the person spreading it. Someone who talks nastily about others *to* you will absolutely talk to people *about* you in the same manner when given the chance. It's why bullying victims are often quiet, while the abusers are waving their ass at everyone who will listen."

This time, his smile is feral and filled with teeth. "We have ways of dealing with people like you describe, little demon. Trust me when I assure you that karma is coming for them soon enough."

Slash's ominous threats are growing on me—they're making me feel safe. How very odd.

Chuckling as he guides me over to a door at the back of the wooden floor, I reply, "I've always sort of subscribed to karma coming for the bad guys, even when the legal shit failed up there. It might take a while, and it might not be *me* who serves the dish, but it will get served cold to those who earn it. You sort of have to believe that a little bit when you live on the surface because so *many* things are fucking broken and unfair; otherwise, you'd go mental."

The smell of sulfur hits my nose, and I frown as he takes me through a locker room I haven't been in yet to a door with a small window in it. When I push up on my toes to look through it, I see a huge swimming pool sparkling in the afternoon light from the ceiling-high windows. Making a face as the smell increases, I turn to him. "What the hell is that scent, man? It's awful."

"Give it a few moments, and you'll adjust. This is common of springs in Hell—sulfur is part of the makeup. You don't realize it, and I doubt anyone mentioned it to you, but there are *many* Hell-specific smells that you have already adjusted to. Your body was doing it from the moment Dr. D let you out of the car and took you to Darkstar. This one is just considered bad on the surface, and so your body and mind are at war in classifying it."

I give him a disbelieving look, but move back so Slash can open the door to the swimming... spring, I suppose. "You're supposed to teach me about shifting. This is so you can hit two imps with one stone, right?"

The sheepish look on his face is adorable, and I have to restrain myself from hugging him. "Well… I… Yes, I wanted to… Fuck, little demon, I just wanted to do this. Is that okay?"

It's very okay that he looks so ruffled and squeezable as he tries to stutter his way through the explanation.

My body warms from head to toe, and I nod, looking up through my lashes shyly. "Of course, Slash. I said I wanted to see your animal, and I meant it. And I definitely need to learn how to work with mine before I do something stupid again. I was only teasing."

His face lights up, and he coughs as he gestures at the water. "That is a Hell-spring, and it is very good for demons to soak in. It is for recreation, healing, power-gathering, and more. They are usually good, but being able to identify ones that have been tampered with is also a skill you may need in the Games. Ones that are not are also good for drinking, though your nose is probably saying they are not."

"No shit," I say as I wave my hand in front of my face. "This adjustment thing needs to kick in soon. It went from sulfur to sewer a minute ago."

Slash chuckles as he watches me shudder. "Give it time, Kit. Patience is a virtue—that's what your people say, right?"

I snort. "They may *say* it, but they sure as fuck don't believe it at any stage. But I get what you mean; let it happen naturally and just calm down. Right?"

"Yes," he replies with a grin. "I am going to remove my shirt and sweats now so I can dive in. Is that okay with you?"

My heart squeezes as he asks permission, when he damn well knows I've been in the bathroom and locker rooms with them half-naked before. Slash is kinder than he gets credit for and more emotionally intelligent than his brothers are aware of. "Yes, big guy. You can strip to get in the pool. I think I can handle it."

He dips his chin, and I swear to fuck, I see a slight tint of redness on his cheeks. Making a dude this enormous and lethal blush has my entire body responding in girlish glee, and I step back. If he's shifting, his senses will sharpen, and despite my Dank potion, I remember his warning to be cautious around their demons and animals. As Slash tugs his shirt over his head with one hand, I swallow hard from the spot I backed into, and curse the dryness in my mouth when words get stuck.

Being in this pool area alone with him differs greatly from the other two situations. He's tattooed all over under his clothes, and though I noticed it before, I wasn't really *looking*. In fact, I was so busy trying *not* to look or look like I was looking… that I missed how fucking cut he is. Okay, I know they're super muscle-y and hotter than shit, but this is… different? Seeing Slash's intricate and likely painful tattoos that dip down his abs to the deep 'V' at the low waistband of his shorts is making me feel lots of things, and I'm having a lot of trouble parsing it all.

"Okay, little demon. I am ready to dive in." He looks at me for a moment, and I worry that he's figured out I'm ogling him. But then he just says, "You will need to come back where you can see and hear better. That is too far. Have I scared you? If so, I will—"

"No!" I blurt out as my body rushes forward without consulting my brain. "No, I'm sorry. It was knee-jerk, not about you. Tell me about what you're going to do. Talk me through it, step by step."

He blinks, his brow furrowing. "That will be very difficult. I have not had to *think* about shifting for so long that your country wasn't even founded yet."

There's the confirmation that these guys are really fucking old in human years and still not old in demon lifespan in a way that I cannot ignore.

Thanks for making it weird, big guy.

"Never say that again," I grumble as I rub my palms on my arms. "I know it's true logically, but my brain still isn't ready to wrap around the fact that demons are like centuries old when they graduate college because that's how damn long you live without dying in suspicious circumstances."

Slash winks at me, tilting his head as his eyes sparkle. "We are all certainly old enough to be so far back in your family tree that it was a seedling—and by you, I mean humans, not whomever your biological relations are."

"Stop that," I hiss as I stomp closer and smack him on the chest. "It's so fucking weird."

"But I enjoy your outrage, little demon. It tickles my funny bone for you to be so incensed about our age. I am not sure if it's because of human teachings or something else, but it's amusing."

My eyes narrow, and I poke the enormous demon in the chest despite it being bare. "Don't tease me about this or I'll… I'll…."

"You'll what?" he asks with his brow raised and teeth glinting in the light.

A bolt of inspiration hits me, and I feel a very Grinch-like smirk curl my lips up. "I will call you 'Daddy Shark' and introduce the song with that in it to the entire caliphate—starting with Salem and Oriel."

He snorts. "I highly doubt that, little demon. I don't know this song, but you will not use that phrase in public. It will embarrass you far too much. I see things you do not think I see."

Keep telling yourself that, Daddy Shark. I'm a petty bitch when I've been challenged.

Jaws
Slash

I don't understand why the little demon is so adamant about denying our age difference, but humans raise their children with extremely bizarre hang-ups.

Kit is over their legal age, and my brothers and I are well over Hell's regulations; there's nothing odd about our association. Of course, I don't know that discussing Hell's laws and rules with him will engender any better responses as they're… lax, at best. But demons see things in ways that humans do not, and it is our nature to err on the side of darkness versus light. Kit hasn't been here long enough to see the entire picture of this realm, but he won't like a lot of it when he does.

I fear most demons cannot live up to the code he created for himself after his assault.

But at this moment, I'm too nervous to have a philosophical debate about what is good and what is bad, especially regarding things like age that cannot be changed. My shark *and* my demon are both eager to connect with him, to show themselves to this new person who has become a central figure in our lives. I stretch up on my toes, cracking my neck as I prepare for the shift when I hit the water, then I look down at my little demon.

"Are you ready?"

Kit nods, stepping back from where he was aggressively crowding me to make his point. "I think so. Is it weird that I have vague ideas in my head based on… like movies and stuff? And I don't know how the real thing will compare?"

"No," I say firmly. "It's not weird, as I'm certain you have ideas about crows or pandas or cobras or peacocks, yes?"

He gives me a grateful smile as he sighs. "Yeah, and they were all very different. I mean, you guys can get way bigger, and there's like the half-shift thing, and um…"

I arch a brow as I tease gently, "We can chat about it or I can do it. Which would you prefer?"

"Oh!" His eyes widen and he waves his hand. "No, go do it. Um, yeah. Let's make it happen or whatever."

Chuckling, I wink at him and then dive into the Hellspring, letting my half-shift happen as I swim through the rejuvenating waters. When I bust through the surface, my face has changed: my teeth are in sharp rows, and my mouth is wider while my features mirror that of my great white. Kit gulps as he looks up to see me—I'm much bigger in this form, and I'm not a small demon to begin with.

"Holy fish sticks, Sharkman," the little demon says as he nervously shifts from foot to foot. "You're so fucking enormous right now. It's like… it's hard to even imagine this. But I guess I could have… Jasper is pretty fucking big in half-dragon, too."

The sound my laughter makes in this form is a raspy rustle that makes ripples across the surface of the pool as I submerge myself so I'm on his level. Only my head is sticking out of the water now, and that makes it much easier to breathe and control myself as Kit stares. "The others can get bigger than they've shown you. We are all being careful not to overload you, Kit. No one wants you to *fear* their animal or demon; in fact, that may be our worst nightmare. Being part of our caliphate means you must trust us, and if we frighten you, that will never happen."

"I hate being so defective," he grumbles as he scuffs his shoe on the ground. "Okay, let's do this. Give me the full monte and don't hold back. I have to see it to believe it, you know? I don't want to be shocked into an attack if this happens in the Games."

The little demon is far braver than he gives himself credit for.

"I will go under and return as the animal." The moment I relay my intent, I duck under the tingling spring water and allow my shark to emerge for the first time in weeks. I have not had the time to come and swim with all the upheaval, and he is *eager* to be free, especially with Kit here. Swimming toward the edge of the spring with my huge fin sticking out of the water, I wait for his reaction to bounce off the water so I can hear it.

"A bigger boat isn't gonna do it," Kit says, and when it gets to me, I have to hold back a laugh. "I'm gonna need lots of bigger things. But… courage isn't the absence of fear, but triumph over it."

I don't know why he said that, but it sounds like a quote. Perhaps Zavida will tell me later, but for now, I swim even closer to where he is. Being three times larger than a normal shark has probably scared the shit out of him, and I'm going to feel the vibrations of him running for the hills and slamming the door soon. My assumption proves to be false when a yell of 'Cowabunga!' echoes off the spring water and a body comes flying into the pool nearby.

He's getting in the fucking pool with me? Really?!

Stunned beyond belief, I keep swimming—that's what sharks do—but I wait to see what is going to happen next. My animal weighs over eighty tons, and I maneuver very well in large open waters, but not so much in this pool. It's large, but not large enough for me to be comfortable in for too long.

"Slash?" The water ripples as Kit swims closer, and my animal flicks our tail like an excited puppy as I sense him getting closer. Suddenly, there are arms draped over me and fingertips touching my skin lightly. "Damn, this is cool. I guess you don't talk in this form cuz of the water, and since I don't breathe under there like you, we're limited. But, um… if you can hear me, this is so, so, so fucking cool. I mean, I've barely even been to the zoo at home, and I'm swimming with a shark as big as a fucking dinosaur!"

The relief that floods through me is immense, and it enables me to push back on the shark enough to return to my half-shifted form. Kit squeaks when he goes from holding on to the shark to me, and I let out the rusty chuckle again. "I wanted to talk, little demon."

"Um… yeah. Yeah, that's good. I mean, I get it."

He looks panicked now, and I tilt my head in confusion. Is he less comfortable with the half-humanoid, half-shark than with the giant animal? That seems very odd. I do not understand why that would be. "Are you okay? I did not expect you to jump in, but I feel very pleased that you trusted me enough to do so."

The little demon looks around, then bites his lip as he frowns. "I…"

"Tell me. I will not judge you if this form is difficult for you to be around—"

"No!"

I blink at his vehement response. "Okay. But you appear to be close to panicking, and I do not want that. Perhaps I went too quickly and you need me to slow down."

Kit makes a frustrated sound and then he swims backward away from me as he rakes his lower lip through his teeth. Once I see he's treading water well, even in our demonic spring, I float quietly while he gathers his thoughts. Finally, he gives me a sad expression, and it makes my heart stop in my chest. "Slash, I have to tell you something. I've been hiding something, and well… in this situation, I won't be able to do that anymore. I… I haven't told *everyone* yet because I need to trust them a lot to feel safe doing it. And, um… I feel like I can tell you now."

My visage melts fully into humanoid as I look at him in concern. Whatever this is, it's very important to him, and I need my judgement to be unclouded by my animal so I can respond. "As long as it's not that Jasper was right about you being a spy for Darkstar, I do not believe it will change anything."

He blinks and shakes his head, his short hair flipping water at me as he does so.

"No, no! Not that—*never* that."

I grin toothily, relief flooding me yet again as I look at him. "Thank fuck. He would have been completely obnoxious if his ridiculous claim were true. No one would have been able to be around him for at least a decade without that coming up. I'm not prepared to live through something that irksome once more."

Kit frowns, arching a brow. "It's happened before?"

"We're ancient, little demon—*many* things have happened before. But yes, we have disagreed on additions to the caliphate in the past who did not turn out to be suitable. Unfortunately, the prince is right more often than he's wrong, and he is not a gracious winner."

"*Shocker*," he says as he grins a bit. "But that isn't the secret, and I'm going to hold you to the promise that nothing else will be a big deal."

I shrug. "I would not have said that if it were not true. Tell me your secret."

"I'm not a guy."

My brows furrow, and I consider that for a second before I shrug again. "Okay."

"*That's it?* Okay? That's all you have to say?!" Kit's eyes widen as he gives me a genuinely surprised look, and I meet his gaze without guile.

"Yes. Did you want me to have a more dramatic reaction or be upset?"

The puzzled expression only gets worse, and suddenly, he's darting at me in the water until we're within centimeters of one another. "You do realize I mean... biologically, right? Like I'm a girl? With boobs? And... other things."

I snort before I can stop it, and Kit frowns harder. Once I am back in control of myself, I look down at him earnestly. "I don't know why you think I would be upset about this. More concerned, yes, and definitely many things make more sense than they did before, but... I am absolutely not mad in the slightest. Curious how and why, maybe, but... not mad. No matter what physical features you possess, you belong to our caliphate, and that is sacred."

"Oh," he says, and his chin drops as his eyes fix on the murky waters of the spring. "That makes sense, I suppose. I'm a... brother or I guess... a sister now? So you're good with me because we're all bonded and stuff."

Kit being a girl has not made his reactions and emotions any easier to decipher.

"Little demon, that's not why it's okay, nor is what makes more sense to me." His eyes skate up my chest to my face, and he waits for me to continue quietly. "Knowing that you are a girl makes the pull from my shark and my demon toward you classifiable. I have not been attracted to men prior, and you drew them so completely. Now I understand why every ounce of my focus cuts to you the moment you enter a room or speak. I would have adjusted eventually were you *not* a girl, but this is *much* less to figure out."

"Huh?"

He looks confused, and I chide myself internally for being unclear. "Kit Camponella, my animal and my demon find you mesmerizing, and since I have not been attracted to men before, I was very confused. I would have learned the right things and followed my instincts had you been male, but *not* being male is much less confusing to me."

"Slash, are you saying you wanted to kiss a boy and didn't know what to do about it?"

"I suppose that is accurate, no matter how odd it feels for you to say it out loud."

Kit ducks his head and murmurs, "Would you like to kiss a girl instead?"

I have the feeling some of my brothers have been doing more than studying with our femme in disguise, and I'm going to thump them.

Together
Kit/Kat

I can not believe I just said that. What possessed me to—

Before I can continue my packed thought train, Slash's arms gently pull me closer and his face descends to press a very soft, surprisingly hesitant kiss to my lips. I swallow hard when he pulls back a bit to look at me with a shy smile despite his sharp teeth.

"Like that?"

I nod, gathering my brain cells so I can respond. "Yes. Um, exactly like that."

The big guy's hands are settled on my waist, and because I'm soaking wet, it's easy to feel the chill coming off of him. It's probably from the shifting and the water. Dank's pamphlets were full of descriptions of how shifters—particularly strong ones—keep some characteristics of their animals in human form for a time after they turn back. Sharks aren't mammals, so Slash is cold when he's usually warm as fuck. "I should… I should also admit something that I have not said out loud before. To anyone, I mean, even Jasper."

Huh? Oh, this is going to get me in so much trouble if anyone finds out.

"Are-are you sure? I mean, you've only known me for a couple of months and, um… they've been your friends forever. Maybe one of the actual guys is the right person to share with. I'm not—"

Placing one finger over my mouth, he gives me what I think is a fond expression. "Little demon, this is none of their business. But as of now, it *is* yours, and therefore, I want to tell you the truth because I trust you with it. We are equals in this, and now that I have your secret, you should have mine."

"Oh," I say softly, feeling heat rise in my face. "Well, I guess it's okay then."

Slash lifts his finger from my lips and runs his hand through his wet hair as he sighs. "They do not know because… I have been diligent in threatening, cajoling, and scaring the living fuck out of anyone who might have a clue so it did not escape containment. I didn't do so because I am ashamed, but rather because there are… expectations of me from many sources. If I were not living up to them, it would have caused more trouble than it was worth. Yet, I could not force myself to live for others and not myself."

I frown, my brows furrowing. "Slash, you said you're *not* attracted to guys, but this really feels like a coming out speech. And… I'm definitely not judging you for being bi or pan or… well, anything. You're a scary motherfucker, but there's a big heart in there. I've seen it in how you take care of people. Whatever this is? It doesn't make me like you any less. I don't think the guys would care either, but whatever you need, I'll help."

He lets out a sharp, rusty chuckle, and I know that's his animal pushing at him. I don't know exactly what his demon sounds like, but I bet it will be different, too. Slash is a unique man, and I'm lucky he's being so candid with me. Shaking his head as his amusement wanes, he says, "No, Kit. I was telling the truth before. I do not need to be ashamed about who I like or don't, but… I am expected to behave like a royal male and the son of the most powerful soldier in Hell. If I didn't, both my father and the King would question us."

"Uh-huh," I say as I look at him skeptically. "Well, you and Jasper are the big bads, and everyone knows it, so I think you've done a good job. It's not a secret to me, though. I'm smart enough to realize when the two of you are performing for a crowd rather than showing your true selves."

Slash arches a brow, smirking. "Good to know, but that *also* isn't the secret."

Getting frustrated, I thump his chest with my fist as I growl, "Oh, for fuck's sake. Tell me and rip off the bandage. Are you engaged to some court bootlicker back home? Do you have a weird lump I haven't seen? Is your favorite porn about licorice whips? Come on!"

"Is my—what?!" His eyes widen and I can tell my big mouth overrode my brain again as he tries to assimilate my wild guesses. "*No*… to all of that. Little demon, I'm trying to say that I have… done things, but not *all* the things. I *pretended* that I'd done all the things because we are expected to sow our oats and be the image our fathers projected onto us. But I… I have not done everything that I claimed because I have issues somewhat like yours."

Holy Poseidon's pregnant seahorses—Slash is a virgin.

Blinking as I absorb that statement, I shake my head and then squint at him suspiciously. "Not that I don't trust you, but dudes can definitely say that and we'd never know. Why should I believe that when the other guys have said differently? Hell, *rumors* say *differently*, too."

"Where are you getting rumors like that from, little demon?" he asks sternly, crossing his arms over his broad chest.

I roll my eyes at him. "Did you forget my hearing is getting better? I hear people whispering, and they assume I can't because they think I'm human. It's kind of useful, though the fucking lion thing blew that out of the water."

Suddenly, Slash's jaw drops, then he laughs. In fact, he laughs so hard that he backs up and puts his hands on his knees to hold himself up. I have no idea what's so damned funny, but I cross my arms over my chest and tap my foot as I wait for him to catch his breath. When he does, he gives me a sorrowful yet completely amused expression as he scrubs his palm over his face.

"Little demon, Zavida has convinced Jasper that you have no mane because you are younger than us and your lion is juvenile, too. I don't know if that was a gambit to give you time, and he knows, or if he just made a leap of logic and followed, but…. Oh, the prince is going to be very, very pissy when he figures this out."

My eyes widen. "Oh, fuck me raw. Jasper's going to *incinerate me*, especially if he's told anyone that shit. Slash, it was nice knowing you, man."

The shark shifter barks another laugh, then comes back close enough to pull me into his chest again. "Kit, I will not allow him to stir-fry you; I promise. I believe now that I have reviewed my thoughts that Oriel and Salem will also be quite put off by that situation."

"Probably X and Anton as well," I mumble. "But, um, Anton doesn't know yet. Xerxes and I are waiting to reveal it."

"Those two and their games," Slash mutters. He tilts his head, looking at me seriously. "Then Anton, Zavida, and Jasper are the only ones who do not know, yes?"

I nod, licking my lips. "I want to tell everyone, but I have to feel safe enough to do it. Does that make me selfish?"

"Hardly. I've known my caliphate for longer than you want me to say, and they obviously believe that I played around as much as Jasper did." He frowns and adds, "Well, he did for a long time before coming here. Oddly, he's been fairly devoted only to Zav since you arrived, and we've all shunned the females we came into contact with."

"That's not my fault," I scoff. "None of you have left me alone to hardly piss since I walked onto campus. I didn't steal your social lives; you turned them in because Jasper thought I was a spy."

He brushes a lock of hair off my forehead and asks, "Did we, though? Or perhaps we were hit with something so unexpected that it still hasn't really occurred to us what it might be?"

What the hell does that *mean? Dank is going to be so tired of me and my litany of weird girl talk with him.*

"I don't know how to respond to that," I mutter as I dip my chin. "But if you guys *want* to do parties and... whatever... I won't stop you. I have lots of books to read."

The big guy drops his hand on my shoulder and uses the other to lift my chin again. "I should go on the record to say I *hate* those things, and was not complaining. But also, so do a lot of my brothers; we attended because we had to be seen. We are not now because this revival of the Games and your arrival have become more important than appearances. I have not heard a single complaint from *anyone* about not going to smelly, beer and sex-smelling dorm parties, little demon."

Oddly, he's right as far as I've heard, too. Not one of the caliphate members has mentioned going to parties or doing anything other than our normal routine together. But for the mandatory Samhain ball and that damn surface meeting thing, we've been very comfortable and happy being home-bodies. I never considered how damn weird that was until just now; they're all royals and this is their college— yet they're spending time in the dorms with me every night.

Anxiety.... anxiety..... anxiety.... so much worry about what that means and what I'm ready for.

"Kit." I look up and see Slash's reproachful expression. "Stop obsessing. If any of us wanted to do something, we would. We do whatever we want all the time, do we not?"

"Even when I want to throat punch people, yes," I grumble. "I suppose that's true."

"Then do not allow voices of doubt in your head to accuse you of things you did not do." Slash grins toothily. "Eventually, you will do enough things on your own that you do not have to take credit for shit you did not decide. It is coming as your power develops, and then you can internally kick your own ass. Agreed?"

I snort. "Getting my powers will not change who I am, Slash. I will not start doing wacky shit and have to apologize."

"That's not what I meant. I am saying as you get your powers, your confidence is growing. You will be strong in mind and body, which will give you the ability to stand up for yourself even more." Both of his hands come up to frame my face, and my body vibrates with pleasure. "You will do things that are good and things that are bad—regardless of intent, we all do that. And when you fuck up with demonic and shifter powers, the ripples across the water are larger. So yes, you will eat crow."

My eyes widen. "I did *not*! We kissed—that's all!"

The room is silent for a moment, then Slash breaks into that laughter that, to this day, I've only seen come out for me. He fills the room with his humor, and I struggle to hide from him as my face turns bright red. I've obviously made a wrong assumption about his words, and man, is he taking it well. When he settles again, he taps my nose with his finger.

"Little demon, I have never met a single soul or soulless being that makes me laugh as you do. I never wish for you to stop because it delights me." Now I'm really red, and he clearly enjoys the fuck out of it. "However, I would not expect you to have taken such a step with Oriel yet. I know how damaged you are, and also that Salem and Oriel would never push you. As for us? We will move slowly together and keep moving until we are comfortable. Does that sound amenable?"

"It does... because it's nice not to be the only one who isn't completely experienced and totally in the know about all this shit," I mumble.

Slash grins down at me as he holds my flushed face. "Ah, but I do *know* about it all. I simply have not *done* it all. I think I will enjoy directing it, though. Don't you?"

Nice one, Daddy Shark. Now I'm going to be thinking about that all fucking day.

BAD INTENTIONS
XERXES

I am *not* a happy camper. In fact, I'm not a happy anything because I'm soaked in sweat and bruised to within an inch of my life because this asshat *Major* has pushed our prince to make us fight until we're all going to need healing potions. It's not very easy to do that to demons, especially hybrid ones like my caliphate and me, and every inch of my body aches as I pant from the bench on the sidelines. Our only breaks have been in between fights, and that's only if you're bleeding—which I am. Otherwise, you have to do laps around the damn arena.

Poor KK would grit her teeth and kill herself to make it through—or get knocked out.

My eyes move to my leader, noting how he looks as if he's going to shatter his fucking teeth if they grit any harder. He's angry about this class session, and he is going to be extremely difficult to deal with afterward. Jasper doesn't enjoy having his hand forced by anyone, and definitely not the watchful eyes of his father's stool pigeon and our stupid headmaster. Together, their presence is going to injure more demons than train them, and that's proven by the constant flow of infirmary workers carrying people out on stretchers. Luckily, none of those people are from my caliphate, but we're taking a hell of a beating.

"Hopefully, Kit is doing better with the big guy than we are here," Salem mutters as he joins me, nursing a bloody cut under his eye that's dribbling down his face. "I would *not* be okay with him being here during this gauntlet. I don't even think the Games are going to be this vicious. Magic will help those who are distance fighters, and this fucker is making everyone go hand-to-hand even if it isn't their skill set."

I nod, pushing the towel against my nose as the blood gathers there. "Exactly. This isn't about training; it's about finding weaknesses in every student they're watching. If they had notebooks, I'd assume they're making a list for later, but they don't."

"Doesn't mean they aren't using a bounce spell or something," the panda grumbles. "Some lesser demon could sit in front of a book in another room watching the notes scribble themselves as the dickwaffles watch us. The question is… why?"

"Because they want to figure out how to harm us in Lucian's case," Zavida says as he stumbles over with a dazed expression. "As for the Major? I haven't figured that out yet. I can't see why he'd want to find weaknesses other than to report to the General and King? But what does that get them? No idea."

"Do you think our parents are actually plotting against us, too?" Salem mutters carefully. "Or at least… the worst of them?"

I don't want to give that thought credence, but… they took Hell by coup starting with the Games, and some of them are ass-tastic even for demons.

"They could be," I admit, pushing dirty hair off of my face as I sigh. "Mine, Annie's… Jasper's, Slash's… Zav's…" I'm not sure about Salem or Oriel's folks; they never make a fuss at the royal stuff, so they're not actively fighting the bullshit, but they don't seem nearly as invested in making those guys miserable as much as forcing them to work in their line's specialties. O's folks are the question marks, truthfully, because his dad is fucking awful, but that's always in service of thievery and their guild shit. "I don't know about the others' involvement."

Salem sighs and rubs blood from his knuckles into the black and white strands of his hair as he shrugs. "My folks always go with the flow, even when they don't agree. If the King says so, they'll stay in the ballpark. So probably."

"Oriel's dad wouldn't want to lose the future leader of the guild, but his guild wouldn't have shit to bid on without the royals," Zavida mutters. "The King could cut them off anytime, so… yeah, probably all of them."

Now that we've identified why the fuck this asshat Major is here, I feel even less comfortable with our new member's training. If Slash isn't helping her learn to shift, I'm going to deep fry that aquatic asshole. KK *has* to get better with what little power she's displaying and *fast*, or these 'training' sessions will become her doom. I'm not sure if they'll allow her buddy, Dr. D, to just hang around the sidelines to clean her up, either.

Although Dr. D scares the piss out of most people; I could be mistaken about that.

Filing that thought away to tell Jasper later on, I push to my feet wearily as I check the position of the sun. "We have a little longer in class. If we can make it to the end, most of us could skip the late afternoon classes and go back to the dorm. It'll take a bit to clean up, but then by the time Slash brings KK back from the gym, we'd be ready to order a damn pizza or something."

"Worried you won't look so fabulous today, X?" Salem smirks at me, and I roll my eyes at him in annoyance.

"I prefer not to walk around caked in dirt and dried blood; so sue me, fucker."

His eyes widen, and I chuckle as he realizes just how damn tired I am by my tone. "Damn, X. You're never this cranky. That almost channeled Jasper."

"You're straining yourself holding back the shift," Zav says softly. "But I get why. You want to save some things for the real deal."

Our many-tailed hacker is right, and I'm paying the price for it as we speak.

But I'm not the only one holding back, now am I?

By the time the class finally ends, Annie and Oriel have taken their licks as well, and we look like a group of refugees from a no-holds barred fight club. I suppose that's what the Major and Lucian made Jasper turn this class into, and I'm ready to get this shit out of my hair and off of me.

"Are we all okay?" Annie asks as he studies me with a careful eye. I know he's worried that while I'm not the smallest, like Zav or KK, I'm not a fighter by nature. Hand-to-hand is a particular dislike for both of us given our parents, and this has been a lengthy, very arduous period.

I nod as I pick up my bag, stuffing my regular uniform into it without bothering to change. "It will be fine, love. Everyone is upright and lacks mortal wounds, so after we eat and rest, all should be well again."

Zavida takes his cues from me and shoves his clothes in his bag. "I take it we're not going to the classes this afternoon slash evening? I can definitely get behind that idea. I'd prefer to follow X's plan of cleaning up and meeting in Salem's room."

My lips twist as I look at him with a knowing expression. "You too, huh? Are we sure the prince will be okay with this? Or can you rebel without getting in trouble?" The Kitsuné gives me a dirty look, and I laugh softly, then wince. "Okay, okay. I think we should all ditch and wait for KK in their room. All in favor?"

Annie raises his hand quickly, and a happy little buzz in my chest kicks up. "I'm in. We will not need Supe Law if everyone is preparing for a post-Games war, anyway. It'll all be in the wind once that shit starts."

"No shit," Oriel says as he flexes his wings, checking to make sure their range of motion is good.

He shifted more than most of us—well, he and Salem. Most demons have seen their shifted forms in various situations over the years, and they don't have to hide. Slash and Jasper have an equally public shifter persona, but theirs is more terrifying than anything else. Annie, Zav, and I hold back and use magic from our demon lines rather than shift since our animals appear to be less dominant.

Of course, anyone who knows us well would know that's a stupid assumption, but we don't let people get close enough to find out. It's strategic.

O growls as one of his wings sits a bit crooked, and I arch a brow as I ask, "Should we ask the doc to meet us at the room?"

"No," he grumbles as the feathered appendages disappear into his back. "It will be fine after a few hours, like you said. Just pisses me off we were put in such jeopardy to satisfy two old fuckers measuring their dicks at one another. I have no interest in being fodder for their wrinkly asses."

Chuckling, I wait for the others to grab their stuff and then throw my gross hair over my shoulders. "Agreed, man. But we didn't have an option, and neither did Jas, so let's maybe... cushion that so KK doesn't go for his gonads and get into a big fight when he couldn't have stopped it if he wanted to?"

Salem blinks, then groans. "Holy fuck, he's gonna lose it for sure. First, Jas made him go train with the big guy—which we know isn't fun—and now he's missed everyone getting their asses kicked. Pizza is *not* gonna do it to soothe that shit, X."

We all look at one another, and I shrug. "Don't look at me. I'm not the Kit-o-pedia. Someone makes a suggestion; we have to make sure he doesn't get scared and upset."

Oriel holds up a finger. "I can find another trinket. He likes my hoard of trinkets."

"Jackass," Salem mutters as he sucks in a breath then lets it out. "I can DormDash some crunkleberry stuff. He loves those, and they make him silly. Maybe cake? Who doesn't love cake?"

I nod, approving of their suggestions. "Okay, what else?"

Zavida bites his lower lip, then raises his hand like we're in class. "I can pirate some movies from the surface he mentioned liking? A movie marathon might be good?"

"Excellent," I reply as I turn and look at Annie with an amused expression. "I made new pajamas I was gonna save for the next crisis, but I can give them to him now. What about you, my rainbow mate?"

Anton straightens, shaking his head so his grime-encrusted colorful hair flips over his eyes. "I found some books he wanted to read at the library that I haven't given him yet. I read them first and... made some annotations that might help. I think he'd like that."

Beaming, I walk over and kiss my reserved mate's cheek lightly. That's practically a declaration from him, and I'm probably the only one who realizes it. "I think Kit will appreciate your help with his research very much."

"Anyone have a clue what the fuck Jasper or Slash will contribute?" Oriel says wryly. "I mean, besides Jas causing chaos since he's gonna be in a *mood* over this."

I frown, then I look at Zavida curiously. "Do you think he's going to be violently furious? Because that's definitely going to harsh the vibe, man."

"No," the Kitsuné says softly. "He's going to be furious and silent and ashamed. Remember the time the king crashed his birthday party when he was fifteen and we all ended up being sent to survive for a week in the Wastes alone? That Jasper is who will show up tonight, for certain. His guilt about not being able to stop this is going to strangle him."

Sighing, I gesture to the tunnel leading out of the arena. "Then we need to get moving and get back to the dorm. If we can set up the room with all that shit and maybe some stuff to comfort Jasper, too, we can avoid an ugly unnecessary confrontation. Slash will probably help keep the prince level as long as the training session didn't go poorly."

Of course, with our current luck, it will have gone so badly that the shark and our newbie will come back in the pissiest moods ever and peace will fly out the window.

My Turn
Kit/Kat

"You know, you didn't answer my question."

Slash looks at me, his brow cocked up as I hide behind the second row of lockers in the pool area. My head is peeping around the corner of the bank of them as I change the soaked clothes from my jump into the spring. "I didn't answer what?"

I squint at him, raking my lower lip between my teeth as he gives me the toothy grin that makes my insides flutter a bit. "Do you think I have more than that, um, lion form? Like really? Because that shifting stuff is hard, and I don't think I'm good at it. But then… I don't think I'm good at the demon stuff, either."

His chuckle is fond as he pulls a tee shirt over his head, covering the immense chest littered with beautiful ink, and it feels sad as I lose my view. "I think you expect everything to come easily because so many things having to do with school have always been that way for you. Zavida says it's because humans would call you gifted? I believe it's that you have so many hidden powers that have not yet emerged, but that is not what you asked."

"It is not, and my stupid 'giftedness' is more of a curse than a blessing. It hasn't helped me with anything besides being alienated most places, so fuck that," I grumble as I duck back behind the lockers and head for my clothes pile to pull them on.

My current companion is very literal, and he's definitely the best person to ask if the 'multiple species' thing is likely because he won't cushion his response.

"Whatever went on up there is now history, little demon. Consider yourself… leveled up?" My lips curve as he attempts gamer speak, but I wait for him to finish before I respond. "Yes, that's what the others call it. You have 'leveled up' and since we've seen traces of the demonic magic and now this shifter side, but you are *not* fully free? I believe the theories are correct—though I do not know what other things you'll manifest. It could be so many things, and we have no new leads about your provenance, only the proof from the tree."

Once I've covered myself, I shove my wet clothes into one of the plastic bags in the dispenser on the wall. It will keep my stuff from getting soaked by the wet things, and I can toss it in the laundry when we get back to the dorm. "Dottie? Dottie? Where are you?"

My kinkajou did not follow us into the pool area, and I guess that should have clued me in about what it was going to be like in there. But I didn't really think much of it when I was preparing for Slash to turn into a big ass shark, and definitely not once we were knee-deep in the 'Kit isn't a boy' conversation. However, now that we've spent the past two hours trying to teach me how to call the animal inside of me on command with minimal success, I'm missing her support.

"She is probably still in the outer area," Slash rumbles from the other side of the lockers. "The smell of this spring is difficult for anyone without demonic blood. The sulfur in the water is part of it, but also I believe there's hex work in the tiles surrounding it. Hellspring water is quite valuable to magic users, I've been told, though it's common and plentiful for us in this realm."

Picking up my bag, I walk around the row to give him a baleful expression. "Demons are that worried about people stealing something you call 'common' that they protect it from their trusted familiars? Man, you guys are *really* paranoid, and coming from me, that's saying a lot."

The shark shifter sighs, shaking his head as he stuffs his things in his bag. "Don't be obtuse, little demon. We simply don't want people getting it for *free*, and familiars can be duplicated by various magics and powers. Beings are welcome to buy it at a premium in all the places where it is sold."

I laugh softly as he grins again, enjoying his playful response. This really is a side of the serious man that I don't think anyone else sees. "Yes, I forgot demons will part with anything for the right price. My bad."

Slash arches a brow. "Not everything, and that is very good for you, Kat Camponella."

"I knew telling you my real name was a bad idea," I mutter. "You're going to fuck that up in public one day; I can feel it."

"But I won't sell you out to Darkstar for a guaranteed Games win to piss off my father so…"

My nose wrinkles, and I stomp over to smack him in the abdomen—which hurts my hand more than him. "Mutually assured destruction secrets, remember?"

He flashes even more teeth. "For now, little demon, but not forever."

I had to say it out loud, didn't I?

By the time we find Dottie perched on top of the pull-up machine and head out of the building, it's getting late. We probably won't be late for dinner because some of the guys have one more class before they're off, but the quad is much less crowded than earlier. I'd be surprised if a lot of the demons here aren't packed into the *Triclinium*, fighting for a place in line for whatever the special of the night is. I'm thankful Jasper only insists on lunchtime meals mostly—the food isn't terrible, but I *hate* being surrounded by all those enemies.

Of course, I'd feel that way even without the massive cabal plotting against the rulers of Hell, but that's not the point.

"I think the others believe you were going to, like… beat me into submission or something," I say as we get closer to the dorm. "They were all kind of weird about you teaching me to shift."

"Unsurprising."

Frowning, I huff when he doesn't expound. Dottie chitters and snuggles closer to my neck, then pulls back, making a face. "Oh, sorry, girl. My hair must smell bad, right?"

The response from my kinkajou makes Slash laugh, and I give him an exasperated look. He just ignores me until Dottie makes a loud noise again, then finally relents. "Fine. Yes, I think they feared I would be quite hard on you. But… I do not think that is why they were being strange."

"Huh?" I ask as I tilt my head. "What do you mean?"

"Little demon, you have shared things with several of us now, and that will affect how we respond to you spending time with others. It is in the caliphate's nature to share, but not of demons in general, especially those with powerful and dominant bloodlines."

When he opens the door to Canto IV, I squint at him curiously. "Are you saying that everyone is jealous? Of me? That's ridiculous."

"Not of you, Kit. They want to spend time with you—alone, together, teaching, studying, *other things*. All of that makes men behave... oddly." This time his expression is indulgent and smug, which makes me want to smack him again. Since my hand is still throbbing, I forgo it, but I sniff at him as I enter the building. "You can be huffy about it if you like, but it will only get worse."

"Worse?!" I squeak, then cough to hide it. "How could it be any worse? That has to be why Oriel and Salem are muttering about one another, which I also missed."

"Probably," the shark demon replies as we head for the elevator. "However, at this moment, you don't have the Prince of Hell in the mix, and that will make everything much more complicated."

As we step into the car, I whirl around and look up at the big man incredulously. "Jasper will *never* be... part of this! I mean, I'll have to tell him eventually, but...he's not...I'm not... Slash, we don't even like one another!"

His big hand lands on the shoulder opposite Dottie, and he stares down at me with an indulgent look in his eyes. "If you say so, little demon. However, I have strong suspicions that you were brought to our caliphate for a reason —and that even if you believe this was a coincidence, it was not. I am not... mythological in beliefs as some others are, but my gut told me that I should not cast you as Jasper wanted. Now that we have shared, I think the reason for that is deeper."

"Deeper?" I ask quietly. "What does that mean, Slash?"

He shakes his head. "I am uncertain yet, so I do not want to give the possibility wings to fly away. But I will tell you once I have more evidence that I am correct. It does not change my promise to you either way, so don't fret over my silence."

"You're telling someone with anxiety and PTSD *not* to fret over the unknown? That feels like an ambitious request." I smile a little, hoping to entice him into sharing with me for my curiosity's sake alone. "We have trouble with those sorts of demands, to put it lightly."

The door opens to our floor, and he's about to answer when Salem appears, his face focused on the inside of the elevator. When he sees us, he curses softly, then kicks the trash can nearby. "Damn it. You guys aren't DormDash."

I blink in surprise, looking at my normally easygoing panda demon as he pouts. "No? But... we are... *us*, Salem. Isn't that enough?"

He runs a hand through messy, wet strands of black and white hair and then nods. "Well, yeah. I mean, *you* are always enough, KK. But... I'm waiting for an especially delicious delivery for tonight, and these motherfuckers are even later than you two."

Slash narrows his eyes at the panda, then crosses his arms over his chest. "That's why you attacked the furniture rather than greeting us?"

His snark gets him a sheepish grin from my roommate, whose petulant frustration melts under the heat of the big guy's glare. "Sorry. Again. I mean... I didn't mean to scare you. But... Why are you so late? Did Slash overwork you? Are you okay? He's a taskmaster, and if you're too exhausted to have fun, I'm going to be very—"

"Ahem."

I snort when Salem backs up as Slash wards his odd hyperactivity off again. "Salem, did someone give you one of your drinks late in the day? You're not supposed to have them after mid-afternoon, and I've been gone awhile."

The panda frowns as he holds his arm out to me. "No. But this afternoon was a bit... difficult, and when we got back here, the guys and I put together a plan to soften the blow of how bad today sucked for all of us. I mean, we've all had Slash's version of training, and he's so fucking hardassed, so you have to be dying to relax. We knew you would be and also... Jasper's tense, too."

Slash cuts his eyes to my roommate, his interest very piqued. "Why is the prince worked up?"

"The Major *and* Lucian showed up to class," Salem mutters. "I'm probably the least shitty-looking of everyone, so he's drinking scotch and blaming himself. Big surprise, right?"

"Fuck," Slash says as he swipes his hand over his face. "We do not have time for him to nurse his wounds over things he cannot change."

"Yeah, well…"

I look at the two of them, thinking about how good they've been at accepting me and helping work through my shit. Oriel and X have been very good, too, and even though I was bristly at first, they've all done their best to make sure I stay safe and secure. Hell, they even risked their asses at the ball and in front of Lucian.

This time, it's my turn to fix something, and Jasper Eversore is the recipient of that debt—Hell help us all.

I See You

Salem

I'm shocked at how well Firecracker is doing after spending several hours training with our de facto commander. She's walking okay, doesn't seem to lack a will to live, and isn't wheezing. When Jasper let Slash run us through paces in the past, that is *not* the condition we came back in and none of us was in as much danger as my roomie is.

However, I suppose even the icy big dude could get beguiled by the alternating fiery spark and soft vulnerability of our Kit Kat..

My lips curve up as she braces herself for the chaos that is currently our dorm room. I know she'd rather have time to decompress and prepare to be around so many wild personalities in a small space, but I said Jasper needs help. Like the staunch soldier Kat is, she's stomping toward the door with her spine straightened and what can't be more than a whisper of a plan to pull him out of the failure funk. It's admirable, if not a bit naïve, and I'm very interested to see exactly what she does to get his attention.

"Little demon, perhaps you should—"

"Nope."

Slash blinks then looks over at me, his blue eyes wide with obvious concern for the small demon striding into my room like a mouse headed for… well, a dragon. Apt description, I guess. I chuckle as we follow her in, then lean in to whisper, "Everyone has to learn to stand on their own two feet, right, General?"

His eyes narrow. "Do *not* call me by my father's moniker—I have not earned it in *any* conceivable fashion."

Oops. That wasn't supposed to hit a sore spot, but it did because of the Major, I'd bet.

"Sorry, man. Didn't mean it that way." I give him a sorrowful expression, and the shark huffs as he makes a beeline for his favorite seat near the prince. Slash is making certain he's within snatching distance on purpose, I fear, in case the grumpy shadow dragon loses his temper with KK.

"Salem, where the hell are the damn—" Jasper looks up at the newcomers blearily, jerking his chin with a grunt at Slash. His second eyes him carefully as he sits down, and I imagine that's how his animal looks when it's tracking prey. He's sizing the prince up even more now that he realizes how blitzed the guy's gotten since we got back. "Oh, *finally!*"

Kat arches a brow at the hazy dragon demon and shrugs as she drops her bag next to her chair. "You asked Slash to train me and that's what we did. We took it seriously, Jasper. Isn't that a good thing?"

Hmm. A little snark, but she's feeling him out like someone who is well-versed with testing a drunkard for meanness before they move into range.

"I don't like that," Oriel mutters as he comes up to me. "Not one bit. Slash is giving Jas the stink-eye, and KK is watching him like a gazelle on the Serengeti."

"Ah, but he's *not* a gazelle," I reply with a small grin. "We know he's the hunter deep down, and I feel he's been in this situation before—successfully, if this strategy tells us anything."

X comes out of the kitchen, their hair braided and comfortable, *not* in gross clothing but in perfect order as they stop to comment. "Kit Kat knows what he's doing without a doubt. Look at the body language, boys. Coiled but firm, calculating risk… I daresay our fishy brother has taught him *something* during this session."

Suddenly, Kit whirls to face us, her expression irritated. "This is not a Nat Geo special. Stop acting like weird meanie girls gossiping in the background. He might not be sober enough to get it, but I can certainly hear you."

I smile, batting my lashes at her playfully. "But KK, I'm enjoying your Steve Irwin-like approach to our hell-flavored version of an angry croc. It's very amusing."

Dottie scampers off her shoulder, across the floor and onto the counter to face the three of us. The small animal makes an impossibly disappointed face—for an animal, I mean—and shakes her tiny fist at us as she makes chittery sounds.

Shit, we made her mad—my bad.

"Hey, hey!" I say to the tiny rodent as I hold my hands. "We were just playing, Dottie. No need to fuss. How about I get you some yummy treats from the cabinet?"

Oriel snorts, elbowing X as he mutters, "Even the pet has him whipped. It's hysterical."

"*Don't* piss Dottie off," Kat hisses at us as she shakes a finger in our direction. "I'm going to go change so I don't smell like… hellspring water or whatever. She doesn't like it, and I don't want that to be a problem. Limit how much more booze he drinks while I do that and consider my options."

"Or you could just let him marinate," Anton says mildly. "He is making a *very* illogical choice, and he wasn't even the one who got his ass beat for hours. That was us, and while we look better now than we did before…"

X leans in to kiss his cheek and pat his shoulder. "Yes, he's being quite self-centered and self-pitying, but that's not something we're going to handle tonight. It seems Kit Kat is up at bat this time."

I frown, caught between wanting to see her try and knowing that we usually fail at culling Jasper's self-pitying shit, and we've known him forever. I don't want KK to internalize that and fuck up her own progress.

Plus, I think Slash might actually kill him if she does.

"Okay, I'm back—what the fuck are you guys doing?"

My eyes stay on the floor because I'm not saying this was my idea, but it wasn't *not* my idea. Hopefully, she doesn't figure it out—or someone doesn't rat me out. But I really think that if we're going to make all this shit work and get through this fucking nightmare as a caliphate, we need to figure out the rest of our shit.

Zav looks up from where he's been fiddling with the huge TV on the wall, pushing his glasses up as his tails swish. "I put together some movies. It's been a bad day and… well, I think we deserve to wind down and destress. You know… together."

Nice one, brave little fox.

Oriel waves at Kat as she slowly walks out of her room towards us, the change in her scent from hellspring swimmer to spritzed with spicy bathroom stuff obvious. "I have something for you, too."

"It's not my birthday, and didn't some philosopher say 'beware of Trojans and horses' or something? That was in class recently, right?" Her eyes narrow as she looks from one of us to another suspiciously. "And I'm not the one who's—"

"Ah, ah," I interrupt as I waggle a finger at her. "Let's not kick up bad vibes by finishing that sentence. We're all pretty calm right now, as you notice."

Looking around again, she takes in the dimmed lights and the incense oil Xerxes fetched from their room to help set the scene. "I suppose so. But then, I'm not sure what a demon brothel looks like, so I could be mixing it with… this."

Slash snorts, slapping his knee as he grins. Everyone turns to stare at him except Kat, and the big guy crosses his arms over his chest. "I told you that it felt like an Arabian Nights knock-off. You laughed at me, and I feel very vindicated."

"But comfy on your stack of cathouse pillows, I suppose?" This time, I snicker as X gets their dig in with a smug smirk. X and Anton were adamant about setting a scene, and it was lucky that KK took a bit to get herself cleaned up so we could transform the space while she was fiddling. It was *supposed* to be ready when she first walked in, but my ass was waiting for the crunkleberry delights in the hall so…

C'est la vie—we're all good now, even if she thinks it looks like the best little whorehouse in Hell.

"This is a very nice gesture," Kat says as she pads over to the circle of comfy blankets and pillows and things on the floor. Her eyes skate from the stack of books by Annie to Zav finishing his TV shit and then over to my trays of yummy foods and drinks I placed just out of accident range. "It's like a weird-ass guy slumber party—I mean, I think. I never went to one, so I only know from TV, but…"

"You've never been to a slumber party?" Oriel's brows shoot up, and my leg moves quickly to kick his shin before he spills the whole 'girl' thing like a dumbass. That dude is not the one I expected to be bad about secrets, but by the way X is sniggering, I guess I was wrong. "I mean, I thought guys did… something like that, too… up there?"

"Wow." X doesn't even have to say anything else to draw attention to how lame *that* sentence was. They tilt their head at the spot we left for Kat, smiling prettily. "Since O is incapable of keeping his foot out of his mouth, come sit with us and we can show you all the fun stuff."

"What about Jasper?" Kat frowns as she looks at the grumpy prince where he's sulking like a dark cloud on the horizon. "It seems like he needs more cheering up than I do. I'm pretty okay."

Jasper snorts, arching a brow at her. "Shifted on your own, then?"

Slash makes a warning sound, but Kat waves her hands as she steps into the circle and walks over to our leader. She looks down at him with her arms crossed over her chest in the baggy sweats, foot tapping. "No. Not really. But I tried, and I made progress. That's all I can ask of myself when I'm learning something new—at least, according to the coach *you* assigned to me."

Uh-oh.

"Mmm. I'm sure that will save your ass in the Games when you can't do anything and we have to save you. Or it'll make us feel better when someone gets *maimed* trying to save you. Then you'll feel like me, and it will all make sense." The dragon reaches for his glass, but Kat gets in his way, and his eyes fill with irritated fire. "Move, shrimp."

"Look, dude," she says as she steps closer and sinks to the floor on her knees in front of him. "I know you had it fucking rough as a kid, and you don't talk about it. Out of everyone, I *really* understand that—we're not exactly the same, obviously. But I. Get. It."

The prince gives her a dirty look, but he stays eerily quiet as Kat looks at him seriously.

"There are probably terrible things that only Slash knows, or Zav knows, or maybe even *nobody* knows about what your fuckface dad and his merry gang of murdering rebels did to you and whoever else they abused to get their rocks off for centuries. I'd probably want to hurl my guts up and then rage about how bad it sucked for hours if you told me."

All she gets is a snort, but the rest of us are watching with bated breath.

"So, no, I'm not going to play 'my trauma is worse than yours' with you because you got liquored up and want to make yourself a villain." Kat blows out a slow breath, and I worry for a moment she's lost her thread, but then she says, "Just because people *want* you to be something doesn't mean you are. They don't get to define us under their terms—victim, villain, prude, prince, thief, turncoat, rebel, reject, lazy, liar, soldier, spy… It doesn't matter, Jasper. We are who we are, not what they would have us be."

"What if I'm not who I would have myself be?"

I blink, eyes going wide as I look over at Slash. He doesn't seem to know where this is going either, but he looks like he's going to spring into motion if need be. Zav, however, has turned away from the screen, and his expression is…hopeful.

"Then stop letting other people define you and take back the reins. Otherwise, you're making a pawn out of yourself and thanking them for the privilege." Kat shrugs again, and I notice her posture relaxing a little. "Your father's bullshit isn't your responsibility, and you can't let him live rent-free in your head. That fucker can afford to pay for his own lodging."

That gets a snicker out of the drunken royal, and I feel myself relax a little now, too.

"And how would you suggest I do that when I am forced to watch his minions torture my caliphate—my *chosen* family—for amusement and yet I cannot prevent it?"

"By first admitting that your guilt isn't the main issue here, knothead." Slash chuckles, and even Zav laughs softly as Jasper frowns. "And then maybe… I don't know. Be normal and ask someone for a hug or something. Let someone help you process the emotion healthily instead of loading up on Johnny Black and acting like one of my fucking foster dads. Satan wept, Jasper, it's not hard."

"Ask for help."

"*Yes.*"

"That's what Zavvie says."

Kat snorts. "He's smart and has cute tails, so why he puts up with you, I don't know."

"Would *you* help someone like me?"

If you're wondering, now the room is silent as a tomb and not one jaw isn't on the floor, so… guess this is happening.

GRACE

KIT/KAT

In the realm of all things unexpected, that question ranks up there. I mean, Jasper has mostly been a dick to me from the moment I stepped out of Dank's car, and much of the time, he's flaunted whatever he could to piss me off or upset me in some way. From edging too close to my boundaries and issues to mocking me, he's even drawn the wrath of my kinkajou because he wouldn't stop jabbing at me. But right now, in this room, he looks defeated and weary. He looks like a guy who has been holding himself up by his claw tips for so long that he isn't even sure when it started or how to stop doing it all on his own.

And his friends look completely baffled by that and the glimpse of his vulnerability that is peeking out at me.

Zav's hopeful expression flickers in my mind, and I know that he, above anyone else, probably knew this existed inside the prickly-ass dragon. His relationship with Jasper has probably been loaded with attempts to bring out the abused kid inside who elected himself the savior of his friends and the entire realm of Hell. I can't excuse Jasper being such an asshole to everyone—especially me—because he's got some super buried, ugly-as-fuck trauma that no one knows about. But I can make good on my own words and help when he asks for it.

"Yes," I say simply. "I would help someone like you, despite all the shitty stuff you've done and said, because I've seen little snippets of the real person hiding behind all that mean armor. I see it in how you treat Zavida when you don't think anyone is watching, and how you found me when that… demon was going to… do bad things."

Jasper grunts, looking uncomfortable.

So I go on, my voice getting a bit stronger in the silence. "I've seen it in your protective behavior in front of the royal parents and the secret room you guys prepped at the Samhain ball in case I got overwhelmed. I know you were out of control when my powers slipped because those guys attacked in class, and I think it was because you were upset the caliphate was getting hurt. You care about people, Jasper Eversore, and you try really hard to hide it so no one can use it against you. Again, yes, I would help that guy if he were asking me."

His bleary eyes meet mine, and I see something fearful in them that I haven't witnessed before. "Maybe I am asking. Maybe it wasn't hypothetical. What then?"

I see this will be up to me to figure out how to show him I'm not lying—great.

"I'd say that I'm game, as long as Zav can be part of it, too." There are snickers behind me as I say that, and I roll my eyes hard enough to injure myself. Dudes are the worst, even in the most serious of moments. "Do you agree to let us help you right now? Because… I'm going to admit that if you do and you go back to being a total shit heel tomorrow, we're gonna have real fucking problems. You need to get that through your sauced brain before you answer."

There's a low whistle of appreciation, and I look over my shoulder to see Oriel flashing me a thumbs-up. Slash looks equally pleased, and knowing the rest of the guys support me helps my shaking insides *a lot*. I know this is a step towards sharing my big truth with Jasper, and his ability to commit to being a better guy to me and all of us is very important to me in that regard. I can't trust him with that if he doesn't stop ping-ponging between decent and a fuckhead. Before I go back to the prince, I look at Zav to make sure he's okay with my inclusion of him in this effort. His smile is huge, and his tails are swishing happily like a damn puppy, so I breathe a sigh of relief.

"Looks like Zav agrees with me, so the ball is in your court now, Prince Pricklypants." I smile a little, trying to mitigate my own issues zooming around inside of me as I wait for him. The teasing is gentle because I want him to know that I'm not asking him to change who he is entirely—just to behave like someone with a lick of emotional intelligence and a heart.

A ghost of a smirk passes over his face, and he shifts in his pile of cushions and pillows. His tail uncurls, moving around me to open up the space in front of him more. "I will do my best to temper the bad habits. I have been trying more recently because… I did not miss that *you* have been working on your own reactions with no one requesting it. It occurred to me that if you can work through bad shit… I should be able to as well."

I take that as a cue to move just fractionally into the cleared space, nodding. "I believe everyone can do the work, and I don't ask for things I'm not willing to give—even grace."

Out of the corner of my eye, I see a reddish flash of movement, and within a blink, Zav is kneeling beside me. He's giving me the distance I need, but also showing Jasper that he's going to be there with me if this works. I smile at him, then bite my lip before I hold my hand out. Zavida's expression is a little surprised, but he takes the offer and looks at his lover. "I think you deserve more than you ask for, Jas. Not the spoiled rich kid act, but like… things you really need and want."

There we go, fiery fox man. Help me get him there.

"Being close to me puts an even bigger target on your back," Jasper rasps. "Especially if I am not being derisive in public after this."

I chuckle softly. "I'm sure you can find things to snark at me about that aren't truly mean or hurtful to keep your cover, Jasper. But letting people in? That takes a lot more strength than enduring dumbasses calling me the 'Caliphate Concubine' when they think I can't hear it."

His eyes narrow as he growls, "Those mother*fuckers*… I thought Slash shut that shit down."

This time, I'm shocked, and I turn to give the guys behind me a dirty look. "Damn it, you guys *knew* about that one? Even the T-shirts?"

Slash looks sheepish until I say 't-shirts' and that's when I'm afraid he's going to stomp out the door right now, in the middle of our big break-through with his bestie. I wave my hand at them, hoping they realize I don't want to deal with that right now. What is happening *here* is so much more relevant to our surviving the Games and whatever happens afterward—at least, I think it is. We all have to be on the same page, and Jasper has been the big holdout.

"No, we did not know about… merchandise," Slash grumbles angrily as he settles back on his pillows. "However, deaths will be swift and consequences will be felt."

"And I'll steal all that shit and burn it," Oriel adds gleefully. "No charge, KK."

The crow's got jokes.

"Okay, okay. You can… avenge things later." I blow out a brain-clearing breath and turn back to the prince. "Look, those idiots aren't the first ones to do things like that, and I'm sure they won't be the last. I can handle that stuff—really. But can *you* handle being thought of as attached to me when they'll all be… like that? Will you be able to build trust and share things as we get comfortable? The others will tell you that we've shared some stuff, and you'd have to do that, too."

Zavida frowns. "Some of us have. But… I'm willing to do it when you're ready."

I squeeze his hand lightly, hoping to reassure him. "We will, Zav. You're doing great."

Jasper finally groans, looking at the two of us with a helpless expression. "I can't resist the two of you looking at me like lost puppies. Fuck! Okay. I will… do whatever I have to do. Just help me figure out how to handle this before everything gets so much worse when the Games start."

Looking over at Zavida, I dart my eyes from him to Jasper and back. He dips his chin, turning red as he nods and lets go of my hand. Slowly, so I don't spook myself *or* the cranky dragon, I inch forward on my knees until I'm within centimeters of the prince. When he doesn't move, but also doesn't flinch, I drop down and scoot in, leaning my chest against him. It scares the fuck out of me because he's so volatile, but both of us need to give for this to work.

"Oh." His voice is shocked for a second, but his tail curls back in, wrapping around my feet as I settle in. For a moment, neither of us move and the tension where we're touching is making it hard to breathe. But then he murmurs, "Zavvie?"

The Kitsune moves in a flash to mirror me on the other side of him, somehow getting inside the circle of Jasper's scaly tail while draping his fluffy ones over us. "Always, Sir."

I feel a rumble against my back, and I turn, squinting up at the dragon. "Don't get any ideas. Zavvie is yours, but I'm comforting you via touch and proximity, buddy. I'm not some office bunny you can coerce."

Jasper blinks, then actually laughs. "I forgot about that shit."

My expression sours, but I stay close, lending my support despite the bad taste in my mouth.

"What 'office bunny' are you referring to?" Slash asks curiously, and Salem leans forward with an angry look. "The Prince *hates* students in his office. That cannot be correct."

"Yeah, what the fuck, Jas?" Oriel says with a frown. "What were you thinking?"

Xerxes sniffs, and Anton looks perturbed, but they say nothing.

"I—" Jasper sighs and tilts his head back to look at the ceiling. "It was *staged*, okay? I was hoping to annoy the piss out of the shrimp, and it worked. I was being a petulant, suspicious ass. Are you all *happy* now?"

I blink. "What?"

The Prince shifts a little, and it almost feels like he's trying to make sure I won't rabbit away when he replies. "I'm a rich asshole, like you love to remind me. I'm also paranoid and spiteful sometimes when I feel threatened in some way. You showed up, got stuck with us, and no one would believe me about you being a spy. I did a lot of petty stuff to piss you off, hoping you'd reveal yourself."

Zavida wrinkles his nose as he murmurs, "I helped with some of it, but not that. We did a lot of searching in the human archives trying to find out your family heritage. In Jasper's defense, we have had quite a few spies sent to infiltrate the caliphate over the years. His dad *really* hates that none of the parents can break through our bond to figure out what we might be doing."

I think about that for a minute. Of course, I knew he helped the prince with stuff by now, and I also suspected Jasper spent much of his time fucking with me because he had deep trauma. Admitting it is a good first step, as is admitting his actual intentions with no need for us to prod him. If I don't accept that he wasn't actually boning someone in the office, then I'm not giving him the grace I was preaching about. And Slash *did* say that the prince was staying with Zavida mostly since they arrived, so…

Damn it.

"Fine. You didn't do that, and I'm going to trust you."

The dragon demon looks shocked as he pulls back a little. "That easily? You're just… taking my word for it?"

My lips quirk up as I nod. "Yes. I am. That's how trust works."

"He did not question me when we spoke during training." Slash gives me a toothy grin again, and I duck my chin to keep Jasper from seeing the look in my eyes. "I told him things, and he simply believed me."

"Me too," Salem says. "At the Faerie place."

I turn back to Jasper as the others add their sentiments, shrugging a bit. "Not to sort of steal your line, but the question is 'can you do that for me', right?"

Take that, Prince Pricklypants—it's your turn for an enormous leap of faith.

Working It Out

Zavida

Jasper Eversore, prince of Hell and heir to the Wrath line, doesn't just 'take people at their word', yet that's exactly what Kit is asking him to do. He doesn't *know* why that's so hard for Jas—and I'm not even sure that I do. I've been involved with him as a lover for many centuries now, and as a friend before that, but I don't think he's admitted everything to me. I don't think he's told Slash everything, and I would have rated the shark demon the other person closest to my love.

He simply cannot trust anyone not to use his vulnerabilities against him, so he doesn't give them up.

But there's a weird feeling in the room right now—Kit and I sitting with him, our brothers watching and supporting us, and the events since Kit arrived hanging in the air like flashing lights trying to guide him. Jasper has always rebelled against adding new people once the caliphate was formed, but Xerxes *insisted* it wasn't complete. I don't know how they knew, but when an empathic cobra says something with that kind of unshakable surety, we've all learned to listen. So we tried to find the missing piece in middle and high school, especially once Jasper was at Discordia ahead of us.

It didn't work, and my spiky lover dug and pried and protested until he found every hidden shadow that prospective members had buried in their souls. He's never been quite as… vehement… as he is with Kit, but the rest of us have never disagreed with his assessment this strongly, either. The truth is likely that Kit is hiding something big, but it's not what Jas thinks, and that's where our dichotomy is clashing. However, my other brothers are staunchly behind him, and as I've been working to rebuild the bridge after letting Jasper lead, I think they're right.

Kit is the missing piece of our puzzle, and it's why we've all been so drawn to him since the beginning—and why Jasper is so terrified of him.

"I don't know how to do that," Jasper says with a frown. "I don't know that I've *ever* done that."

I stay quiet, pressed against him in the most unobtrusive yet comforting way I can. When he's this upset, the prince often needs someone to be close but allow him to muddle his emotions out on his own. He doesn't even say them out loud sometimes, but he needs the physical support that I guarantee not a single asshole in that castle ever gave him when he was small. His mother was never of much use, and the King spent most of his time either gathering power to prevent someone from performing the same coup he did or doing awful things to mold Jasper into a clone of himself. Mind, we all have shitastic parents, but Tarron Eversore was definitely the worst of the bunch.

"Maybe you didn't feel safe doing it," Kit says as he gives Jas a gentle smile. "And I get that. I haven't felt safe around guys, especially within touching range, since the… thing. You guys have been slowly helping me through that, better than four years of therapy ever did."

Slash makes an annoyed sound across the room, and I peep out of my tails to look at my brothers. They all look as infuriated as the shark demon, especially Salem and Oriel. It's true none of us likes the way a great deal of males behave—human or demon—but I don't think I've seen any of them act like they're going to rip someone in half with their bare hands like this before. At least, not if it wasn't in defense of our caliphate members. I know Kit's one of us now, but… there's a sinister chill in the air that feels more emotional than brotherhood.

It feels like vengeance and possession—enough that it brushes against the strands of envy that weave through me because of my lineage.

Jasper shifts a little, and uncertainty fills the immediate space around us. "But you're okay with this, yes?"

I blink, looking at my love with what has to be pride in my eyes. Jas isn't a fucking creeper, but checking to see how what he wants will affect someone else isn't something he often does. It took a long time for him to feel comfortable enough with me to do so when we're *not* in the bedroom, so this is kind of amazing.

"Thank you for asking, but yes. I came to sit with you, and I'm doing okay. Like I said, the others have been getting me acclimated to touch without going into full-on panic mode."

"And doing a damn fine job of it," Salem mutters. "You're *welcome*."

Kit's face turns a fun shade of red, and I squeeze my tails happily when it's not me feeling shy about such things for once. "Yes, well… You're in a good position, being my roommate, Salem."

"Lucky bastard," Oriel grumbles as he leans back on his pillows. "You get KK all to yourself a lot, and the rest of us have to make do."

"Guys—"

Salem grins cheesily, stacking his hands behind his head. "I do, and it's fucking awesome. Eat your hearts out, assholes."

Jasper growls suddenly, and Salem's smugness fades as the tip of the dragon's tail tucks around Kit and me. "Watch it, Stryker. Changes could be made if it's distracting the caliphate."

"They absolutely can *not*," Kit says as he smacks my lover's shoulder lightly. "You can't pass me around like an object you want to add to your hoard. Instead, you could just say you'd like to spend time with me like Oriel did. Well, sort of did and sort of whined, but close enough."

"I want to!" X exclaims as they wave their hand. "I mean, Annie and I definitely do. We can work on the magic stuff, like Jasper suggested, and mental shielding. That's going to be important for close-quarters stuff in the Games."

"We must continue training," Slash adds, though the corner of his mouth is curved up in an interesting smirk I can't quite place. "We started with shifting today, but much more work is necessary."

"More of us than just you shift, Scrum," Oriel says as he looks at Kit. "And I can also work with him on thief-type things. It'd be good if he learned to pick pockets and locks and such."

I frown and then look at Jasper. "Tech. I can work with him on that *and* on the catch-up stuff about supernaturals and powers. I'm the best at teaching."

"For fuck's sake… you'd think we're fighting over a new puppy," Jasper says as he looks up at the ceiling and sighs. "We will all do our parts to work with you, shrimp, and thus, will all get to spend time with you. Does that work or not?"

Kit tilts his head, looking up at the dragon demon in amusement. "Does that include you? Because I have noticed the distinct lack of interest in claiming coming from behind me."

The flash of his dragon lurks in my love's eyes at KK's words, and I squint as I observe them. Jasper's dragon is one of the most mercurial I've ever seen, but it did *not* like that suggestion at all. Sighing, our emotionally damaged leader looks down at me, then over at Kit silently for a moment. Finally, he nods. "I believe I would like to work with you in combat one-on-one. My skill set is varied, and I'm the most trained in using both magic, physical, and weaponry-based combinations. That would allow us time to… connect more. If you agree."

"You want to give me fighting lessons?" Kit almost squeaks as he looks at the prince. "Dude, you're like… so much bigger than me. Aren't you going to squash me flat?"

Jasper arches a brow. "You don't seem concerned Slash is going to eat you. How is this different?"

That makes Kit choke, and I reach over, patting his back just in case. When he gives me a thankful look, I smile and dip my chin. I don't know what my role is with him and Jasper here—exactly—but I like that he asked for me to be here. Anything I can do to help them overcome this stubborn ass conflict they were embroiled in is fine with me.

"Uh, I don't… I mean, I don't know!" Kit looks frustrated then wrinkles his nose. "Because the big guy has always been nice to me and shit, probably."

Something about that doesn't ring true, but I'm not an empath, so I can't dispute it.

"Jasper would not dare harm you, little demon. He would face the consequences from the rest of us should he do so." Slash flashes his shark-y teeth this time, and I shiver. He is *not* joking in the slightest; if Jasper fucks this up and hurts Kit in any way, his best friend is coming for him.

"Don't be dramatic," Jasper mutters as waves his hand. "Of course I'm aware of the size difference and the experience difference and all of that."

"Did he just say…" Salem leans into O, snickering behind his hand as he and the crow look at one another like bosom buddies with an inside joke. My brows furrow as they laugh, and it spreads to X, then, surprisingly enough, gets a rusty chuckle out of the stoic shark.

Now I'm really *suspicious, because Anton isn't laughing, nor am I. They're all hiding something.*

Jas, however, rolls his eyes at all of them and turns back to Kit. Our fellow cuddler looks extremely fidgety and pink, but he clears his throat to croak, "Okay. That's gonna fall under I'll trust you, then."

"You're making me look bad, shrimp." The smirk that takes over my love's face is devilish, so I stop worrying about the others and focus on how much better he looks than when we got to this room earlier. "I haven't taken a leap of faith for you, and you're taking *two* for me now. I'm not a royal who enjoys being in debt."

"Jasper, you're not a royal who enjoys much at the moment, and *that* is why we're doing this." Kit pushes his floppy hair out of his eyes and sighs. "But teaching me will help me get a stronger basis for the classes you TA and the stupid Games. That's a good payback in my book, especially if you behave while we do it so we can build the whole 'trust' thing."

"Everyone is teaching you, so no dice." The prince frowns as he looks around for a moment. "And everyone had a surprise for you tonight but me. That's another mark against me because Anton had books, Zavvie found movies, Salem brought sweets, and Oriel... what the fuck did you do again?"

The crow eyes Jasper carefully as he pulls out a very soft-looking stuffed animal with glittering jewel eyes. It's probably a raven, but it looks enough like a crow that he can say it is. "I brought spoils from my hoard—and I even made sure it's clean and magic-residue free."

Kit's eyes widen as the emo demon hands it over, and he squeezes it to himself tightly like it's going to anchor him to reality. "Oriel! This is... really... Damn. It's really helpful."

"I know. It gives you something to hang onto if you're crashing out here."

Jasper growls again, and his expression turns to a pout. "See? How in Hell's rings am I going to pay back debts when I'm being constantly outshone? This is bullshit."

I lean in, looking at him seriously while Kit is admiring the sparkly and squishy gift. "You're the Prince of Hell, Jasper. I imagine you can think of something nice to give him, if you really want to be even. Monetary value isn't the reason he likes that thing, even if it has black diamonds for eyes."

His lips curve as he looks down at me fondly, and I feel my tails swish happily. I *like* Jasper showing emotions—especially ones that don't fall into his Wrath line. If Kit is helping him bring them out, it will only benefit all of us, including me, and it would cement my belief that he really is our last puzzle piece.

I just have to encourage everyone to continue behaving like we weren't raised by fucking psychos, so we don't scare him away.

Panic Room
Kit/Kat

Squeezing the stuffed bird tightly, I press my lips together as I try not to show the massive amount of emotion rocketing through me.

Since I arrived at Discordia, I've gotten more gifts and kindness than I have in… ever. The guys weren't all welcoming from the start, nor have they always behaved like I'd prefer. But over time, the relationships between us have slowly grown to be so fucking important that it scares me, and now, even Jasper is acting like he has a shred of decency. I don't quite know how to handle it because a part of me—this small, sparkling pink part that feels like it's cracking through the other dark colors inside—is flooding me with what I assume are 'girly' feelings.

That part is probably responsible for all the steamy, tingly feeling about them, too, and it needs to get a grip.

"KK? Are you okay? You look… angry and happy simultaneously."

My gaze moves to Xerxes, who has the hint of a smirk on their lips as they study me. I forget they are extremely talented in deciphering emotions because of their lineage, and hiding things from them is next to impossible. I nod, swallowing the lump in my throat and then clearing it. "Yeah. I mean, I will be once I get some of those tasty snacks Salem got. It's not like you to order things rather than make them. What happened?"

Salem wrinkles his nose and sighs. "Time, KK. We decided to do this with very little time to prepare, and you know that I only bake from scratch. It's that sliver of pride in me, so I had to order out rather than cheat by using something truly awful like a mix."

I frown at him, wagging a finger. "Don't be so judgy. Some people don't have the time or physical ability to cook like you. Pre-prepared meals or mixes make it possible for those with disabilities to experience the same joy you do in the kitchen."

The panda gives me an exasperated look as he holds up a pretty tray of sparkling, sugary treats. "Duh! I *know* that, and I'm not being salty about everyone having the chance to get their Julia Child on. I'm just a cooking snob in *my* kitchen and in how food is prepared *here*. However, I should add that this shit comes from one of the most coveted bakeries in this section of Hell… but they rarely serve the elite, only the normies. Their shit is *so* much better than the fancy-pants places most of us annoying rich guys buy from —trust me, you'll *love* these cupcakes."

I wait for him to bring the plate closer so I don't have to move. Jasper and Zav are whispering to one another, but I don't think they would be happy if I scampered off. I'm doing my best to shut them out so I'm not eaves-dropping, obviously, and I don't want to shatter this very cozy moment. Once Salem gets close enough, I take one of the pink, purple, and blue confections that smell like heaven and make my stomach rumble eagerly. He looks at me with a soft heat in his eyes, and I blush as I duck my head.

These damn boys are going to give everything away before I'm ready to tell the others, I swear to fuck.

"There you go, KK, but… just as a warning? Eat slowly. They're made of —" His eyes widen when I look at him after a big bite of the large cupcake. "Uh, they're made with crunkleberries, crunkle syrup, and crunkle icing?"

Oriel blinks. "Well, that's going to be fascinating."

"I estimate the effects will set in within about five minutes, especially with that concentration," Anton says as he tries to hide a smile. "Salem, you've just gotten KitKat high."

"No. No, no, no," I groan as panic floods me. "The last time someone gave me a lot of drugs… it did not go well."

My body locks up, and I look around with a wild expression. I feel scared and trapped, even though my brain knows that I'm safe. Instinct is pushing hard to get me to move, to hide, to get the hell out of here until I'm locked away from the men who can hurt me.

But then the arm around me tightens, and I feel the broad chest rumble a little before lips touch my ear to murmur, "You are safe. You are among friends. You will not get hurt here. Breathe, shrimp."

Jasper's voice, baritone and soothing, is a surprise, but it has the intended effect. My muscles relax slightly, and I lean towards the sound as I swallow with my dry mouth. I can't respond—not yet. I'm too busy closing my eyes so the spinning of the room doesn't make me barf the damn tasty as fuck cupcake all over us.

"KK, I didn't know you'd take such a big bite so fast. I'm sorry."

The echo of Salem's voice sounds far away, but I feel the truth in it. That helps a bit more, and I'm able to unclench my jaw so I don't ache later on. I blow out a slow breath as I go through mantras in my head one by one, using my exercises to help me undo my trauma response without sliding into a full attack. I know my sweet panda didn't mean to trigger that, and I've eaten the berries happily before, so he couldn't have realized that in this concentration it would feel similar to a bad thing. It was an error in judgment to let me take the cake after a workout, without giving me the Alice-style instructions first.

"He's not mad, Salem," Zav says softly. "This just triggered something, and he's working it out. It will be okay, right, Kit?"

I think I nod, but I'm uncertain as I push away the memories of swirling rooms and half-remembered words that prefaced the incident that broke my brain. The snippets that come remind me that it felt very different from the effects of crunkleberries, and I need to hang on to that as I come out of the haze. The roofies made me feel heavy and sleepy, confused and unable to move my limbs. These berries feel light and fizzy in my head, and if I weren't having a panic moment, my body and mouth would move just fine. It's not the same.

It's hard to get my stupid brain and primal panic button to agree on that, though.

"Shrimp, you need to open your eyes. Seeing who is here and who is *not* here will help you manage the reaction." The prince's voice is filled with confidence, and it tells me that at some point, he's done this. I have no idea what made him have PTSD attacks or be caught in memories that physically hurt, but my gut says he knows what he's talking about. So, I open my eyes, and my free hand grips the material of his sweatpants as I ground myself.

The world is hazy and trippy, but I see Salem watching me with a sad expression as he bites his lip. It makes me want to hug him and say he's forgiven, but I can't yet. Xerxes and Anton are curled together, keeping a sharp eye on me and the surrounding space, so I assume they're making sure my magic will not spike. That's a guess, but since they're the experts in that arena, I think it's a solid one. Slash is tense in his seat, his body looking prepped to spring forward and snatch me if need be. I don't know where he'd take me, but that makes my chest squish a bit. Oriel's eyes are narrowed, and he's murmuring something to himself silently—which might be why the bird I'm clutching is exuding warmth against my stomach.

"Now tell yourself that what you see is real and what your mind is seeing is not," Jasper says. "Get control of one sense so you can slowly regain mastery of the others. It will help you drown out the flashbacks if you replace them with reality."

Yeah, the prince definitely knows what fucking happens during one of these attacks, and I'm going to kick his ass for being a dick when I had them before.

"Little demon, you are always safe with us. Even when the prince was being a dick, he did not physically harm you. We are your caliphate; you are ours to protect and care for."

I want to tell Slash he's edging dangerously close to wording that will trip someone's wires, but I'm still a bit shaky and haven't found my voice yet. So I look at him, unclenching my hand from Jasper's pants, and give him a weak thumbs-up. That makes him chuckle, and I think my lips curve a tiny bit.

"I saw that, KK," X practically purrs. "You smiled a little, and that means you're coming back to us. While I'm sure you'd be *much* happier curled up with Annie and me in positive emotions, you have to admit that Zav and Prince Pricklypants are doing a good job. Your hands didn't even shake."

They're right, and that is pretty amazing. I had to hold on for a few moments while I righted the ship, but I didn't shake, and I sure as hell didn't black out. This is progress—real, *tremendous progress*—and it's because I'm surrounded by all of them. Maybe there is something to the mysterious things Slash was saying in the pool about purpose and shit? I don't know, but I'm slowly slipping back into reality without my usual symptoms taking over my entire body and making me a sack of potatoes.

That's a powerful indicator that getting closer to these guys is a good thing, right?

The universe doesn't answer my mental question; it never does. I'm left with looking at the anxious demon shifters and raking my lip through my teeth before I croak, "Thank you."

It's not a lot of words, but it makes all the guys in front of me look super relieved, and before I know it, a soft, fluffy set of tails appears in front of my face. I'm a little confused why Zav has me hiding in his tails instead of himself, but when I turn my head, the Kitsuné is looking at me shyly. His face is red as he darts forward to press a whisper-soft kiss to my jaw.

"I'm happy to share my hiding spot if it helps you when your emotions are jumbled like mine," he murmurs, and my jaw drops.

The voice in my ear is rumbly again on the other side of my face as it says, "I can share my Kitsuné if you can keep trying to let me be better. I will fail often, as I frequently do when I stray from my training, but you can tell me when I'm fucking it up. But the loyalty and allegiance my caliphate shows you, Kit Camponella, is something so intense that I fear I could never sway. They are both strong and fragile, which you now hold as much responsibility for as I do."

I choke as I try to respond to quite possibly the nicest thing Jasper's ever said to me, and Zav gives me a gentle smile. It seems as though the redheaded hacker also realizes how important that tiny, barely audible speech surrounded by tails is to me and our group. Finally, I'm able to whisper, "I don't break things, Jasper, even if I'm broken. I think we're all trying to heal together. As long as you join us, we will be stronger than before the cracks."

An unexpected, yet soft flutter of lips against my ear makes my whole body light up, and the effects of my attack fade like the sun on the horizon at dusk. I've never experienced something that sent the fear and terror packing so quickly, and I turn to look at the prince with wide eyes. "How the *fuck* did you do that?"

"Easy," he says with a smirk. "I may be from the Wrath line, shrimp, but my demon eats and breathes fear. That's my gift that I keep inside in favor of my shadow dragon; it's only for the most dire of circumstances."

Since when the fuck am I 'the most dire of circumstances' and when was this confusing asshole going to mention this?

I Don't Want To Be Here Anymore

Salem

Whistling to myself, I finish whipping up the breakfast for Kat before I head to the *Triclinium* with the guys. She's staying in the room again today, but since we've all got entirely unmissable classes because of fucking Darkstar and that asshole Major, we have to leave her in Dottie's care. I don't like it, but given yesterday's nonsense, even Jasper had to relent. Kat has a note from the scary doc; we do not. But we can make certain she's okay by keeping in touch with texts, and Slash will head right back here during his two-hour free block to take his turn on KK duty.

It's only two hours, Salem; get a grip.

My brain is trying to convince my heart and the fear in the pit of my gut, but it's not doing so hot. After our little bonding sesh last night, it finally feels like we might all be on the same team—*for real*—and I don't want some dumbass to fuck it up. By the time she nodded off from tiny bites of my tasty berry cakes and exhaustion last night, my girl was actually smiling, and so was the pissy prince. That's sort of a miracle, and I refuse to sit idly by until it's a common occurrence, not an occasional one.

"Salem, you didn't have to get up early to do this," Kat says on a yawn as she pads out of her room with Dottie in tow. The small animal scampers over, climbs the stools and perches on the counter as she waits for her breakfast. "Man, you've spoiled *both* of us."

Grinning, I shrug as I lick my fingers. "I aim to please, Firecracker."

She dips her chin and hops onto the stool, looking sprier than yesterday. That pleases me, and I add a bit more Cantù berry and cream to the pile of pancakes for her. "That's not the woo-woo stuff, right?"

I chuckle and shake my head. "No, it isn't. We reserve that treat for times when you are safely surrounded by us, so nothing bad can happen. Also, I vow to make sure you know how strong the concoction is before I hand it to you. I'm still really fucking sorry about that, by the way."

Kat pushes her hair out of her eyes, and I notice that for once, she doesn't have bags under them. "Salem, you didn't mean to do that. It was like a bad comedy of errors, man. And… I really haven't discussed the whole bad times thing, and that makes it hard for you guys to dance around it without sometimes hitting a landmine. We're fine; I promise."

Wrinkling my nose, I fill her plate with the fluffy stack, the beast meat sausage and the Stygian eggs scrambled with sweet cheese and Fae berries. It's a fancy-ass meal with expensive ingredients, but I doubt Jasper will bitch about my food budget *now*. "Eat. You're still getting your strength and your magic back. You'll need to up your food intake with shifting practice, and even more if Jas is really going to privately train you for battle. He reverts to the training he had sometimes and forgets that not everyone is a goddamn dragon."

"Do they have really good stamina or something?" Kat asks as she takes a bite and groans happily.

"Interesting that you would ask that today," I reply with a smirk. To be honest, I'm not upset about KK getting closer with the rest of the guys in the slightest, only allowing my panda to feel his 'mine' feelings in a non-aggressive way by snarking. He's a little possessive of our girl, especially since he's never given a red, randy shit about anyone before.

Her eyes fly open as she flushes, the next bite stopping on the way to her mouth. "*Salem!* Stop being… flirty in front of people all the time. You and Oriel are going to out me before I'm ready for the others. One night with Jasper behaving like a decent person isn't enough to… I need more time."

I walk over and lean on the counter, looking at her with my head in my palm. "You realize that there's only three of us left that don't know, right? We're getting close to having no 'big secret' to be afraid of, and that means we can be affectionate whenever we want. Are you always going to turn into a tomato?"

Kat huffs and shoves the bite in her mouth, but can't hide the groan as she tastes the food again. Once she's swallowed, she gives me a dirty look. "I can't be mad at you when this food is like a fucking party in my mouth. I'm with Oriel… you're a big, fluffy cheater, Salem Stryker."

Hearing my full name on her lips makes me grin, and I shrug shamelessly. "Never claimed to play fair when the others have so many tricks up their sleeves, Firecracker."

"Tricks?" she asks curiously. "What tricks?"

This time, I'm the one who huffs. "Oriel with his damn gifts from the secret hoards. Xerxes makes you fabulous clothes. Zav let you hide in his cutesy tails. Slash and his protective big-guy thing. Hell, even Jasper and the whole wounded rich boy past. I'm just a cook with a poofy tail, KK. I can't compete."

"It is *not*, nor will it ever be, a competition." Her fork clatters as she leans on her elbows and looks at me over her half-gobbled plate, expression serious. "Salem, you were the first person to really accept me here. Everyone said you'd be mean and kick me out, but you taught me to cook and did all sorts of things that said I was welcome when no one else was saying it. You have something they don't and can't replicate."

Now I'm feeling all mushy inside, and I don't think she's ready for that just yet, so I mutter, "Thank you for saying that, Firecracker."

Once she's smiling again, I stand, walk over to press a kiss to her temple, and then I get to cleaning up the kitchen. If I don't, I'll be too involved to grab my stuff and leave with the guys, class be damned.

And I definitely can't be randomly absent with Darkstar as the professor this morning— that wouldn't go over well at all.

"AND THE *REASON* WE'VE ALLOWED THAT FALSE INFORMATION TO PERSIST, OF course, is to keep the surface-dwelling humans in line," Darkstar says as he looks around the room. "They're far too weak-minded to be let in on the secrets of the realms or even those beings in their own space. In fact, many of those so-called 'lost ones' that the Society is so eager to scoop up and train end up being guests of their own prisons because they've been far too damaged by their time living with those meat sacks."

Ouch. He's on a roll today—I wonder why?

"If he believes that, why did he bring KK from the surface?" I whisper to Oriel and Slash.

"Don't be dense, bro," Oriel mutters. "Even Darkstar has to obey the seers when they tell him someone is supposed to be here. He fucking hates it, but those guys are appointed by the court. All the heads of the schools have to listen when they tell admissions to send letters."

"Indeed, they do. Denying the seers would be tantamount to saying the King is wrong. Darkstar wouldn't risk it." Slash folds his arms over his chest, eyes forward as he replies in a low tone. "The little demon lucked out by having the doctor be assigned to fetch him, though. That was very fortunate."

"How he wrapped that terrifying fucker around his finger, I'll never know." Oriel draws a flaming skull on his notes, and I smother a chuckle.

Biting my lip, I consider what I'm going to say before I ask, "Do you think the doc knew the *secret* the minute he picked KK up?"

Slash snorts and shakes his head. "No. I do not."

"I think KK is pretty easy to like, and he doesn't treat the doc like a freak. That's how he ingratiated himself with the old birdman." Oriel looks at me and shrugs. "Doc probably knows by now, though. Jas will flip when he realizes that tidbit. I hope he doesn't fuck everything up being mad at everyone."

"The likelihood of his fury is far greater than his calm," Slash says in a sigh. "I agree Kit should not tell him until they are much more settled in this detente."

"Duh."

The crow and the shark glare at me, and I hold my hands up. "I mean, I'm not wrong! I was a bit surprised it went so well last night, especially after the snafu I created with the berries. But I'm all in on getting the two stubborn people in our group to stop pretending they hate each other. I don't want to screw it up *or* for them to screw it up because we didn't help."

"I think Zavida's support will mitigate that." Slash tilts his head and frowns. "Are Darkstar's speeches suddenly much more… pointed today?"

Oriel snorts as he flips a coin over his free hand like an old-timey poker player—but faster in a freakily skilled show of dexterity. "His mask is slipping, and I don't know what would make him bolder about his hatred of those in other realms. The Major made him look stupid, so he should be in snivel-y-mode. Why is he so confident in showing his ugly side?"

It's a good question and one that we need to find an answer to—Darkstar changing his tune this completely is concerning.

"However, despite the uselessness of the humans as allies or colleagues across the realms, they *are* very integral to maintaining the status quo in Hell. As you know, there are entire industries in our home dedicated to humans needing our services and goods. Working for the royal Court or other consortiums that employ demons who have the species and lineage gifts for acquiring power from other realms is quite lucrative. Many of you will graduate from here with offers from those firms because of what you are and who you are descended from—you should be honored."

Squinting up at the front of the room, I feel my intuition spike at that statement. This is Mythology class, not career services or even some sort of business class. We're supposed to be learning about the differences between reality and what the surface folks (or other realms) believe about history and the stories from it. Why did I just feel like I was in some sort of recruitment commercial?

Slash grunts as he stabs at his phone. "I am texting Jasper about this. I dislike Darkstar favoring anyone. That is suspicious."

"Perhaps Zav needs to do some deep-diving on the outside companies doing bargains and deals and all of that shit?" Oriel elbows the big guy, his eyes serious. "Maybe that's where some of the money to help a rebellion is coming from. Siphoning it from that industry would be easy, I bet. It's not done with traditional payment, and those contracts can be traded for cash— a good way to launder it."

I pinch the bridge of my nose, not liking the sound of the thief's guess. Obviously, he's funded up there with all the shit the Geminis have their fingers in, but he'd need more to stay in the loop. I hate politics, and I hate serious stuff like this even more. I just want to cook my food and be with my friends—not fight a damn war, but… The day's finally come where we're going to be part of it whether I want to or not.

"Yeah," I say as I slouch in my seat. "Well, I suppose Zav will need to set up his what-sits to track money from a lot of places once we have a better idea of what allies he has down here. The Games might reveal that, I think."

"How?"

I make a face as Oriel draws me deeper into speculation. "Because Lucian will hold his own form of court for most of them and the crowds will get bigger the further into them we get, right? That means he'll give special treatment to his favored people in his section when there are events. We should be able to… I don't know, tech something or spell something so we find out who it is."

"That's a good point, Salem. Very smart."

I know the big guy isn't being sarcastic, so I'm feeling pretty good although we're stuck here until this windbag shuts his pie hole.

Glitter and Gold

Kit/Kat

The knock on the door scares the crap out of me. I jump about ten feet in the air, disturbing Dottie in her snoozing place above my head, and damn near fall out of the chair. I was reading one of the books Annie gave me last night, using his really neatly printed annotations to cross-reference with my textbooks. Keeping my mind busy helped me not be anxious about being alone in the room, when there are many shitty people on campus—both visitors and permanent residents. I obviously didn't let the guys know I was skittish; it would have led to fights about skipping class and the watchful eyes on us.

But yeah, my brain was taking little side quests to What-If Land, so I had to occupy it.

"Coming," I call as I blow out a breath and slow down my heart rate before I walk to the door carefully. The knock makes me suspicious because my caliphate knows the code; they don't *need* to knock to get the damn thing open. I pause by the reinforced wood, listening with my new sharpened hearing skills and sniffing to see if I can identify what the fuck is on the other side.

"Saltwater?" I mutter before I look at the door in confusion. "Slash, is that you?"

"Excellent job, little demon. You were cautious about opening up to someone unknown and used your new abilities to mitigate the risk."

His rumbling praise makes my stomach flutter, but I yank the damn thing open and I glare at him, anyway. "Why are you testing how I deal with visitors? No one dares to come onto this floor. Jasper would fricassee them."

The toothy grin also makes my body shiver, though I try to shake it off, and he arches a brow. "Do you think those with ill-intent are going to stay away because of the prince's temper? If that were true, *no one* would ever attack you, nor would they spread rumors. Yet, even the weakest demons take part in the gossip mill when they think we cannot hear them."

I frown. "If you hear them, why is it still happening?"

"I have been forbidden to eat them, and we find other ways to make them suffer. Jasper believes too many missing students would draw unwanted attention, especially this close to the Games." Slash's scowl tells me they disagree on that topic, and I wonder what the other guys have said about it.

Damn men and their secret meetings—it pisses me off something fierce.

"I'm a big… boy, Slash. I could be in those discussions; no, scratch that… I *should* be in those meetings. It's bullshit."

The shark demon comes into the room, shutting the door firmly before he turns to look at me seriously. "They are not meetings, Kat. Those were random conversations held in passing when you happened to not be around. That might sound fishy, but it is true. I would not purposely exclude you with your safety, even with our new shared secrets."

My face flushes as I step closer, looking up at the gigantic man until it almost gives me a crick in my neck. "You'd better not. That promise about it not changing things holds even when it involves defending myself and risky shit. I don't want you guys to fashion me into some damsel in your heads once you know the truth. I've always had to protect myself, and even more so since the incident. I *have* to take care of myself or I feel helpless again. You get that, right?"

His jaw grits as he walks over to pick up Dottie and sit her on his broad shoulder. "My instincts dislike that sentiment; I have to admit. However, my brain understands what you are saying, and I will do my best to give you the chance if need be. But you also must listen when I say that our demons and our animals will naturally want to protect you like Salem did in the Fae place. We cannot stop them from doing it. That doesn't mean we believe you are weak, little demon. It only means we value you greatly enough to put ourselves in harm's way so you are safe."

Ugh. Why does he always have to make sense and be sweet about this shit?

"It's not fair that you're good at being practical when you're also being nice," I grumble as Dottie chitters happily from her perch up high. "And you're a traitor, girl. You didn't even complain that he picked you up!"

Slash chuckles as he pets her head with one finger. "She knows I mean you and her no harm. Therefore, she can trust me to carry her while you gather your things. It is time to go to the gym again for our sessions. We have a lot of time today that should not be wasted."

"Boogers," I grumble as I stomp toward my room to get my stuff. "I was hoping you'd hang out with me while I catch up on reading. Annie's notes in the books are helping me make connections way better than my classes are. At least, the ones taught by assholes."

His laugh follows me into my room, even when I close the door. Heading to my dresser, I shed my comfortable dorm room clothes for ones that are good for moving in the gym. I don't know if he will want me to shift or not, but if we do light cardio, I'll need to be in things that don't leave me drenched in sweat. Once I'm bound tightly, boxer'd up, and wearing the gym uniform under my sweats, I look in the mirror. I need another haircut—apparently, one of those parts of me is encouraging it to grow like it never has before. I won't pass for a dude nearly as well if I don't ask X to trim and buzz me a bit.

I hope they can keep it looking decent, but if not, we'll have to think of a better solution going forward.

"Are you done yet?" Slash calls from the living room. "I did not think you would take *longer* to get ready now. Will that be normal?"

My eyes narrow, and I grab my bag, stomping out of the bedroom to see an amused-looking demon waiting for me. "You did that on purpose."

"Perhaps," he says with a shrug. "But you are here now and we can get moving."

"In a minute," I mutter petulantly. Ignoring his chuckles, I head into the kitchen to tuck snacks for Dottie and me, a bottle of the water treated with Dank's meds, and reluctantly, one of Slash's granola bars as well into my bag. "I promised Salem I would keep extra food on me. He's convinced that I'm going to hit like… a magical growth spurt or something because the lion appeared?"

Slash nods in approval, his expression solemn. "The panda is right. You will, and it will get more intense as other things continue to develop. Put two more of your snacks in the bag, just in case the practice drains you. While I don't mind carrying you, I do not believe you'd enjoy it happening as we cross campus in broad daylight."

"Gee, what made you think that?" I mumble. Slash gives me a reproachful look, so I do as he asked and stuff some more of Salem's pre-made goodies in my bag. "Is that good enough?"

He tilts his head, then shakes it. "No. Two more waters as well. I want to make sure you are staying hydrated. Not just because I am being a pain, but because I'd rather you have it and not need it than be ill."

It's hard to argue with such no-nonsense caution, and he damn well knows it. Bastard.

"Fine, fine," I huff as I shove more into the bag. "Are we good now?"

"Yes, thank you." That said, he turns, heading for the door to open it, and I follow along, caught between feeling girly and cared for while also being annoyed that I didn't think of it all myself.

Being hyper-independent around these dudes is a real pain in my ass.

"Okay, little demon. The door is locked, and I have made certain it cannot be opened without going through me. Time to show me the big cat."

I'm standing in my boxers and the makeshift gauze binding glaring at Slash. Obviously, I can't rip up my damn binder over and over, but I've been assured the boxer briefs are easily replaceable. There's a lot of skin on display, which makes me itchy and nervous, but it's also something I'm not good at yet, which makes that feeling worse. Luckily, the shark is patient as fuck with me—something I fear Jasper won't be—and he's not staring at all the pieces of me that are normally covered.

He really is a kind man, and he hides it so well that it's a shame.

"So I have to close my eyes and think of her, focusing on that color inside me where I think she came from…"

"If that is how it happens, yes. The colors metaphor confuses me slightly, as that is not something I experienced when I first shifted." Slash frowns as he studies me for a moment, obviously waiting for the change. "You can begin whenever you are ready."

"I'm *trying*," I grit out as I squeeze my eyes closed and picture what he said in my mind. "This *is* what happened in my head, but… I don't know why I can't always get it."

I feel him coming closer; the air getting colder and warmer simultaneously. His voice is deep and rumbly as he says quietly, "Your first shift came when you were overcome with emotion. That part is not uncommon, I believe. You could do it with me in the pool area because there were also a lot of feelings. That is what is missing—you have to summon her with all of those things, until you are so good at calling that she comes every time."

Sighing, I nod, and then delve back into my mind. Nervousness is a feeling, and it's definitely flowing through me while he's this close and I'm *this undressed*. So I follow that thread, letting my brain meander along that trail until I hit the colors swirling inside of me. They're not red and black today, though, and I don't know what to make of that. I don't want to fail at shifter practice, so I embrace the other colors, pairing with an internal plea to help me figure this out.

That's when I feel the change begin, and my body sparkles with excitement.

I open my mouth to say something, forgetting that I sure as hell don't have enough knowledge of how this works to talk as an animal. The only thing that comes out is a big huff, but it doesn't sound right. Moving my legs, I make sure there are four, but it still doesn't feel right.

What the fuck is going on now?!

"Little demon…" Slash says, his voice full of awe. "You…."

My inability to ask him what the hell I did is frustrating, and I hear another huff as my legs stomp. Finally, I give up and open my eyes to a room full of goddamn rainbows and glittery sparkles that seem to fall from the fucking sky.

Am I high? Did my water have secret crunkleberries in it? I'll kill Salem…

"You shifted." Slash shakes his head and then rubs the back of his neck as he stares in shock. "But this is not your lioness, Kat. This is… magical."

Stomping again in irritation, I note that I definitely have a tail. It's swishing as I throw a tantrum, the only way I can in this form.

"They're so rare. *You're* so rare." His eyes narrow, and my big guy looks even more worried than he did when I got hurt. "We cannot allow people to know, little demon. They will hunt you, drain you, and leave you for dead. This changes everything."

He keeps dancing around it, so I stomp over and huff at him nearby, hoping he gets the damn point. When I step back, his expression is sheepish. "I should have known by the tattoos, but we didn't… you weren't a *girl* in our heads then."

I'm going to lose it if he doesn't say it soon.

"Kat, you're an alicorn."

HOME

ANTON

The Arms class was brutal, and though none of us got *injured* this morning, the exhaustion showed on my brothers' faces as we left the arena to head for our various classes. Slash pretended to be stoically unaffected by the fact that he got to fetch KK for shifting work for several hours, but even Jasper rolled his eyes at the act. Once I noticed it, there was no way anyone else could miss the tiny spring in the big guy's stomp as he left.

Kit is doing an excellent job of finding the right way to approach each of us to develop a stronger bond; I wish I were as intuitive as he is.

"Babe?"

Blinking, I look up from my phone to see Xerxes standing next to the doorway of my Design Lab. "Fuck. I was too buried in my head again. I need to be more cautious."

They smile fondly, reaching up to ruffle my hair just a smidge—not enough to set off my issues, of course—and I make a face before I straighten the colorful strands carefully. "You were. Slash and Jas would be super pissed, but luckily, I had time to stop by before my Women's Fashion class. You're heading downstairs for Drawing, yes?"

I nod, stepping closer so they can hug me. X has always been conscientious about my quirks, and they know that initiating too much touch when I am not ready can throw my entire vibe off for the day. Xerxes tugs me into their arms, squeezing a little, and I return the action once I relax. It's the dance we do when we are publicly intimate, and we've perfected it over the years. At times, I wish I weren't so particular about things, but X hasn't ever cared. They simply accept me, funny habits and special instructions and all— something my parents or siblings never have.

The family we make can have stronger bonds than the family we are born into.

"You're thinking again, Annie."

I pull back, straightening my uniform to give him a sheepish expression. "Yes, it's hard not to with so many things going on simultaneously. My brain catches on something, then spirals out until I've gone to the end of the line, and once that happens, I can put pieces together. Not all the time, of course, because I don't always find the end for a while."

"Shall I walk you downstairs to your class, then? Coco won't mind if I'm a few minutes late. My projects are so far ahead because of the… adjustments I've made to include KK's things as part of my portfolio, that no one could accuse me of slacking."

Nodding, I take their proffered arm, heading for the stairs with my love. "How are you getting away with making things for Kit in a *women's* fashion class? That seems counterintuitive."

X blinks, then coughs as we descend together. "Uh, well. He's so small, and I've dubbed the pieces my 'inclusive' clothing line that will capture the 'sexually adventurous' customers. Not my words, mind, as sexually adventurous doesn't *have* a fucking gender, but the diva refuses to use proper terminology. She's not the most enlightened of our kind, and her opinion of her own fame is more than I think she deserves."

I smile, my lips twisting a bit as I realize that he's being both honest and petty concurrently. "Black and white basics aren't very difficult to create. Her reputation came more from her time period and those who wore the items, I believe. It was one of those 'perfect storms' that create a legend rather than sheer talent."

X nods, tossing their hair over their shoulder. "And she didn't exactly cavort with the most honorable of people, either. KK would lose his mind if he found out who's stuck down here teaching as purgatory."

They're right—Kit's sense of justice is highly developed, and it's one of the things I worry will make his demon transition difficult.

"That's a problem for another day," I reply as we finally hit the bottom floor. Opening the door to the hallway, I wait for Xerxes to pass and follow. "I believe he's gaining flexibility slowly, though. His lack of fury at the destruction Jasper caused during the standoff in the dorm, shows he is re-evaluating how he looks at proper punishment."

"Yes, but we don't want him to lose what makes him special. I worry about that," my lover says softly. "Kit has so many things to heal from, and there have been even more curveballs flung at his face than an umpire. He needs more time to process, but we simply do not have it with the Games looming. I'm certain they're going to start after Krampusnacht."

That hadn't occurred to me yet, and I feel absolutely ridiculous for missing it. The time from Devil's Night to now has practically flown by, and we haven't prepared our new brother for the holidays, exams, or anything we'd usually be doing at Discordia at this point. We've been focused on the fucking bullies, Darkstar, and the damn Games to the exclusion of important shit. I frown as we approach the door to my class, shaking my head.

"We have to remind the others of what we've all forgotten."

X sighs, watching my fingers fly over the keys of my phone as I text the group chat without Kit. "I'm not looking forward to explaining this; are you?"

"Not even a little," I reply distractedly. "Who is the best choice to broach it?"

The look we exchange tells me neither of us knows the answer to that question—fabulous.

AFTER X LEFT FOR THEIR CLASS, I SPENT DRAWING CLASS WORKING ON THE designs for the end of semester project while my brain went on wild goose chases. Even when I was young, I could separate the function of my art from the insanity of my unfettered mind. It's an odd ability, and most people, even Xerxes, don't quite get it. The only person who comes close to understanding is Zavida; he also codes like his fingers are on fire while his brain wanders off. We're alike in that way, though I believe my disassociation is far worse than his unless he's wearing the headphones. That helps him block everything out, whereas I'm able to sink into my focus and ignore the entire world with no external assistance.

Again, I believe Kit was spot on in determining that my caliphate and I are not like our parents because we diverge from their typical behaviors and psychology so completely.

But that's not a surprise so much as confirmation for me. I certainly knew from a young age that I wasn't like my parents, Aegon and Anastasia, nor were my siblings—Achille, Adara, Asse and Alkemene—anything like me. I was the odd man out in every conceivable way, yet the traditions forced my summoners to accept me as the heir or find a way to get rid of me without being caught. I'm surprised they didn't manage the second, but I think my divergence wasn't as clear until I was old enough that it would be noticed if I went missing. Once I was entrenched with the prince and the other heirs, we looked out for one another, foiling any pissed parent's schemes to activate succession.

Jasper was very clever in his ways of helping those of us who weren't physically difficult to handle, avoid as much harm as possible. As much as I know he's imperfect, he was born to lead, and that has been obvious since we were quite small. He and Slash took up the mantle of protectors, even when it cost them dearly at home. I suppose that's why we never once complained when Jasper was being a jackass to everyone; we all owed him our lives in some form or fashion.

However, *now* it's like that burden has lifted and everyone has found a purpose bigger than gratitude. Kit Kat appeared and *poof!* The veil lifted, and all of my brothers realized we'd been hindering the prince's development by letting him treat us poorly. His sharp tongue and quick wit were matched well by the new guy, and no one else had the stones to consistently get in Jasper's face to call him out. Given that Kit is small and powerless but stood his ground, it felt weird not to do so myself. I guarantee the others experienced that epiphany as well because no one, not even Zav, lets the shadow dragon be cruel in our circle anymore.

We sort of owe an enormous debt to KK for that alone, but in watching, I think there's more.

I look at my work, tilting my head as I realize what I'd done. The building I've been designing for my architecture portfolio is based on the fantastical drawing I've been doing for the semester here. Not that I've told anyone— even X—but this is the compound I want to build for my caliphate someday. Obviously, we will have to live in the palace at some point in time, but none of us believed it would happen right after we finished Discordia. We believed it would take many years to get to the point where we had enough resources and support to challenge our parents' rule, and we'd need a home base away from them as a haven.

So I've been designing our future home as part of my classwork. By the time I graduate from Discordia, the plans should be perfected. However, while I was thinking about how my caliphate had changed, my hand changed the sketch on its own. The middle of the compound is expanded now, and the wings dedicated to everyone's pursuits now ring that section like spokes on a wheel. It's almost as if the various amenities—professional kitchen, art studio, gym, tech center, etc—are orbiting the center structure.

I think I just reorganized our future home to include Kit without thinking about it.

"Huh," I murmur as I look at the drawing with discerning eyes. "That could actually work."

Biting my lip, I sketch out a few other additions, including a room to build an interactive playroom for Dottie. Kit's relationship with the small rodent is important, and if I'm making a space for him in our future, there needs to be a place for her as well. My brows furrow as I consider how helpful the kinkajou is to him, especially with regulating his moods. Perhaps on the next trip to visit The Keeper, I should query him on how I might find out if I am an acceptable demon for such a thing. It might be useful, even if I'd need to adjust to having someone that depends on me for continued survival.

"Keeping things clean, too."

"Did you have a question, Mr. Aldaric? *Quelle surprise.*"

Shit. I said that too loudly and got the attention of Professor Landis. She's half Muse and half drude, which means she's a great art professor, but if you piss her off, your dreams are where you'll pay. Salem and Xerxes can fight that shit off, but I hate conflict that cannot be resolved quickly. Landis is petty enough to keep trying to get in until she feels vindicated. Sleep is hard with the way my brain works, and I'm not willing to risk it for a hollow victory when she's being snarky.

"I do not, Professor." I look up from my sketch, meeting her gaze with as little emotion as possible.

If I don't pique her interest further, she'll fuck off to help the more effusive students, and I can go back to focusing. Drawing is a required course for my studies, and despite my experience and title, the fuckers in admissions wouldn't let me skip it anymore than they did my brothers and their entry-level courses. It's a waste of time for us to be taking many of the '101' cour-ses, but here we are. I'm sure Darkstar had a hand in that decision, and if I could kick his ass for it, I absolutely would.

Luckily, there's only a few more hours of class until I can head back to the dorm and decompress with my brothers.

Of course, wanting to decompress with other beings present isn't something I did before KK arrived, either, but it's definitely what I want to do now.

Pink Pony Club
Kit/Kat

I make a frustrated noise and stomp my front feet hard, hoping he gets my point; I don't know what the fuck that is. It's not a lioness, but it has four legs and a tail and… I think about my body for a moment. Wings?! Holy fuck, I have wings. Is… Am I like a pegasus? Maybe, but if I was, he would have just said that, right? I wonder—

"Little demon, alicorns have been extremely rare since the human medieval ages. The species they combine—a pegasus and a unicorn—has never been plentiful. Many myths speak of their powers, so they have always had to elude humans *and* supernaturals, though for different reasons."

I'm a unicorn-pegasus?! That's why I had those insane cutie mark tattoos pop up; it makes perfect sense now.

Moving around a bit again, I stomp my feet and feel the wings flap. I'm terrified of figuring out how to fly, and I guarantee I'm going to screw up shit with this head weapon. I huff a breath again, the sound of my horsey frustration registering with my ears now. Now that I know why everything differs from how I felt when I was a lion, I'm not sure how or why I got this response to my request to shift. The guys already thought I was a target for getting the invite without my demon, having more than one shift, and being part of their caliphate. Adding the layer of a super rare shift just ices the danger cake, man.

Slash frowns as I prance around the room, fluffing the wings and tossing my head. He walks over and carefully puts his big hand gently on my muzzle. I lean into his palm, making a calmer sound as it helps me stop wigging out in my head. "I would like for you to try something, Kat. It is not something that everyone can do. In fact, I cannot, nor can *most* of our caliphate. Jasper and Oriel are the only ones who have the necessary power and genetics needed for it to be possible."

I have no idea how to frown as a horse, so I just do my best and then press against his hand.

"I want you to take all the thinking in your head—the voice you hear that I do not—and focus on pushing it through the barrier to your animal. That sounds quite stupid, I understand, but since you have so many rare gifts, I am curious to see if you would fall in this designation as well."

He wants me to talk as a pretty pony shifter?

My ears twitch as I give his request a try anyway, though. Slash is patient with me during these sessions, and if he thinks it's possible, I have to listen. Picturing a barrier between the colors that represent all the new stuff emerging inside me, I jabber in my mind and push it gently. It doesn't work at first, so I flare my nostrils and shove the words harder. An odd sensation ripples through me, and suddenly, a perky high voice says, "I don't think it's working, Slash."

The shark shifter blinks at me in surprise, then his hand moves from my muzzle to clap over his mouth. Snickers escape anyway, rough and deep as he looks down at me. I try to horsey-frown at him, but I still don't know if it's working. He laughs and removes his hand, shaking his head with a soft look in his icy eyes. "You seem to be wrong, little demon. Though in this form, you sound *much* more like your feminine self. It's probably normal for this species—though Anton may confirm my supposition."

"Annie didn't give me anything about alicorns."

Slash looks down, his lips quirking at my high-pitched, silly voice. "He wouldn't have focused on things that are near extinction. You won't see them on the Games teams nor as challenges or obstacles. No one risks getting themselves killed in this sort of event. Unicorns charge incredibly high prices for their various powers and spell ingredients."

This is becoming too much, and I don't know how to deal with it. A low whinny escapes as I scrape my hooves over the ground, and I toss my head. Slash moves closer again, his hand running lightly over my mane.

"I know this is a lot, little demon. You are going through so many changes at once. It would scare anyone."

Not nearly as much as it does me, but I understand what he means.

"It's time to go back to your normal body, Kat. Focus again, and this time, you need to visualize yourself in your Kit body." He stops, then chuckles. "You know what I mean."

I do, and I appreciate that he's trying so hard to say things the right way. Honestly, I've gotten used to being both Kat and Kit, so neither feels wrong to me. Closing my eyes, I do as he says. It doesn't work immediately, so I keep breathing and focusing on the images in my mind. I'm not sure how much time goes by; it's not fast. But I keep the image in my mind and my inner voice coaxing until a tingle runs over me. It turns into heat, and my skeleton cracks as I finally get it to work.

"Excellent, little demon!" He moves back as my body reshapes itself, and I wing a prayer that he turns away when I end up naked.

I'm not quite ready for the full monte with him yet, but I do trust him not to take advantage—which is pretty big.

My limbs buckle after it's done, and I land on the floor, smacking my ass hard. "Gonna have to learn how to stick the landing. This floor is really hard."

"Your hoodie is to the right," Slash calls over his shoulder. "Tell me when you're ready to discuss your accomplishments."

I scramble over and pull the huge sweatshirt on, covering myself to my knees. This is good enough for now; it covers as much as the now ripped gauze and boxers. "Okay."

His toothy grin greets me when he turns, and the anxiety ball in my gut unwinds. Slash being himself without a single hint of remorse is comforting as fuck. "You did well, despite the surprise transformation."

"I'm not fast enough," I mumble as I scuff my foot on the ground. "I'll still be a liability to you guys."

"That is why we keep training."

Sighing, I run my hand through my hair. "Yes, but an alicorn isn't exactly a scary power. What if that's what I shift into during the fights?"

The big guy gestures at the bench, and I follow him over to it. We sit down, and he puts his arm around my shoulder. "Alicorns have a lot of sought-after abilities. I am uncertain which ones are true and which are myths. However, I believe you know who can help you find out."

"Really? Do you think it will have things I can use in the Games? It feels… silly and not at all useful for something like that."

He nods. "I believe so, yes. But even if I am wrong, the lioness and your magic will certainly be strong offensively."

"That's true," I reply as I lean against him. "If I can figure out how to use them reliably."

"Now we're back to training, little demon."

"Okay, okay." I sigh and pat his huge thigh lightly. "I get it. Find out about the Pink Pony Club later and work on technique and speed now."

He rumbles a chuckle, standing and offering his hand. I let him tug me to my feet, then push up on my tiptoes to kiss his cheek before I scamper back to my spot on the floor.

Time to make this shit happen or die trying.

By the time our three hours are almost up, I'm worn out. I shifted into the anime pony a couple of times and got back to my normal body, though I'm still not very fast. The room looks like a strip club—it's covered in glitter in a way that is going to make some custodial demon *very* unhappy. But I feel victorious because I did a lot better this time than I did yesterday. Progress might not be coming quickly, but it is coming.

"We need to get you back to the dorm," Slash says as he hands me the second water bottle. "But you must drink while we walk."

I pick up my bag, whistling for Dottie. She gives me a look that says she doesn't want to touch the sparkling floor, and I laugh. Walking over, I hold my arm up so she can scramble down it to my shoulder. "I know, girl. The Pink Pony is messy AF, right?"

Dottie chitters her agreement, and Slash looks around with a frown. "I will text Jasper to find someone to clean this up as soon as possible. I'm uncertain anyone will connect it with us, but it would be better if it were gone before others come in."

"No shit," I mumble. "If this place were co-ed, we might have better options for putting the blame on cheerleaders or something. Sadly, that will not work at sausage school."

Slash chokes, his eyes going wide. "You have been hanging around Salem and Oriel too much."

Shrugging, I give him a shy grin. "I'm trying to immunize myself against all the boy talk. If I'm spitting dirty stuff, too, then I won't get so blushy about it. And you know, maybe I won't be so prudish about sex stuff. I need to get less…affected by it."

He arches a brow at me, his smirk making my stomach flutter. "Why is that, little demon? Do you have plans I am not aware of?"

I wrinkle my nose as I walk up to him, smacking his arm. "Shut up. You don't need me to say why. I'm not *that* immune yet."

Laughing as he opens the door, Slash transforms into the quiet, threatening bodyguard he is when we are in public with effortless grace. His posture is stiffer, and the aura of menace he exudes blankets the hallway. "I believe in you, little demon. You are stronger than your trauma, and we have all noticed that you are healing. It is at your own pace, but I do not think any of my brothers are concerned by that."

As we board the elevator, I tilt my head at him. "You think? It's not annoying that I'm so damaged."

"We are *all* damaged." He reaches over to scratch Dottie's head since we're alone and shrugs. "You are no less accommodating with our issues. The way you handled Jasper and Zavida the other night was impressive. I have not witnessed the prince being so open with anyone—ever. I do not think it will be easy, even now, but you may do something none of us have been able to achieve."

"What's that?" I ask curiously.

Slash gives me a grin, but his eyes are earnest. "You might get him to truly open up about the horrors of his home life. If so, he might come to terms with it, and that would be quite a coup."

"I'm not trying to perform a coup successfully." I frown as I fiddle with the strap of my bag. "I just want to get better, and I want him to do that, too. I think it will be good for everyone if Jasper can stop reverting to his dad's bullshit brainwashing."

"It will, and you mistake what I meant." The big guy pauses, thinking for a few moments as the elevator dings and we exit. He doesn't speak as we walk through the lobby and down the steps, but once we're a good distance from anyone else, he says, "I meant you would accomplish something amazing and, by doing so, it will benefit the caliphate."

"Whew," I breathe. "*That* I agree with. My fear is that if bad shit goes down, he'll break his promise and it will hurt me. I'm fragile, and while I'm doing better, a stunt like the office thing would end our truce. I don't think I could stand for him to go back to being cruel now."

"He knows better."

I arch a brow as we cross the middle of campus. "Why?"

"Because if he does, he will have to deal with me."

Okay, then.

Anxiety

Jasper

The worst part of today is the ridiculous amount of free time I have.

After the Arms class, I had as many unscheduled blocks as my second, but I promised to allow Slash to work with the shrimp alone. That concession didn't bother me *before*, but after last night, I find myself insanely curious about what they're doing and if the kid is progressing. It made me itch to stay in my office and write up reports on progress for students, then go to lunch with Salem and Oriel before my Dark Magic lecture.

To be fair, they were grumpy as fuck, and I'd bet a shiny gold soul it was because Kit wasn't there.

My caliphate has completely and irrevocably shifted our focus to the kid, and while I understand it, the part of me raised by the king is having trouble with that. The Games will begin after the holidays—there's no doubt in my mind. The Major's arrival and the uptick in Lucian showing up to be a dick-waffle during class tell me they both know shit we do not. I haven't heard a peep from my father since he granted our surface pass and I sent him a glossed-over report with as much omission as I could get away with.

Trouble is brewing in multiple areas of concern, yet my step is lighter and my dragon is calmer than it has been in… a very long time. I don't want to consider what that means, so I have thrown myself into every task and class with fervor so I have to focus there instead of on my emotions. The acceptance of his offer to help surprised even me, but Zavvie was also quite pleased with it. He made certain to tell me how proud he was on the way back to our room this morning during our early session and again after Arms class. My Kitsuné is smart enough to do it privately, but he definitely wanted to express how much he liked my acquiescence.

Which means he, too, is hoping to get closer to the shrimp, and he wants to do it together, as Kit suggested.

I've tried to picture how that would work with our dynamic, and it's both exciting and confusing. The kid is so damaged that I don't have the faintest clue what would work and what wouldn't—it will require a very thorough conversation and clear boundaries. I've never entered a scene without that, of course, because of my trauma, but... I don't want to be the cause of a setback for someone so fragile. It's a war raging within me—the fear of being my father paired with the brainwashing of his edicts for my entire life-span. Being with Zavvie hasn't required such precise control, and I don't know if I'm capable of it if emotions run high.

"Fucking Tarron," I mutter to myself as the class ends and I stand. My seat is close to the back, purposely in the shadows so any practical applications of the subject are far from other grad students. My control of magic is excellent, but when I am embroiled in this kind of inner conflict, mistakes are possible. I need to escape if the need to shift arises. Luckily, that also keeps the others from hearing me curse my father and gives me a quick exit to stomp out of.

"Jasper, wait!"

Zav's voice catches me, and I stop, waiting for him and Salem to catch up. Pushing his glasses up, my lover gives me a scrutinizing look that I know means he's onto me. "Don't you two have classes to get to? I'm the only one with free periods next."

"Yes, but you were simmering the whole damn class, man." The panda arches a brow at me as we fall into step. "You can't go barging into the room and be shitty with KK because you've got your tail in a knot."

That wasn't my plan, but whatever.

"I will not go back to the room and be a dick, okay? Just because I have things on my mind doesn't mean that I will revert to old habits."

Zavvie frowns at me, still suspicious. "It's your pattern, Jas, and you know it as well as we do. Don't ruin the chance to overcome shit now."

Throwing up my hands in surrender, I huff. "Fine, fine. Yes, I'm having... issues. It still does not mean I was going to be shitty."

"That's more than we usually get, so good on you."

I roll my eyes at Salem as we get into the elevator. "Thanks. Very confident praise there, Stryker."

"You can't be mad that we are basing our concerns on *centuries* of repeated patterns, Jasper." Zavvie looks up at me, his tails swishing as he gives me a small smile. "No one is accusing you of bad intent as much as bad habits that were drilled into you by your asshole dad."

"That's why we put up with it." Salem reaches into his bag and hands me the bar with my ribbon color. "Here, have a snack and, like, chill. It always helps."

He's always got us covered that way, and I don't think I tell him enough how useful that is.

"Thanks, Salem," I mumble as I unwrap the snack. "You're good at keeping us fed."

"Holy fuck, an acknowledgment! There we go, Prince Pricklypants!"

I sneer at him and then take a bite of the treat, chewing before I respond. "I'll still kick your ass."

"Of course you will," Zav murmurs as his cheeks heat. "And some of us will enjoy it."

Damn his fucking afternoon classes—now I'm horny and I'm on my own.

WALKING ACROSS THE CAMPUS TO THE DORM IS MORE NERVE-WRACKING than I expected. I don't get why I'm so nervous, but I suppose it's because Zav and Salem were so worried I'd be an ass. They weren't being assholes; I know—but my own internal conflict is making it hard not to be on edge. My eyes sweep over the crowds moving through the quad, watching for threats as usual, but also checking for unusual behavior. Having someone from my father's court here is amping my distrust, which isn't helping the spiky anxiety over exposing myself to possible betrayal last night.

I guess they weren't wrong to speak up, but that doesn't make me feel any better.

Sighing in irritation, my tail flicks as I stalk towards Canto IV. Perhaps I should find something specific to do so I don't fuck this up. I can't ask Kit to go work on physical training on the field; he's been working on shifting for hours and will be exhausted. We can't go to the *Triclinium*; I ate earlier, and Slash likely made him eat the moment they got back to the dorm to refill his energy. I growl as I head up the steps, and it causes the crowds to part around me like magic.

"Move," I snarl as I enter the building. Demons scatter, and I stomp over to the elevator, glaring until the other people waiting move away so I'm alone when the doors close. By the time I get to our floor, I've gone through every idea, and I'm fresh out. I have no idea what I'm going to do to make certain that I don't screw up the truce without meaning to.

Pausing at the door to the shrimp's room, I run my hand through my hair. I pace back and forth for a moment, ignoring the keypad as I mutter to myself more. I'm never this insane, and there's no actual explanation for why agreeing to let the guy inch closer to me is making me a goddamn psycho.

The door opens and I whirl around, my eyes wide as Kit peeps out. I scowl at him, growling low. "You aren't supposed to open the door for anyone who doesn't have a code!"

His brows raise as he tilts his head in confusion. "But you have a code, Jasper."

"I didn't *use* it, did I?"

Rolling his eyes, he leans against the doorframe. "I used the damn peephole. We heard the elevator ding when you got up to the floor."

That's a pretty good excuse, but lots of demons can convincingly appear *to be someone else.*

"Do you know how many demons—much less those with hybrid magic or shifting powers—could pull off a convincing facsimile of one of us? Hint: it's a lot."

The shrimp sucks in an annoyed breath as he stares at me. "But they would have set off the sensors that X and Annie put in, and you didn't."

"There are those who could disarm them. It's impossible to know what anyone is hiding here. Think about the things that we're hiding from every-one." I frown, stepping closer as I look down at him. "Shrimp, we're all worried about keeping you safe—at least until you can reliably defend your-self. You can't blame us for that; human bodies are so fucking fragile."

He ducks his head, muttering, "I know that, and it's really…nice. I'm trying not to put myself in danger, but also hate being the weak link. I did a good job at practice, but I'm nowhere *near* where I need to be. It's demoralizing, even when Slash tells me I'm doing well."

I press my lips together, suppressing the urge to laugh. My best friend *never* compliments people during training, no matter *how* fucking well they perform. I don't think the kid has a clue how incredibly weird hearing that is. The dude always acts like *his* drill sergeant father, almost down to the insults he throws out when you fail.

"What? I know it's stupid, but I can't help feeling like a failure."

Coughing as I rub the back of my neck, I gather myself before I respond. "It's not stupid, and if Slash said you're doing well, I guarantee you are. He doesn't hand out praise often."

"Really? He definitely does a good job of motivating me without scaring me," Kit says as he finally meets my eyes again. "Actually, he's probably the best teacher I've ever had. I haven't told him that; he'd be uncomfortable, I think. But it's true because he's patient and works hard to keep me from sinking into negative shit."

I need to see this, but I don't think the shrimp would like it if I had Zavvie plant cameras in the gym—damn this conscientious behavior thing.

"Well, tell him." Kit looks skeptical, but I shake my head. "No, you should. I'd bet no one ever has. It's just not how things are done in royal circles, and none of us has ever been great at expressing emotions because of our childhoods. I'm not the only one who struggles with it, just the slowest to adjust."

His smile is broad as he looks at me, and I don't know why. His little rat comes scampering over, crawling up his leg to his shoulder to look at me, and I'm surprised when it settles without yelling at me in rodent. "Dottie approves, so maybe, um… Maybe we should go do one of our practices? I think I've recovered enough from my shifting to do a little work."

"Are you sure?" I look at him with a narrowed gaze. "Zavida will be furious if I push you too far and you relapse or something. The others won't be happy either."

The shrimp chuckles, pushing his hair out of his eyes. "They will, but as long as you listen to me when I tell you something is too much, we'll be okay. And of course, Dottie will totally tell on you if you don't. She really likes Salem and Oriel, so they'll know."

I suck in a breath, then let it out slowly as the wheels turn in my head. My training was *not* kind or gentle, and I have no idea if I can keep old habits from cropping up, especially if we're alone. It would be terrible, and I'd ruin everything—the rest of the guys would *lose* their shit. "I don't… I don't know if that's a good idea. We need to start, but alone? It might not be the best—"

Kit snorts, stepping into my space to put his hand on my bicep. "Jasper, I realize this will not be easy for you. I'm in your classes. But I think *you* need to know you can do this, and *I* need to feel like I'm getting closer to protecting myself. Putting it off until both of us don't feel nervous about it won't fix anything."

Good thing he's so damn confident; now I need to live up to that and not fuck this up entirely.

Training Season

Kit/Kat

The campus is bustling as Jasper walks Dottie and me across the quad to the arena. I know he just came from here a while ago, and I appreciate him trying so hard to live up to the promises he made last night. But his nervousness is brushing against mine as we enter the stadium; I have to take a few deep breaths to help myself calm as we head straight for the field. My experiences on the pitch have *not* all been good by any stretch, and the thought of other people seeing me get decimated by the hulking prince isn't my idea of a fun time. But the place is empty, and even when I squint, I don't see anyone hanging about in the stands.

Maybe this won't be as humiliating as I anticipated.

"Set the rat down and stretch," Jasper rumbles as he walks around the sideline looking at the racks of weapons thoughtfully. "Even if you were shifting, this is different, and I'm sure the doc would be mad if we showed up with any injury."

"Dank won't be mean and don't call Dottie a rat."

His snort echoes as I do what he said despite my retort. Giving her a bag of treats to munch on, I put my kinkajou on the bench where she can watch. Once she's settled, I plop on the ground and start the sequence of stretches I've been taught one by one. Jasper turns, giving me a pleased expression as he sees what I'm doing, and then goes back to eyeing the weaponry.

"I thought we were doing physical defense and stuff first," I mutter as I work on my calves. "Why are you browsing knives and stuff?"

"Because you need to warm-up and also because we will alternate between hand-to-hand and various weapons as we train. It is important to provide well-rounded lessons if we want to get your knowledge base moving faster."

Okay, that makes sense, and he didn't even act like I'm a dumbass. Nice.

"Do you fight in human form often? I mean, if I were a dragon, I'd choose that over getting clocked in the face every day of the week."

The prince laughs, the sound sharp as he growls, "Dragons, even half-shifts, do not *fit* in every situation, shrimp. Size is a factor in many situations, but also, they are an extremely difficult animal to master harmony with. Their instincts are to raze and destroy completely—mine is powerful enough that it's often using… What do your people say? Using a nuke to drive a nail? Yes, that's it."

I frown as I continue loosening my muscles. "They aren't really my people, Jasper. You know that as well as I do. I'm part demon and part shifter; I was *never* human to begin with. If I have to come to terms with that, so do you."

"True," he replies absently. "I suppose you had no control over being left up there for a bunch of donut-eating dullards who obsess over the most trivial things possible. If you'd been abandoned in Hell, you might have at least gotten the basic knowledge of your real species and home before you reached college."

"Duh. That might not have been any easier than foster care up there, but I wouldn't be so 'fish out of water' now." I grunt as I work on my quads, moving to a squat before I mutter, "And maybe I wouldn't be so fucking broken, who knows?"

His shadow suddenly looms over me as he says, "Trial by fire can produce the strongest materials and beings in every realm, shrimp. Perhaps the Fates needed to make you able to withstand the flames to do whatever your destiny is. It sucks, but it's no less probable than thinking you were purposely screwed over."

I laugh, shaking my head as I look up from under my floppy hair. "Don't tell me Jasper Eversore is an optimist. That would be weird as fuck."

"Absolutely not. But I am a realist, and I understand that positive intent and negative intent have equal chances in the chaos that is the universe. That doesn't mean I *believe* positive shit first; I simply recognize that it can't be ruled out without more data."

"Now you sound like Annie. He's very data-centric." I think about that for a moment and add, "It's calming sometimes because he doesn't freak out often. He looks at the facts dispassionately, and it balances X's endless enthusiasm."

Jasper watches me as I move to a standing position and do the stretches there. "You're a bit like both in your ability to see everything, but also communicate with everyone in their preferred style. At least, I assume that because you wormed your way into all of my brothers' good graces fairly quickly. You'd have to adjust to their quirks without being patronizing."

I narrow my eyes on him. "Zavida told you that. No way you noticed it on your own, Prince Pricklypants. You've been too focused on how I'm going to 'betray' you to see the way I interact with people."

His smile is sheepish as he shrugs. "Guilty. I listen to Zavvie when he is adamant about things, and he's been quite vocal about my behavior regarding you for a while. I suppose it took having to watch the beating our caliphate took for it to click that despite our immense power and experience, we could still be killed or defeated if we don't… coalesce better."

"Bzzzt! Wrong answer. Try again," I sing-song as my arms and shoulders loosen up. "You're giving the answer you *should* give, not the real one."

Looking annoyed, he runs his hand through hair, tail whipping as he mutters, "Also, I needed support as this is pushing all the buttons I keep protected inside. Or something. Zav said that too, but he's right, I guess."

Man, Jasper really hates *people knowing he's not impenetrable—even more than me.*

"Right… that's it. Step *into* the strike with your weight thrusting forward…"

I pant as I mimic Jasper's example, putting my weight behind the sword as I stab the dummy. "This thing weighs as much as I do, I swear to fuck. My arms are going to be noodles tomorrow."

"You can lift it and swing it, shrimp. That means it's viable for use, even if it's only in a pinch."

Groaning as I go back to the beginning stance, I wait for him to tell me to do it again. The dragon demon has stripped off his shirt, revealing his gorgeous tattoos, and it's been distracting me ever since. I have no idea why he's sweating more than me, but the scent is also making the colors inside me swirl around excitedly. I've had to tamp that down while also telling my lady bits to fuck off so my brain can comprehend his damn words for almost an hour now.

My arms will not be the only things that are going to be mush by the time we get back.

"This time, I want you to stab, then deflect quickly, and get out of range. Your footwork must be light with and without a weapon, but it's harder when your stamina is running low."

Sighing, I grit my teeth as I force myself to continue, following the instructions as best as I can. I'm not too tired to continue, mind, or I would tell him, but I'm getting there. "This would be easier if I weren't struggling to keep this damn thing aloft, you know."

"Easy doesn't save your life," he replies firmly. "If you can do it on the difficult setting, you can do it when it doesn't take as much energy."

"Yes, taskmaster," I mutter as I set the pose again and wait for him to nod. The second time, I'm faster, and I growl under my breath when he's right. The repetition of each move helps me cement it in mind and body, while also building my strength. His relentless demands aren't to make me unable to hobble home as much as they are designed to challenge me.

That doesn't mean I don't want to punch him in the nuts right now, though.

"Water time," I gasp after the next run. "Definitely and assuredly water time."

With a sharp bob of his head, Jasper acquiesces as promised, and I drop the broadsword on the ground. I walk over to my bag, pulling out a bottle to throw to him, and then grab my own. My throw isn't exactly screaming 'this kid is ready for the majors', but he doesn't comment as he catches it. Jasper has been weirdly detached since we started the session—not at all as open as he was before—and I swallow a huge gulp of the liquid as I consider that.

"You're… trying really hard." His jaw ticks as he dumps a little of the water on his head, and I have to bite the inside of my cheek not to make a sound as it sluices over him. "Despite your lack of previous training and physical power, you're putting every ounce of effort you have into this. That is impressive."

I blink up at him, my mind warring between Jasper giving me a compliment and his ridiculous water show. My entire brain is shorting out as my mouth hangs open, and I have to look like a goddamn trout sitting here. Closing my eyes, I shake my head as if that will get all the conflicting shit out of it, then clear my throat. "Um… thanks. And, uh, I appreciate you being patient. I'm not a slow study most of the time, but physical sports and such have never really been my forte."

He snorts, and I open my eyes to see him smirking at me, all tattoos and water droplets and low-slung joggers. "Gee, I never would have figured that out on my own, shrimp."

Danger, danger, danger, Kat Camponella! Avert your fucking eyes!

Listening to my panicked brain, I dart my gaze to the ground as I chuckle nervously. "Yep, I hide my non-sports loving side pretty well. Luckily, the whole shifter thing is helping with that, right?"

I feel his stare on me as I find anything in the world to look at besides him. My body is both exhausted and humming with excitement—two things that do *not* go together and won't end well. Having him watch me struggle isn't helping, and I squirm in my seat as I try to figure out what the hell to do. I take another drink of the water, praying it lowers the temperature a bit so I can finish this lesson without embarrassing the fuck out of myself.

"Shrimp, are you okay? You look like… well, you sort of look like you need to take a massive shit, and—"

"No!" I shout as my eyes widen and I look at him. "No, no. Not that. Don't be gross. I'm just… uh, tired. But not *too* tired, so once I'm hydrated we can… continue."

His expression goes from teasing to suspicious in a blink, so I knock back another drink from my bottle to cover myself. "Dude, having to poo isn't a big deal. Is that something they shame you for up there? Fuck, humans are weird. It's a bodily function."

I don't have an answer for that without giving myself away, so I just shrug as I set my bottle on the bench. "I didn't want you to think we had to leave yet. We've got like…thirty more minutes before the others will get out of Intro to Fae. I figure we can squeeze a lot in during that time."

"Oh, don't worry. I plan to wring every second of energy out of you until you're ready to collapse." Jasper grins evilly, and my insides hum again. "Now put the sword on the rack and we'll go back to hand-to-hand. You're going to keep me from pinning you to the ground."

Sweet Lucifer's robes, I will not survive this without making a fool of myself, am I?

I HOPE UR MISERABLE UNTIL UR DEAD

Xerxes

Friday is the day when a lot of my classes don't align with the rest of the caliphate. I have labs and studios relating to my design focus, and few 'general' requirements. They even go later than the rest of the guys' sessions, which puts me behind on everything that's happened.

I wasn't concerned about it until KK arrived and we accepted her into the fold. Now, it bothers the fuck out of me, though these classes definitely make it easier to create clothing that will work for various events and potential needs. Being non-binary myself creates a special latitude in what I create, no matter what class it's for, and the professors simply have to accept what my vision is—even if they grumble and bitch under their breath.

Being part of the royal court helps, obviously, because no one wants their shit getting back to the people who commission the most fashion pieces in the entire realm.

However, today is particularly irksome as I know KK was going to work on shifting with Slash. He missed our law class, despite Jasper's orders, and now I'm itching to know how that went. After that, Kat should have had a great deal of alone time in the room, and I can't help wondering what she's doing. I know she planned on studying the books my lover painstakingly notated for her, but that only stretches so far. I doubt she sat around bored, but the concern about how strong our safeguards are and how determined the beings who wish to harm her are has monopolized my thoughts.

When I come back to reality, I realize I've been staring at the Games uniform I'm working on altering for Kat like a gormless fool for fuck knows how long. I'm not the type to get lost in my head like Zav or Annie, but the stress of worrying about how we're going to protect KK has taken over my brain today. I know she's getting *something* from the doc that must be helping her stay hidden, but she hasn't confessed exactly what she and the terrifying masked physician discuss when they are alone. In fact, while she's been opening up a lot more recently, she's still swarming with secrets that I don't believe any of us are privy to yet.

Her trauma is bone-deep, just like the rest of us, but it's unraveling slowly. Unfortunately, time is not on our side.

Sighing, I adjust the drape of the pants, studying them as I work out how I'm going to replicate the damn things with material that is infused with more protective fabric and enchantments. I know I can't use this *actual* set of Games clothes to make KK's better version—it's not made well, nor are the materials worth shit. I have to alter this to the specific cut and fit I want and then completely remake several sets in the expensive, preventative materials that I've already ordered from royal suppliers. Using this project for my portfolio means I can spend whatever the fuck I want on it and no one will question the requisition for outrageously costly and rare ingredients.

The polo and pants aren't anything special, and the only marking is the Discordia logo. That's pre-programmed into the embroidery machines, so I don't have to worry about stitching it. Other than that, they're plain black with no embellishments. Luckily, they didn't ask anyone to do anything complex because they assumed they'd need bulk quantities when participants go through them like water during the various challenges and whatever. That cheap-ass corner-cutting makes it very simple to replicate on the surface.

"I want this to fit snugly enough to allow for protection, but not to give her away. The undergarments are going to be far more difficult to deal with, but I'm working on that in the Nazi-lover's class." I muse aloud as I tilt my head, squinting at the pants in particular. I want to add some hidden compartments for small weapons and secret things Annie and I can give her to stow away for emergencies. He's a whiz at potions, and small vials and bottles tucked away could be the difference between escaping and getting killed.

There's a knock at the door of my studio, and I whirl around, glaring at the locked steel door. Studios are kept secure to prevent design theft, so I will have to walk over and find out who's rapping at my chamber door. I put down the chalk pencil I was using to mark the fabric, tossing my hair over my shoulder as I get close enough to open the slit. My breath comes out in a soft whoosh when I see Annie looking at me through the gap.

"What are you doing here?" I grumble petulantly as my heart stops thumping. I'm not afraid of being attacked, but I do *not* want some asshole to steal my fucking shit. It's important for my grades, but even more pertinent is making certain Kat is as safe as possible when we compete. I'm convinced it will begin after the holidays, and I have to finish, sew, photograph, and bring my adjusted uniforms to our room before they do.

"It's late, and you've skipped all your afternoon classes to work in here. We should get back to the dorms so we can have dinner with the others."

I frown, pulling my phone out to look at the screen. There's still plenty of time left on my studio time, and I'm not sure why he's here so early while claiming it's late. "I have an hour left, and you're out of your Fae class an hour early. After that, I have a two-hour period. What are you talking about?"

Annie shrugs, grinning at me boyishly. "We heard Slash skipped Law, too, so we ducked out of Cedar's lecture early. You should come too. We're going to see Kit and get dinner ready. It was a group decision."

Snorting, I arch a brow. "It was, huh? One no one ran by the prince, right?"

"We don't have to run every decision by him," Anton says as his chin juts out stubbornly. "He's the leader, but not our goddamn dad."

Yep, Annie's headed toward full-on obsession with our secret girl, and KK needs to tell him soon so he doesn't feel betrayed.

"Okay, love. Let me put away my stuff, and I'll be right out."

Tonight's dinner and our time together afterward is going to be fascinating.

Once I'm ready, I exit the studio and set the security. Annie offers me his arm, and I take it as we walk down the hallway to the elevator together. There are very few people on my floor this time of day on Fridays —I swear, they gave me the worst possible schedule for the day before the weekend on purpose. Knowing Darkstar and his lackeys in the admin departments, it's not entirely out of the question.

"You're working on the uniform for the Games," Annie says. He doesn't expound, which is normal for him, and I smile.

"Yes, I'm re-designing it so there are more options for keeping Kit safe. Extra pockets, better materials, enchantment patches… everything we need to help him before he sets foot on a competition field."

Anton nods, processing that for a few moments before he says, "It's a good plan. Jasper will be concerned with area-of-effect attacks and defense, while Slash will coordinate and execute from the ground. Anything that can give him a defensive advantage is worth focusing on. I suspect we will not have long after the break to prepare. They think they're being sneaky about when the Games will begin, but it's extremely obvious."

I nod as we get on the elevator, and it lurches and then begins the descent to the main floor. "Those dipshits completely cannot hold their wad. Sending The Major was a huge red flag, and I have no idea why the King and General didn't realize that. Most students wouldn't grasp the significance, but certainly the staff, Darkstar, and our caliphate would."

"Perhaps that was their intent?" Annie holds the doors open for me when the elevator dings, and I think about that. "Sending him signaled to us that they are aware of the committee's plans, and that the Games are nigh. It also told Lucian that he's not as safe in his machinations with the committee as *he* believes. It's a dual-purpose middle finger."

As we walk across the lobby to the doors, I consider the theory further. "It could be. It kicked us into gear, sent Jasper into a spiral, made Lucian stomp around bickering with the Major in front of us… There's a lot of moving pieces that his arrival set into motion. I'd wager the idea to do it did not originate with the General or the King."

"Shit," Annie sighs as he runs his hand through his rainbow locks. "Oriel's dad. Furfur was *definitely* involved in this plan. Of all the parents, he's easily the most devious. He must be plotting with Slash and Jasper's asshole fathers to change the chessboard. Not out of character, unfortunately."

"True." I look around the quad as we walk down the stairs, my eyes narrowed as I take in the small groups walking to various destinations. "Do you think the Bloodstones have spies within the student body? Oriel hasn't balked at any of their jobs since he arrived, to my knowledge. There isn't any reason for his dad to assume he's not 'following orders' or whatever."

Annie bumps my shoulder with his. "Love, none of our parents truly requires a reason to spy on us. You know as well as I do that they've been doing it since we were young demons. They won the Games and led a coup to take over Hell. They had to build powerful families full of heirs, but they feared those heirs from their births and summonings because of their paranoia. That's why all the firstborn heirs are hybrids, in my opinion. I've long believed that it was because they believed it 'dilutes' our power."

"For fuck's sake. You think they 'bred' us weaker—in their opinion—so we couldn't dethrone them all?" My brows furrow as I try to imagine he's wrong, but I can't.

As we get closer to Canto IV, Anton finally responds. "Yes, I do. I believe one of them came up with the idea, and they all decided together as a caliphate to 'poison' the bloodline of the first heirs. Unfortunately for them, they failed, especially given our caliphate formation and the amount of things we have kept hidden from them. They didn't account for how badly Tarron would abuse Jasper and how deeply it would seat his desire to send them all to the pits."

"The General didn't do them any favors with Slash, either. He's hated everyone in his family and the crown from the time he and Jasper bonded." I chuckle, shaking my head ruefully. "That's pretty funny given the General and the King pushing them at one another."

"It's easy to miss the forest for the trees at their level. Both of them have grown accustomed to having others do the work for them, but this plan was only shared among the couples and their spouses. There weren't any lackeys to risk their lives by pointing out the holes in their schemes."

My lips curve as we walk up the steps to Canto IV, thinking about how satisfying it will be to see them all fall flat on their faces. "Is it hubris to feel so happy about their eventual ousting at our hands? I don't care if it is, honestly, because they've all spent most of our long-ass lives making us miserable."

"We have to keep Kit away from them," Annie murmurs as he opens the door to the dorm. "None of them can get their dirty hands on him. It will be awful, and… I don't think any of us could live with ourselves if they hurt him like they have us."

My mate has never spoken truer words, but I have no idea how we're going to accomplish his suggestion.

Trapped

Kit/Kat

"Again!" Jasper says as he jumps to his feet.

The fucker has been pinning me to the ground every round with a smirk that grew increasingly infuriating with every failed attempt to win. He's not being an asshole to taunt me, though; this time, he's doing his best to rile me so I fight harder. I know what he's doing, and yet I'm still not angry enough to do more than duck a few hits and land a few punches before he gets me.

It doesn't help that the more we spar, the hotter he looks and my body has told my brain to fuck right off.

I set my feet for another go, gritting my teeth as I reach for the darker parts of me. It would help *a lot* if the strength that makes my lioness come out or whatever the fuck happened during that battle would show up to throw some power my way. Alas, nothing inside of me seems to want to beat the fuck out of the prince. If you'd told me that even a week ago, I would have laughed in your face, but here we are.

"Use your emotions, but do not let them overtake you, shrimp," Jasper says as he falls into his stance.

"Thanks for the advice, Emperor Pout-patine," I mutter as I advance on him. The jackass is really fast for the biggest demon I know, and like Slash, it's clear he's been trained for this since he could walk. His movements are fluid and easy as he ducks my first punch, and I growl as I dance out of his way when he whirls around. His tail is a built-in weapon, too, and I have to watch it as much as his fists.

Being struck with it stings like a bitch, even with the non-spiky part.

"Is that a reference? You and those human movies… It's lost on me, unfortunately." His smirk deepens as he tries to sweep my leg in the distraction, and I barely escape his maneuver without getting trounced once more. "Oh, very good. Your speed is improving a bit."

"Yay," I grunt sarcastically as I watch him, looking for another way to strike. "I'm not slow enough to flatten immediately; how exciting."

"Tuck your thumb! You're going to break something."

Rolling my eyes at his non-response, I do as he says while I circle the ring we're fighting in. He set it with his magic so I'd know where the bounds are, but I don't think anyone I fight in the Games will stick to a set space. My comment on that was ignored, so I guess he's working on something specific that I don't need to know about. "I'm likely to break something anyway, Jasper. You're about fifty million times stronger than me, even when you're holding back."

"I won't let that happen," he says as he darts forward, and I have to duck and roll out of the way. "Look at that! You're learning."

I get to my feet, my tired body wishing the half hour would be up, but I school my features not to show it. Jasper might give me quarter in this practice, but real enemies will not. I have to focus on pretending this is real. "Isn't that what this is supposed to be? A lesson?"

Before I can blink, he's in my space and knocking me to the ground again. I groan as his huge frame presses me into the field, both out of exhaustion *and* the pent-up tingling racing through me from these moments where I've been shocked to find that I'm definitely *not* terrified of the dragon holding me down.

Fucking hormones, I swear to shit. I have no idea how people live with this all the time.

"Did I hurt you?" he asks, his eyes going wide as he doesn't move as usual. The color of his eyes has changed, and there's a rumble to his voice that is decidedly not normal.

"No, I…" I swallow hard as lovely sensations flood my limbs and my body clenches eagerly. "Um, no. You didn't hurt me, I'm…" I can't seem to finish a sentence as I look up at him while the weight of his heavy-ass dragon-muscled body presses me into the ground. My pulse spikes and my gut flutters as I lose control of myself entirely—something that usually only happens when I have an attack.

This is not *an attack, though, and I'm damn near frozen in place as it grabs hold.*

"Shrimp," he says softly, too softly for the surly asshole who likes to torture me. "I…"

"What a fine display of dedication!"

The funny feelings dissipate like mist on the moors as a loud, booming voice echoes throughout the stadium. Jasper's face reflects panic—which I haven't seen on him before—as he scrambles to his feet. I'm left dazed and certainly fucking confused by the abrupt switch, sucking in a breath as I work to right the world so I don't sway when I get up. The prince, however, is dusting himself off as he stares up at the stands toward what must be the person who spoke. The panic has morphed into his usual arrogant scowl, and I realize that he's about to put on a show for our uninvited spectator.

"Major. What a pleasant surprise," he growls as his tail whips in a way that I *know* means exactly the opposite of his words. "What brings you to the arena during my private session?"

Holy fuck, that goddamn court dude everyone is so worried about is here!

I push to my feet, willing my body and every part of me to give me the strength to also put on an act for this dangerous motherfucker. We don't need him spreading shit to Jasper and Slash's dads, nor do we need him deciding to monitor me. I have to be just beige enough for him to ignore me completely in favor of the dragon demon despite my ball of conflicting emotions and bone-weary condition.

"Taking on extra duties to ensure your caliphate is top-notch. Very noble… something your father would find pleasing, no doubt." The huge soldier stomps down the last rows of the stands to leap over the edge and hit the ground without even flinching. "This is your newest member, I take it."

Jasper nods, walking over to get his water, and I follow suit like a good little caliphate member. I assume that mirroring his behavior without the royal attitude is probably safest, and keeping my mouth closed for as long as possible is an even better idea. I toss back a swig, wiping my mouth on my sleeve as I avert my eyes from the Major. I hate playing this submissive role to my very core, but I also made a promise, and part of it was to do my best not to bring more shit on our heads if possible.

Whether I'm successful at it depends entirely on how this motherfucker behaves, though.

"We have a duty to perform to the highest of our capabilities in the Games," Jasper says smoothly. "I work with all of my brothers to refine their talent and develop their weak spots."

"Do you now?" The Major says as he saunters over. His casual question sends up a million red flags in my brain, and I turn away from him to ensure that my reaction isn't visible. His intonation and gait are supposed to lull us into a false sense of security—of that, I'm certain. I had foster fathers who played this game when I was very young, and figuring out how to avoid bad consequences when they put on the mask of friendliness was something the kids in those houses learned quickly.

Jasper sends his empty bottle hurtling towards the trash bin, and I know he's using it to drain off his anger. Of course, it lands in the damn thing perfectly as if he's a fucking NBA All-star, but that's not my worry at the moment. My concern is the speed of his tail tip, which I can see out of the corner of my eye, and how fast it's moving as he gets more and more irritated.

"Perhaps I'd enjoy a demonstration of your technique, Your Highness. You've been taught by the best fighters in the realm since you were a newly summoned lad, and I would like to see your methods."

Fuck. Fuck. Fuck. He can't say 'no', and he won't be able to hold back as much as he was before.

I turn to look at the two demons, my jaw set as I stand ramrod straight. "Prince Jasper may request my participation in any training he sees fit." That hurt my soul; I *hate* appearing to be a spineless sycophant, especially for a dickweasel like this. But I know by the look in Jasper's eyes that he's trapped, and we won't be able to fly under the radar if he refuses. I'll have to let him do this to keep the caliphate's cover, and there's nothing either of us can do to stop it.

"Of course, Major," Jasper replies as he moves back into our circle slowly. His entire body radiates tension as I watch him set his stance, and I know to the bottom of my soul that this is going to trigger the fuck out of me no matter how hard he tries to prevent that.

But I can't show it, and I have to perform well enough to seem *like I'm not the weakest link—no pressure here on day one of training.*

Walking into the circle, I pause at the edge to close my eyes. The guys have encouraged me consistently to talk to my animal, talk to my magic, and to reason with it as I do my emotions when I'm having issues. That's worked occasionally, and with varied results that are not predictable. But right now, I *need those* parts of me that I do not have full control over to listen in a way that they never have before. They have to help me get through this goddamn demo while dancing in a field of landmines that affect all of my men. So I dig as deeply as I can inside my mind, my heart, my soul, and even the colorful stains within me to plead for that aid. I beg them to give me enough strength and stamina to make a very mid showing so this shit-head goes away.

Then I open my eyes and walk to the center of the ring, dropping into position.

Jasper's eyes are dark, swirling with colors that have to be both his dragon and his demon. I don't think any part of him wants to do this, and he's fighting like hell to keep that a secret from our spectator. His fists are high as he looks me in the eye, and within seconds, we've both made a move. He is faster, but I dodge it—barely. I move away from him again, using the distance to see if I can catch telegraphed moves like he taught me, but Jasper can't level himself down like he did before.

The first blow rocks my socks off, sending me staggering until I bounce off the barrier the circle creates. My bell is rung, but I focus on the demon circling, *not* the fucking birdies around my head as I get back into the game. He gave me enough time to reset by slowing down a fraction after the punch, but that's about as much leeway as he can get away with, I think. Moving quickly, I run forward, sliding under his arm as he strikes and grab-bing an ankle as I go past.

It makes him stumble, but he catches himself easily and whips around. I'm not nearly as fast getting to my feet as he is, so it leaves me at a disadvantage that has him on me within seconds. I'm pinned and up looking at him, my frame trembling with both fear and fury at the situation we're in.

"Oh, that was too easy, Jasper! Let him up and go again. The boy is weak, and he's going to get you killed."

The smug taunt from the Major is the last damn thing I hear before blood rushes to my ears and I feel the sensation of losing control again, but this time, it's not my pussy getting overly excited. No, now I'm filled with a rage so deep that it coats my insides with sludge as it races through me, and I know that without a doubt, something terrible is going to happen. I try to fight it, but there's nothing I can reach for, nothing I can hold on to in my mind or body—it's like I'm completely detached from it all.

This is awful, and I have no way of stopping it; I can only watch from a distance in abject horror.

Chaos

Zavida

Anton and Xerxes have just arrived at the dorm when the shockwave hits. I'm almost knocked off my feet by the sudden jolt, and when I look at Oriel and Salem, I know they've been rocked too. That can mean one of three things: Slash, Jasper, or Kit have been attacked. We're all clamoring for the door at top speed, almost getting caught in the frame as we rush out of it. Salem is leading the way as we take the stairs— no one is going to stand in the damn elevator when it's very clearly an emergency.

By the time we're running out the front doors, I realize I don't have shoes on, but then, Oriel doesn't have on a shirt, Salem is wearing an apron, and the other two still have on uniforms. We're a mismatched bunch of idiots following the trail of the caliphate magic towards whatever has activated the panic button. Oriel growls as he lets his wings out, taking to the air, and Anton joins him in a surprising contrast of dark and light.

I'm running hard when I see the big guy exiting the main building, his enormous bulk moving at a speed that most wouldn't think is possible. But Slash swims at light speed and can move almost as quickly on land—when he chooses to. He's normally careful and practiced in his motions, but like the rest of us, he's figured out that we're only missing two people who could cause the bond to tremble with alarm.

Neither of whom we can lose without enormous consequences—and I don't mean just the caliphate bond.

"I thought they would be in the dorm," Slash snarls as he falls in with X, Salem, and me. "Why are they not in the safest place on campus?"

"We don't know," I reply as our direction turns unerringly toward the stadium. "Maybe they decided to work on the physical, like Jas said?"

"The little demon was exhausted after shifting. He did not make a good choice."

"Slash, my man, I don't think KK being tired is why the metaphysical Bat-signal is calling us to the stadium." Salem rolls his eyes at us, and a loud screech from the sky brings us back to our target.

Oriel is pissed, and, oddly, Anton has joined him in the animalistic fervor.

"I didn't think Annie was this… involved," I say to X as their hair streams behind them. "He so rarely shifts in public, so people don't stare and make him nuts. This is awfully emotional for his usual behavior." X gives me a smirk full of snake fangs, and I blink. "Nevermind, I guess. You're pretty lit up, too."

"Zav, our leader and/or our… brother… may be hurt or in danger," X hisses. "There is no better reason to allow our true forms to take hold."

I'm not sure I agree because we have no idea what we're walking into. This could be a trap—holding one or the other to draw us in and get information we've kept concealed. "What if it's not what it seems? We give the enemies weapons they did not have before."

"That is true, Zavida, but our responsibility is to them, not to our secrets." Slash looks irritated, but his words ring true.

Even if this is a set-up, we can't ignore the bond's call.

"We are going in from above, use the parapets and structures to stay out of view," Anton yells from the sky. "Take the main entrance and keep quiet as you enter carefully. Oriel can caw when it's time to hit the field."

"Got it!" Salem yells back as he looks to the rest of us. "Slash and I go first, followed by X and Zav. We're bigger and can take direct hits more easily if there are ground assailants. Xerxes, get the powers warmed as we move. Zavida… you know what you need to do; you have advantages we may need."

"The family line magic will go first. You know I prefer keeping species-based things quiet."

Slash gives me a toothy grin. "If we must, we will all peel away the curtains we use to hide our depth of abilities, Zavida. We cannot allow anyone to harm, kill, or take the Prince hostage."

"He can defend himself, big guy," Salem says as he glares. "KK is my concern."

That earns him a bunch of mumbled agreement, and Slash stops at the entrance to the arena. He turns to look at each of us. O and Annie fly high above. "Jasper is powerful and strong, but any of us could be disabled by the right opponent. Neither of our brothers are acceptable sacrifices to anyone —not the crown, Darkstar, rebels, or even unknown enemies. Use every power you possess to ensure that they both survive and are intact after we engage. Do not hold back, no matter who we need to battle. Am I clear?"

I raise my hand. "Even the Major?"

Slash grins again, his eyes full of ice as he snarls, "Especially that son of a bitch. If he's attacking our caliphate, we are within our rights to defend, no matter who it is. That is the law of the realm, Zavida. Even the King must follow it."

The problem is, the King has never followed a rule in his entire existence, which is how he became king in the first place.

As we enter the tunnel into the arena, a loud crash echoes through the building, followed by the sound of a dragon roaring. I swallow hard, knowing that Jasper shifting into his dragon means shit is *going down* on that fucking field. My gaze flicks to Slash, remembering the last time he had to be air-lifted to calm Jas out of the sky, and he gives me a sharp nod. He's preparing for the worst as we wait for Oriel to give the signal to move out of the relative safety of the shadowed tunnel and into the open air of the stadium.

The shriek of an extremely distressed peacock is followed by a loud crow caw, and that has us all moving at top speed out of the darkness. Anton is not the type to panic, and that sound is *not* one that I've heard him make before. My tails billow behind me as I run out with my brothers, eyes darting around the immense space in worry.

I don't even know what to do with the visual once I can see what's happening; I'm completely stunned in place.

My caliphate brothers are just as shocked, and we all stand there, gaping at the scene like slack-jawed yokels. It's simply too much to process simultaneously.

Oriel and Anton are only half-shifted, using their wings to carefully circle the outside ring of the arena. They haven't moved in closer because *two* enormous, shadowy dragons are flying in the middle of the sky, shooting shadows at one another as if they're having fun. There's a hint of fire on one side, while the other seems to sparkle in the sunshine in a way I've never seen a shadow-powered demon do.

But that's not even the most shocking part of the scene—no, that's the absolutely dead body of the Major, third in command of Hell's armies sprawled on the ground like a giant stuck pig that's been spit-roasted for dinner.

I open my mouth to speak, but nothing comes out. Kit is a fucking *dragon*, and not only that, but can apparently wield shadows as Jasper can. That means the list of rare abilities he now possesses is growing, and the target on his head will only increase. Worse yet, something happened here that was so egregious that one of the two *killed* the third-highest military leader in the realm, and they don't seem remotely concerned by it. In fact, the two animals in the air are far more interested in what looks to be a dangerous game of... tag?

"Fuck me running," Xerxes breathes as they stare up at the sky in awe. "I mean, I thought maybe... but... this...."

"It changes everything," Slash says with a grimace. "As does other information we did not have before today. But none of that takes precedence *now*, brother. We have a *much* more pressing issue at the moment."

"The body," I say as my tails puff and cover me in a protective stance. "We have to figure out what the holy fuck we're going to do about the body."

Salem snorts. "Zav, the body will not matter if we can't explain *why* this giant asshole isn't around anymore. We've got a million methods of disposal at our fingertips for a body; we don't have an excuse for this motherfucker being dead that won't invite scrutiny with an investigation."

The panda is right, and I push my glasses up as I think about the scene. "We need help—lots of it, and quickly. While the six of us who are *not* in lizard form are formidable, we know Jasper will be off when he comes back, and who the fuck knows what's going to happen with Kit. We need allies who will help us cover this goddamn murder up and help dispose of the corpse in a way that won't point at us."

Xerxes blinks and reaches into their pocket, holding up their phone. "The Doc! I have his information from when I was on KK watch. I can call him."

"The Keeper," Slash rumbles as he, too, pulls out his phone. "His contact was given so we could arrange the little demon's lessons."

"Anyone else?" I ask hopefully.

They all shake their heads. For once, our standoff-ish inability to allow anyone access to our circle is actually hurting us rather than helping. The only reasons those two people *might* be willing to help us are, ironically, flying over the stadium engaged in shadow battles without a care in the world.

"Okay," I sigh as I run my hand through my hair. "Oriel and Anton are probably watching to make sure no one else comes into the stadium up there. I'm going to need you two to contact the outside help, while Salem and I go examine the damn body. It would help to know *why* and who killed the Major before others arrive."

Slash and Xerxes nod, heading into the tunnel with their devices to do as I asked. Salem chuckles as the two of us walk across the field to the prone demon, giving me a smirk.

"Really weird for you to be in charge, eh?"

I scowl at him as I work to keep my tails from twitching. "Yes, but it's not like I don't have the capability. You're not exactly the usual 'hero' either."

He grins, shrugging as we reach the big-ass body. "True, but I'm ass over end about my KK, and I'm not shy about anyone knowing it, man. You and Prince Pissypants have been much less vocal. See, I honestly don't give a single, solitary *fuck* about disposing of this asshat if it keeps Kit safe. Hell, I'd dispose of a *fleet* of bodies to make sure of it. You, however, are most concerned about the person least likely to take the blame for anything, Z-man. Jasper won't be punished if he killed this dude—at least, not in any lasting way. But if it was KitKat? Off with his head wouldn't come close to what would be in store."

Frowning, I stomp up to him, looking up with fiery eyes. "That's not true, Salem Stryker. Of course I care about my mate getting in trouble, but I am *exceedingly* aware that Jasper's untouchable aura doesn't extend to us and especially not to Kit. Why the fuck do you think I'm involving outsiders? This cover has to be *perfect* because if we fuck up one single thing, we might earn Kit a death sentence—something I don't think *anyone* in our caliphate could handle. In fact, I think it would damn near kill us. So... back off, asshole!"

Salem's eyes widen, and he just stares at me for a moment. My entire body is vibrating with anger, and when his lips curl up, I want to punch him in the dick as hard as I can. But I don't, because he claps me on the shoulder with a chuckle.

"Now that's what I needed to hear, man. Let's get to work."

I have no clue why that worked, but now that we're aligned, he's right—we have serious work to do.

Secrets

Kit/Kat

I have no idea what in the actual *fuck* is going on right now.

Okay, that's not true; I know fully that I'm flying through the air in a giant body that apparently belongs to me.

However, the ability to control what I'm doing has been taken away by the infuriated lizard that popped out of me earlier. The dragon was so blindingly enraged at the Major's abusive tactics that this girl came rushing out in a flood of fury and weird black fiery power. Before I could process what happened, she grabbed the son of a bitch and squeezed the life out of him. That's when we took off into the sky, and Jasper shifted to follow us as we circled the stadium.

I thought we were going to crash and die, but instead, his dragon coasted alongside us until our wings steadied. The absolute *joy* that filtered through my dragon as we soared through the air, chasing one another and shooting shadows playfully was indescribable. I've truly felt nothing like this; it's beyond any positive emotion I've ever felt.

But I don't know how to take back control or what to do if I manage it.

Ducking a shadowy warning as it passes by me, we flap our wings hard, then bank left to avoid the next turn his dragon executes. We don't have his precision movements down yet; in fact, I'm pretty pleased we're still in the air and in the game. The dragon tosses our head, making a huffing sound as we do a loop-de-loop so our body ends behind his. I suspect the prince is going easy on us, but every time we pass near one another, I feel his dragon's happiness like a wave of energy pushing toward me.

A movement on the ground catches our attention out of the corner of our eye, and I realize that the rest of the guys have arrived. Looking around, I see Oriel and Anton in the air, monitoring the boundaries of the arena as we dart around. They're watching for other demons, and I suppose that's to keep anyone from discovering the body I left down there before taking to the skies.

Probably not the brightest move, but I didn't have a choice in the matter.

"Jasper, for fuck's sake, man! You gotta land. We need you, not the lizard, and KK has to shift back. C'mon, dude!"

I think our face smiles as Oriel pleads with the prince. His dragon huffs, stubbornly leading mine away from the half-shifted crow demon. Jasper's dragon doesn't get allowed much time here, I remember the guys saying, and now that it's found a friend? It's not letting go just because O asked nicely. My dragon is of a similar mind, it seems, because we're just following him happily. My internal pleas are ignored as I try to reason with her, and I wish I could speak so I could say something Jasper might hear inside.

"Prince, we must land. Get your dragon under control and do what you know is necessary."

That's Anton this time, and he's using logic—something that isn't surprising, but also isn't what Jasper's dragon gives a shit about. I wheedle with the enormous beast controlling my form, asking nicely and demanding. It's not working because she's eager as fuck about getting loose, just like Jasper's beast, and together, we're being led by the reptilian equivalent of dangerous, excited puppies.

I have no idea what the fuck we're going to do; neither of us seems capable of stopping this display.

"*Ab antiquis usque ad bestias, vobis impero ut audiatis et oboediatis![1]*"

The booming words aren't in a language I know, though I *think* it might be Latin. However, for the first time since I shifted, my dragon is paying attention. It's like her ears perk up inside of me and everything stops—including both of our enormous, scaly bodies. She turns her head, looking down at the field curiously, and Dragon Jasper does the same.

"*Tempus tuum hic finitum est, bestia fidelis. Transforma te et iterum dormi.[2]*"

Feeling the immediate change in my body, I panic. We're high enough in the air that we will *definitely* die if we shift and hit the ground. I have no idea what to do, and my dragon doesn't listen to me yet. Our head whips around to gaze at the bigger onyx dragon, and he bobs his head at the field before tucking his wings to head downward. My panic subsides as she follows Jasper in the dive, taking us to the grass a lot more elegantly than I would have expected.

When our feet touch the grass, the change begins without a second to spare, and I scream as my body reshapes itself into a form that isn't big enough to crush a house. Panting as it finishes, I've barely opened my eyes when I feel a cloak drape over my shoulders, covering me from all the eyes staring down at me in shock. I clutch the sides, pulling it around me as I shiver. I think I'm recovering from the warmth that the dragon body provided—something I didn't even realize until it was gone.

"H-h-h-holy…. f-f-f-f-fuckkkkk," I stutter around my thick tongue.

"Don't rush it, Master Kit. I am here, and we will discuss everything you need to know."

The voice startles me, and I turn, wincing at the pain in my body from the fight that's come roaring back in this form. Dank is standing there, his mask off, and his weird, skeletal, fiery-feathered form revealed. The damn cloak must be his, and I don't know if I've ever felt so grateful to see someone. When I first got here, this would have scared the fuck out of me, but now? I look up at the ancient demon with a huge smile.

"I… Dank.. dragon?"

His spooky visage forms what I'm pretty sure is a smile as he nods. Flaming feathers molt and fall as he does so, making me frown. Is being without his protective garb hurting him? I don't know. Hell, I don't even really know what kind of demon he is, or how ridiculously old he must be. I just know that even if it is harming him, this kindly old demon made certain that no one saw me for real if I didn't want them to.

"Yes, Master Kit. You have several secrets, and some have become… less hidden today, it seems."

I snort and then grunt as it makes my torso ache. Probably cracked those damn ribs again. "Yeah, it's been a real peach of a day, Dank. Did… they call you?"

"Aye! They called him *and* me." The gruff voice of the Keeper echoes behind me, and I blink in surprise. "I didn't know you'd made such good friends with the royal physician. Had I known, I would have added a few suggestions for you to ask him during our last visit."

His enthusiasm is a bit much for me right now.

Swaying at the sudden influx of emotions and power around me, I put my hand out in case I crumple, but there's someone behind me immediately. I turn my head slowly, smiling when I see Salem grinning at me. "Thanks, Salem."

"Don't worry, KK. We'll always catch you, even if some dickhead is leading you into a dive you might not have the mechanics to handle yet."

There's a growl from the periphery of the circle at the dig, and I sigh in relief when it tells me that Jasper is okay. "I appreciate it. I really have no idea how I managed that. The dragon was in the driver's seat from the moment it popped free. I could only watch and yell inside, but it didn't give a fuck what I said."

"That's not surprising, lad. All new shifters struggle with control and trust with their animal, and the more powerful the beastie is, the harder it is to learn." The Keeper backs up, his bearded face barely concealing the smirk. "I believe it would be worse for someone who has more inner beings than they know what to do with."

"Gee, I can't imagine," I mutter grumpily.

"Master Kit, may I speak with you privately? I would like to examine you briefly to ensure we are not ignoring serious injuries and to discuss your condition with you. The others can decide what they will do to clean up this… situation… while we do so."

I would kiss that flaming bird demon if I didn't think it would burn me to ash.

"Yes, that sounds like a good idea, Dank."

Slash lumbers over, picking me up without a word, and stomps over to the bench with me in his arms. The big guy is clearly upset, but he's gentle as can be, cradling me close, and then finally depositing me on the toilet in the bathroom of the changing area. "Close the door and be cautious. I must go assist the others, little demon."

Since we're not in view of the others, I dart forward, kissing his cheek lightly as I whisper, "Thank you."

"As the panda said, we will always keep you safe."

I smile to myself as he pulls back and exits the small restroom, so the doc can enter. As soon as he's inside, Dank chants a few words in the demonic language, and the door glows purple. I assume he's using magic to lock it in a more serious manner than the handle, so I just sit on the cold ceramic lid as I wait.

"You have chosen your allies very well, Katarina," Dank says in his rusty voice. "I believe those young demons would truly sacrifice themselves in order to keep you safe. They are not lying to you or themselves anymore, it seems."

Scoffing uncomfortably, I scuff my foot on the ground. "Maybe. I mean, some of them. I don't know about everyone. They're all being better, though."

"You're not giving yourself or them enough credit. However, such is the fallacy of youth, I believe." He laughs, the sound making more feathers fly, and I frown. "Do not worry about that, Katarina. My feathers have molted and grown back so many times over my long life that I lost count before the current royals took the throne."

I guess that might be a hint to some, but it leaves me completely at a quandary on age and shit.

"Okay, I just… it looked painful, and I thought giving me your cloak and keeping your mask off probably made it worse."

Dank laughs again. "No, those are devices for *others'* comfort. You do not look at me in abject horror as so many do. I am perfectly comfortable and not in pain. You, however, cannot say the same, I gather?"

My nose wrinkles as I whisper, "Jasper and I were practicing sparring. It was fine until the Major showed up out of nowhere."

"I see," he hums as he pulls the cloak off of my shoulders so he can see me. "And then what transpired?"

The darkness inside me rears up again as I think about it, and the doctor puts his hand on my shoulder, making it melt away somehow. I give him a wide-eyed expression, but he just goes back to examining me. "Um.. well, The Major ordered Jasper to spar with me again, and um… He said the prince couldn't hold back this time. It was an order, and I could tell Jasper didn't want to do it, but we couldn't say no."

Pausing, Dank looks at me sympathetically—I think—and shakes his head. "The soldiers loyal to the crown, especially those in the highest ranks, have lost their way. Sadism, cruelty, and lust for power run amok in their midst. Ordering a powerful, elder demon to attack a young one is never helpful and often leads to the thinning of their ranks rather than filling them. You cannot lead soldiers you gravely injure or kill."

"That's what I thought, but obviously, this asshole wasn't taught logic," I grumble. Dank's hands move to a spot that makes me cry out, and he stops, turning to look in the bag on the floor. "He seemed determined to fuck me up, and it's probably because we metaphorically gave the King the middle finger on Halloween. Well, Jasper did, and I was involved."

"Ah, so you believe he was instructed to look for you during his visit and make you pay for that affront."

"Definitely."

The bird demon tsks as he mumbles, "Young royals should know better than using those who are not ready for vengeance in their schemes. However, I am certain the Major was quite shocked when you not only withstood the assault, but shifted into a powerful beast as well. Am I correct?"

My face heats as I look at the floor. "He didn't really have a chance to think much, I don't think. I shifted into a dragon—which I didn't know I could do—and well, you saw what my dragon did. It was over pretty fucking quickly."

"I see." The doc tilts his head as he waits for me to meet his gaze. "Why did your dragon do that?"

Shrugging, I say, "He was an asshole."

"Perhaps, but that does not warrant the rage that forces a shift of such a powerful animal. Think harder, Katarina."

I frown, biting my lip as I consider what was going through my mind when the dragon took over. When it comes to me, I blink and then swallow hard before I answer. "I didn't like that he violated Jasper's boundaries. It was obvious he didn't want to hurt me, and the Major was forcing him to."

"Have you ever been in a situation like that before?"

My body locks as I remember the incident, and I feel my pulse spike. "Yes."

"And what happened then, I wonder?" The demon muses as he applies cream to the injuries carefully. "What did you do when it happened before?"

"I didn't know until just now, but… I think I set the place on fire," I whisper.

I've never seen a flaming bird skull look quite so pleased as he does right now, but it's almost like Dank is gloating.

---

1. From the ancients to the beasts, I command you to listen and obey!
2. Your time here is over, faithful beast. Transform yourself and sleep again.

Your Betrayal

Jasper

My dragon is displeased that we're stuck waiting, and for once, I agree with him.

Of course, we're aligned for completely different reasons, and that's going to be a problem —eventually.

Looking around at the mess my caliphate and these… helpers… now have to clean up, I'm finding it hard to control all the emotions rioting inside of me. However, it's not time for that; it's time to work together to get rid of the Major's fucking body before someone stumbles onto our treasonous act and trips an alarm. While Darkstar has no love for agents of the court, he won't hesitate to use this situation to his advantage.

"Slash, now that you're back from coddling the shrimp, gather the others."

My second gives me a suspicious look, his expression turning cold as he nods sharply. He lumbers over to the rest of my brothers, bringing them into a circle with the Keeper around the corpse. Once they're all in place, I lift my chin and glare.

"What is our plan?"

The Keeper scratches his beard, and then says, "Have to be a disposal job. If we move it and try to cover it up, it will bring hellfire down on the whole campus. At least if he's just missing in action, people can assume things until someone actually decides it's worth pursuing."

The demon makes a good point—if he falls out of contact with Slash's dad, the General might ignore it for a while, thinking the Major is snooping or whoring about.

"Fine. What are we using for disposal and how are we getting it to the place where it will happen without being seen?"

"We could stow it under a tarp and hide it until nighttime." Oriel's wings fold against his back as he tilts his head to look at the large body. "Once it's dark, there will be fewer people around, and it will be easier to transport without being caught."

Slash shakes his head. "Still very risky. He is quite obtrusive."

"Lots of weapons at hand. We could chop it up," Anton says as he stoops. "There are sharp enough implements in the cabinet, and while some take the parts away in bags, the others could clean the mess."

"Nae, lad. The best way to get rid of pieces is a fairly good clip from here— we'd need to use the Wastes or my razorback devil pigs."

I arch a brow at the Keeper, considering his input. "The pigs would be a good way to get rid of every single piece of him without leaving a trace."

Xerxes waves his hand. "If we chop him, Slash could eat him. The gym springs aren't that far. Shift and easy peasy… no parts."

My best friend shudders. "While I will eat those who force me to, I would prefer not to ingest someone who has been… a difficulty in my life. It would be like eating my pain."

I have no idea what the fuck that *means, but I can guess where the theory came from.*

Growling in annoyance, I look over to the changing area impatiently before turning back to them. "What else, then? The pigs and Wastes are too far, Slash is unwilling…. We need a solution quickly."

Salem coughs, giving me a confused look. "Why the fuck don't you just burn him, Jas? You *are* a goddamn dragon."

I suck in a breath, telling myself not to lash out simply because he asked a question that assumes I'm not very bright. "Because it will leave a magical signature that we cannot fully erase, Salem. We can do our best, and it might fool *most* demons, but if the court sends the powerful trackers, they will eventually untangle the hexes and enchantments. That puts us back at square one, only with bigger problems."

He looks chagrined, rubbing his hand through his hair. "Sorry, Jasper. I didn't know that. It just seemed like an easy fix, man."

"The Prince is right—both about the magic and losing time." The Keeper looks around before he whistles so loudly that we all wince. His bird comes rocketing through the air to his side, making that noise that irritates the hell out of me. "Arces will scout for us. That will give us time to scramble if someone is coming towards the arena."

As soon as he finishes his sentence, the bird takes off again, soaring into the sky on its mission. I frown, considering the familiar for a moment before I ask, "Where is the rodent?"

Slash glares at me again and rumbles, "Dottie is with the doctor and Kit. She followed behind me, and I let her in before I returned."

"Geez, I didn't even—now I feel bad," Oriel mutters. "Poor girl is probably losing her fucking mind."

The Keeper grins at him. "Don't worry. Familiars are so in tune with their companions that they can sense when injuries are serious. If the lad had been gravely harmed, the little lady would have been making a fuss the likes you've not seen before. Size doesn't matter when a familiar is truly determined."

Also, something good to keep in mind as it explains why the damn thing had the stones to shove a fruit in my nostril.

"Now that we've established that, back to the topic at hand," I say, getting their attention once more. "This fucking corpse has to go, and we still don't have a viable plan."

"We sure as hell can't *Weekend at Bernie's* it," Zav mutters, and Salem snorts at a joke I don't understand. Oriel is still chuckling while my brainy mate walks around the inside of the circle, his tails swishing, as he thinks. "Our inability to use magic without being caught at some point is really limiting us."

"No shit."

Zavida whips his head around and gives me a stink eye that would wilt a garden full of flora. "Sarcasm is not useful at the moment, I believe. Creativity is better used to help us brainstorm."

Ouch. He's definitely not letting me off the hook for being frustrated.

"We have to be missing something. We've thought about magic, physical labor, weapons, gag movie plots, and consumption." Anton stands next to Zav as they both gaze at the body. "He's huge, so anything we do has to be geared towards removing something of his mass."

"I still think we can move him at night." Oriel gives them a stubborn look, his feathers ruffling. "I'm the one who operates in the dark here all the time. I know where the security is, where there are guards and where there are holes… I could easily guide us around them."

Before I can correct him, Slash jumps in. "You can guide us around them in the *sky*, old friend. You do not sneak around Discordia in this form. You fly as the crow, and transform when you are safe. Your methods will not apply directly to this situation."

The dark-haired demon frowns, then looks thoughtful. He holds up a finger and then puts it down as he sighs. "Okay, the big man is right. While I know the routes and shit airborne, I haven't studied the ground specifics as closely. I might be able to guide you, but I don't feel one hundred percent now. Though, you bet your sweet asses that I'm going to correct that over the next week or so."

Everyone falls quiet when he admits that, and Anton grins. "I would have had a much tougher time admitting that, O. KK would be proud of you."

The last thing I need is them falling into a wankfest over their emotional growth and how happy it would make the absent member of our caliphate—at least, right now.

"Enough of that," I bark as I rake my hand over my hair. My tail twitches as I pace back and forth, angry that we don't seem to be able to figure out something that should be so simple. "Focus! If we can't do this without losing the thread, we cannot function on the Games field. Not being able to think quickly as a unit will get us killed in that forum."

"He's right," Slash says reluctantly. "Our lack of cohesion now is a bad omen for our performance there. We will deal with that after we resolve our current issue."

"Maybe a different point of view would be helpful?"

We all whip around to see the very distraction I was fighting against dressed in someone's oversized sweats with a cloaked demon and a pissy-looking kinkajou in tow. Rolling my eyes up to the sky, I push all my emotions back into the box again before they take over. I was hoping we'd figure this out before Kit emerged from the bathroom, but as usual, the universe cares not a whit for how its timing will affect the people walking around in it.

"KK!" Salem cries as he abandons his spot in the circle to walk over and pick the kid up and spin around. "You're okay. I was worried, little dude."

Snorting, I look away as the others clamor to give their congratulations.

They get a few moments to greet him before I turn back around and growl, "What did I say about *focus*?"

Dark brown eyes narrow at me as the newly emerged shifter crosses his arms over his chest. "What crawled up your ass and died, Jasper?"

Counting to ten… remembering painful injuries… thinking of horrid things…

"Nothing. I would like to get rid of the body you left for us to deal with so none of us end up in the royal dungeon with scheduled executions." I arch a brow and shrug. "Though honestly, I'm not sure *everyone* would end up that way considering their parents."

"Rich asshole," Kit mutters, and I'm surprised to hear the crusty old bird-doctor chuckle behind him. "Just because you have a pedigree doesn't make you any less a part of this—what happened to all that brotherhood and chanting shit?"

Zavida leaves his spot studying the Major, his tails flicking happily as he walks over. "He's just worried, KK. This is a big deal, and we've had a hard time thinking of a way to fix it without either getting caught or leaving a trail that points to us. Usually, we're able to accomplish stuff like this without a lot of effort."

"Perhaps it is because you were incomplete until now," the doctor says as flaming feathers float off of him. "If you have completed the caliphate ritual, your group efforts will need to be coordinated together to succeed."

I give the old demon a disbelieving look. "Are you saying we won't be able to think on our own anymore? I don't recall ever hearing that a caliphate bonding caused that."

"Nae, Prince. The doctor means that your teamwork will fail if you don't work together—and right now, you're not functioning as one." The burly bestiary demon looks at my brothers, then me, and finally, Kit. "There's a storm brewing, and you're fractured. Cracked foundations won't hold up under pressure."

"We're not cracked," Salem says with a frown. "In fact, we had a really good bonding time the other night. It's getting better."

Dr. D laughs again, flames flaring on his cloak as he shakes his head. "Do not be obtuse, young Stryker. It is quite apparent that whatever happened here today has caused this rift, and if you do not resolve it, I fear we are all going to share the darkest level of the palace torture chamber together— even the haughty prince."

"For fuck's sake, *what*?!" Kit stomps over and pokes me hard, knocking me off balance a little. "It has to be you, so… tell me what it is. Are you feeling less special because poor, parentless, non-royal me is a dragon, too? Have I hurt your pride because I didn't struggle to fly with you or whatever? Out with it, Jasper! Tell me why you're acting like a fucking prick again!"

My eyes darken as I look at the newest member of our group, the fury inside me fighting with my demon and my dragon as I say, "Because you lied to me… you lied to everyone! When were you going to tell us you're *a fucking girl… whatever your name is!*"

Everything goes still as my words leave my mouth, and when I look around, I'm horrified to see the results of my outburst. They all knew… at least, *most* of them. Zavvie is blinking in confusion, and Anton looks taken aback, but the rest of my brothers *and* these damn 'helpers' know. None of them warned me, nor did they insist that this faker give up the secret.

I'm surrounded by people who betrayed me, including my inner beast and my demon, and I have no idea how I'm going to survive this.

OH NO!

I guess you'll just have to see what happens in the bonus… and maybe the holiday novella…

Go here for the bonus

Go here for the holiday novella

GET A SECRET
BONUS SCENE!

For another secret bonus scene that follows *this book, click the link below, sign up for my newsletter, and get your freebie.*

Get your bonus scene here!

Reviews, Print, and Merchandise

If you have enjoyed this story, please review it.
It helps other readers find my work,
which helps me as an indie author.

Thank you!

Reviews are appreciated on the following platforms:

TikTok
Instagram
Facebook
Bookbub
StoryGraph
Threads
Tome
Lemon8

To purchase print copies or merchandise, go to The Worlds of Cassandra Featherstone

Some pronunciations are very basic, but my editors believe they should all have it to be uniform in style. Obviously, I know you know how to read 'Bob', but it's just weird for things not to match, 'kay?

Characters, Pets, & Creations

Katarina Camponella (kat uh REE nuh CAM POH NELL uh) foster kid living with the Jamesons; now learned to be at least part demon with some kind of magic

Nicknames: Kat, Kit, Kit Kat, little demon, shrimp, firecracker

Blake Jameson (blay-k Jay-meh-son) twin foster brother of Kat; plays football, popular kid; absolute ass; accepted to Alabama to play ball

Bryce Jameson (bry-ss Jay-meh-son) twin foster brother of Kat; plays football, popular kid; absolute ass; accepted to Alabama to play ball

Brett Jameson (Breh-TT Jay-meh-son) foster father of Kat; clueless; does whatever their mother says

Allison Jameson (al-uh-SON Jay-meh-son) foster mother of Kat; snobby; only like the prestige from having the two foster boys who play ball; disdainful of Kat

Professor Horatio Alecto (hor-ay-she-o uh-leck-to) professor at Discordia; Dean of Admissions; sends a letter to 'Kit' Camponella

Mr. Jenkins (Jeh-kinz) school guidance counselor; obviously overwhelmed and near retirement

Dottie (dah-tee) random kinkajou that shows up and is trying to break into the Jamesons bedroom floor safe; Kat finds her, and she refuses to leave; later, she's told it's a familiar

Sheriff Bob (Bahb) Useless, prejudiced town sheriff

Wilbur (will-BURR) deputy sheriff; four years older than twins; bully with a badge

Becky Sanderson (beck-ee San-der-son) town busy body

Lucian Darkstar (loo-see-en dark-stah-r) Headmaster of Discordia; sketchy AF; pit demon

Dank (DahNK) demon sent to fetch Kat; wears plague mask; aka Dr. Danckwardt

Silvera (sil VAIR UH) demon who does Lucian's bidding; fear demon

Beccarus (Beck-A-roos) toadie to Lucian; demon in Headmaster's office; chaos demon

Jasper Eversore (jas-PURR EVER-sore) Prince of Hell; leader of caliphate; dragon/demon hybrid; four years older than the others; working as teaching assistant while taking graduate classes to be with caliphate as they go to school; controlling asshole; fear demon

Nicknames: Asshole Demon, Prince Dickface, Prince Prick, Prince Prickface, Prince Cocknozzle

Scents: vanilla, musk, vetiver, bergamot, Sicilian mandarin, ylang-ylang, and honeyed neroli

Piercings: Lip, ears, tongue (both humanoid and forked dragon), Jacob's ladder and magic cross

Special equipment: stimulatingly bumpy, large as fuck dragon dick with vibration and knotting

Salem Stryker (Say-lem Str-eye-cur) Panda/demon hybrid; likes to cook; Kat's roommate; dream demon

Nicknames: Lazy Demon, Sleepy Bear,

Scents: Sicilian Lemon, Citron, Grapefruit, Bergamot, Green Mandarin from Italy, Juniper Berries, Cypress, Ylang-Ylang, Musk

Piercings: ears, navel, nipples, Apadravya

Special equipment: fluffy panda tail when aroused

Anton Aldaric (an-TOHN all-dur-icvk) peacock/demon hybrid; designer; lover of X; incubus

Nicknames: Flirty Demon, Annie

Scents: egyptian cassis, pepper flower, pink pepper, jasmine, geranium, rose, balsams, myrrh, amber

Piercings: ears, nipples, deep shaft, Reverse Prince Albert, tongue

Special equipment: cock pocket

Xerxes Zenobes (zerk-zees zee-not-bzs) cobra/demon hybrid; lover of Anton; enby; dream demon

Nicknames: Pretty Demon, X

Scents: Crushed red currants, broken twigs and blooming dahlias

Piercings: one nipple, frenum, pubic, Lorum, ears, eyebrow, nose

Special equipment: hemipenis

Oriel Bloodstone (or-ee-elle blud-stohn) crow shifter/demon hybrid; likes to steal shit; emo looking; quiet; shadow demon

Nicknames: Goth Demon, O

Scents: Clove, black pepper, rose, incense and amber

Piercings: nipples, septum, ears, eyebrow, labret, lip, magic cross, hafada

Special equipment: unknown

Zavida Draven (zah-VEE-duh reh-ven) kitsune/demon hybrid; hacker; gamer; sleeps with Jasper; very smart; chaos demon

Nicknames: Gamer Demon, Zav, Zavvie, Z

Scents: cinnamon, red pepper and saffron

Piercings: Prince Albert, nipples, tongue

Special equipment: knotting

Slash Scrum (slah-shuh) Jasper's second in command; Fireball champ; shark; demon hybrid; vengeance demon

Nicknames: Big Demon, Big Guy

Scents: amber, sandalwood, musk, rare pure Indian agarwood, pure Turkish rose, patchouli ylang-ylang and frankincense

Piercings: unknown

Special equipment: unknown

Professor Alabaster (al-UH-bas-ter) Deconstructing Human History professor; chaos demon/demi-god hybrid

Professor Kindervalt (kin-der-Walt) Demonic Languages professor; hybrid dream demon/giraffe

Professor Wormwood (werm-wood) Curses & Hexes professor; mage/dhampir hybrid

Professor Basquez (bas-Kez) Culinary Art professor; ancient; stodgy; hates cell phones; bores Salem to tears; crossroads demon

Professor Romero (rom-may-ro) Dark Lit professor; fallen demon

Professor Lillibet (lil-ih-bet) Intro to Supes professor; succubi who feeds on boys in class; jerk to girls

Bastion Queznar (bast-ee-on qwehz-nahr) greed demon in Thieves Guild; species racist; drude

Cornelius Rhodes (cor-nee-lee-us row-dz) leader of the Southern demon contingent; crossroads demon

Phelps Brewster (fell-ps brew-stir) Leader of the Midwest demon contingent; dream demon

Allegra Masterson (UH-leg-ruh Mass-tur-sun) leader of the Eastern demon contingent; pit demon; ugly as hell

Professor Salazar (SALL-uh-ZAR) Dark Magic professor; chaos demon with bent for making people nutty for his amusement

Professor Cedar (CEE-dur) Intro to Fae professor; hybrid Reaping Fae and incubus; actually a cool dude

Ivan Roquefort (ee-vahn ROH-kh-fort) demon in Kit's Waeapons class; super jackass;

King Tarron Eversore (tay-ron ev-er-soar) full nightmare demon; upset last royal rule in Hell; asshole; Jasper's father

Queen Daramah Eversore (dare-ay-mah ev-er-soar) Queen of Hell; arranged marriage; succubus; Jasper's mom; pays no attention to him or the kingdom

Professor Holmes (hole-m-zuh) Supernatural Law professor; minor crossroads/sloth demon hybrid

Magnus Chilton (mag-NUSS CHILL-ton) a drude; Zavida's family line; in Arms class

Kristian Hoebert (kriss-tee-in HOE-bert) an incubus from X's family line; in Arms class

Aesyllian Furon (AY-sill-ee-on Few-RON) hybrid Midnight Fae and vengeance demon from Jasper's family line; in Arms class

Wilhelmina 'Billie' von Henrich (will-HELL-meen-uh Bill-ee VAUGHN Highn-rick) Cubi from Xerxes' line; attends Brimstone Academy

Professor Gaius Octavian (guy-US OCK-tay-vee-un) History of Warfare professor; crossroads demon

Anastasia Aldaric (ahn-UH-stah-zia ALL-dare-ick) Anton's mother; matriarch of Pride line; thinks of him as a failure; possibly bi-polar; rage phases well known

Aegon Aldaric (AYE-gone ALL-dare-ick) Anton's father; second in command in Pride line; useless and spineless; rarely around; suspected to have married Anastasia for political reasons; his attendent is rumored to be his lover; never around when Anton was little

Budet (boo-det) demon from Gluttony line; opponent in Weapons class

Guillermo (gee-air-moh) brown recluse spider shifter; tailor to Geminis; ancient as hell

Laurel (lah-rel)racoon shifter; assistant to Guillermo

Delamar the Deciever (day la marr) redcap at the apalachin guarding the Fae lands

Morgana LeCiel (mor-GAN-uh lih CEE-el) hybrid gargoyle/gorgon shifter; adopted by gargoyle and witch parents; educated and previously employed at Swallowtail Academy; killed her dragon fiancé Magnus; stood trial before Society and sentenced to clean up State U; has one unruly gorgon snake in her hair called Dez;

Nicknames: babe, Salaadir, M, Lass, Lady M

Slade Finn (slay-duh fihn) siren grad student who works at campus coffeehouse; meets Morgana and invites her to dinner with his pined for room mate Ignatius Briarton; son of crime lord family in Bay City

Nicknames: darling man, guppy, songbird

Ignatius Briarton (ig-NAY-shus bry-er-TON) professor and head of Witchcraft & Wizardry department; mage; womanizer; lived with Slade since they met when he was undergrad; snobby elitist; rich old family

Nicknames: Iggy, Professor

Lucas Wolfberg (loo-CUSS Wolf-berg) grandson of Wolfenberg dynasty; polar bear shifter; star hockey player for State U Bonecrushers; accused of murdering rival team member at State U rink; mates with Morgana on accident; gets poisoned; has shitty playboy/girl parents

Nicknames: Papa Bear

Prince Liam Spéirgheal (Lee-UM speej-gee-al) one of the Princes of the Daybreak Court; attending grad school for interspecies diplomacy Masters; lives in staff housing close to Morgana

Nicknames: Prince, Li

Kaspar (cass-par) storm dragon; security detail for Liam; been with family since a kid; grumpy and suspicious

Nicknames: Kas

LOCATIONS

Woodlawn High School- school where Kat goes to school

Common Grounds- coffeehouse and diner where Woodlawn moms hang out

Woodlawn Mall- where Kat goes to create her Kit persona

Short Cuts- where Kat gets her haircut for Kit persona

Raging Trends- scene kid store in the mall

Wally World- mega store in town

Discordia University- premier demon college that invites Kat to attend

Canto IV- Section of Hell Discordia is located in

State U- Supe college

Bamford Academy- reform school

Canto IV- the dorm they live in

Library Enclave- Building where many lectures take place

Magic Enclave- building where magic classes occur

Triclinium- cafeteria building

Infirmary- a bad place to go for treatment

Dr. Danckwardt's Office- the elite royal doctor's clinic

Arena- where the weapons and physical classes occur; also a large meeting space

Temple/Altar- ancient space where rituals are performed

Brimstone University- female elite demon college

Wastelands- place where punishment occurs; near Discordia; desolate region where some of the lowest demons live.

Purgatory Pizza- best pizza in Hell

Rigoletto Abbigliamento e Accessori di pregio clothing store in Bay City

Bay City supe city on West Coast where they portal in

Autumn/Harvest Court one of four courts of Faerie

Midnight Court one of four courts of Faerie

Court of Reaping one of four courts of Faerie

DISCORDIA SPECIFIC-TERMS & ITEMS

Crunkleberries- used in desserts, Kit loves; they make her a little high;

Black Underworld Cow- meat eaten by demons from Hades' special cows; akin to Kobe beef here;

Meat Bag- slang for human

Beast Meat- from unidentified Hell beasts; used for food;

Bat wings- used as food like chicken wings

Fear fish- fish used for food from River Styx;

Batberry- used to make wine in Hell

Cantu berry- used in foods, desserts, and snacks

Emerge- come into supernatural powers; usually in pubescence

Society- highest Council of mixed supes from all realms who help keep their worlds a secret from humans and protect the supernaturals

Fireball (aka Magic Battles)- the sports league of Hell's schools

Chasm Worm- another meat used in foods

Hybrid- supe of mixed species

Pits- the fiery place where pit demons live and reign over the beings sent there

Faeberry- used to make wine; from Faerie; smells like sugar, strawberry, grapes, and honey;

Crawling Thorn Briar- crawling thorn patch used for both food and captivity in Faerie

Tripleskia- a supernatural with three or more supernatural sides; extremely rare.

Dark Cow Milk- milk from Black Underworld cows used for a variety of cooking and drinks

Stalk Cassandra Featherstone in the Dark Corners of the Web

Join my Facebook group and follow me everywhere!

Want More?

Sign up for my bi-weekly manifesto for a free series sampler:

Join my Ream as a FREE follower or exclusive subscriber to get access to cover reveals, WIPs, Serial Stories, and personal chats from me!

Sneak Peek: Come Out & Prey

Just A Girl

Delores

Sighing, I look around my bedroom at the posters and decorations covering my walls. My obsession with pop music, musical theater, and high school rom-coms sickens my parents. They would prefer me to be into heavy metal and horror movies like the other kids my age.

Being the only child in a family as prominent as mine is difficult when you don't fit the mold. My parents—like their parents and all my friends' parents

—are apex predators. Preds rule our world, and the division between us and prey is so severe that we regulate them to a completely different echelon of society. Prey shifters are weak and beneath our lofty abilities. The ruling class of elite predator families stretches back generations, and they've evolved into a bunch of assholes who only care about succession and greed.

My animal has not manifested yet, but it will soon enough. Luckily for me, none of my friends have manifested their inner animals, either. I'm part of the in-crowd at school, and my boyfriend, Todd, is the most popular guy in my class. While he and I aren't officially engaged yet, we've talked about it enough that I know it's only a matter of time before he puts a ring on my finger. I should be on top of the world, but I can't help but feel like my life just doesn't fit me the way it's supposed to.

Every teenager wishes their life was different, but I dream of becoming an entirely different person. Not inside, mind, because I'm pretty comfortable with who I am. I don't want to be part of this legacy, this society, or even this family. They are all focused on competing to be the richest, the deadliest, or the most powerful, and I want no part of it.

I walked over to my closet and pulled out the outfit that I had chosen for my tour of Apex Academy. My mother hired her personal designers to create a custom school uniform for today and expects me to present the 'appropriate' image of the sole heir to a Council seat.

I hate having to pretend to be like them because I'm nothing like them.

Regardless, I pull on the short, pink pleated skirt, three quarter length sleeve blouse, knee socks, and Mary Janes that comprise the uniform for my exclusive private high school. Since I'm using a 'college visit' day to tour the Academy, I'm expected to represent Shifter Secondary as well.

Shifter Secondary is the most exclusive high school for unmanifested shifter teens on the East Coast. Unfortunately for me, it was not my parents' first choice for my education. They hoped I'd follow in their footsteps by choosing to force my animal to emerge early. If I had done that, I could have attended *Apex Academy Lower School.*

I didn't have the stomach to use my body in that manner at fourteen.

Their heirs followed my lead, which made my mother and father furious and their hoity-toity council colleagues angry. My closest friends, the Heathers, also refused to force their animals to emerge, as did Todd and his friends. That was the first time the adults in our circle decided I was a bad influence. After that, I had to toe the line at every turn, ensuring that I followed all the strict rules and regulations that govern the heirs to council seats.

Everywhere I went, I had to dress in a manner befitting the next Drew to sit at the table. They forced me to take dance lessons, piano lessons, diction lessons, and other more humiliating tutorials to prepare for the day that I became a true predator. In our society, teenagers have no say in how we prepare for our animals to emerge.

Your parents make all the decisions, choose your friends, choose your mates, and decide every detail of your life down to what you eat every single day. At least, that's how it is in my family, because my mother is from the old world.

She came over from Slovenia when she was incredibly young and met my father on the society fundraiser circuit. Her idea of preparing her daughter for the future involves lessons in makeup, clothing, jewelry, and on how to keep your mate satisfied. Lucille is completely unconcerned about whether I end up happy, only that I attend to my council seat and my husband's *needs*.

Once I get dressed, I grab my vintage Vuitton bag and peek at the mirror for a last check before I head downstairs. I tuck my perfectly highlighted blonde tresses behind my ears, and the smokey eye and winged liner are on point with this year's fashion trends. I apply a quick swipe of cherry red lip gloss and open my mouth, inspecting my teeth to make sure they are pearly white. Even though once I develop threatening incisors or sharp fangs, something will inevitably cover them in blood, my parents want my smile to look like a toothpaste commercial.

It's all such utter bullshit.

I take a deep breath and turn on my heel, heading for the door. I can already hear my parents yelling in a Scotch and vodka induced rage in the drawing room. It's only eleven thirty in the morning, for Hera's sake.

Lucille and Bruno don't fuck around with cocktail hour. They are nicely sauced by ten a.m. every day, without exception. I can't remember a time when my parents didn't get drunk off their asses at an event or party, much less in our 'home'. They liquor up and fight until they part for the day, and then start again once they arrive home from their daily commitments.

I brace for the barrage of criticism my mother will subject me to when I cross the threshold. Closing my eyes, I whisper words of encouragement to myself via lyrics to some of my favorite songs, desperately trying to hype myself up before she can tear me down.

"Delores! I hear you breathing at the top of the stairs, darling. Come down this instant and let your father and I inspect your presentation."

My mother's purr *sounds* friendly, but believe me, it's not. I roll my eyes as I make my way down the stairs, knowing my mother won't hesitate to send one of the staff if I don't acquiesce to her command. Most of their staff would gleefully jizz themselves with being chosen to drag me downstairs for inspection.

At this time of day, the only servant in the drawing room will be Matilda—my ex-nanny turned personal assistant—and that request would test her loyalties. As the only person in my household who has my back, I don't want to put her in that position, so I answer. "Yes, Lucille. I'm on my way."

I'm not allowed to refer to her as 'mother' because it makes her feel old. 'Lucille' is always what I've called the woman who supposedly gave birth to me. I'd be tempted to disbelieve we shared any DNA at all if it weren't for our similar bone structure. She's about as nurturing as a rattlesnake, and if it weren't for Matilda, I might have died as a child. If the kitchen staff whispers are accurate, I have to accept that my mother neglected to feed me much of the time.

"You coddle her far too much, Lucille," my father growls. "As the heir to our family seat, Delores will come without being instructed to do so. We will not tolerate her insolence after her animal emerges. She will behave as I command or suffer the consequences."

The last of Bruno's rant echoes off the marble walls of the foyer as I step onto the hideously expensive, endangered teak floor. Schooling my features into the mask of indifference I wear whenever I have to deal with them, I enter their den of drunken fights with my spine steeled for an emotional assault.

"I apologize for my tardiness, Father. I only wished to perfect the image I will present during my tour of Apex Academy. I realize it is imperative I impress the Headmistress and her staff."

The humanoid features of his face shift seamlessly, and the hungry crocodile inside of him gives me a toothy smirk. "You will impress them, daughter, or so help me… I'll send you to Bloodstone Isle."

My stomach drops like a stone as I barely suppress a shiver.

Bloodstone Isle is a reformatory school. It's surrounded by spells and enchantments to prevent students from escaping—a feat that has only happened once in its one thousand years of existence. The most feared cat group in the shifter world—the Khan ambush—runs the school, and they're rumored to consume errant students when the Council allows it.

It's the threat both rich and poor shifter parents used to keep their children in line. Wealthy parents like mine use it as a method of controlling any heirs that refuse to conform to the rigid structure of our society. Predators don't value the lives of those who are weak, and they label heirs who refuse to take their rightful place at the top of the food chain weak. Everyone knows Bloodstone is full of criminals, miscreants, and psychos, and even they don't seem to survive.

Bloodstone is a death sentence—pure and simple.

"Y-yes, Father. I understand," I croak out. As if the pressure of touring my new school isn't enough, now I worry the Dean will relay something to my parents that gets me shipped off to Death Island.

"Bruno, darling, if you scare her, she'll frown. That causes wrinkles. Delores, chin up and smile for us."

Swallowing the lump in my throat, I flash my mother my brightest smile. Her blood-red lips curve, and her leopard fangs burst free as she all but purrs. "I will not have you sullying the family name, Delores. It's bad enough that your education gave you ideas about your value beyond breeding stock. You will take the seat on the Council when it is time, but the husband we select will control the business—as nature intended. Do you hear me?"

My eyes narrow briefly, and for what is possibly the millionth time this week alone, I nod at my mother to appease her temper. "Yes, Lucille."

"Excellent!" The leopard fades as she claps her hands. "Matilda!"

The tiny woman steps up, her eyes wide behind her glasses. She's a pred, but the smaller size of hawk shifters puts her in the servant class. I believe she genuinely lives in fear of one or both of my parents deciding to eat her. "Yes, madam?"

"Fetch Bruiser. He will accompany Delores to the academy for her tour. Tell him to take the Escalade—it won't do for her to arrive in a tiny car—it will draw attention to her extra weight. We must make an impression."

Matilda nods, and I feel the fear radiating from her, and I don't blame her. Bruiser is one of my parents' bodyguards and our frequent chauffeur. He's a Komodo dragon shifter and the house staff are terrified of him. It's hard not to be, given that he prefers to play with his food, then eat it after it's dead. The kitchen crew believes he 'handled' the gardener that looked too long at my mother when I was ten. He disappeared without a trace.

Once Matilda scurries away, I watch my parents drink and bicker about their plans for the day. Bruno is going golfing with a congressman, and Lucille is going to the spa. We all know that both outings will include stops at the homes of their current pieces of ass for a quickie, but no one talks about it. The appearance of the loving couple has to be maintained, although neither of them has slept in the same room since I was a baby.

They don't give a damn about fidelity; I learned that at an early age. Children often discover things they shouldn't because of adults discount their ability to understand the conversations happening around them.

I stopped keeping track of who they're boning long ago, because I'd need an assistant to keep the affairs straight.

While my parents' marriage is a sham, I remind myself that my boyfriend, Todd, isn't like them. Yes, his parents only own half the live entertainment industry, but my father allows me to see Todd. The other parents will force the Heathers to accept an arranged betrothal, and I'm grateful I'm lucky enough to have found the perfect match on my own as my high school sweetheart.

"Delores, Bruiser is ready to escort you to Apex. He's pulling the car around now," the hawk shifter says softly.

Snapping out of my reverie, I smile at the trembling woman. Bruiser must have scared the living hell out of her. For no other reason than it amused him, I'm sure. He's as much a brute as his name implies, and I don't look forward to riding alone to the academy with him.

Something about that shifter gives me the creeps…

Sneak Peek: Blood on the Ice

Killer Queen

Morgana

Looking around the campus with a critical eye, it isn't hard to notice the differences between the campus of Swallowtail and State U. The major difference is age, of course, but even secondary schools overseas are unlike the blatant marketing machines that are American universities. State U doesn't resemble the colleges I've seen in American movies or on TV, though much of that is the Society's doing.

However, banners, statues, plaques, signs, and even architecture are emblazoned with the school's motto—*Honoris. Veritas. Potentia*—as if constant reminders will enforce the virtues it extols. *That* differs from the places in Europe I attended or worked in.

"Getting used to the sales aspect of education here won't be your biggest challenge and you know it," I mutter to myself.

When the outcome of my trial led to a guilty sentence, I didn't expect the punishment they handed down. Instead of being jailed for the murder of my ex, they decreed I would replace him as the Dean at State U. I wasn't the only one who disagreed with my purgatory—the vote on the High Council was split down the middle until a mysterious figure cast a vote in favor of my exile. They summarily dismissed me from Swallowtail Academy and sent me home to pack my shit for a journey overseas to the nest of corruption created by the man I thought I would marry.

Not only am I the youngest Dean to ever hold the title, but I'm the only hybrid to head one of the Society's schools.

Placing me at the helm of the crown jewel of their American institutions made their unorthodox punishment even more bizarre, but I've never believed the group that guides our kind to be infallible. The irony of replacing the being responsible for all the university's current issues with the fiancee who killed him hasn't eluded me. It's like my penance for not blowing the whistle on him instead of taking my vengeance in blood.

They did not impress hard line elders with the eventual outcome, but that had to be expected. Some supernaturals don't believe in the young being given positions of power, especially when that young candidate is also a woman and a hybrid. Given that I believe Magnus had cronies at various levels of government he was paying off, some of them must be worried I'll expose them to prove I was right to remove him from this world. Either way, the assholes who are screaming I'll ruin their precious programs and reputation haven't shut up since I left the trial chamber.

Let them whine about their outdated, elitist standards. I'll show them.

I turn away from the greenery of the campus, leaving the balcony to take a seat at the enormous desk in my overly plush office. Knowing the way parents and donors behave in this country, I assume every inch of this space has been purchased not by the college, but by donors who had 'one little request' for my ex. Magnus Corona was well-known in academic circles for milking the wealthy Americans until they ran dry, but his lack of ethics couldn't go on forever. My greedy, dragon lover went on the lam after a series of scandals involving kickbacks, illegal sponsorships, sports, and sexual harassment. The last one is why I hunted him down and eventually watched the last breaths he took on this planet with vengeful glee.

I'll start looking for a decorator immediately. If it's not in the budget, my trust fund will cover it.

Like most lost ones, they left me on the doorstep of a very talented witch and her gargoyle mate. I never found my 'real' parents, but growing up on Swallowtail's campus was not a burden. It was different when my adoptive parents were professors there—three hundred years brings a lot of changes. When I graduated, I attended Oxford and came back to work there in administration because I missed the old buildings and libraries.

That's the gargoyle in me, I know.

My adoptive mother is blind—except for the gift of future sight. Being a beautiful, blind witch couldn't have been easy when she was teaching, but she met my father in college and they've been together ever since. When they graduated, they came back to Swallowtail to teach. Eventually, she became the head of the Witchcraft & Wizardry department at the Finishing School and my father was the chair of the Physical Education & Training program. Over the years, my mother's gifts made their investments and ventures fruitful enough to retire while they could still enjoy it. They live on a small island in the Mediterranean where supes of their caliber like to soak up the good life.

Once I get settled here, I might invite them to come tour the campus. My father would particularly enjoy the Gothic structure of the buildings; they were constructed to evoke the feeling of Oxford and he loves those old buildings. I give the picture of them on my cherry wood desk a half smile and sigh when I realize it's going to be awhile before I can extend that invitation.

First, I have to figure out how to get this ship back on course. Loyalty divides the staff; the students are due to arrive in two weeks, and I have a lot of house cleaning to do within these hallowed walls. It's going to ruffle feathers to do the things that are necessary to keep our supernatural accreditation *and* our human sports certification. I'll have to let some staff go, shuffle departments and assignments, and bring in new people to monitor certain aspects of the college's accounting to satisfy all the requirements we need to meet by the end of the semester.

State U has never been forced to toe the line quite as closely as we must now, and that is all because of Magnus Corona's lack of scruples and inability to think without his dick.

Not that any of his adoring fans will believe it for a second—and that is the rock I'll have to push up the hill for the foreseeable future.

"They'll have to get on board or get the fuck out," I say as I compare the list of coaches, trainers, and support staff for the football team. "I don't have a choice and neither do they."

When I finally finish going over the massive budget for the major boys' teams, my brain is damn near fried. I cannot fathom how colleges here justify the expenditures of these programs compared to the paltry sums I saw on the balance sheets for academic programs. Americans truly have lost their focus on education, and it doesn't surprise me at all that Magnus could manipulate this to his advantage. There's so many discretionary funds and black holes in the books that I'll have to find someone much more numerically inclined than myself to help me wade through this shit.

It's almost like it left room for loopholes and nefarious deeds.

Pushing to my feet, I rise from the high-backed leather chair and slip my shoes back on. I've been at this for hours and because I don't have office staff, no one was there to remind me I should eat or take a break. I had to fire everyone who worked in Magnus' immediate circle—both out of principle and necessity. I can't prove they knew what he was doing, nor that any of them would try to harm me as retribution, but I'm also not stupid enough to let someone with loyalty to my ex pour my goddamn coffee.

Coffee.

The word makes my blood hum and I know it's time to find sustenance— particularly caffeine. I locate my phone on the massive desk and slip it into the pocket of my suit pants. My appearance has been a topic of gossip on campus since I arrived—social media is a terrible curse when you're in the spotlight, even if it's for the right reasons. I've seen staff and alumni commenting on the 'uptight murdering bitch' strutting around campus dressed like someone from the *Addams Family* as if their vitriol isn't public when they post on Facebook.

My lips curve as I look down at the bespoke Tom Ford suit, Zegna tie, and Louboutin heels. Dressing the part has always been a theme of mine, but Magnus preferred the 'rumpled academic' look. He allowed the staff to run around looking like grad students and that will soon end. If they hate me for looking sharp compared to my frumpy ex, they're going to hate the new dress code when it rolls out in a week. I will not go as far as the Society schools did at home or in other countries, but I refuse to have the press haunting our grounds while taking pictures of grubby looking professors and coaches for their rags.

If this is the crown jewel, it needs more polishing than the Council realizes.

Before I go out, I shake my purple and black curls out of the messy bun, letting my hair settle over my shoulders. A quick check with the selfie mode on my phone tells me my makeup doesn't need to be freshened—thank hell—so I close the camera and put on my sunglasses to keep my sensitive eyes from the waning sun.

I'll need the State U app to find a place that's out of the way. I open it and cringe—the damn thing is hideous in form and function. I make a mental note to interview app designers and web developers; the website has to be as poorly maintained as this bullshit. Yet again, I marvel at the level of incompetence men can show without consequence. It finally loads the map and I scroll around until I find a coffee shop on the edge of campus. I don't want to go to a break room or the food court—there will be far too many eyes on me and I'd like to relax.

Noting the landmarks around the shop, I walk out onto the balcony and touch the amulet at my neck. My wings spring free, sprouting through the suit without a single tear, and I leap into the air. Catching a wind shear, I glide to the far end of the commons, then bank to the right towards the arts building. They nestled the little beanery I identified between the theater and the gallery, so I pull my wings back to descend slowly as I approach.

When I land, the magic of my mother's amulet helps me slip my appendages back in gracefully and walk towards the door without missing a beat. I open the door, take off my sunglasses, and stride in with confidence. I'm not here to throw my weight around, but I can't let anyone see me sweat, either. I look at the menu board before I lower my gaze to see the barista behind the counter.

Holy. Mother. Forking. Shit.

The guy behind the counter is beautiful, and I don't say that lightly. His long blond hair is pulled back in a ponytail, but somehow, it doesn't look douchey. Paired with his patrician features and thin silver framed lenses, he projects the air of a student, but not a new one. My guess is a grad or doctoral student and this is his side hustle. The muscled forearms and powerful hands tell me he's not just a bookworm, so I ponder what discipline this lithe, gorgeous supe is studying. When I finally drag my eyes back to his, the aqua color of his is mesmerizing.

"Can I take your order, ma'am?"

Yikes. That destroyed my brief fantasy.

"Um, yes, sorry. It's been a long day. I'd like a triple espresso and a club sandwich, please." I feel my cheeks heating not because I was staring—he's got to be used to it—but because I got caught checking out one of the students.

It's not forbidden at State U, but I am the murdering bitch with ice in her veins that's here to destroy everything the university stands for. Or, so the article in the *State U Review* said last night. There's no way this gorgeous coffee-serving man doesn't recognize me and I'm sure I'll get an earful about my evil ways once he's done making my order. In fact, I should continue watching to make sure he doesn't mess with my food for revenge.

Yeah, that's why I want to watch him.

"I don't blame you for coming here. It's not one of the campus hot spots. Mostly we get professors, arts kids, and the occasional normie who wants to hide from the masses."

I blink, realizing he's nailed my reason for choosing this shop without even trying. "I think it's rather cozy."

"You don't have to pretend, Dean LeCiel." His pretty eyes meet mine again and I feel that heat creeping up my spine. "I'm aware of how contentious your appointment was. It doesn't bother me, honestly. I've been a student through much of your ex's reign and since the music department was of little concern to him, I don't have any allegiance to the former administration."

Definitely a doctoral candidate. His thesis is probably massive.

Covering my mouth as the unintended double meaning of my words occurs to me, I wait until the urge to giggle like a teenager fades. It would be extremely unprofessional of me to comment on his… attributes… especially since that kind of bullshit helped bring Magnus down. Of course, that doesn't mean I'm not wondering now…

"Dean? Hello?" The hot barista is waving his hand as he looks at me curiously.

"I'm sorry to be so rude. I didn't catch your name?"

There we go. That sounded totally normal.

"I'm Slade," he replies with a slow smile.

That doesn't surprise me in the slightest, and I wonder if he might be part Fae. Not giving me his real name is part and parcel with them, and so is the ethereal beauty. "You may call me Morgana when I am here. I think titles are dreadfully stuffy, but…"

"Set boundaries early because you have mutinies to deal with."

Frowning, I tilt my head. "You aren't reading me with magic, are you, Slade? Even during my ex's time, that kind of invasion of privacy wasn't allowed."

"No, no!" He stops making the sandwich and gives me a sheepish look. "I inferred it. I mean, I don't run with the undergrads or the popular crowds, but I hear things. It wasn't hard to figure out that you're at the hole in the wall shop so you don't have to be on stage while you eat or that you're going to make big changes because of all the charges against the former dean."

I nod, observing him. "I believe you, though I probably shouldn't. Betrayal hides in obvious places; I'm living proof of that."

His features look sharper as he smirks. "There are those of us who don't believe what you did was unjustified, Morgana. Living here at State U will provide you with plenty of evidence to give the Council that will mitigate your actions."

"That's both my desire and my deepest fear, Slade. There's only so much bad PR this place can take before the Council shuts it down and moves on."

A coffee cup and a plate with my sandwich slide across the counter as he murmurs, "You'll have to decide if that's what you want when the time comes."

"I know."

Get it on Kindle Unlimited

Get Season Two on Ream

Sneak Peek: Failed State

Every Day is Monday

Sydney

"Jesus fucking Christ," I mutter as I slog through the streets of Tempest Seven. "Just because they locked us up like animals doesn't mean we have to live like them."

Pausing in my walk to the education center, I look around myself in abject disgust. The inhabitants of this end of Tempest Seven aren't the bottom of the proverbial barrel, but outside of the 'lockdown losers', people stuck here never seem to get out of the cycle of poverty and despair. I don't think it means we have to throw garbage everywhere and give the drones nice shots to prove to the humans that we're as unworthy as the leaders of this stupid country say we are.

What would it hurt to tidy up, even if we don't have much?

Honestly, I believe it's only a third rooted in laziness. I think the other parts are exhaustion and hopelessness. Since the First Infected Being Sweep of 2020, supernaturals all over this country were tracked, catalogued, reassigned, and declared property of the government. By the time they ran the second through fourth sweeps, the population of some supernatural species dropped by fifty percent. The rules on how to track us down and receive your bounty were infuriatingly vague, which gave the most violent psychopaths in the world a free license to kill, maim, rape, and disappear anyone caught on the 'Non-Human Watchlist'.

I was a baby when my mother left, but my father taught me everything I needed to know about being a shifter. Unfortunately, he was one of the people who ended up on that list and was killed in the Second Infected Being Sweep of 2020. That sweep was brutal, and since I was a 'half-breed' orphan, I was placed in the orphanage in Tempest Seven. From the moment every child and teen arrived, they were forced to attend the Federal Enrichment Assimilation & Re-Education Center.

Our human professors taught us that being born this way is a punishment from their God, especially if you were a mixed type. At first, we tried to tell them about our various species, but it became clear very quickly what would happen if we didn't fall in line. You either learned to smile and nod, providing the rote answers and scripts they gave you when tested or interrogated, or you died.

Now, in 2024, there are no rebellions against the Federated Human States of America, nor are there any aid workers from other countries left to help or try to get us out. The world has given up on the former United States— it's been ruled a failed state by the United Nations and cordoned off at every border on land and sea.

We're on our own in the former land of the free and home of the brave.

"As if anyone would want to come here anyway. Shit went downhill fast after that baboon was elected," I mutter to myself. I realize I've spoken louder than I thought and I look around carefully, making certain I'm not near a Confession Enforcement zone or any other beings. My breath releases slowly when I confirm that I'm totally alone and not in a hot zone.

No one watches out for others now; the temptation to gain things your family or group needs is too high. A random person would dime me out for a week's supply of crackers and I can't blame them. Food and drink are rationed, our clothes are drab and provided, and the world is dimmer since the Sweeps. They force us to stay small so they're in control, and we have to live with it because of the fucking Markers.

My hand flies to the back of my neck, grunting in irritation as I scratch at the tattoo that covers the skin where the implant is located. These were the second step on the path to the current tyranny of our 'benevolent' government. That spray tanned fuck won the election because the humans here were that goddamn stupid, and then the virus hit. COVID brought America to its knees and like all good con artists, President Taterman used the distraction to funnel money into secret programs under DARPA.

Men who stare at goats my skinny ass.

They released a widely contested study that blamed the virus on the 'infected'. Unfortunately, they defined that as beings living in our country that had paranormal capabilities. The rest of the world laughed at the senile old fuck until the media hype was so huge that the various species around the world convened a leadership meeting. With so many cameras and videos everywhere, it was only a matter of time until a random human caught one of us doing something and bam! A viral TikTok would expose all of us whether we were ready or not. The vote was close, but the supernatural community decided to come out of hiding to protest their innocence.

'The Unveiling' was the most watched TV event in decades, and the consensus was our leaders had done the right thing. At least, until the next study was released. This one made Taterman damn near salivate as he screamed into the TV cameras about the 'unclean' liars and thieves who have been hiding in plain sight, taking our jobs, and stealing the lives humans should have. It quickly devolved into a mass panic and our kind were left scrambling.

We'd told them who and where we were, like a bunch of fools.

Thus, the evil assholes at the top started their mission to protect the humans from us and reclaim their country. Supernaturals in other nations were fine, but the atmosphere here became dangerous within the blink of an eye. Taterman stacked his own deck in the courts and the legislature by fearmongering, especially since the world was still reeling from a pandemic. Eventually, he was able to get the support he needed for the first Sweep.

Secret Supernatural Enforcement Agents used databases, social media, DNA websites, immigration records, and everything they could to gather the biggest dragnet of personal information ever assembled. Civil rights advocates and other world leaders were vocally opposed to such violations, but nothing could stop the juggernaut of hatred. Once they identified every supe in the nation—to the best of their ability—that's when they stripped our citizenship, robbed us blind, and re-assigned every single one to the sectors they'd been building in secret.

Let's be honest—they're supe prison camps.

But the humans felt safe once more because while we were all being shuffled all over like cattle, the rest of the scientific community worldwide started to get COVID under control. Taterman crowed about the United States' involvement, taking credit for slowing the spread by locking up the infected beings. No one but his nutty followers believed him, but at that point, it didn't matter.

So when they came to implant the Markers, no one spoke up.

We all have them, and depending on what you are and how powerful you are, they are different. But resting above the spot where they cut us open to shove in the controller, there's a matching tattoo of the logo that is now on the flag of the Federated Human States of America... but that came much, much later.

Democracy dies in the dark, the old slogan said... and here lies her rotted corpse.

"Hey, Syd. It's a beautiful day in the neighborhood, huh?"

My brooding gets interrupted by the arrival of Thad, my friend since we got placed here four years ago. He's a bear shifter and the size of a small SUV, but it doesn't bother me. I survived the sector version of high school partially because we stuck together. My brains and his bulk were a good match and it kept us from getting cornered by the gangs and cliques.

Okay, fine, it kept me from getting cornered. Obviously, Thad held his own without me.

"That sentiment hasn't been applicable for half a decade, man." I toss my braid over my shoulder and wait for him to catch up. It's our second week at the F.E.A.R. Academy's college level program and being late is more than frowned upon. I have to give us extra time every morning because Thad lumbers out of bed like his animal—slow and grumpy. "We gotta get moving."

The dark haired shifter looks at me, scratching the piratical scruff he's usually sporting. "You're ridiculously concerned about rules for someone with such a rebel spirit."

"Rebels die, Thad. I'm very aware of that." Turning on my heel, I head toward the huge building at the end of the main drag with a heavy heart. Losing Dad was hard and I'll never forgive him for assuming humans are anything but ignorant beasts that barely rise above their simian relatives.

We continue walking in silence until we reach the steps. The line is stretched down them as the guards run the wand over each student to check for weapons. After that, we put our bags on the conveyor belt for the magical detection while the security mages in government issued loyalty collars scan us for anything the wands wouldn't catch. It's not quick, but it keeps fights in the schools non-lethal most of the time.

That's the official reason, but the real purpose is to allow the staff to abuse students if they step out of line. The Markers not only brand and track us, but they siphon energy and power in small bits to keep us all weak enough to be controlled. Weapons would even the score and the humans who run these stupid ass brainwashing cults would be at risk.

"Look who's last at the trough again." The wry voice of the only demon in Tempest Seven gets my attention. Huck Monroe saunters up, tilting his worn black cowboy hat back as he smirks at me. "Y'all are just cruisin' for a bruisin'. I swear, you don't have the sense that the Devil gave a goose."

My eyes narrow at him briefly, then I turn forward and shuffle along as the line moves. "You don't have to hang out with us, Huck. In fact, it'd be great if you fucked off and stayed there."

Thad laughs, bumping his shoulder against the annoying fear demon's and I sigh. Huck was sent here during the First Sweep, like us, and he's been a Southern bramble in my side ever since. It's my bad luck that Thad enjoys his folksy charm and it means he sticks to us like glue during school hours.

"Sometimes you're meaner than a wet panther shifter, Sydney Jolie. I should take you at your word and mosey off, but I like your boy."

Huck's pitch black eyes are hidden by his Ray-Bans, but I know they're sparkling with amusement. He finds my dislike funny, and I don't get why. But then, I don't get a fucking thing about men, especially supes, nor do I want to. Life in our sector is hard enough without having to consider birth control or babies or even finding privacy. I'll save that for the day when I get the fuck out of here.

"I heard they're bringing in a new group of students today." Thad changes the subject quickly, knowing I'll continue to needle Huck and vice versa until one of us loses their temper. "The rumors say the shipment has vamps, losers, and traitors. I'm worried this sector is turning into a dumping ground for psychos."

It wouldn't surprise me if the humans started segregating the camps by species, value, or even criminality. Even after they corralled us into the sectors, the leaders have continued to exert their influence and power over us. The Markers were first, then the lockdowns for the ones they deemed dangerous, and now they're shuffling people weekly at random. I've often wondered if all of this is covering up something like what went on in the 1940s among the humans, but I haven't seen any proof.

Our media is monitored and curated, so unless you know someone with a highly illegal device, you have no idea what's happening outside of the FHSA.

"Next! Keep it moving, you little shits," the yell from the front of the line brings me back to reality again.

"Wicker is the fucking worst," Thad mumbles as we ascend the steps to stand behind the person being inspected. "Watch his hands, Syd."

"I'm aware." Despite thinking we're the scum of the earth, some of the human staff and enforcement in the sectors are fucking creeps. Some supes are willing to trade sex for perks, but that doesn't stop the predators from being creeps to those who don't. "I'll let you go first so Bishop gets me."

"Got it," he says as he muscles in front of me. "Huck, stay behind her."

"Why, I'd be delighted, Thaddeus."

I guess he's useful sometimes, but he'd better not let it go to his head.

Get it now!

ABOUT CASSANDRA FEATHERSTONE

Cassandra Featherstone has channeled her lifelong passion for writing into a flourishing career, a journey that started when she first grasped a pencil as a gifted child with ADHD.

Her debut novel, born during the solitude of COVID lockdown in March 2020, draws on a tapestry of personal encounters and insights that resonate deeply with her readers.

An international bestseller, Cassandra has topped Amazon charts in categories such as LGBT Anthologies, LGBTQ+ Mystery, and Bisexual Romance, among others. Her works navigate the complexities of bullying, PTSD, body dysmorphia, mental health struggles, personal reinvention, and the empowerment of claiming one's own space. Importantly, Cassandra offers a thoughtful and respectful portrayal of LGBTQIA+ relationships, subtly reflecting her own connection with the community through her narratives.

Her literary repertoire spans sci-fi fantasy, urban fantasy, paranormal, and comedic genres in academy whychoose settings, with a strong commitment to portraying consensual, safe, and accurately depicted BDSM and kink lifestyles. Her books are an invitation to explore transformative stories that are both inclusive and engaging.

Often affectionately called 'The Muppet' for her wacky theater kid personality, she resides in the Midwest with her tech-savvy husband, their creatively inclined college student, a literary-minded dog, and four scheming cats.

READ MORE AT CASSANDRA'S WEBSITE OR HER FACEBOOK PAGE. SIGN UP FOR EXCLUSIVE CONTENT AND UPDATES HERE.

FIND HER ON ANY OF THE SOCIAL MEDIA BELOW AS SHE *LOVES* TO CHAT AND *NEVER* SLEEPS!

Shifters Unleashed
Jingle My Balls
Love is in the Air
Silent Night
Snowed In
All Hallows Eve

Shifters Unleashed
Jingle My Balls
Love is in the Air
Silent Night
Snowed In
All Hallows Eve